The
egend of the Gypsy Hawk

The
Legend of the Gypsy Hawk

Sally Malcolm

Book 1 – Pirates of Ile Sainte Anne

Where heroes are like chocolate – irresistible!

First published by the author as *Beyond the Far Horizon*

Published 2016 by Choc Lit Limited
Penrose House, Crawley Drive, Camberley, Surrey GU15 2AB, UK
www.choc-lit.com

A CIP catalogue record for this book is available
from the British Library

ISBN 978-1-78189-265-7

MIX
Paper from
responsible sources
FSC® C013604

Printed and bound by CPI Group (UK) Ltd, Croydon, CR0 4YY

For my children, Jess and Ben

Acknowledgements

With thanks to Laura, my brilliant critique partner, and the wonderful people at Choc Lit for taking a chance on this book.

To Choc Lit Tasting Panel members: Heidi, Elke, Janice, Sigi, Heather M, Siobhan, Sarah C, Caroline, Jane O and Liz R – thank you for giving my manuscript your approval.

Prologue

1848

Midshipman Samuel Reed went about his business with a grumble on his lips and tender thoughts of home and hearth in his head. Too many years he'd been at sea and he'd long felt Her Majesty – God bless her – could do without his lowly services in her vast merchant fleet. Especially on days such as this, shrouded in an infernal fog, made worse by the belching smoke from the *Empire Harmony*'s funnels, and the cold creeping into his bones. Cursed by passengers, too – French ones.

One in particular, surly and full of rebellion, had caught his eye. Trouble, Reed thought, definite trouble. Not that it was any of his concern. Bloody students paid their way and who was he to judge them? If they wanted to raise merry hell in their own blasted land he'd not argue, so long as they didn't try to export their nonsense to British shores. For that, he'd box their sodding ears and not ask Her Majesty – God bless her – for a penny in return.

Still, it was a cold day to be at sea and he could damn them for their part in that, if nothing else.

He stopped by the rail and blew into his numbed hands, his breath doing little to fend off the January chill. It so happened that the rebellious young Frenchman who'd been preying on his mind stood just a few yards beyond, gazing thoughtfully out into the fog as if he might see through it, were he to stare hard enough.

'If you're looking for France, lad, you're looking the wrong way.'

The boy turned, milk-faced in the cold air, dark eyes defiant. 'I see something,' he said in heavily-accented

English, indicating the water with a languid wave of his hand.

Reed glanced at the flat sea. 'A man?'

'*Non, un coffre.*'

'A what?'

'A ...' He frowned and made a rough square with his hands. 'Like a ... box?' He glanced down again, leaning over the rail, and pointed. '*Voyez! Là!*'

Reed looked, mildly surprised to see that the boy was right. An old sea chest floated in the water, bobbing up against the side of the ship. 'Jetsam,' he said, looking back at the lad. 'Lost cargo of some kind.'

He murmured a reply, gazing down at the water – a question, perhaps, in his foreign tongue.

'Don't know what you're saying, mate,' Reed grumbled. 'Speak the Queen's bloody English aboard her own ship.'

The boy cast him an irritated glare, and then flashed a disarming smile that had the look of the devil about it. 'Treasure.' He nodded to the box. 'I think it is treasure.'

Reed laughed. 'Twenty years at sea, mate, and I ain't seen no bloody treasure. Especially not in the English Channel.'

The lad's smile turned crafty, a mere ivory glint in the cold light. 'Perhaps, monsieur, it is because you have not dared to look?'

Reed scratched his head and in the foggy silence heard a soft thump of iron on wood as the box drifted against the hull. His eyes met those of the boy and saw a challenge there – a challenge and a flare of danger, an invitation to adventure. The boy said no more, turning back to the misty sea, but Reed found himself needing to prove his mettle to this strange young lad.

'Harper! Kendall!' he shouted. 'Find a grapple and get yourselves aft!'

It took several attempts and much cursing to haul the chest aboard, but eventually it sat, dark and dripping, on the deck of the *Empire Harmony*. It was old, that much was sure, though not rotted, as a man might expect of a chest that had been long in the water. Its iron bands were not rusted, its lock gleaming wetly as if newly cast.

The boy crouched before it, running long-fingered hands over the lid before hefting the lock. It was ornately carved and the sight caused Reed to draw a deep breath, blinking twice to ensure his old eyes weren't playing tricks in the deepening gloom. 'Let me see that,' he said, kneeling at the lad's side and taking the lock from his hands. 'Bloody hell, look. What do you see?'

The lad was puzzled, and ran a slender finger over the intricate engraving. 'Here is a ... *dauphin*?'

'Aye, a dolphin,' Reed said. 'And the other's a hawk, see? By the shape of the wing.' He wiped a shaky hand across his mouth and sat back on his heels. 'Bloody hell.'

The French lad frowned. 'I do not understand.'

'A hawk and a dolphin, boy. Do you not know the tale of Amelia Dauphin and the captain of the *Gypsy Hawk*?'

The lad shook his head, his attention drifting back to the chest. He took the lock from Reed's hand and as he turned it over it broke in two. No, it didn't break so much as the two halves seemed to fly apart and the lock was open.

Reed said nothing. No one spoke as the lad carefully lifted the lid, not even the sailors who stood around them in a curious half circle.

There was no sparkle of gold, no treasure, and as he peered into the chest Reed saw nothing but a book. Letters on the cover glinted in the dull light as the boy lifted it out. 'My God,' Reed whispered. 'The Articles of Agreement – I thought it just legend.'

The lad's dark eyes lifted to meet his. 'What is this?'

'Freedom, lad. So they say. Mark it well.'

'*Liberté*?' The boy frowned, his slender fingers prising open the book. 'Look,' he said, 'something is written here.'

Reed peered over and saw words inside the cover, written in a curling, flamboyant script. *The gentry must come down, and the poor shall wear the crown.* Beneath them were inscribed the initials A.D. and Z.H. He let out a slow breath, awestruck. 'It's true then ...'

'What is true? What is—?' The lad stopped abruptly, looking out to sea, eyes wide. '*Ô mon dieu ...*' He lifted a shaking hand and pointed into the mist. '*C'est quoi?*'

Reed sucked in a freezing breath and stared. 'Bloody hell,' he murmured, scrambling to his feet. 'Holy mother and child.' Out of the murk loomed the shadow of an old tall ship, her sails dancing in a phantom breeze, before she was swallowed by the fog once more.

'*Bateau fantôme!*'

'Aye, lad,' Reed breathed, 'a ghost ship. Bloody hell, do you know what that was?'

The boy looked at him, wide eyed. '*Notre mort?*'

'No.' He felt a strange elation. 'No, lad. Not our death. For bugger me blind, but I say we just glimpsed the *Gypsy Hawk* herself.'

The boy frowned into the mist, but there was nothing to see. 'That is ill fortune?'

'No, son. Quite the opposite.' Midshipman Samuel Reed was sailor enough not to doubt tradition, nor what some folk called superstition. The *Gypsy Hawk* had not been seen these fifty years or more, not that he'd heard, and for her to appear now, at the very moment this strange lad unlocked the Pirate Queen's chest, was a providential sign indeed.

He glanced over his shoulder at the frightened faces of the crew and realised that he alone knew what it was they'd seen – and even he, old salt that he was, scarce believed his eyes. It was time to pass the story on.

'Come then,' he said, turning around. 'Come then, boys, listen and I'll tell you a tale. 'Twas told to me by my old da, who spent fifty year in the merchant marine, and to him by his da and so forth back to the days when the edges of the map were still sketchy and the world were a bigger place.' He beckoned the men closer and reached for his pipe. 'Come then, and I'll tell you the tale of the Gypsy Hawk and her wily captain – the infamous Zachary Hazard ...'

Part One

1716

But soon the sun with milder rays descends
To the cool ocean, where his journey ends;
On me Love's fiercer flames forever prey,
By night he scorches, as he burns by day.

'SUMMER', ALEXANDER POPE

Chapter One

Possessed of the devil's own luck, and a dangerous beauty to match, Captain Zach Hazard might have rivalled the angels themselves, were it not for the pleasure he took in more earthly matters.

Namely women, dice and rum.

Amelia watched him from the rigging of the *Sunlight*, letting her bare feet swing as she perched on the topsail yard. Hazard had docked at Ile Sainte Anne that morning, ghosting in with the dawn, unheralded and arriving, it seemed, out of nowhere. His ship, his beloved *Gypsy Hawk*, had not been seen on the island for six years and her appearance had set every tongue wagging. The *Hawk* sat high in the water, clearly empty of plunder to trade, and Zach stood on the docks in deep conversation with Jean-Pierre, her father's first mate.

Amelia couldn't see Zach's eyes – his face was lost beneath the stark shadow of his hat – but the wind caught at his hair and the silver ring that glinted in his ear. That same morning breeze also carried a snatch of conversation.

'... has matters of business to attend, but he will see you at noon.' That was Jean-Pierre, arms folded and stubborn; he'd never liked Zach Hazard.

'I'm not here for the good of my bloody health! Tell him it's urgent.'

Amelia smiled; his voice stirred a memory. Last time he'd sailed in their waters she'd been little more than a girl. He'd pulled coins from her ears and made her laugh with his outrageous stories, but that deep, smoke-scarred voice had touched on something new and blossoming. At the time she'd not known it for what it was; now, at one-and-twenty, she understood why his name alone made the women of Ile Sainte Anne giggle.

Not that she would giggle. She was Amelia Dauphin, daughter of James Dauphin and captain of the *Sunlight*. She was the youngest captain in her father's fleet and anyone who said she'd not earned it was welcome to test her mettle with cutlass or pistol. She would not giggle over a man.

Down on the dock, Zach Hazard was getting more heated and aboard the *Gypsy Hawk* his crew were lining the rail, old Brookes peering down from his work in the rigging. She saw no drawn blades, but in the slow morning heat the air began to crackle.

Time, she decided, to intervene.

Slipping off the yard, she scrambled down the mast and landed with a soft thud on the deck. Her first mate lifted a sleepy eyelid from where he'd been dozing by the helm and started to rise, but she waved a pacifying hand. 'No trouble,' she said. 'I'm heading up to my father's house.'

With that she trotted down the gangplank and onto the rickety quay. Her pistol was tucked into her belt, her powder dry, and the boards were smooth under her bare feet – it was a good morning to be alive. 'Zach Hazard,' she called as she drew close. Down at his level the shadow beneath his hat was not so dark and she could see his face more clearly.

Had she not been Amelia Dauphin, youngest captain in the pirate fleet of Ile Sainte Anne, she might have been startled by that face, beautiful despite sin-black eyes and a sardonic mouth. But she was made of sterner stuff and met his frank appraisal with a bow. 'Amelia Dauphin,' she said. Then, as an aside to Jean-Pierre, 'My father has asked you to attend him; I can handle Captain Hazard.'

The two men exchanged a glance and Amelia found herself blushing without entirely knowing why.

'As you wish, mademoiselle,' Jean-Pierre said. But, under his breath, he grumbled his disbelief.

'Nonsense, is it?' she shot back. '*Casse-toi, Jean Pierre!* And it's *Captain* Dauphin, to you.'

Jean-Pierre glared and didn't deign to reply, still muttering into his grizzled beard. She watched his back as he left, just in case. When she eventually returned her attention to Hazard, he was regarding her with undisguised surprise.

She laughed. 'Do you not remember me, Captain? You used to pull coins from my ears.'

For a moment he said nothing; then surprise changed to humour and something silver flashed in the sunlight. 'You keep them there still,' he said, taking a coin as if from behind her ear and spinning it in the air.

She snatched it with a grin and tucked it inside her shirt, watching the way his eyes widened. 'You'll need better tricks than that, Captain Hazard, to impress me now.'

'And what sort of tricks impress you these days, Miss Dauphin?'

'It's Captain Dauphin.' She pushed past him a little closer than necessary and then turned around, watching him as she walked backward along the dock. 'Would you like to see my ship? She's called the *Sunlight*. Or do you think me too much of a child to captain a ship?'

His bold gaze drifted down her body and his mouth curled at one corner. 'There's nothing of the child about you now, Amelia. How long's it been since we last crossed swords? Six years, by my reckoning.'

'We never crossed swords,' she said, puzzled.

His smile was liquid gold and not even remotely innocent. 'We may yet, however. I've a mind to think you're as wily as your old dad, and with those pretty lips a world more perilous to an honest pirate like myself.'

'Honest!' she snorted, turning away from his gaze. A girl might lose herself there and Amelia had no desire to be lost, especially not to a man with a string of broken hearts in every port and his own untouched by any softer feeling. She knew Zachary Hazard far too well to succumb to his charms.

He followed her along the dock, his loose-limbed stride reined in to keep pace with her. 'Much as I'd love to see your ship,' he said, 'I've urgent business with your father, no matter what Jean-Paul—'

'Pierre. It's Jean-Pierre.'

'No matter his name, Amy!' He was impatient. She'd never known him impatient before. Zach always carried with him the laconic heat of the Spanish Main, a far-off place she'd never seen with her own eyes but, through him, had come to know as a land of rum-filled nights and easy profit. That he would be impatient now – and come to them with the *Hawk* empty and lean – spoke of trouble.

'Do you bring ill-tidings?' She looked at him askance, saw the narrowing of his eyes and the tightening of his lips.

'What I bring is for your father's ears only.'

'I'm a captain in his fleet. I'm—'

'It's between him and me, Amelia. Leave it now.'

Frustrated, she kept her mouth shut and they walked in silence along the dock until they reached the narrow path leading up to her father's house on the cliffs. No doubt Jean-Pierre had gone ahead to betray her interference, but she knew her father well and doubted she'd be scolded. He loved Zach like a son, an errant son perhaps, but a son nonetheless, and she knew he'd be delighted to see him despite Jean-Pierre's dark mutterings.

Away from the salt-tang of the docks the air was rich with the scent of vanilla flowers and she breathed deeply. Tall trees shaded them from the climbing sun and she smiled to herself as Zach swept the hat from his head, wiping his brow against the arm of his coat.

'Too hot for you, Captain?' Casting him a sideways glance she wondered that he didn't rid himself of some clothing; his long coat and boots looked out of place in the heat of Sainte Anne. She wore only britches and a shirt, going barefoot even in the forest. Some of the visiting sailors – those unfamiliar with the citizens of the island – thought her wild, but she saw no reason to bind herself in stays and stockings for their convenience. She doubted they'd never seen a girl's ankle before, and if they hoped for more and were disappointed then so be it. They could take their pleasure among the lightskirts at the docks and leave her well alone. She wanted nothing of men, only the wind in her hair and the *Sunlight* beneath her feet.

'Why your father insists on camping out in this stifling bloody heat is beyond me,' Zach muttered, swatting at something on his neck. He peeled away his hand and grimaced, wiping it on his coat. 'Calls himself a bloody pirate, yet he never puts to sea.'

'My father is far more than a pirate!' Bridling at the insult, she turned on him. 'Look around you, Captain Hazard, and see for yourself. My father is a leader, a leader of free men and women – the only people in the world who are truly liberated.'

Zach stopped, regarding her from behind a fall of black hair. His face glistened with sweat, eyes laughing. 'And what do you know of freedom, girl? You who's known nothing but luxury and indulgence your whole life.'

'If this isn't freedom, then I don't know what is!'

He swept the hair back from his face and his lips curled into a smile, sharp as a blade. 'No,' he said. 'I imagine you don't.' He kept on walking, leaving her behind in a stew of outrage.

After a moment, she gathered herself enough to stomp after him. 'What does that mean?'

'It means,' he said, not stopping or turning around, 'that the world's a lot bloody bigger, and a lot bloody nastier, than you – or your dear old dad – know anything about.'

'My father has—'

'Your father—' He turned abruptly, so fast she almost ran into him, and she was forced to brace her hand against his chest to keep her balance. His skin was warm through the linen of his shirt, his heartbeat strong beneath her fingers, and she felt a flash of a different kind of heat. Hurriedly she withdrew her hand, stepping back.

Luckily, Zach didn't seem to notice her awkwardness. 'Your father has hidden away in this little utopian fantasy for a score of years, Amelia. He plays at being king of the pirates and ignores the rest of the world.'

'But the rest of the world does not concern us, Zach.' She smiled, confused by the heat in his voice. 'Their troubles are not ours. We are safe here.'

He shook his head, a flash of frustration quickly hidden behind a twist of a smile. 'We'll just see about that, won't we? I'd hate to have come so bloody far for nothing.'

Captain James Dauphin, the self-proclaimed Pirate King, kept his court in a fortress atop the cliff of Ile Sainte Anne. To the eyes of Zach Hazard it was a preposterous ostentation, but his own opinions, he knew, were coloured by the choices of his father, who had called this place home for twenty years. Zach wanted nothing to do with pirate kings or their castles. All he wanted – all he needed – was a ship beneath his feet and the wind in his sails. That was his idea of freedom, and it had nothing to do with the lofty ideals his father guarded closer than his own life. Closer than the life of his son.

Had he been truly free, of course, he wouldn't be here now in the sweating heat of Africa's west coast. Had he been truly free he'd have washed his hands of the wretched place years ago. But his father was his only kin and, though he knew he'd regret coming back, he'd not been able to ignore the gathering clouds of war. A warning had to be given. Whether it would be heeded was another matter entirely.

Eventually they reached the fortress, its grey stone walls rising above the trees. It might have sat well atop some stark, English hill but amid the lushness of Ile Sainte Anne it looked absurd. To Zach, the fortress had always seemed as big a folly as the ideals it had been built to defend. Nevertheless, he sighed in relief as Amelia led him into the blessed cool of the stone hallway, a sea breeze floating in through its narrow windows and stirring the air. He breathed deep, relishing the sharp sea-tang on his tongue.

Amelia smiled, looking at him sideways, as they stood together for a moment and gazed out past heavy stone towards the bright azure of sea and sky. 'You've been ashore no more than an hour,' she said. 'Do you miss the sea already, Captain?'

The breeze riffled her shirt, pushing soft linen against the slender contours of her body. Zach looked quickly away, licking his lips and tasting salt. 'Like I'd miss the air if it weren't here to breathe.'

She closed her eyes, lifting her arms as if she were a bird. 'Do you ever sit astride the bowsprit and pretend that you're flying?'

He laughed, couldn't help himself. 'Not a fitting place for a captain,' he said, 'but, aye, when I was a lad I did. Or in the crow's nest.'

Amelia smiled, eyes still shut, the breeze stirring her hair. 'There's no feeling better, is there?'

'Almost none,' he agreed, thinking of her taut body beneath the man's shirt and britches she wore. He wondered if she knew the effect all those tantalising glimpses of flesh had on a man who'd been too long at sea. He suspected that she knew all too well.

Amelia opened her eyes and smiled. 'Come, my father will be impatient to see you.'

She walked on and he followed. When last they'd met she'd been but a girl, close to flowering but still a child. Now, however ... Dark curls hung loose down her back, swaying like temptation in time with her hips. Her skin was sun-darkened to olive, unfashionable no doubt in the courts of true kings, but to his eyes her tanned limbs looked as smooth and touchable as silk.

But it was the fire in her eyes that sparked his interest. It spoke of adventure, of a wild spirit. He could imagine her astride the bowsprit, arms held wide and her hair running out behind her in the wind. She was no blushing maid and he stirred at the very thought of her firm, unbound body beneath his hands, and those adventurer's eyes fixed on him, bright as the play of sunshine over water. He'd have taken her to bed with great delight had she not been the daughter of James Dauphin.

Amelia looked back over her shoulder and arched a curious eyebrow.

'Admiring the view,' he said with a smile.

Her expression grew impish. 'Captain Hazard, there are at least twenty women I know who spit and curse whenever they hear your name mentioned. Do not imagine I want to be one of them. I won't succumb to your seductions.'

'Seductions?' He gestured to the windows in feigned innocence. 'I meant the sea view.'

'Oh.' She turned back around with a toss of her hair. 'Well ... Good.'

He smiled again, devilish despite the news he bore. 'Don't blame you, of course. Most women find me irresistible.'

'Do they?' She spun around, eyes laughing. 'Then it's fortunate for me, *Captain*, that I'm not "most women".'

'And it's fortunate for me, *Miss Dauphin*, that I've no interest in wild little barefoot girls.'

She looked as if she would retort, but after a silent moment all she said was, 'It's Captain Dauphin to you, sir,' before spinning around and stalking deeper into the fortress.

Blowing out a long breath, he followed. The crossing from Florida had been overlong – he'd not realised the level of his own frustration. That was all. That was enough to explain this sudden flare of desire. This girl held no special power over him, any girl would do and there were plenty who'd be eager to oblige. More than eager.

He would deliver his warning and be gone, steering well clear of Amelia Dauphin and her adventurer's eyes.

James Dauphin's court was just as Zach remembered it: high windows cut into thick stone walls admitting shafts of sunlight that striped the flagstone floor. First built to protect the colony from other pirate raiders, the fortress now served to defend Dauphin's precious Articles of Agreement. Set down in the time of his father's father, the Articles asserted the right of every man, whether highborn or baseborn, to live and die free beneath the open skies. Driven from England during the turmoil of war, they had found a home among the freemen of the sea and eventually, under James Dauphin, they had become the law that guaranteed equality of wealth and power to the free people of Ile Sainte Anne.

Though the fortress had defended the Articles from those less-enlightened raiders who coveted the island's wealth, Zach feared it would offer little defence against a new and greater threat: the firepower of a well-armed East-Indiaman and her naval escort. For the world was turning its eyes towards Ile Sainte Anne and the freedoms she proclaimed, a fact Zach had to make plain to James Dauphin – and to his own stubborn father.

Pausing in the hall's great arched doorway, he let Amelia precede him into Dauphin's so-called court, giving his eyes time to adjust to the gloom. Dominated by a huge fireplace that was lit despite the oppressive heat, the court was full of shadowy corners and the rattle of dice as men played at hazard and talked in low, easy voices.

He followed Amelia with his eyes as she walked barefoot across the stone, hips and hair swaying, to the fireplace at the far end of the room, where sat the captain's chair. Pilfered, no doubt, from some ancient galleon, the carved wooden chair gleamed in the firelight and upon it sat the man he had come to see. Behind him, a shadow at Dauphin's shoulder, stood the man he had most certainly not come to see – his own father, Zechariah Overton.

'Look,' Amelia said. 'Captain Hazard has come!'

Dauphin rose, hearty despite his years. 'Zach, my boy! What are you doing lurking in the doorway? Come in, come in!'

Aware of eyes peering out of the court's dark corners, Zach doffed his hat and strode into the room. 'Captain Dauphin,' he said, sweeping a bow. Then, with a scant nod to his father, he added, 'Captain Overton.'

His father watched him with bright eyes but said nothing, merely returned Zach's nod.

There was an awkward moment before Amelia said, 'Zach has come with tidings, Father. Ill news, by all accounts.'

'No, no,' Dauphin said. 'We'll have no ill news yet.' He held out his arms and embraced Zach, thumping him hard on the back. 'We need rum! And food. A feast! Tonight we'll feast in your honour. How long has it been, Zach, since last we saw you?'

Zach stole a glance at Amelia. 'Long enough.' She lifted her chin, bold beneath his scrutiny, and somehow it made him smile.

If Dauphin caught the look, he said nothing, just thumped Zach on the back again. 'Too long,' he said, turning to Overton. 'Is it not so, Zechariah? Too long since we've seen the boy.'

His father made no move from behind the captain's chair, only growled, 'Makes a man wonder what manner of news would cause him to sail so far.'

'Later,' Dauphin said, smiling again. 'Time enough for news later. First we—'

'James?' Zach clasped his shoulder, interrupting. 'Loath as I am to say as much, my father is right: the news I bring is dark, it's no reason to feast.'

'But your return is,' Dauphin said warmly. 'It's been six years, Zach, without a word.'

Guilt flared briefly but he had no reply to give. He had turned his back on Ile Sainte Anne and all for which it stood, and his father could not forgive him for it. The day he'd sailed, six years ago, Overton had disowned him and Zach had sworn never to return. Yet here he was.

Dauphin's hand tightened on his arm. 'Come then, give us your news. Perhaps it is best to hear it in the morning, while the sun is bright and the air full of birdsong. Tonight, when it is dark, we shall feast and chase away the gloom, shall we not?'

'Aye, if you wish.'

'I do.' He looked over at his daughter. 'Amelia, order a goat slaughtered and roasted, we shall—'

'Am I not to hear Captain Hazard's news?' she said. 'Have Jean-Pierre arrange the feast; I should hear what Zach has come to say.'

'Amelia—'

'Father.' The challenge in her voice rang clear as a bell, defiance in every line of her body as she stood braced for a fight.

There followed a silent contest of wills, and after a moment Zach was amused to see Dauphin's eyes narrow in defeat. 'Very well,' he sighed, 'we shall meet in my quarters.' He smiled at Zach, feigned exasperation clearly mingling with pride. 'She is her mother's daughter.'

'Aye,' Zach agreed, 'and her father's.'

Dauphin laughed. 'So she is.' He slapped Zach on the arm. 'It does my heart good to see you, Zach. It does it good indeed.'

Over Dauphin's shoulder Zach saw his father watching

them. There was no warmth in his expression, never had been, only a keen intelligence that sliced like a knife. Zach suspected his father knew exactly what he had come to say, and hated him for it as much as he ever had. Truth, when it differed from his own view of the world, was never something Zechariah Overton wanted to hear, especially not from his son's lips. Dauphin's sentimental attachment to Ile Sainte Anne might be hard to overcome, but Zach feared that his father's stubborn adherence to the colony's ideals could prove impossible to shift.

If he was right, then his father might doom them all in the end.

Chapter Two

Amelia loved her father's ramshackle quarters at the top of the fortress. The bookcases had long since overflowed into unstable piles that ebbed and flowed like the tide. One wall was covered in a chart of Ile Sainte Anne and the western coast of Africa, with navigable routes marked through the treacherous waters surrounding the island. Other charts were rolled up and propped in spare corners, and around the small fireplace were gathered a half dozen chairs. Dust motes drifted lazily in the sunlight, warm and hazy and starkly at odds with the conversation taking place.

Zach had chosen the seat furthest from the fireplace, as far from the blaze as possible. His coat was slung over the back of the chair, his waistcoat unbuttoned, and he sat with his elbows on his knees as he spoke.

'... without the need for a trial, they've permission to dispense "justice" as they choose,' he said, voice low and grave. 'Any pirate they take, or any suspected of it, is hauled to the yardarm there and then. Sometimes they'll take a man or two back to Wapping. They think gibbeting a corpse at Blackwall Point for a month or so will keep their sailors honest, but—'

'Wapping?' Amelia asked. 'Where's—?'

Zach glanced at her. 'It's where they hang pirates,' he said. 'Execution Dock. That's in London.' He glanced at her father. 'Have you taught her nothing of the world?'

'Only what's worth knowing,' he said. 'And Amelia need not know of such places as Wapping.'

Zach shook his head. 'Not knowing something doesn't make it less real.'

'But I want to know,' Amelia protested. 'Father, you

don't need to protect me from such things. I'm not a child any longer.'

He gave a thin smile and reached out to take her hand. 'You are still *my* child.'

Overton shifted in his seat, pulling a long-stemmed pipe from his pocket and starting to pack it with tobacco. 'There ain't nothing new about them hanging pirates,' he said. 'That ain't why you came back, boy.'

Zach nodded, his fingers clasping and unclasping before him. Clever fingers, Amelia noted, a pickpocket's fingers. 'They've driven the pirates out of the North Atlantic, pressing hard in the Caribbean. Too many men have seen too many other men hang, and now' – he lifted his gaze and met Amelia's – 'now they're coming here.'

'To Ile Sainte Anne?' Her heart grew cold, like a stone. 'Why?'

'Because they'll let no such place as this remain, a haven for the pirates they're hunting.'

Silence fell, the soft crackle of flames the only sound in the room. Outside, gulls cried and the distant boom of surf called to her from the beach. At last, her father spoke. 'How do you know this, Zach?'

'First heard it in a brothel in Hispaniola,' he said, with half a glance at Amelia. Unaccountably, it made her blush. 'Couple of tars talking about sailing East with the French.'

'With the *French*?' Overton sat forward. 'Not bloody likely.'

'Heard the same a month later in Veracruz,' he said. 'This time from a French officer. Drunk as an emperor, he was, and eager to please. Told me all about the fleet: French, British, even the Dutch.'

'Together?'

'A treaty, to eliminate the threat of Ile Sainte Anne.'

'What threat?' Amelia protested. 'We take only what we need from the merchants who sail these waters, and we share the takings fairly among the crew and their families. We pose no threat.'

'Maybe not to honest men,' Zach said. 'But to the powers of this world grown rich from commerce? Only a fool would think this place poses no threat to them.'

No one answered that, but the looks exchanged between the three men were eloquent enough. Her father and Overton were tight-lipped and stubborn, arms folded. Zach just looked grim, turning away from them with a shake of his head. These were old arguments, she realised; they must date to the times before Zach left. She hoped he'd say something, explain, but he held his tongue and the tension grew thick.

Aware that there were traps underfoot, but determined to break the tension, Amelia said, 'When will they come?'

Zach looked at her in surprise; clearly he'd not expected her to believe him. 'Six months from now,' he said. 'Give or take a month. That's what I heard.'

Overton reached forward to light a taper in the fire, then sucked the flame into his pipe until it began to smoulder. The smoke only added to the heat in the room. He puffed out a lungful and said, 'What's your purpose, then, coming here with this fishwife's warning?'

Irritated, Zach said, 'It's no fishwife's tale. It's the truth, whether you want to hear it or not.'

'Truth,' Overton spat. 'It's what *you* want to hear, 'tis all.'

Zach cast an exasperated look at Amelia, a shared moment that made her swallow a smile. She knew all too well how stubborn his father could be. 'My purpose in coming here,' Zach said, 'was only to warn you. What you do with the warning is your business.'

'Then you've not come to help us fight?' Overton sucked on his pipe stem and smiled when Zach didn't answer. 'I thought not.'

Amelia's own father had listened without comment, as he often did, but now it was his turn to speak. He put a placating hand on Overton's shoulder and said, 'Zach, you have my thanks for your warning. To have come so far is a kindness.'

Zach sat back in his chair, a sardonic look in his eye. 'And yet ...?'

Her father rose, walked to the stand beneath the window and picked up the leather-bound volume that rested there for any man to consult: the Articles of Agreement, the soul of Ile Sainte Anne. He smoothed his hands over the cover and turned back to Zach. 'You know we cannot leave.'

'I know you *will* not leave. What you *cannot* do is win the fight.'

'Must it come to that?' Amelia asked, horrified. 'Leaving or fighting? Are they our only choices?'

Zach shrugged. 'There's a third.'

'Which is?'

'You could hang.'

'Zachary!' her father scolded. 'Enough. I'm grateful for your warning, but I'll thank you not to frighten my daughter on the unsteady evidence of two sailors in a whorehouse and a drunk Frenchman!'

'Six months,' Zach said, rising to his feet. He levelled a finger at her father. 'Mark that, James. Six months and the fleet will be here.'

'Let them come,' Overton said, blowing smoke. 'I ain't afraid to die for the Articles. Plenty of others have.'

'You'll be in good company then,' Zach snapped, stalking towards the door. 'But don't expect me to throw my life away so easily.'

'Zachary!' her father called. 'Please, let's not argue again. It's been six years ...'

'Aye, six years and still nothing has changed. I should never have come back to this castle of dreams!'

'Captain, wait.' Amelia darted from her chair to block his path to the door, a hand on his chest to stop him. She glanced at her father, saw the distress on his face. 'Please, don't go. Not like this. No decisions can be made now and, truly, we thank you for coming so far to warn us.'

He was angry, breathing hard. She could feel the rapid rise and fall of his chest. 'Amy, you don't know what—' He took a deep, steadying breath. Her thumb, she realised, touched the skin at the edge of his shirt, grazing his chest as he breathed in and out, a fact of which they were both suddenly aware.

'Stay,' she said, not dropping her hand, heart hammering. 'They've already slaughtered the goat.'

His expression changed, humour replacing anger. 'Already slaughtered the goat, have they?' He smiled. 'Then I had better stay for the feast.'

She smiled, too. 'Thank you.'

For a tingling moment they just looked at each other; then Zach turned away and Amelia let her hand fall to her side. 'James, I'm sorry,' he said. 'My temper sometimes bests me.'

Her father smiled, relieved as he came to join them. 'Yes, well, you came by that honestly.'

Overton didn't respond to the jibe, didn't move from his chair, blue smoke clouding his face.

Ignoring his father, Zach said, 'I've a couple of bottles of good Cuban rum aboard the *Hawk* – goes well with roasted goat. Or with anything else.'

Amelia smiled. 'I've heard Cuban rum is the best in the world. Here we can only get cane juice.'

He made a face. 'Then a bottle's yours. Be warned, though, it's knock-down stuff.'

'Captain Hazard,' she said, arching an eyebrow, 'I can handle my drink as well as the next man.'

His only answer was a smile that looked all too much like a challenge.

Chapter Three

After a day of dark talk, the feasting and drinking lasted long into the night. On the beach the goat was roasted over a fire that crackled and danced, sending sparks high into the sky and shadows leaping across the sand.

Old Jones was on his fiddle, his music as drunken and reeling as the dancers who whooped and laughed as they spun around the fire. All the islanders were out tonight – fishermen, pirates, farmers, the blacksmith and his wife, and, of course, all the tavern doxies with their red petticoats and bare legs on show. Amelia's father presided over it all with a smile of such pride that she thought her heart would burst with love for him. How could Zach talk of abandoning this place, this life, for anything?

She swallowed another mouthful of Cuban rum, and very fine it tasted. Spiced and exotic. Dangerous, too, the way it rubbed the sharp edges off your mind and lit a fire in the pit of your belly. She took another swig from the half-empty soldier's bottle at her side.

She hadn't seen Zach for a while, not since they'd eaten together on the fine Persian rug laid out for her father, Zach pulling strips of meat from the bone with long, nimble fingers and her watching with more interest than was proper.

Her and every other woman on the beach. She'd seen them around the fire, trying to catch his eye, displaying their voluptuous wares. Amelia pulled her knees up to her chest – what there was of it – and sighed. That's where he was now, she supposed, out beyond the firelight, wrangling with lightskirts on the beach. And with anyone else who offered, of whom there seemed to be plenty.

Not that she was jealous. Not that she had any intention of letting Zach Hazard seduce *her*. Not that he'd want to … What had he called her this morning? A wild little barefoot girl. She took another swig of rum, licked her lips, and wondered idly if his tasted the same, all burnt sugar and spice. Frustrated, she fixed her eyes on the dancers, wild in the firelight.

No one had asked her to dance. The men of the island stayed away from her for fear of angering her father or, worse, Captain Overton. Most of the time she didn't mind because she had the *Sunlight* and that was all that mattered. There were times, however, like tonight, with the rum firing her blood, when she wondered what it would be like to taste another's lips, to ignite the flame ...

Old Jones started playing another air, her favourite foc'sle song, slow and romantic. She got to her feet, a little unsteadily, and headed down the beach to where he was playing and where O'Reilly had started to sing in his rich, melodious voice. He nodded when he saw her approach and she took a breath, joining in as she so often did.

The moon's in her shroud and to light thee afar
On the deck of the Daring's a love-lighted star.

Others came in with the chorus, or clapped along, the swelling emotion as intoxicating as the rum that swung from her fingertips.

So wake, lady wake, I am waiting for thee,
Oh, this night or never my bride thou shalt be.

Then, at the edge of the firelight, she saw Zach watching her. He didn't clap or sing, just watched with the fire dancing in his eyes. Slowly, slowly, he began to walk towards her. Not in a hurry, but steady. Unswerving.

So wake, lady wake, I am waiting for thee,
Oh, this night or never my bride thou shalt be.

She swallowed, lost her place as the new verse began and took another, fortifying, mouthful of rum. It burned her throat, fuelling the fire in her veins. Closing her eyes, she let the music take her, spinning in slow circles as the chorus swelled, and suddenly there was heat at her back, down the whole length of her. Hotter than the fire. A strong arm circled her waist and a voice whispered in her ear, 'Dance with me.'

Her heart tripped over itself, indecent with excitement.

Breathless, she turned within the circle of his arm. Close up his eyes were molten, black and gold in the firelight. Amelia found she couldn't breathe, didn't want to breathe. He pulled the rum bottle from her hand, took a long drink, and then tossed it away onto the sand. 'Dance with me, Captain Dauphin.'

She opened her mouth to refuse, but she'd no appetite for protest, not when heat was building deliciously in all the right places. All she could think was, why not? Why not do this? She licked her lips and saw him watching, felt his arm tighten about her waist, pulling her close enough to feel him, hard and eager. 'I don't dance with strangers,' she said, and they both knew they weren't talking of the 'Barley Mow'.

Zach smiled, devilish and charming. 'Then it's a good thing I'm no stranger,' he said, lifting his hand, tracing a finger across her lips. She tasted the tip with her tongue and thrilled to see him shiver, but his hand kept on moving, to her throat and the little hollow at its base. She breathed, quick and sharp, head tilting back as he circled there and then moved down, lower, along the line of her shirt and, slowly, slowly, beneath it to skim the edge of her breast. There he stopped, his other arm like iron about her waist, keeping her upright, for her knees had turned to rubber and her head was spinning faster than the song.

'Siren,' he murmured into her ear, sending her spirits

shooting skyward like sparks from the fire. 'Have you bewitched me?'

'No,' she promised. 'Perhaps it's the rum.'

He laughed, soft against her skin. 'It's a spirit much stronger than that.'

From behind them, in the darkness beyond the firelight, she could hear husky sounds of pleasure – moans, cries and shouts. She had lived most of her life in Ile Sainte Anne, had seen whores at work and sailors at play. There was little she hadn't seen or heard about and she was not afraid.

Taking Zach's hand, she led him towards the shoreline, into the darkness and the quiet. Here he was all shadows, dark and thrilling. With a touch to her shoulder he stopped her. 'Far enough.'

Heart thumping, she kept her back to him. Waiting. He stroked her hair, pulling it aside so he could kiss the place where shoulder met neck, his hand slipping beneath her shirt, skimming across her skin until she gasped his name.

Then he turned her in his arms. She couldn't see his face – he was only a silhouette against the stars – but she could see the way his hands shook when he touched her.

'Beautiful,' he breathed. 'Too beautiful ...'

His touch was light and reverent as he bent to kiss her, unlacing her shirt and slipping it from her shoulders as he drew her down into the sand.

It was almost too delicious to bear the heat of his mouth and the cool breeze against the places where he'd kissed her. Lower he went, fingers unlacing her britches, slipping them down until she was nude and vulnerable and feeling deliciously wicked.

'This morning I vowed I wouldn't let you touch me,' she laughed, amused by the notion now that she lay there, naked beneath the spinning sky. 'Funny, isn't it? I vowed I'd never be one of those women, the sighing women who cry over you all the time.'

She giggled, woozy and dizzy, dimly aware of shadows shifting, something changing – of Zach, on the sand at her side, breathing hard and watching her from behind a fall of dark hair. He touched her hip, ran a hand over the bone and down onto the plane of her stomach. Lower, she wanted to say, go lower.

But he didn't. He stopped.

'How much—?' His voice caught; he cleared his throat and began again. 'How much have you drunk, Amy?'

She laughed. 'Plenty! Do you have more?'

'Are you drunk?'

'Very. Aren't you?'

He muttered something beneath his breath, then said, 'Not nearly enough for this.' He rolled onto his back, pressed both hands over his face and blew out a shaky breath.

Amelia sat up, confused, sending the world spinning in all directions. She screwed shut her eyes, but it didn't help, so she lay back down again and peered up at the stars turning above her. The sand under her fingers was soft and dry, but cool. She dribbled some onto her belly, felt it pile there. '*I'm* drunk enough. Drunk enough for anything!' She giggled again and found it hard to stop because it was true and because there was sand piling on her belly.

'You're a child,' Zach said, in a voice that was wrong. He wasn't meant to sound like that when he was seducing her, all quiet and grave. 'You're a child, Amy.'

She looked over, saw him sitting up, staring out at the black sea. The moon had painted a long silver stripe across the water, which was pretty enough, but he was meant to be looking at her, not the sea. She touched his back and he flinched like it burned.

'I'm not a child.' She struggled to sit, but this time when the world spun it threatened to throw her off entirely. It wasn't so funny; she felt a little sick. 'I'm one-and-twenty.'

He laughed, a dry sound. 'You're a child, and a summer child to boot. You think you know the world, but you know nothing. I'll not take advantage. I'm not so low as that.'

'Take advantage?' Anger wormed its way through her happy haze and suddenly she was conscious that she sat naked on the beach not a hundred steps from where her father was feasting. She groped around for her shirt, but it was dark and she couldn't seem to keep herself the right way up.

'Here.' Zach pushed fabric into her hand.

It was a tangle and it took a moment to put it on right. Tying it was impossible, her fingers were too confused, so she just clutched it shut and pulled her knees up to her chest. 'You aren't taking advantage,' she said, humiliation rising in her throat. 'I've seen darkness enough washed ashore on this island to know what I'm about.'

He made a gruff, noncommittal sound. 'You'd never forgive me. Once you'd come to your bearings, you'd have hated me for it.'

'You think I don't know what I want?'

'I think you're jug-bitten.'

'So are you!'

'Yes but I'm— I know what I'm doing.'

'Oh? Whereas I'm a silly child who needs protecting from herself, is that it?' She scrambled to her feet, glad her shirt came down to her thighs and ignoring the precarious way the beach was sliding towards the sea. 'Take a good look, Captain Hazard, because that was your one and only chance!'

He didn't get up, just watched her. 'I can live with that. There are worse regrets to have.'

'Such as abandoning your father, perhaps? Or trading everything he believes in for rum and easy profit?' She made the mistake of taking a step towards him and the beach tricked her, flipping her over, and suddenly she was back in the sand, Zach's knees under her belly.

'Elegant,' he said, helping her to sit up next to him. After a moment's silence he added, 'You know nothing of my father, Amelia, or why I left this place.' He glanced at her, his face all shadows in the moonlight. 'There are some things in life more important than a man's ideals, don't you think?'

She laughed. 'No! What could be more important?'

His gaze became deeper, more searching. 'Do you really not know?'

'Gold, I suppose, for you.' She pulled her shirt tighter. 'Rum and dice. Pleasure?'

He shook his head, turning back to the sea. 'Far more important than any such trifles.'

Her head was spinning too fast now, fast as a top, but not so fast that she missed the melancholy in his voice. She tried to speak, but instead made a noise that sounded unpleasant, something like a whimpering dog coughing up a hairball. Her stomach began to pitch and roll alarmingly.

'Lie down,' Zach said. 'Can't fall off the world when you're lying down.'

Somehow there was soft fabric under her cheek instead of sand, fingers brushing hair out of her face and something warm draped over her shoulder. 'Go to sleep, you silly nug,' he said from far away in the spinning night. 'And if you're going to cast up your accounts, don't do it all over me.'

She tried to answer, but it took too much concentration and her sluggish words couldn't beat the collapsing darkness. So she just closed her eyes and let it drown her. In the morning, she'd unravel it all. In the morning.

Chapter Four

Zach awoke to raindrops on his eyelids.

Only it wasn't raindrops, it was Brookes with a flagon of water, standing over him and dripping it into his face.

Spluttering a curse, Zach sat up. 'What the devil—?' He scrubbed water from his eyes and looked around. He was still on the beach and the day was just breaking, already bright enough to be unpleasant with his head tender from drink.

'That weren't the wisest thing you ever did,' Brookes said, nodding off to one side, to where Amy lay sprawled on his coat with her tanned legs bare and her hair tangled in the sand.

Zach rubbed a hand across his face. 'I didn't,' he said.

Brookes merely raised an eyebrow.

'Too drunk,' Zach said. 'Couldn't do it.'

With a nod, Brookes patted him on the shoulder. 'Aye, well lad, the drink'll do that to the best of us. In this case, though, it's probably better that you didn't—'

'Not me!' he said. 'Her. *She* was too drunk, didn't know what she was about.'

'And you played the gentleman?'

'No need to sound so sceptical.' Zach got up, shaking sand out of his shirt and hair. He grabbed the flagon from Brookes' hand and took a long, welcome drink. 'My father won't listen,' he said, changing the subject. 'Thinks I'm telling Dauphin fishwives' tales.'

'Colour me surprised. Did you really expect any different?'

He didn't answer, because he wouldn't have come so far if he'd had no hope at all. Yet he should have known nothing would change; six years was meaningless in the dreamland of Ile Sainte Anne. Here, reality remained as distant as ever.

His eyes wandered to Amelia, fragile-looking in the dawn light. She'd feel wretched when she woke, but for now she just looked piercingly beautiful. He wished he could preserve the image, but no painter could capture the softness of her skin or the way her hair shifted in the breeze.

'Half the crew's got barrel fever this morning,' Brookes said, interrupting his musing. 'Won't be able to start loading supplies until tomorrow.'

The taste of her skin was suddenly vivid in his memory, warm and soft as silk – what kind of fool had he been not to take her when he'd had the chance? She'd been so willing, so eager. So drunk. Not for the first time he cursed the thin vein of morality that ran through his soul. One day, he swore, it would kill him.

'Zachary,' Brookes said, like he'd repeated it several times. 'Are you listening?'

He offered his most disarming smile. 'Somewhat.'

'I said we can't even start loading 'til tomorrow.'

'There's time enough.' He forced his eyes away from Amy. 'Not planning to sail with the next tide, not after the crossing we just had.'

'Aye,' Brookes said cautiously. 'No reason to linger, neither. Not with the navy on its way.'

'Crew needs to rest. You know it. We can afford a couple of weeks, even a month without risk.'

Brookes grunted. 'There's more than one risk in these waters, Zachary. More than one way to run aground.'

'Then it's a good thing,' he said, meeting his old friend's worried look with a smile, 'that I'm somewhat skilled in the navigation of these particular waters. Don't imagine me in any danger.'

'We'll see.' Brookes nodded towards the harbour and the *Hawk*. 'Will you head back with me?'

'I—' He took a step, but couldn't help looking back at

Amy asleep in the sand. 'That's my good coat she's sleeping on,' he said, brazening the moment with a smile. 'I'd hate to lose it. I'll just wait 'til she wakes.'

Brookes said nothing, only lifted an eyebrow before turning and walking back along the beach. Zach watched him go for a moment, and then sank down onto the sand. It *was* his good coat, that was no lie, and if he'd wanted to leave her there he could have done. He simply chose not to.

She was James Dauphin's daughter, after all. He could hardly abandon her alone and still half drunk on his rum, now could he? It didn't signify anything more than a sense of duty to his old friend. Nothing more at all.

Chapter Five

Amelia had several memories of the previous night and early morning, but they all washed up together like flotsam on the beach and she could hardly tell one from the other. She remembered heat and firelight, desire and anticipation – his hands on her body, wicked and delightful. She remembered disappointment. Rejection. Humiliation. She remembered waking, cold and half naked, full of shame and feeling wretched. She remembered the world still spinning as she tried to stagger home, and a strong arm about her waist, holding her upright as she emptied her stomach into the sand. Miserable as sin. And then she remembered her father, full of concern, and the welcome softness of her bed.

It wasn't until the evening that she was able to unpick events, lying alone in the dark of her bedroom while downstairs she could hear her father and Overton arguing, their voices a bass rumble that she could almost feel through the floor.

Like a fool, she'd offered herself to Zach and he'd rejected her. The details were hazy, but she remembered him saying he wasn't nearly drunk enough to lie with her. And she remembered accusing him of abandoning his father. The memory flushed her cheeks with mortification; his barb had pricked her pride but hers was designed to inflict a deeper wound.

A few self-pitying tears threatened, but she wiped them away angrily. She wasn't sorry he'd rejected her, she was only sorry that she'd made such a spectacle of herself in the first place, and for that she blamed the wretched rum he'd given her.

Someone had placed a plate of sliced fruit next to her bed and she tentatively nibbled on a piece of mango. The sweet juice washed away the sour taste in her mouth and revived her so well that she managed to sit up, and though she felt fragile, the room no longer spun and her head only skirted the edges of pain. It was a vast improvement from the morning.

Downstairs, she could still hear her father talking but there were other sounds too. Someone was playing a fiddle, others were laughing, gaming – the usual hubbub of an evening in her father's court. Not that she would be attending; even this close the noise of it made her flinch. No, what she needed was fresh air to clear her head and solitude to contemplate what had – and had not – happened the previous night.

After pulling on her clothes, she crept down the stairs and left the fortress unnoticed, striking out along the short path that ran along the top of the cliffs. There was no moon yet and the stars were draped in diamond swags across a cloudless sky, the humid air alive with the song of night creatures. Amelia took a deep breath, relishing the warm island fragrance. Far below, a gentle sea washed against the base of the cliffs, the muffled sounds of carousing growing fainter and fainter as she walked until all she could hear was the soft boom of the surf and the song of the cicadas. Already, she felt better.

She loved the cliff tops at night. It was quiet here, away from the madness of the docks and the intensity of her father's court. Next to the *Sunlight*, it was her favourite place in the world and it was the perfect place to think.

On this night, she had much to consider. Her own folly aside, Zach had brought ill news: talk of a truce between the Dutch, the French and the British, their gilded kings more afraid of Ile Sainte Anne than of each other. And war, he said, being plotted in the great cities of the world – war against her father.

Beneath her feet the grass was soft and the air rich with

the scent of loam and vanilla flowers. Though it was difficult to imagine how anyone could fear this place, where all were equal and shared what they had one with the other, Amy understood very well that the powers of the world feared equality and freedom more than anything else. They were ideas that could not be stopped by military force; they were ideas that could not be stopped at all.

Her heart swelled with pride at all her father had built here, and, unlike Zach Hazard, she believed it was worth fighting to preserve. She just hoped that a better way could be found. There were too many innocents on the island to risk an outright confrontation.

She turned the problem over in her mind as she ambled along the familiar path towards Black Church Rock, so named because here the grass gave way to a craggy black shard that rose like a spire from the waves crashing around the promontory on the north side of the harbour. To the south, the docks sprawled, alive with light and music, while to the north the fires of Runaway Bay burned bright. Beyond that the dark sea ran out to the end of the world, nothing but stars reflecting in its depths. Sometimes, when she scrambled out to the very tip and looked down to see white foam at the base of the cliff, she imagined that she stood between two worlds: the world of men and the world of the ocean. Occasionally she wondered to which she belonged.

Emerging from the trees she headed towards the outcrop but stopped dead when she saw that she wasn't alone. A man sat exactly in her favourite spot, upon the flat rock close to the end of the headland. He was hefting a stone in his hand, gauging its weight before hurling it out into the darkness. Then he picked up another and did the same. Amelia hesitated. She wasn't in the mood for company so turned to leave, but as she did so the stranger rose to his feet.

'Oh,' he said, in a voice that proved it to be the last person she wanted to see. 'It's you.'

Heat flooded her face, both embarrassment and anger. Her instinct was to run away, but a moment's reflection made her realise that this meeting must happen, and that it would be best to get it over with now, in privacy, rather than to risk a more public encounter. She forced herself to turn back around and stand her ground. 'Captain Hazard.'

'Feeling better?'

'Yes, no thanks to your vile rum.'

In the darkness she saw a glint of ivory as he smiled. 'Nothing wrong with the rum, Amy. It's the quantity that did for you.'

She didn't answer, flushing again in embarrassment. 'I— I don't exactly remember ...' She was unable to look at him as she spoke, unable to forget the feel of his hands on her body. Her embarrassment grew acute. 'I don't think I was myself last night, I trust you'll not—'

'I make a point of never remembering anything I've done when I'm half-cut. Much easier that way.'

She risked a quick glance at him, to see if she understood his meaning.

'Don't remember a thing,' he assured her with a smile. 'Though I do believe I heard you sing at one point ...'

'Not very well, I'm sure.'

They fell into silence. Amelia had intended to be angry, but he'd disarmed her with his unexpected gallantry. Though his rejection still hurt, she found she could not hate him.

'Thought perhaps you'd come here to sing,' Zach said. 'Wouldn't surprise me to find you perched on the end of these rocks, luring passing sailors to their doom.'

She shook her head at the image. 'With my voice, I'm more likely to frighten them away than lure them in.'

He laughed and crunched over the stones towards her,

gesturing to the headland with a grand sweep of his arm. 'I'll leave you in peace, then, to do whatever it is you do here. I've business at the docks that requires increasingly urgent attention.'

'I study the stars,' she said, as he walked past her. 'And I think. That's what I do here.'

He was already behind her when he stopped. She heard his boots rasping on the rock. 'It's a good place for that.' She thought he would leave then, but instead he said, 'And there's much to think about tonight.'

Amelia turned to look at him, unsure of his meaning. There was an earnestness in his expression that baffled her, until she realised he must be thinking of the reason he'd come to Ile Sainte Anne in the first place. 'It's true, then, what you told my father?'

He looked a little surprised, but said, 'I'd hardly have come so far if it weren't.'

'Yet you won't stay.'

'Stay and die, you mean? No, I won't do that.'

She felt a rush of disappointment, despite knowing how he'd answer. He'd been gone six years, after all, had abandoned them long ago. 'Then why come back to warn us? Why take that risk?'

He gave a soft laugh, rich with irony. 'That, Amelia, is a very good question.' He spared her a sideways glance. 'And I have no answer to give.'

'Perhaps,' she said, 'you still feel something for the people of Ile Sainte Anne? For your father?'

'Not for him, no.' He looked away, back out to sea. 'But then, I never did. No more than he felt for me.'

She shook her head. 'That's not true, your father—'

'You know nothing of my father.'

'He's a good man,' she persisted. 'He does good work here, settling those men and women we rescue from the—'

'Enough!' He turned on her, eyes flashing in anger. Then

he took a breath and in a calmer voice said, 'Even bad men can do good deeds, Amy. It doesn't change what he is at heart.'

'And what is that?'

His lips pressed into a hard, tight line and he shook his head. 'Your father and mine, Amy, they'd see the world turned upside down. They'd see kings in rags and beggars upon their thrones. But what thought do they give to those who get trampled in the fight? What thought do they give to those who burn in the fires they stoke? They sacrifice *everything* to their precious ideals, with no care for—' He gave a brief shake of his head. 'The world's not so simple as they'd have you believe, Amy, and there's a price to be paid for their choices.'

'They just want us to live free. Is that so wrong?'

'We *can* live free.' He cast his arm out towards the ocean. 'At sea, we are all free. Live as we please, go where we please, and when trouble comes, we run. But here?' He shook his head. There was frustration in his face, as though he'd had this conversation many times before. She'd been a child when Zach swept out of Ile Sainte Anne six years ago, but perhaps he'd spent ten years before that arguing this very point. He jerked his head towards the fortress and the white flag of liberty that hung limp in the breathless night. 'When you raise a flag against them, that's when they'll come for you. When you rally others to your standard, set yourself up against them, that's when they'll come. And who will protect these people then?' He kicked a stone with the toe of his boot and for a moment looked more like a petulant boy than a man of the world. 'Folly. Arrant folly. Told them that six years ago, of course. Not that they ever listened to a word that left my mouth.'

Amelia found herself smiling. 'What father ever listens to the wisdom of their child?'

'Certainly not mine.' He lifted his eyes to hers, rueful

for a moment before turning more speculative. 'You won't always stay here, though, will you? You'll sail. You weren't born for the land.'

'This is my home ...'

'It's just a place, and a dangerous place at that, marked now by those who would see it burn.'

'I don't fear them.'

'Don't you?' He studied her face with an intent expression, as though he were trying to read her very soul. 'Then you're a fool, Amy, because when they come – and they will come – it will be the end of the world.'

'Are you trying to frighten me, Captain Hazard?'

'Yes,' he said, drawing nearer. 'Because you should be afraid.'

Her heart began to race. Like fire he was, up close, a startling and compelling heat. Despite all that had happened, she was drawn to him, and that frightened her more than the thought of ten thousand warships on the horizon. Determined that he should see nothing of her feelings, she jutted out her jaw. 'We will fight them, Captain Hazard, if we must. We'll seek peace first, but if they bring war here then they will wish they had not!'

He barked a laugh. 'And how will you fight an armada?'

'Any way we can. Believe me, Captain, there is nothing I would not do to save Ile Sainte Anne. I would die for it.'

'Then I'm sure you'll have the chance. Along with every other soul on this island.' With a shake of his head he turned away from her, staring down at the docks. The *Gypsy Hawk* was moored at the southernmost side of the harbour, lamps lit, and suddenly she knew what he was thinking.

'You're leaving already.'

'I've given my warning: you've six months, perhaps less, before they come. Time enough to run.'

'My father won't run, and neither will I.'

'Then you'll die.'

'Better to die free.'

'Better yet to live free. Better to run when—' He stopped, stock still and peered into the darkness. 'What the bloody hell is *he* doing here?'

She followed his gaze, throat closing in fear. Had the enemy come so soon? 'What? Who is it?'

He spared her a glance, half-amused and half-sour. 'There – look. I know that ship.'

'Where?' She did her best to follow his gaze, but his eyes were sharper than hers. 'I can't see a ship.'

'Coming in behind the *Hawk*.'

A moment later she saw the sleek prow of a brigantine emerge from the night, lit only by the *Hawk*'s lanterns. She was running dark and Amelia wondered how Zach had seen her at all, let alone recognised her. She squinted to read the name, but it was too far away.

'French privateer.' Zach's voice was stony. '*Le Serpent de la Mer* – captained by one Luc Géroux.'

'I know that name.'

Zach cast her another look. 'Do you now?'

'Is he not the Marquis de Bernez?'

'So he'd have you believe.'

She watched the corsair ship slide into anchorage, sleek and powerful next to the weathered bulk of the *Hawk*. 'I've heard that Captain Géroux has been terribly wronged by his father and brother, disinherited and exiled from his homeland.'

'A tragic tale indeed.' Zach folded his arms across his chest. '*I've* heard he was born on the wrong side of the bed sheets to a Parisian whore and reels in gullible women with stories of his pitiful past, all the while picking off honest pirates at the behest of the highest bidder.'

Amelia flashed him an angry look. 'Trust you to look on the darkest side of the story.'

'It's where the truth's usually found.'

'Captain Hazard, you're a cynic.'

'Aye, it's why I've lived so long.'

She smiled but had no answer to that, so instead said, 'Since this is Captain Géroux's first visit to Ile Sainte Anne, I'd better welcome him before Jean-Pierre sends him away.'

Zach said nothing until she was almost at the tree line, then he called out, 'He's not here to help you fight, if that's what you're thinking. Luc Géroux only ever acts in his own best interest.'

'Then you and he have much in common.'

Against the dark horizon he was little more than a shadow. Only his eyes caught the starlight, glittering like black amber. 'Be sure to ask him what Letter of Marque he carries. Perhaps it is you he has come for this time.'

By the time Zach returned to the *Hawk*, the *Serpent*'s crew were preparing to moor in Ile Sainte Anne's protected harbour. Barked orders drifted across the water to unstow the anchors, unsling the lower yards, and send down the top ropes.

It was deftly done. Professionally, Zach could admire the corsair captain's seamanship, but that was all he could admire. He knew the ship well, had fought her three times in open water. Twice he had won, once he had not and that time only Brookes' swift thinking had saved him from the deadly nevergreen.

That the *Serpent* should now be mooring within cannon range of the *Hawk* ... Well, it didn't sit right. It didn't sit right at all.

'Géroux showing up here will raise a breeze.' Brookes' words echoed Zach's thoughts as he came to join him at the rail, watching the *Serpent*'s crew hang the anchor to the longboat. 'I say we sail tonight, find a safer anchorage to rest the crew.'

Zach shook his head. 'If Géroux was here for us he'd have come in, guns blazing, not moored on our stern. He's here for some other purpose.'

'A purpose we don't want to know about, I dare say. Which is all the more reason to sail tonight.'

'With half the crew still ashore?' Zach glanced over at his old friend. 'Besides, sail where? Back to the Spanish Main or the Floridas, where the seas are full of navy frigates?'

'To the Indies. Madagascar. Take our chances with the East Indiamen. They'll be ripe for plucking in a month or two, on the way to the pilgrimage.'

'Aye, running well armed and with a naval escort too.'

Brookes turned, leaning one arm on the rail, and studied Zach with sharp eyes. 'Géroux coming here is no coincidence, not with the combined fleet mustering.'

Zach couldn't deny it.

'What will you do?' Brookes pressed. 'Sit here and wait for his masters to come for us? That's madness.'

'We'll not do that. We'll run, as always. Keep one step ahead.'

'To run,' Brookes said, eyebrows rising, 'we must have a heading. South? Back west? Where will we run?'

It was a good question and Zach had no answer. The world was shrinking; they were pressed in from all sides. Where was there left to go for men who refused to obey the laws of tyrants? He glanced towards the lights on shore, towards Dauphin's stone fortress, and thought of the old man sitting by his fire, of his unfettered daughter and the freedom they imagined they'd found here. It was an illusion about to be shattered and, for the first time since leaving this place, he felt a weight of sadness at the prospect. 'I don't know,' he said at last. 'I don't know where to go.'

With a sigh, he looked over at the *Serpent*. A second longboat was being lowered now – the captain going ashore, no doubt. He imagined Amelia on the quay, waiting to welcome Géroux to the island, and felt an unexpected and unwelcome pang of envy. Irritated, he quickly tamped it out. Why should he care if Géroux lured her in with romantic tales of his tragic past? Zach had no claim on Amelia Dauphin.

'Captain?' Brookes was regarding him with shrewd eyes and not a little unease.

Aware he'd been drifting, Zach pushed aside all thoughts of Amelia. 'There is a place,' he said, smiling at the memory. 'A little slice of heaven in the Mediterranean; an island too small to be noticed. A place where a man might live free, and happy too, with a fishing sloop and a woman at his side.'

Brookes snorted. 'An island? If it's marooning you want, Zach, me and the crew can arrange it.'

That was no idle threat; the crew had little patience with a captain's indecision. Even less with his bad choices.

'Anyway,' Brookes added, 'you'd never give up the *Hawk* nor the sea. It's in your blood, as it's in mine. We're born for it and for nothing else, you and I. It's why you left this place to begin with, is it not?'

'One reason.'

'And you should leave again. Sail tonight. You've given your warning, and there's no more to be done.'

'Abandon them to their fate, you say?' He looked over at his first mate, at the lines of experience etched into his face, and knew that he was right. 'Run before the storm and the devil take the hindmost.' He'd lived by that rule since he'd sailed from the Port of London on that bitter winter night long ago. It had saved his life many a time since, and yet ...

Impatient, Brookes levelled a finger at him. 'Think on this, lad: were the situation reversed, were you in mortal peril, would Dauphin and his people risk themselves to save you?'

Once he'd thought not, but in his mind's eye he saw

James' sincere welcome, Amelia's fierce integrity, and thought that maybe they would. 'I've been absent too long,' he said. 'And I can't leave without knowing Géroux's purpose here.'

Brookes scowled. 'And if his purpose here is the bounty on your head?'

'Then we'll scupper his bloody ship and be done with him, won't we?' He turned away from the rail, looked back towards the island and the lights along the shoreline. 'My father's here, would you have me abandon him to those who would see him hang?'

'You hate your father. Besides, I don't think it's your father you're unwilling to leave behind.'

'Meaning?'

'Have a care, lad. There's been many a sailor lured to his death by just such a siren as Amelia Dauphin, perched upon just such a godforsaken rock as this.'

'Come now, do you really think me as big a fool as that?'

'I think you're as big a fool as any man of nine-and-twenty what's cursed with a face pretty enough to invite trouble.'

Shaking his head, Zach smiled. 'We'll be heading south by March, I swear it. As soon as I know what Géroux wants here.'

'Or who.' Brookes stomped away from the rail. 'Best hope it's not you, eh?'

'Perhaps I'll be lucky,' Zach called after him. 'Perhaps he's here to take my stubborn bloody father!'

Brookes didn't turn around and Zach's humour sank beneath his disapproval. For one thing was sure: Luc Géroux had come to Ile Sainte Anne for a purpose, and that purpose would do no one but himself any good.

Chapter Six

Runaway Bay was exactly as the name implied: a haven for runaway slaves, outlaws, and misfits of all stripes. Ramshackle huts clustered along the shore, wood smoke drifting from the shacks further back in the trees beyond the water's edge.

The bay itself was sheltered by a narrow opening that widened into a small, shallow cove on the north side of Black Church Rock. Several *boucans* were set up at one end of the beach – a permanent fixture – and the smell of smoked meat hung in the warm morning air. Amelia felt her stomach begin to growl and threw an apologetic smile to her companion, Captain Luc Géroux.

'If we're lucky,' she said, 'we'll find breakfast here.'

Géroux returned her smile with a polite incline of his head. 'I can imagine no better place, nor any better company.'

Géroux had proven to be thoroughly charming, which was fortunate, for Amy had decided to find him so from the first moment he'd set foot on Ile Sainte Anne. He smiled and spoke of the wonders of Venice, Paris and Rome. His accent rolled pleasantly from his tongue and, unlike most of the sailors on the island, barefoot in their ragged slops, Luc dressed in linen shirts and silken waistcoats, his hair tied neatly at his nape. He looked and acted every inch the gentleman, and Amelia was happy to be captivated by a man so very different from Zach Hazard.

'We don't seek riches,' she explained as they walked, 'only to share fairly the wealth rich men take from the poor and hoard to themselves.'

'You call it fair,' Géroux said mildly. 'But I think the traders you board would disagree, no?'

'They have plenty,' Amelia said, bristling. 'Far more than they need.' She indicated a couple of old salts sitting nearby, mending sails. 'Those injured or too old to sail are still cared for here. No one begs for food, no one starves on Ile Sainte Anne. We each have what we need and no more, as set down in the Articles of Agreement.'

He lifted an eyebrow. 'Even your father, in his castle?'

'Well, he—'

From the foreshore came a sudden cry of greeting and Amelia saw people run from the tree line to watch a longboat arriving around the bay's headland. Children darted in and out of the water, their laughing shrieks carrying over the noise of the surf better than the softer tones of their parents. Women gathered in groups, skirts hiked to avoid the water, talking and laughing as they watched their children play. Despite the ragged appearance of its inhabitants, Runaway Bay was always a merry place.

Géroux laughed. 'And all these people you have rescued?' he said, waving a lace-cuffed hand towards the beach.

'Not all,' Amy said. 'Some have found their way here alone, fugitives from the powers of this world, seeking the freedom we offer. But others …' She broke off and looked at him, at the mild interest in his sea-grey eyes. 'Others we have freed from those terrible ships that fill their holds with human cargo. You do not defend those traders, I hope?'

'No,' he said. 'For that, I admire you.'

'Admire my father,' she said. 'Admire Captain Overton. Without them and the Articles they swore to protect, this place of freedom would not exist.'

He gave her a gracious smile.

Her eye was drawn by the longboat again, still yards from shore. Someone now stood balanced at the prow, and with a jolt of recognition she realised it was Captain Hazard.

'What now?' she murmured as he leapt into the water, up to his knees, and strode the rest of the way ashore.

He was met by a crowd of laughing children, and more than a few women, and greeted them all with his infamous charm, acquiring a girl on each arm before he'd reached the shore. Amy felt that she should be exasperated, or affronted, but somehow found herself amused. He was Captain Zach Hazard, after all; she'd never wish him anything different than what he was.

'And so you must be Captain Géroux,' said a warm voice beside her, interrupting her thoughts.

She turned with a smile to the woman she'd come to see, one of her oldest and dearest friends. Familiar bright eyes crinkling at the edges, her smile as broad as her round face, Addy stood with an infant perched on her ample hip and another clinging to her skirts. Her mass of black hair was held back by a scarf, a clash of green and blue against her dark skin. 'I am Adamaris Sesay,' she told Géroux, 'and you are welcome to Runaway Bay.'

'Thank you,' he said. 'It is my honour to be here. This seems a happy place.'

Addy laughed, a rich, contagious sound. 'It can be,' she said. 'And will be tonight, with the *Hawk* and her captain in port.'

Amelia glanced towards the shore, towards Zach. 'You know Captain Hazard?'

'Amy,' Adamaris scolded, her attention drifting to the foreshore. 'I've known Zachary since he still wore the name Overton and stormed ashore like a hurricane, set to claim the life of his wicked father.'

Amelia stared at her. 'He— What?'

'Or perhaps he was washed up by mermaids,' she said with an unapologetic grin. 'The sea is made of legends, eh? And it, by turn, makes its own.'

She nodded towards Zach, all swagger and strut as he supervised the off-loading of the cargo, trailed by a gaggle of girls – a legend indeed.

'Come,' Addy said, touching Amelia's arm. 'Eat with us.'

At the top of the beach, rocks had been assembled in a rough circle, at the centre of which lay cold ash; the site of the evening fire. Now, in the warm morning, women and children were scattered about the stones, eating a breakfast of rice and fruits. There was much laughter and the children seemed to belong to everyone and no one, the occasional sharp word snapping them to order when their games became too boisterous.

'Come, come,' Addy urged, moving into the circle and depositing the child on her hip in the lap of a yellow-haired woman with crooked teeth. 'Sit and eat.'

Amelia did both, dropping into the warm sand with half a juicy mango in her hands. 'How is Freema?' she asked, glancing at the infant gumming her way through her own mango next to her. 'She looks better.'

'So she is,' Addy said, tousling the child's hair. 'The fever broke last night and she slept 'til dawn.'

'I'm glad,' Amelia said, touching her hand to the girl's sticky cheek and getting a grin in return.

'There are so many children here,' Géroux said, looking around him in smiling bewilderment. 'To whom do they all belong?'

Amelia laughed. It was true: there were plenty of children in Runaway Bay. The women came and went: some down to the water's edge to help unload the cargo; others mended nets; while up near the trees others ground grain into flour. And children darted between them all, avoiding chores where they could, content to play and leave the women to their work.

'Many women here have menfolk at sea, or dead,' Addy explained. 'It's not an easy task, to raise a child alone.'

'No,' Géroux agreed, shifting a little awkwardly on the rocks. Amelia glanced at him, but his thoughtful gaze was fixed on the grey ash of last night's fire. 'No it is not.'

'But here,' Addy carried on, 'the children belong to us all. As it should be, hmm? No one owns a child. Not here. These children run free.'

'Here,' Amelia said with swell of pride, 'we all run free.'

'I hope—' Géroux cleared his throat and looked up, but his smile appeared too bright for the mellow light of morning. 'I hope it will always remain so.'

Addy gave a disgruntled huff. 'Freedom,' she said, 'is a thing of great value, but fragile as a shell in the sand, easily crushed beneath men's boots.'

Amelia glanced at her, surprised by her uncharacteristically dark tone, and trying to read her expression. She wondered what she'd heard, and from whom. 'You sound like Captain Hazard,' she said. 'But I believe our freedom is stronger than you think. No man can crush an idea beneath his boots.'

Addy didn't openly disagree, but she made a sceptical sound in the back of her throat and Amelia looked away rather than argue. Her gaze drifted down the beach, back to where Zach stood by the water's edge, alone now and apparently deep in thought. He'd discarded his coat and stood barefoot, his shirt fluttering in the breeze. He looked free and wild, every inch a man of the sea, and she felt drawn to him just as she had that night on the beach. As if sensing her gaze he turned, unerringly meeting her eyes with a frank look. She wondered if he felt it too, this strange attraction, or whether it was only in her imagination.

'Zachary,' Addy said, 'lives his own kind of freedom, hmm?'

Embarrassed to have been caught staring, Amelia turned back to her friend. 'He values the freedom to do as he pleases,' she said, more sharply than she'd intended, 'but no deeper meaning of the word, I think.'

Addy shook her head with a fond smile. 'There's no anchor yet that's held him in place, it's true. But he's an older soul than you know, child, and he may yet find what he seeks.'

'And what is it he seeks, aside from women and gold?'

The look Addy gave her was arch, brimming with hidden smiles. 'Freedom, of course.'

'That, he already has.'

'So he thinks, but there are many kinds of freedom in this world, Amelia.'

'Many indeed,' Géroux said, spreading his bejewelled hands before him. 'The world is changing, no? Soon, commerce will make kings and queens of us all – there is no greater freedom than growing rich from our trade with the world.'

'That depends,' said a voice from the shore, 'on the manner of goods you're trading. And on the price you're willing to pay.'

Zach approached, his predatory prowl belying the easy smile he gave them. In the low morning sunlight Amy could see golden strands glinting amid the dark locks of his hair, gilded like his skin.

Beautiful.

The thought popped, unbidden, into her mind and she chased it away with a scowl and hoped he hadn't noticed.

At her side, Géroux rose to his feet. 'Captain Hazard.'

Zach sketched a mocking bow. 'I assume you're not here to hang me this time?'

'We all make a living as we must, Captain.'

'Aye, and you make yours by trading the lives of other men.'

'If such men are careless enough to bring themselves to the attention of the Admiralty Court, then that is their own concern.' Géroux gave a tight-lipped smile. 'Why should I not assist the navy if they pay me well enough to do so? We are both men of business, Captain Hazard.'

Zach was silent, his expression stormy, and across the cold fire Addy watched both men with bright amusement. She favoured Amy with a wry smile and climbed to her feet, placing herself firmly between Zach and Géroux. 'Peace,' she said. 'The Articles call for peace among the brethren on this island and so it will be, hmm?'

Zach gave a nonchalant shrug, although the muscles in his shoulders did not relax. He switched his gaze from Géroux to Amy. 'And what brings you down from your castle so early, Captain Dauphin? Must be something particular.'

'I'm showing Captain Géroux our island,' she said. 'But I come here every day.' She moved to stand close to Addy, touching her warm arm. 'These are my friends, Captain. My people.'

The reason, she said with a look, *that I will not abandon this place.*

He understood her meaning, she saw it in his eyes. Something softened in his expression, a smile that didn't quite reach his lips, an intimate smile that was for her alone. It sparked a flare of unexpected warmth deep down in the pit of her belly.

Géroux cleared his throat and Zach looked away; the moment was over.

With a brazen grin he turned to Addy instead, who was watching them both with enough enjoyment to make Amelia's cheeks flush.

'Silks,' Zach said, sweeping his arm towards the cargo now sitting on the beach. 'Some Spanish silver and sugar.' He flashed Addy a wicked smile. 'Cuban Rum.'

Her eyebrows rose. 'And no small amount of guilt, hmm, after six long years and not a word to your friends?'

Zach pressed both hands to his heart, eyes aglitter. 'But you were always in my thoughts, I swear it.'

Addy's disbelieving smile was one that a mother might reserve for an errant child. 'Your promises are worth no more than footprints in the sand,' she said and lifted her hands to cup his face, pressing a kiss to his forehead. 'You were missed, Zachary, and not just by the giggling girls who know no better.'

Amelia felt a little awkward, witnessing such an unexpected and tender moment. It was easy to forget that Zach had lived a life here of which she knew little – and a life beyond the island of which she knew nothing at all. She wondered how he could talk so easily of running from this place, from these people who clearly loved him still.

She wondered if she could persuade him to stay.

Days slipped like sand through the glass and once their coin had been spent in the inns and whorehouses of Ile Sainte Anne, Zach's crew became impatient to sail. Géroux's presence unsettled them all but, more than that, it had been too long since they'd taken a prize and a crew was only as loyal as the weight of the gold in their pockets; wise captains kept their pockets heavy.

Zach knew that. He knew that the day would soon come when he must leave Ile Sainte Anne in search of richer waters, and yet he did not sail. He felt anchored, as though he'd run aground on uncharted shoals and was unable to float free.

It was a profoundly disturbing sensation.

He had some idea of the cause, of course. But it was a secret he liked to keep hidden as best he could, even if he couldn't keep it entirely from Jedidiah Brookes. In fact, Zach had taken to slipping away from the *Hawk* before the sun rose, just to avoid the disapproving gaze of his sharp-eyed first mate.

Most days he spent with Amelia as she went about her business on the island, sometimes aboard her ship, sometimes settling disputes ashore. He sailed with her once, much to Brookes' consternation, lounging on the quarterdeck steps as she took the *Sunlight* to the mainland to trade silks for grain.

The sight of her at the helm, the wind in her face and her

smile fierce, stirred a feeling in him deeper than desire. It would be something, he found himself thinking, to sail life's waters with such a woman at his side.

His evenings he spent in the Anchor, one of the island's dockside taverns, avoiding Brookes' pointed looks and the grumbling of his crew. He liked to watch Amelia in the tallow light, her eyes bright as she talked of the future and laughed at the tall tales he spun just to make her smile. Sometimes she sang, albeit not very well. Sweet enough to his ears, though, and he dared not think too much on why that might be so.

Géroux sometimes came with her to the Anchor, when he could drag himself away from her father's court. Then, Zach kept his distance, watched from the shadows with a cold and crawling unease coiling in the pit of his stomach. On those nights he drank too deep and told himself it was the island's future he feared for, not Amelia's. He told himself he wasn't jealous; he had no right to concern himself with her future, after all, for he had no intention of staying and she would never leave.

But it was the mornings he enjoyed best, walking the empty foreshore as the horizon brightened from azure to gold. Walking alone.

Alone with Amelia.

Whether he planned it or she did, Zach wasn't quite certain. Neither spoke of it, yet somehow each morning he would find her sitting on the beach of Runaway Bay, staring at the breaking day. And somehow, he would find himself sitting in the sand at her side until the sun rose, the children stirred, and the island came alive.

It brought him pleasure and pain to be there with her, to feel the gentle softening of her heart toward him and yet to know what lay ahead.

'My father,' Amelia began one morning, after a long and easy silence, 'has become quite taken with Captain Géroux.'

'So I've noticed,' Zach said. 'Géroux barely leaves his

side, unless it's to be at yours.' He slid a sly look towards her, to see how she took his observation, and saw her frown. 'And what of you?' he said with some trepidation. 'Are you equally taken with him?'

'Not so much as I once was.' She gave a self-conscious smile that he well understood. 'Yet some of what he says ...'

'Let's not argue about that.' Zach sighed, turning away from her and back to the sea. 'You know what I think of his talk of trade and business.'

She breathed out a long breath. 'I just wish you would ...' Another sigh, her hand dropping from her knee to toy with the sand between them. Her fingers looked pale as bone in the predawn light.

'What?' he said. 'You wish I would what?'

She shook her head. 'Open your mind.'

He laughed at that, too loudly for the dark of the morning, and swallowed it quickly. 'Amy, there's no man alive with a mind more open than mine.'

'But not to this,' she said, turning to face him. Her knees touched his thigh, warm through the rough fabric. He wondered if she noticed it too, if the contact burned her like it did him. 'What if Luc's right, what if there is a way to protect Ile Sainte Anne?'

'And what if there were a pot of gold at the end of the rainbow?' He softened the jibe with a smile. 'Wishing something were true doesn't make it so, Amy.'

'That doesn't stop me wishing you would stay,' she said. Then she shook her head and looked down at her hands as if embarrassed, down at her knees pressed against his leg. She moved back a little, but he reached out to stop her.

'Amy ...' He hardly knew what he was about, but her skin was warm beneath his fingers and there was a tension between them, charging like lightning before a storm. Unfinished business, he thought. He should have bedded her when he had the chance. 'Amy—'

'My father thinks Luc can protect us.' She blurted the words, her eyes fixed on her hand held in his. 'He has powerful connections, influence in high places.'

'Maybe he does, but at what price his protection? You can be assured that the trade will be entirely in his favour.' His fingers laced with hers. 'What is it he wants, Amy?'

She looked up at him, her lips tight and her eyes solemn. Something dark sank into the pit of his belly as realisation dawned, cold as a winter's day. 'Ah, I see.'

'It's how business is conducted, is it not?'

'Aye, among folk who know no better,' he said angrily. 'I thought the people of Ile Sainte Anne were free, or does that not apply to you?'

'Of course it does,' she said. 'My father would never force me, it would be my choice.'

He snorted, got to his feet; he couldn't bear to look at her any more. 'Just because you choose to walk into the cage, Amy, doesn't make it any less a prison.'

'I'd give my life for Ile Sainte Anne,' she said, defiant as a child. 'Marriage would be a far lesser sacrifice.'

'Would it?' He picked up a handful of stones from the sand, hefted the weight of them in his palm. 'Seems as though you'd still be giving your life.'

'Some part of it, perhaps, to protect the people of the island, to protect Addy and the children. I have a duty to them,' she said. 'You know I do.'

'*Duty.*' He spat the word, felt it heavy and bitter on his tongue. With an angry flick of his wrist he sent a stone skimming over the waves. 'All manner of sins are committed in the name of that bloody word.'

'Sins?' She scrambled to her feet behind him. 'What do you mean?'

A second stone followed the first, bouncing once, twice from the crests of unbroken waves. 'It's of no matter,' he said because ahead of them the sky was turning golden, the sun on the cusp of rising, and he'd no wish to return to the dark place from which his anger rose.

She touched his arm, turning him to face her. 'Tell me.'

'I said let it—'

'Tell me what you meant.'

Her firm hand on his arm, the challenge in her eyes, provoked him. He met her glare for glare, heartbeat for heartbeat. 'Loyalty,' he said, daring her to object. 'Freedom, desire – aye, even love; I've seen them all sacrificed to the spurious claims of duty.'

'Spurious, you call it?' Arms folded across her chest, she lifted her chin as if ready for a fight. 'On that we can never agree. For me, duty will always have the highest claim.'

'Aye,' he said, a hollow weight settling in his chest, a familiar sadness. 'It seems you are too much like your father, and too much like my own.'

She looked at him, her eyes wide and serious. 'Your father,' she said after a moment, and more gently. 'He left you as a child to come here. Is that what you meant by sins?'

On the horizon, the rising sun spilled gilded light across the water; another day had dawned, another day he had lingered too long on this island of dreams. 'I should go,' he said, half to himself. 'I should leave this place.'

'Your father loves you, Zach. I know it.'

He felt a bitter, unwanted smile creep onto his face. 'Not so much as he loves the Articles, Amelia. Sacrificed us all to that dusty old book.' It was an old pain, one buried deep, and it surprised him that she could pry it loose. Alarmed him too, that she had that power.

Her fingers touched his arm, brushing his skin, touching something buried deeper still – tenderness, perhaps, or affection. Maybe something more. He swallowed, felt himself leaning into her warm caress, at risk of falling.

'What he has built here is good,' she said, close enough

now that he could almost feel the words as they left her lips. 'It's—'

'I know what it is.' He closed his eyes against the swell of emotion. 'I know what he built here, Amy, but I know what he destroyed in the process and I cannot balance the two.'

She was silent and for a while all he could hear was the hiss of the surf on the shore, the breaking of the waves. Then she said, 'But do you never think of what your father lost? What he sacrificed to build this place?'

His eyes flew open. 'What *he* sacrificed?' He pulled away from her, saw her flinch at his sudden anger. 'Believe me, my father sacrificed nothing he was not eager to lose.'

'But Zach—'

'There are more important things in the world than this place, Amy!' he snapped. 'And things of greater value than rules and books and bloody *principles*!'

'Such as your own self-interest, I suppose?' she said, his anger sparking hers. 'Such as doing as you please instead of what is right?'

He gave a smile; it tasted sour. 'I'm not ashamed to act in my own self-interest.'

'*That*, I can believe,' she said, turning to walk up the beach to where the people of Runaway Bay were stirring. 'But I cannot respect it.'

He watched her go in silence, watched her scoop up a sleepy child in her arms, and told himself he had no need of her approval. What did she know of him, of his life? What did she know of the world beyond the sheltered shores of Ile Sainte Anne? Nothing. Nothing at all.

Turning his back on her, he turned his eyes to the future, to the sea and the horizon. But instead of beckoning him on as it always had, it looked vast and empty.

Behind him, Amelia's laughter carried on the breeze and he glanced over his shoulder, saw her playing in the sand with the children who had appeared from the tree line as if summoned by the dawn. And he felt something sharp catch in his chest, something as unstoppable as the rising sun.

He tried to push it away, but it would not go. And, though he knew he should return to the *Hawk*, he found himself walking back up the beach towards Amelia, who knelt in the sand, fending off several over-excited children. He said nothing, just lifted the most rambunctious lad up onto his shoulders and offered his free hand to Amelia. It was an apology of sorts, though he'd not say as much.

After a pause, she took his hand, wrapping her strong fingers around his and pulling herself back to her feet. She smiled, still angry but softer now, and did not let go of his hand until the child on his shoulders squirmed and he was forced to grab both the lad's ankles.

Amelia sighed. 'I wish I could convince you to stay.'

'I wish I could convince you to leave.'

'And abandon these people?' She toyed with the fingers of the child on his shoulders. 'You know it's impossible.' Her gaze held his for a fleeting moment. 'I feel we are meant to be allies, Zach, and ... and friends. It's a shame that we seem destined to take different paths.'

'Destined?' He huffed out a sigh. 'No such thing as destiny, Amy, only choices. We're all masters of our own fate in the end.'

'Somehow,' she said, with a sad little smile, 'that makes it worse.'

Chapter Seven

Amelia saw little of Zach in the days following their argument. He appeared to be avoiding her. No longer did he meet her on the beach at dawn and sit with her to watch the sun rise; no longer did he visit Runaway Bay, or talk in the taverns about her future and the island's.

Yet the *Hawk* remained moored in her berth and Zach did not leave. That gave her more pleasure and comfort than she felt was entirely right.

Occasionally Zach visited her father's court, arguing vehemently with Luc Géroux. He rarely spoke to Amelia directly, yet their eyes often met and she always knew what he was thinking. She knew he disliked her growing friendship with Luc, and often felt his dark gaze lingering on them as they talked. But she refused to let his disapproval keep her from doing what was necessary to protect her home. Amelia Dauphin understood her duty, and the more Zach disapproved of it the more she was determined to continue.

Perhaps that was why, contrary to her usual custom, she stood gazing into a looking glass at her own reflection. She barely recognised the woman staring back, for she was wearing a dress.

Luc had made her a gift of it, cream silk and lilac flowers – the height of fashion at Versailles, he told her – so it would have been rude not to wear it. Anyway, despite the restriction of skirts and bodice, Amelia found she rather enjoyed the transformation. With her hair braided and twisted on top of her head she thought she could pass for a lady at court. More or less.

Her bare toes wiggled beneath the skirts as she had no shoes except the boots she sometimes wore to walk the island. Luc would have to allow her that little nod to the freedom of Ile Sainte Anne.

Lifting the elegant skirts, she left her room and made her way down the narrow stairs that led to the hall below. She felt a little silly in such finery, but knew it would please Luc. She knew, too, that in pleasing Luc, it would also please her father. Besides that, Luc talked sense. Where Zach gave bleak advice to abandon the island and the Articles, to flee before the enemy arrived, Luc suggested a better plan. Trade, he said. Trade with the imperial powers, deal with them as equals and live at peace with the world under his protection.

To her ears it was a persuasive argument. Trade, not war, must be the way of the future. But Zach disagreed, loudly.

She stopped at the foot of the stairs, sighing as she heard his voice rise yet again in the hall below.

'... arrant nonsense and you know it! Why would they trade when they can take what they want by force of arms?'

Weary of the argument, Amelia hoped her entrance would at least subdue it for a while. Putting on a bright smile, she stepped into the hall and waited to be noticed.

Her father sat in his customary place by the fire, Overton watching like a hawk at his shoulder. Luc held the ground before them, with Zach some distance away, in a patch of sunlight by the window. His gaze was turned out towards the sea, as if he were contemplating making a dash for the *Hawk* and taking his own advice to run.

Her father saw her first, his eyes melting with emotion. 'Oh!' he breathed. 'Amelia, you look beautiful.'

She smiled and attempted a clumsy curtsy. 'The *dress* is beautiful,' she conceded, smoothing her hands over the ivory silk. 'Thank you, Luc. It's a lovely gift.'

'I'm afraid,' Luc said, offering a courtier's bow, 'that the beauty of the dress merely gilds the lily.'

At the window, Zach growled low in his throat and when

Amelia looked over she saw his gaze sliding away from her and back out to sea. 'Captain Hazard doesn't agree,' she said, provoking him to turn back around.

Luc took her hand and led her towards a chair at her father's side. 'Then Captain Hazard has been too long at sea, no?'

Zach watched them with a guarded expression, and after a moment said, 'What Captain Hazard thinks is that this is hardly the time to be playing at courtiers.' He sketched a gesture towards her dress, his gaze holding hers and shading the meaning of his words. 'It's pretty enough, if you like your women trussed up in stays.'

Angered, Amelia coloured but before she could reply Luc said, 'You, sir, are no gentleman to speak so before a lady.'

'Never claimed to be any kind of gentleman.'

Her father frowned as Amelia took her seat at his side. 'Have a care, son. You're speaking of my daughter.'

Zach offered a scant bow of apology and turned back to the window. The sunlight slanting through the glass burnished his skin to bronze, and in the sculpted angles of his profile Amelia saw again that sudden, startling beauty. Despite everything, it was impossible to deny that he was alarmingly handsome and her stomach gave its usual sharp flutter in response.

Irritated with herself, she returned her attention to Luc. Smiling, he said, 'I was just telling your father of a friend – a captain – with much influence in the *Compagnie des Indes Orientale*. He is, even now, docked in Porto Novo on his way south, and is keen to know better the people of Ile Sainte Anne.' As he spoke, he came to stand between her and the window, obscuring her view of Zach. Whether it was intentional or not, she didn't know. Luc smiled down at her, though there was something in his storm-grey eyes at odds with the expression. 'He is a good man of business and it is but a few days sail to Porto Novo if you wish to meet him.'

'A few days' sail!' Zach turned again from the window and prowled closer. In his slim-fitting britches and shirt, barefoot and tangle-haired, he struck quite a contrast to Luc's studied elegance. 'And how long will she stay in his brig afterward?'

Luc spread his arms. 'You think I set a trap?'

'Wouldn't be the first time, would it?'

Silence drifted in the wake of his accusation, unspoken words sparking between the two men. Zach's hand rested lightly on the hilt of the short blade he wore and there was vengeance in his eyes. Behind her father's chair Captain Overton turned his head, sharp gaze fixing on his son. She wondered if he expected bloodshed.

No one else moved. Outside, the cicadas sang above the distant crash and boom of the surf and Amelia wished she were there, down on the beach with the wind in her hair, not trapped in the stifling heat of the court. She shifted in her seat, the uncomfortable dress making it difficult to breathe.

'Come now.' Her father broke the tension. 'We'll have no settling of old scores here, Zach. Captain Géroux means to offer us friendship and protection.'

Zach kept his eyes on Luc and his hand on the hilt of his sword. 'Have you nothing to say on this matter?' He directed his words towards his father. 'You've had dealings with Géroux and his like, have you not?'

After a pause Overton spoke in his familiar growl. 'I've only this to say: any man what lets himself fall into the hands of a privateer deserves to feel the hempen collar about his neck.'

Amelia saw a flash of hurt in Zach's eyes, but it quickly turned to indifference. His posture stiffened, however, taut as a bowline.

Luc smiled, triumph curling the corners of his mouth. Deliberately, he turned his back on Zach and addressed himself to her father. 'It is simple, my friend. There is but one language all men speak, and that is the language of commerce. We are living in a modern world, and in the modern world there is no longer any need for conflict. Why fight when we can bargain instead?'

Zach's fingers flexed away from his blade, but his expression grew darker by the moment.

'Then you propose,' Amelia said, 'that we should trade with the French East India Company?'

'Of course. With the British and Dutch too. Why not? You cannot fight them. How many are you here? Two hundred? Three?'

'Three hundred and fifty,' she said, with some pride.

'Then you cannot hope to fight. But trade! Ah, yes, with my help, that you can do.'

Her father shook his head, his lined face aged by sea and sun but his eyes still diamond bright. 'Trade with the devil, you mean? There's no freedom in that, sir.'

'Perhaps they are not so much the devil as you think.'

Zach spat a bleak laugh. 'And perhaps they are, but either way they are still your master. A man cannot be a little bit free. It is all, or it is nothing.'

'Free?' Géroux spread his arms wide, taller than Zach in his heeled boots, dominating the room. 'You think you are free, do you, aboard your ship? Well, you are not. You simply mistake running for freedom. I, Captain, am free because I do business with those who would otherwise enslave me.' His gaze shifted back to Amelia and her father, his expression turning grave. 'This is what I have said to you, no? This place, this idea of freedom, cannot stand. It is a reed against a hurricane. Your salvation lies in commerce – give them something they want, and you will survive. It is the only way.'

James Dauphin's expression was grave and behind him Overton scowled, reaching for his long-stemmed pipe and starting to pack it with tobacco. 'This is nonsense talk,' he warned. 'Mark it, James, this is havey-cavey business.'

'Perhaps,' her father said, and reached out to take Amelia's hand, squeezing it between his calloused fingers. 'But we are old men, my friend, and the world is changing.'

'What we believe in won't change, nor ever will.'

Luc made a bow in deference to Overton's words, though he clearly disagreed, and was silent.

Across the room, Amelia found Zach's intense gaze locked on her own. He looked very much like his father in the shadows of the court, dogged and intransigent. There was irony in that, in the fact that Zach rejected all that Overton stood for and yet sided with his father against the opportunity Luc presented for peace and prosperity. Both, in their own ways, were too wedded to the past.

With effort she turned from Zach, letting her attention come to rest on Luc. In her heart she felt that he was a good man, and if he was right, if he could protect them, help them to prosper, then was it not worth the price he asked?

Her father's fingers squeezed hers and she took a deep breath, making her choice. 'Captain Géroux,' she said, 'it's so hot in here. I think I'll walk down to the south beach. Will you join me and tell me more about your friend in Porto Novo? I think I would like to meet him.'

The pleasure on Luc's face was obvious, a smile warming his eyes. '*Je serais honoré*,' he said, holding out his hand to help Amelia rise. But she didn't miss the triumphant look he shot at Zach, or the baleful glare he received in return.

Zach's disapproval stung, but she did her best to ignore it and to focus instead on the future Luc promised. Her mind was alive with bright images of her people, her free people, trading sugar, spices and silk with the great powers' mighty ships. If she and Luc could bring it about, it would be glorious indeed.

Taking Luc's arm, she let him lead her out of the hall and

into the dappled sunlight beyond. Though she felt Zach's hot gaze on her the whole way, she dared not look back. The future was there to be taken, and Amelia was pirate enough to want to take it for herself and for the people of Ile Sainte Anne. No matter the cost.

And no matter what – or who – she might lose in the process.

Chapter Eight

Though the population of Ile Sainte Anne was small, it was of a hard-drinking sort and well able to sustain two dockside taverns. Of the two, Zach preferred the Stone Jug – it was darker, seedier and easier to get lost in than the Anchor. It also benefited from the distinct advantage of not being frequented by Amelia Dauphin.

And tonight Zach wanted to be as far from her as possible. For she had made her choice, thrown her lot in with Géroux, and Zach would not – could not – bear to linger any longer.

The *Hawk* was preparing to sail and they would leave with the dawn tide.

Brookes had been overjoyed by the news, but Zach felt only empty. Part of him was anchored here and he feared that, when he sailed, it might rip the very heart out of him. He was profoundly miserable.

With a sigh, he sank lower in his chair, lost in the shadows at the back of the Jug, and nursed his cane-juice, a drink so vastly inferior to rum that it didn't even share the same name. It was potent enough, however, and more readily available here than good grog. He wasn't fussy, not tonight. He needed something harsh to scrub his mind clear of the regrets that plagued him.

He should never have followed them from the court that afternoon, should never have watched them together on the beach.

Swallowing another mouthful, he screwed shut his eyes. It did no good. He could still see them at the water's edge – Amy and Géroux – standing close and talking earnestly, Géroux slipping his arm about her waist, tilting her face so that he could kiss her. Right there, with the setting sun burnishing her hair and turning her skin to amber. Right there, for all to see. Right there for *him* to see.

He pressed the heel of his hand to his eyes, but it had no effect. The image did not fade; his jealousy did not abate.

Jealousy. Him! It was ridiculous.

Yet he couldn't get the memory out of his head, couldn't ease the knot around his heart. Couldn't forget the confection of silk and lace into which Géroux had bound her, and couldn't ignore how much he wanted to free her from its constraint. Amy Dauphin was not born for such things; she was born wild and free. Born to be naked and glorious, skin blanched pale as cream by the moonlight and hair dark as night. A witch, beautiful and enchanting. And *his*. Above all, she was born to be his.

He swallowed another mouthful of cane-juice, but it could not wash away the envy in the pit of his stomach. Brookes was right, he should have sailed weeks ago and saved himself this trouble.

A couple of lightskirts plied their trade in the tavern, hanging on the men playing at hazard, hardly pretty but available. *That* must ease his tension, must it not? They fell a poor second to his memory of Amelia, as rancid as cane-juice next to spiced Caribbean rum, but if there was no rum to be had ...

He drew a coin from his pocket and let it glitter in the lamplight until one of the women looked his way. Spinning it upon the table he smiled and slapped his hand down over it, a jerk of his head beckoning her closer. She came with a swish of her hips and a smile that wasn't entirely false; he had a reputation, after all.

'What's your name?' he said as she sidled in next to him.

'Lilly.' Her face was pinched, eyes shadowed, and she spoke with a familiar accent. She'd known the world, this girl. Known the cold.

'Sounds like you were born on Newgate steps.'

'Stepney. You from them parts too?'

'A long time ago. Left when I was a nipper.'

'Who wouldn't, if they could?'

That was true enough. 'You're a long way from home,' he said, turning the coin over on the table. She was watching it with eager eyes. 'What brings you to Ile Sainte Anne?'

She shrugged, bony shoulders slipping out from beneath her overlarge dress. 'Reckoned if I was to be a whore might as well do it somewhere warm.' Her hand touched his leg, as if to remind him of their business. 'Me aunt found me and brought me here, an' it's better than where I was.' She nodded her head towards the upstairs, where her 'aunt' oversaw the rooms. 'Half a crown for an hour in bed, one and six for a dry rub against the wall outside.'

He didn't answer, looked instead at the coin turning over in his fingers. The taste of cane-juice was sour in his mouth and he wished he had a swallow of something better to wash it away. Such desire as he had felt dissipated, leaving only the gnawing hunger for what was impossible. It was not the kind of need easily sated by such a woman as this.

'You miss your girl.' He glanced up and she smiled and nodded. Some of her teeth were missing at the back; he could see gaps when she smiled. 'I can always tell the ones what's missing their girl. If you close your eyes you can pretend I'm her, if you like. Don't mind what name you call me.'

Zach shook his head. 'I've got no girl.'

Her head tilted, like a bird's on her skinny neck. 'Did she throw you over, then? More fool her, I say, with those pretty eyes of yours. And them hands.' She touched his fingers where he toyed with the coin. 'Bet you know what to do with them an' all.'

Zach laughed, partly because she was right and partly because it was ridiculous to be talking so with a London street whore, here in Ile Sainte Anne, when his heart was so tangled up in Amelia Dauphin that he could hardly think straight.

'If you want her back,' she said. 'Why don't you take her?'

'Perhaps she doesn't want to be taken?'

'Then she must be blind, or stupid. Have you asked her?'

He shrugged. 'She's got someone else now.'

'So? Maybe she don't know you still want her.'

It was possible, he supposed. Possible that she didn't know how he burned for her, but more likely that his longing counted for little against the weight of her bloody duties. He took another swallow of drink and slid the flagon across the table to the girl, Lilly. 'Maybe she wouldn't want me even if she knew?'

Lilly smiled her gap-toothed grin. 'Don't know why not. You've the prettiest face I ever saw.'

Zach shook his head and tossed her the coin. 'For the advice,' he said as she caught it and hid it in her skirts.

'Advice?' Her hand touched his thigh again, wandering higher. 'You don't want a tumble? Help ease your cares.'

He took her hand, lifted it to his lips and kissed her knuckles. 'I wish you good fortune, Lilly, but I think there's only one way to— Perhaps I'll take your advice, eh? Throw myself at her feet. I've only my dignity to lose.'

Her eyebrows rose. 'She's here, then? On the island? I was thinking she was back home.'

'She's here,' he said, standing up. 'Though I won't be, not for much longer. We sail at dawn.'

'Then you'd best waste no time. Shame though – there ain't many here I'd turn a trick for with pleasure, but you'd have been one.'

He offered a bow. 'I'm flattered.'

Lilly laughed. 'Whoever she is, your girl, she's a fool to throw you over. You tell her so from me. A bloody great fool, unless she's got herself a prince instead!'

A marquis, Zach thought sourly. Nearly as good, and infinitely better than a pirate.

He started to leave, then stopped. 'A word of advice in exchange for yours, Lilly. Take the next ship out that'll have you. Go south – Madagascar, maybe. Or west to the Atlantic colonies. Just don't stay here.'

Lilly frowned. 'Why not?'

'Because there's a storm coming, and I don't mean the weather. In a year, this whole place will be gone.'

She looked at him as though he were mad. 'And how do you know that?'

'I can hear it on the wind, girl. And I don't say it lightly. Get out of here while you can, or you'll not live to see another summer.'

Inside her bedroom the lamps burned low, warm light glittering against the golden hairbrush and comb that lay upon the simple wooden trunk that served as both her dresser and closet. They were Luc's latest gift, and she dared not guess their value. He'd taken them as part of a large prize, he said, captured near Hispaniola, the rightful property of some long-dead Spanish queen.

Amelia ran a finger over the intricate engravings, her mind drifting on fair winds. Tonight, Luc had kissed her. Not like Zach had kissed her on the beach, full of fever and urgency, but with care and respect. A gentleman's kiss.

Tomorrow she would sail with him to Porto Novo, upon his sleek, modern brigantine, and there she would meet with his associate in the French East India Company. Her father was uneasy, and Overton flatly objected, but it was Zach's response that knotted in her chest.

She'd expected him to protest when she announced her decision, to growl disapproval from the shadows of her father's court, but he'd said nothing, just stared at her with that challenging gaze of his until she'd been forced to look away. Then he'd left her father's hall and not returned. The *Hawk* was still anchored in the harbour, but Amelia had seen the crew busy in the rigging as the sun bled into the horizon and she doubted the ship would still be there at daybreak.

Sitting in the quiet of her room, she saw his face in her mind's eye, serious and intent, and couldn't bear that he would leave thinking ill of her. Yet how could she help—

'A pretty trinket,' a voice said, as if summoned from her daydream. 'All glitter and gold on the outside, but what lies beneath? That's the question.'

She spun around and there he was, lounging against the window frame, watching her through sardonic eyes. In the confined surroundings of her bedroom, Zach Hazard was larger than life, the fresh scent of the ocean clinging to his coattails. He flashed a smile. 'No "Good evening, Captain Hazard, so pleased to see you"?'

'Surprised to see you,' she said, trying to ignore the flush of excitement heating her cheeks. 'What are you doing here?'

He didn't answer right away, sauntering across her bedroom as if it were the most curious place in the world. His lips curved into a dissolute smile as he trailed his fingers along the edge of her bed; she thought he might be a little drunk. Then the trunk that served as her dresser caught his attention and he strolled closer, casting a professional eye over the brush and comb that had been Luc's gift.

'Don't even think about taking them,' Amelia warned, wishing she had a sword to back up the threat, but she only had silk skirts at her side.

Zach turned a wounded eye on her. 'Not worth the effort, it's all glitter and no value.'

Her eyes narrowed. 'You came here for some purpose. If it wasn't to rob me, then what?'

Turning away from the trunk, he continued his perusal of her room. 'To offer a final warning, before I sail.'

'You're leaving, then.' She already knew it to be true, yet still felt a sharp pang of disappointment.

He flung her a brief, questioning glance. 'No reason to stay, is there?'

'You could help us—'

'Help you do what?' Zach made a gruff sound, a sour laugh. 'Die? You'll need no help with that. And I'm not fool enough to put my faith in Géroux. Nor should you be.'

She said nothing for a moment, studying his profile half turned away from her. His lips were turned down, brow creased by a frown. 'My father tells me that you were Luc's prisoner once, is it true?'

'True enough. A mere matter of business, he would say. The Admiralty had a fine price on my head that Géroux had a mind to collect.' He glanced at her, and in the lamplight his black eyes gleamed gold. 'It's twice as much now.'

'He's not here for you.'

'If he's not, then he's here for a bigger prize.' He frowned, making a show of thinking hard. 'Now I wonder what that could be?'

'Me? No, the Admiralty has no interest in me—'

'In Ile Sainte Anne, it does, in your father and his notions of freedom. It's not you the Admiralty wants, Amy, it's this place.' He moved closer; she could feel the heat of his anger across the narrowing space between them. 'It's the idea of this place they fear, and that is what they will destroy.'

'But Luc—'

Suddenly Zach reached out, spun her around until her back was to his chest and she saw herself reflected in the mirror. 'Look,' he whispered against her ear. 'Look at what you've become, Captain Dauphin. Look at what Géroux is doing to you with his pretty gifts and honeyed words. The fatted calf being led to the slaughter. Do you think this will save you in the end?'

She saw the exaggerated rise and fall of her chest above

the restraint of her bodice, the way her hair was piled upon her head – a woman of society, the good wife Luc wanted. And behind her stood Zach, wild and dark, his face against hers and one hand flat across her corseted stomach, keeping her flush against him. 'Captain Hazard,' she gasped, 'I demand that you release me.'

His eyes glittered. 'Had you a sword at your side you could demand it. As it is, all you can do is hope.'

'*You* had better hope,' she growled, trying to ignore the heat of his iron grip about her waist, the warmth of his chest against her bare shoulder. 'You had better hope that my father does not walk through that door. He loves you as a son, but he would hang you from the yardarm for this.'

In the mirror his smile darkened as he eyed the length of her exposed neck. 'Then why don't you scream?' He gently blew a teasing breath against her skin. Her whole body shivered involuntarily, and Zach grinned like Lucifer himself. 'Go on then, scream. Call for help.'

Finding her breath in ragged gasps she said, 'I choose to be merciful.'

'Ah.' He studied her neck intently, leaning closer all the while, until slowly, agonisingly slowly, he pressed a heated kiss against her skin. 'Sail with me. Tonight. Now.'

The suggestion astounded her, only adding to the dizzying sensation of his kiss. 'Sail with *you*? Why?'

'Because you want to. I know it.'

She did. In that moment she wanted it all: freedom, adventure. Him. If she gave in now, if she opened herself to his kiss, then it would all be hers. She would burn bright, like the stars. For a night. Or a week. Maybe even a month.

Yet it would not last. In the end the blaze would consume her, destroy her, and leave her life in ashes. Her father's hopes, Ile Sainte Anne, everything she valued, would be destroyed in that glorious inferno, and when the fire had burned out – when Zach had moved on to new waters – she'd be left alone.

His teasing fingers tugged at the neck of her dress, inching it lower over her shoulder, and he murmured something against her flushed skin that could have been her name. Her head was spinning, her body turning to liquid, and she knew that this was the fork in the road, the pivotal moment. Her whole life hung in the balance.

'Zach ...' Weak-kneed she stumbled forward against the trunk, holding herself there while she tried to catch her breath. 'Zach, please stop ...'

Behind her was silence. She could hear nothing above her own breathing. When her head had cleared enough she lifted her eyes to the mirror and saw him reflected there, watching her, face impassive. Had she not been close enough to see the rapid rise and fall of his chest, she would have considered him perfectly composed. 'Sail with me,' he said again, a rough-edged whisper. 'Sail with me tonight.'

Slowly, still leaning on the trunk, she turned around. 'That's impossible.'

'Nothing's impossible.'

She smiled fondly – sadly. 'Not for you, perhaps. But I'm not like you, Zach. This is my home; these are my people, and I must protect them however I can.'

'Even if that means jumping into bed with Luc Géroux?'

Her cheeks flushed, but she refused to be ashamed. 'Who I share my bed with is none of your concern, Captain. But at least Luc doesn't council running from our enemies like cowards.'

'Not like cowards, like pirates.' He stepped closer but made no move to touch her again. 'Tell me, what is it you dream of in that bed of yours, Amy? Do you dream of a trader's ledger? Of sugar and silks and spices? Do you dream of Luc Géroux?'

'I …' Her lips were dry; she touched her tongue to them and his hungry gaze dipped to her mouth.

'Or do you dream of the wind in your hair and sea spray on your skin? Do you dream of open seas and the freedom they bring?' His eyes lifted back to hers. 'Do you dream of me?'

She couldn't take a step back because the trunk was behind her, but she squared her shoulders and prayed for strength. 'I have duties here I will not abandon.'

'The Devil take your duties!' he snarled, seizing her by the shoulders. 'Amy, what is it you *want*?'

He held her gaze for a long, scorching moment, but she would not yield. She fought the desire tooth and nail. 'It doesn't matter what I want,' she said at last. 'I must do what I think best for the island, for my father and my people.'

'No matter the cost?'

She lifted her chin, defiant in the face of his scorn. 'I will pay any price for their future, Zach.'

'Aye, but not only you!' He let her go and turned away, something dark flashing across his face, deep and old and heavy with hurt. 'You are your father's daughter indeed.'

'I make no apology for that.'

His frustration was evident and he stood with his back to her for a moment, scrubbing a hand through his hair, but when he looked at her again the heat in his eyes had cooled. 'The *Hawk* leaves with the morning tide,' he said in a low voice. 'If you change your mind—'

'I can't,' she said. 'You know I can't.'

'You won't, more to the point.' He ran his knuckles across her cheek and into her hair, raising goose bumps on the back of her neck. She feared – hoped – he might steal a kiss, press his lips to hers; it was a theft she would welcome more than she ought.

'Don't leave,' she whispered. 'Stay and help us face the storm that's coming. My father could use your counsel. We could use the power of the *Hawk*'s cannon.'

'I can't stay,' he said, hand falling away from her face. 'You know I can't.'

'You won't, more to the point.'

He held her gaze and it seemed for a moment that she could see into the very heart of him; it was a dark and lonely place. 'I know what it is to be trampled by another's duty,' he said, 'and it's better by far to live unshackled and alone. My father taught me that lesson well.'

She caught his hand in hers. 'But, Zach, can we not at least be friends?'

'Friends?' He shook his head and took a step back, retreating until their fingers parted. 'You are what you are, Amelia, and I am what I am. We cannot fight the tides that pull us apart.' A smile touched his lips, sad and final. 'But if you'll not run, then I'll leave you with this warning: for every deal you make there's a price to be paid. Take care it is not so high that you lose everything you value in the bargain.'

'Zach—' she began, but a rap on the door cut her off.

'Amelia?' It was her father. 'Amelia, may I enter?'

'One moment,' she called, running to the door. 'I'm just dressing.'

She turned back to Zach and hissed, 'You must go.'

But the room was already empty, the sea breeze blowing in past her curtains and riffling the silken skirts of her dress. Running to the open window, she looked out but it was a moonless night and the trees were black silhouettes, hiding their secrets.

He was gone and she would never see him again.

A pain pierced her heart, sharp as a blade, but she refused to succumb to it. She refused to mourn his loss, no matter how deeply she felt it; she would not be one of those lovelorn women who sighed at the name Zachary Hazard. He had made his choice, and she had made hers. Besides, there were other men. Men who would help them to fight, not run away from the threat. Men who understood that life meant more than living only for the moment, however glorious that moment might be.

The wind rustled through the trees, whispering of a rising storm, and behind her the door opened. 'Amelia?'

She turned from the window, composing herself. 'Father.'

He hesitated on the threshold and glanced past her, through the window, then back to her face. 'Are you well, child?'

'Yes,' she lied. 'Quite well.'

With a distracted nod he said, 'Good, for I have a matter to discuss with you. A pleasant matter, I hope.' His smile was uncertain as he came further into the room. 'Amelia, Captain Géroux has asked for your hand in marriage. And I have consented, if you are willing.'

'Marriage ...' Though she'd expected it, the word caught in her throat.

'You have captured his heart, my dear, and who could blame him?'

She sank down onto the edge of her bed, skirts tangling around her legs.

'Luc is a powerful man, and an alliance with him ...'

'Yes, I know.' She glanced at him. 'Then you agree that we must seek to trade if we are to survive?'

'In truth, I don't know. These are dark days, Amelia, and I am an old man. Maybe I would be wise to listen to the advice of younger men.'

She looked up, saw the uncertainty on his face and felt a weight descend on her shoulders. 'You fear there's truth in Zach's warning.'

'The Articles have always had the power to frighten kings, Amelia.' He sighed and sat next to her on the bed. 'Ile Sainte Anne must have allies. Friends. And Luc Géroux has those in the highest places.'

She nodded, glancing down at the silk of her skirts. The

delicate pattern blurred before her eyes, the skin on the back of her neck burning where Zach had kissed her. 'Luc has been kind to me,' she said, calm despite her chaotic emotions. 'And he means to help us. I ... I do not love him, Father, but I respect him and believe that he can help our people.' She looked at him and saw the swell of pride in his eyes. 'I understand my duty.'

Her father took her hand, pressing it between his own. 'Sweet child.'

But he couldn't hold her attention; it drifted away, straying to the open window. Outside, the night wind whispered through the palms, bringing with it the salt-tang of the docks, the promise of freedom. The memory of Zach's kiss.

In her room, all was still and her breath came up short against the stays of her dress.

She wouldn't leave. Damned obstinate girl. Zach stalked through the trees, down towards the docks, slapping away the biting insects that infested this godforsaken island. She wouldn't leave, so she'd die here – Amelia, her father and Zach's own father too. They'd all die when the storm came, when the East Indiamen laid low their fortress town with cannon and hard, soulless men who cared nothing for the so-called freedoms of Ile Sainte Anne. Then she'd see; then she'd understand the folly of listening to a man like Géroux. Then she'd wish she'd sailed aboard the *Hawk* to enjoy the only real freedom left in the world.

But by then she'd be dead.

The thought stopped him, pressing in on all sides like the sticky heat of the forest. He could hear the wash of surf on the beach, the slow crash-boom of it, feel a storm wind coming in from the west, running fingers through the treetops far above. Yet all he could see in that dark night was flames, Ile Sainte Anne burning, and Amelia along with it.

Damn fool girl.

'So, you mean to leave then, do you?' The voice, like the scraping together of rocks, was his father's.

Zach turned with a start, hand on the hilt of his sword, and cursed for revealing even that much of himself. Overton stepped out of the darkness, lean as a bone, skin like worn leather and eyes sharp as the blade at his side. 'No reason to stay,' Zach said. 'I've given my warning; if you won't listen, what more can I do?'

'Warning,' his father growled. 'Do you think I don't know what's coming, Zachary? Do you think I don't know what the Articles mean to the powers of this world?'

Zach shook his head. 'You intend to die for them, I suppose?'

'Someone has to.'

'No,' Zach said. In his mind's eye he could see Amelia being led to her death by his father and his obsession with the bloody Articles. He took a step closer. 'Listen to me. No one has to die for them. They're only words, they're not worth—'

Out of nowhere, a hand slapped him hard across the mouth, knocking him off balance. Zach staggered, tasting blood, and spat it out onto the ground. 'Son of a—'

'Only words?' his father growled. 'Only words with the power to unseat a king? Only words that proclaim a man's freedom? Never speak so again, boy.'

Heart racing, furious, Zach balled his fists at his side and willed himself not to strike back. 'You never were a father to me,' he spat, 'never cared if I lived or died.' He glared at his father, saw the slight narrowing of his eyes, the slight flinch on that hard face. Good, he intended to wound. 'But be grateful that your stinking blood flows in my veins, because if you were any other man you'd be lying dead at my feet right now.'

If his words struck home, his father didn't show it. 'Do

you think to threaten me, boy? I've more blood on my hands than you can imagine and I could open you from gut to throat in a heartbeat.'

Zach spat again, touched the back of his hand to his split lip. 'I've no need to threaten you,' he said. 'You'll all be dead within the year, you and everyone else here, and your bloody Articles will be smoke on the breeze.'

'You think they'll be so easy to destroy?' Overton gestured out towards the beach. 'There are places on these islands that no man knows but me, secure places. The Articles will endure, Zachary. They'll live on until all men understand their truths.'

Zach shook his head, turning away. He could stomach no more of his father's nonsense, not tonight with the taste of Amelia's soft skin still fresh on his lips. It was past time to be gone. There was truly nothing left on Ile Sainte Anne to hold him. 'Hide them if you wish,' he said, starting to walk. 'But when this place is ashes there will be nobody left to find them.'

'The Articles are your legacy, Zach,' his father called after him. 'Unworthy though you are, the Articles are yours to pass on when the time comes.'

Zach barked a dark, humourless laugh. 'My legacy? The steps of Newgate gaol were my legacy, *Father* – poverty, death and grief was the legacy you bequeathed your family. Keep your poxy Articles; I want nothing of them.'

With that, he stalked away through the trees, towards the harbour and the *Hawk*. He thought his father might follow, but he didn't and in the end Zach wasn't surprised. His whole life, his father had cared more about this place and his precious bloody Articles than he had ever cared about the life of his first-born son.

Chapter Nine

Zach was as good as his word. The *Hawk* sailed with the morning tide, sails gleaming in the dawn light, and Amelia watched from the cliff top with a heart bereft and angry. The boom of the cannon, a three-gun salute, marked his farewell as the *Hawk* left the harbour, bearing south until she was lost behind the curve of the island.

He was gone and the sea stretched empty before her.

Time passed as it ever did on Ile Sainte Anne. Amelia made her visit to Porto Novo and watched, fascinated, as Luc's friend in the French East India Company greeted him with smiles and pleasure. There were others in port too, the British not least among them. Amelia watched from the shadows as the scarlet-uniformed officers took Luc aside and presented him to a tall, thin man dressed all in black. They spoke together for some time, in low voices, and something about that conversation disturbed her. Perhaps it was the stiff way Luc held himself, the tension in his jaw, but whoever this man was she doubted he was a friend.

She asked Luc about it later, as they sailed home to Ile Sainte Anne, but he waved away her concerns and said they'd spoken only of trade and the sharp edges of the modern world.

And it was easy to forget that dour man when Luc talked with excitement and renewed faith of their plans for the future.

Her father, though more cautious, began to be hopeful too and only Overton, like his son, remained stubbornly opposed. But his opposition could not stop the path of progress. Once her father had agreed that Luc should help Ile Sainte Anne trade with the imperial powers, it seemed proper that Amelia's marriage to him would mark the start of the island's new future. The date was set for their wedding and, four months after Zach Hazard had sailed from Ile Sainte Anne, Amelia felt that her life was once more on an even keel.

If she occasionally dreamed of Zach – passionate dreams, leaving her sweaty and frustrated amid her tangled sheets – it was no matter. He was gone, he would not return and dreams were only dreams.

On one such night, with a high wind whistling through the stone walls, she awoke from her fevered sleep with a start, sitting bolt upright in bed, heart pounding. For a yearning moment confusion reigned. Her body was still ripe with desire, the memory of his lips on her skin so sharp that she could barely draw breath.

Then reality penetrated the dream, casting it into the wind. Outside there was a clanging of bells, shouting, and the running of feet. It could mean only one thing: a ship was foundering in the treacherous waters off Black Church Rock.

Jumping out of bed, Amelia threw on her clothes, slung a length of rope across her body, and darted down the stairs and out onto the path leading to the cliffs. The wind was blowing hard from the east, and more than likely it had driven a hapless trader onto the rocks.

The night was dark, storm clouds hiding the moon and stars. Only the distant flash of lightning lit the scene, revealing staccato images of horror to terrify any sailor. The ship was grounded and breaking up under the force of heavy seas – her mainmast was gone, sail flapping like rags in the wind – and her hull was pierced and taking on water. Even over the crash of the sea and the roar of the wind Amelia could hear men screaming.

She battled her way to the end of the headland. Already there were islanders scrambling over the rocks at its base, some with lines to throw to the sailors and others intent on salvage.

Though she knew the path well, she took the winding route down the cliff with care. On a calm day she would sometimes dive into the waters below, but it would be death to fall into these dark and heavy seas tonight. Soon she had reached the foot of the cliff and was scrambling over sea-sprayed rocks towards the foundering ship. Others came along the beach; she could see their torches, ragged in the wind as they ran.

The noise was astonishing, like being inside a thundercloud. The boom of the sea on the rocks filled her head, and only the shrieks of the sailors and their dying ship could pierce the noise.

Her clothes were drenched, hair whipping into her eyes. She pushed it back with her fingers, cursing herself for not braiding it, and clambered closer to the stricken ship. Jean-Pierre was ahead of her, shouting orders into the wind, torch held aloft like a beacon. Among the rocks floated bales – silk, perhaps – and men perched far out, hauling them ashore. There were sailors, too, scrambling up onto the rocks, while others floated lifeless in the sea.

Ahead, the ship loomed black against the night sky. She looked enormous, rolled onto her side, belly split like a whale rotting on the shore. Keeping low enough not to be blown off her feet, Amelia climbed closer. The rocks were slick and she made slow progress, but unlike most of the men of the island she knew these rocks well and could go further out, closer to the ship and her crew.

She could see men, shadows and flashes in the lightning, crowding close to the rail of the ship. Her deck was canted seaward almost ninety degrees and they hung on its landward rail in desperation, too frightened to risk the drop into the sea. If she could reach them and tie off her line between the rocks and the rail they could make their way along it to safety.

Working fast, she secured her rope around a sturdy rock

and tied the other end around her waist. She was light and quick; it would not be difficult to climb up onto the ship once she had crossed the stretch of churning water. The sea was rushing through the channel, fast and deadly, but she knew these rocks and it was no more than waist deep, shallow enough to wade. If she could keep her footing she could reach the wreck and climb up along the fissure in her hull; it would be the work of a moment, even in the dark. Crossing that treacherous channel of water, however …

A hand seized her arm and she spun, startled to see Luc standing behind her. 'Amelia!' He had to shout to be heard over the wind. 'What are you doing?'

She gestured to the men. 'With a line, they can reach safety.'

He squinted through the darkness. 'Impossible,' he said, tugging her arm backward. 'Come. Come away.'

Angry, she shook herself free. 'Not impossible for me.'

'I won't let you—'

'They'll die!' she shouted through the storm. 'Would you just leave them to die?'

'Men die at sea!'

'Well not if I can help it.'

He might be her betrothed, but he couldn't stop her and she climbed over the last of the rocks, down into the water. There was a fierce pull on her legs as a wave rushed through the narrow channel and she had to hold on to the rocks to keep her feet. Above her she could hear Luc swearing in French; there was a glimpse of movement, and then she felt the line on her waist go taut. For a moment she feared he was going to haul her in like a fish, but when she looked up she saw that he'd braced himself and was paying the rope out little by little so that if she fell he would be able to hold her. She smiled and felt a rush of warmth in her chest; Luc simply nodded and watched as she made her way across the torrent to the wreck.

Twice she fell, knocked sideways by the waves racing around the ship. Water closed over her head and in the darkness up was down and fear was a scarlet flutter in her chest. But each time she found the line at her waist and hauled herself upright as the water receded.

Luc had saved her life, of that she was certain. Perhaps she *had* been somewhat rash. No matter. She lived, and that was all that counted.

The wreck loomed over her now, the barnacled hull sweeping up into the night. Far above, the stranded sailors shouted, their language unknown to her but their panic obvious. With water streaming down her face, she reached out and grasped the broken boards of the hull. It was slick and black, but where the boards were splintered she could easily grasp hold and heedless of the shards of wood scraping at her hands and feet she hoisted herself up and out of the water. The line dragged heavily on her waist and looking back she could still see Luc, torchlight glimmering against his wet hair as he watched her climb. Higher now, the wind snatched at her with long, ruthless fingers, and she had to hold tight to keep from being blown back into the water. But climb she did, sheltering inside the ship as she made her way up the crack in the hull.

The ship, though, wasn't still. She moved each time a wave broke over her and the wood snapped and complained, water racing in and out of her hull. Pausing, Amelia glimpsed a flash of light from the starboard side of the ship. For a moment she was confused, then it came again and she realised that she was seeing lightning through another rent in the hull, this one on the opposite side. The ship was breaking in two, speared on a rock and being hammered by the relentless ocean. Amelia could feel the hull shifting as she climbed and doubted the ship would last much longer.

She hurried. No one left aboard when the ship broke up would survive.

At last her climb became more of a clamber as she crested the curve of the hull and made her way to the deck that listed down towards the ocean. One of the sailors clinging to the rail gave a shout when he saw her – perhaps he imagined he'd seen a phantom? Other frightened faces peered at her from the storm as she slid along the hull towards them.

On her knees, she grabbed the rail with one hand and the arm of the man who had shouted with the other.

'I have a line,' she yelled. 'I can help you.'

He stared, not understanding. To his eyes, she supposed, she appeared like a wild boy rising up from the sea as if from nowhere. Since explanation was impossible, she started working on the knot around her waist. She'd tied it well and it came away easily beneath her practiced fingers. Hauling on it until it was tight, she tied it off securely to the rail and then motioned to the first of the men.

He understood instantly and untied his belt, looping it over the line and then around his chest. With care he made his way across the slippery, exposed hull of the ship and then slid along the line until he was out of sight.

Amelia waited, felt the ship shifting as another wave crashed into her windward side. Something below deck creaked and snapped – she felt it through the soles of her feet. Around her, the men hunkered lower.

Then it came, three tugs on the rope.

'You,' she pointed at the next man. 'Go.'

Eyes wide with fear, he did the same as his shipmate, slipping on the hull and sending the rope bouncing with his uncontrolled descent. He must have made it, however, as the rope was tugged three times again. And so it went on.

There were five men in total and one by one they made their escape to land. Amelia would not leave until the last of them was gone, and as he made his careful way off the ship she found herself alone.

Alone in the midst of a storm.

She should have been more frightened than she felt, but there was something so thrilling about the roar of the sea, the howl of the wind, and it ran through her veins like fire. She turned her face to the wind and laughed, yelled a wordless shout into the teeth of the storm. Let the wind tear at her hair, at her clothes. She longed to spread her arms, to fly.

Then she heard a noise, a sound from below deck – a cry for help?

The rope tugged three times. It was her turn to leave.

'Hello!' she shouted. 'Hello there!'

Of course, it would be impossible for anyone to hear her above the noise of the storm. She should get below herself, so she could be heard.

The rope jiggled again, three times. Impatient.

She jerked it back once, and then slid down the deck toward the nearest open hatch. She'd just call down, in case someone was trapped. Another wave hit the ship, sending up a vast plume of spray that got into her eyes. She wiped her face and grabbed hold of the edge of the hatch, poking her head inside. 'Hello, is there anyone there?'

The only sound that came back to her was the boom of the waves inside the wreck and the creak of protesting wood. Suddenly, the deck shifted. With a jerk, she lost her grip and began to slide down the deck, towards the hungry sea. Desperately, she tried to stop her fall, bracing her feet against the root of what had once been a mast. Snapped now, it stuck out like a fallen tree and she balanced on it, her back pressed against the deck. Above her the rail and the line to safety seemed very far away.

She cursed, thoroughly.

Light split the sky again and, for an instant, she caught sight of another ship, well clear of the rocks, riding the storm. Then it was gone.

A new panic set her heart racing faster. There were many

tales of unnatural ships that haunted wrecks, looking for the dead. Well, if that was what she'd seen then the ghostly captain would have many new recruits this night, but she did not plan to be one of them.

Determined, she turned her attention back to the hatch above her head. The deck was too slick to climb, but it was strewn with broken rigging, so all she need do was grab hold of one of the snapped yards and make her way back up to the rail.

Simple.

Or it would have been if the ship hadn't chosen that moment to split. With an enormous rending sound, the stern broke away, turning sideways under the force of the sea. Amelia saw it racing towards her; if she didn't move she'd be crushed between the two halves of the ship. Her choice was immediate and desperate. There was no time to even shout out, she simply launched herself from her precarious perch on the splintered mast and dived into the raging sea, trusting in nothing but fate to save her.

'Haul the fore-sail up and furl it!' Zach yelled as he staggered across the heaving deck to take the wheel. 'Square the yards, and get strops round the mast above the booms!'

Brookes grabbed his arm, soaked to the skin and clinging to a line. 'We'll never outrun it, Zach. Are you mad?'

'Reef the sail!' Zach shouted in response. 'Haul on board the tack, tend the braces and haul up the mizzen. Throw out the warps and get a tri-sail rigged!'

'Zach!' Brookes yelled, fear dark in the man's eyes. 'In the name of mother and child, we must make port!'

Laden with cargo to trade – their venture to the east had proven profitable – the *Gypsy Hawk* rode the huge seas with all the grace of a pregnant cow. Perhaps it would have been more prudent to make port at Ile Sainte Anne, but Zach intended to avoid that place at all costs.

'Captain!' Brookes shouted through the rain. 'This is madness!'

He was right, but Zach had no desire to encounter the siren of Ile Sainte Anne. Nor to see her in the arms of Luc Géroux. Four months since their last meeting and still he felt the danger of her. These treacherous seas were nothing compared to his own treacherous heart. Best steer well clear.

'She'll hold!' he shouted back to Brookes, both hands on the wheel. 'The worst is past, another hour or two, no more.'

'But Zach—'

'Sail ho!' The shout came from the port rail; no one was aloft in this weather.

Zach peered out into the black just as a flash of lightning split the sky. There was a ship on the rocks, breaking up in the storm.

Brookes made a swift warding gesture.

'We're well clear of it here.' Zach knew these waters well, even in perilous weather. Lightning zigzagged across the sky, and in its light he saw men moving across the canted deck of the ship. Poor buggers.

Brookes spat on the deck, for luck. 'They'll be sleeping with Old Hobb tonight.'

It was true enough and there was nothing the *Hawk* could do for them. To draw close enough to pick up survivors would imperil the ship, and the seas were too big for a longboat, the rocks beneath them too hazardous. The risk was too great.

'Take the helm.' Handing the wheel off to Brookes, Zach made his way towards the ship's rail, holding tight to a line lest he be washed overboard.

'Zachary?' There was a note of unease in Brookes' voice, as if he could guess the path of Zach's thoughts. 'Captain, there's nothing we can do for them!'

'I know it.' Nevertheless, he cast a glance at the longboats and wondered. But, no. The *Hawk* pitched sharply and he staggered, a wave crashing over her prow as if trying to pull her under. She rolled and Zach heard the cargo shifting, though it had been firmly tied. 'Shiner!' he yelled. 'Send a man below, secure the hold.'

Shiner bellowed orders and Zach found himself at the rail gazing out at the dark island. He could pick out the white of the breaking waves as they crushed the wrecked ship, and he tried not to imagine Amelia Dauphin perched on the rocks, singing sailors to their deaths.

There was another flare of lightning across the sky, a long flickering fork of light. Then he knew Amelia had been in his thoughts for too long because it seemed that she stood upon the upturned deck of the foundering ship.

He blinked, swiping a hand across his face to dash the water from his eyes, and looked again. All was dark, and then another flash of light and he saw a figure on the deck, near the remains of the foremast. Cursing his own madness, he pulled his glass from his belt and waited for another flare of lightning.

It lasted only an instant but it was enough.

For some unfathomable reason, the girl was aboard the wrecked ship. There was no doubting it was her, scampering about alone on the deck.

'What the devil is she doing?' he cursed, hesitating between putting his glass away and looking again.

Lightning flashed; he looked again.

The deck was at a sharp angle, and it seemed she was unable to climb up to the top rail. Little good it would do her anyway for the whole ship was breaking apart. She would be crushed, drowned. There was no chance for anyone aboard that doomed ship and in the icy grip of the storm Zach Hazard felt a rush of dread.

'Lower the longboat!'

Confused eyes blinked at him from Shiner's ugly face. 'Captain?'

'I said lower the bloody longboat!' He stripped off his belt and everything else save his shirt and britches and shoved them at Shiner. 'Don't lose them.'

Another flash of lightning split the sky, followed by a terrible rending crack as the spine of the wrecked ship snapped. Zach felt it like a fist in his gut. 'Longboat, now!'

In a flurry of activity, the longboat was lowered. The *Hawk* pitched and rolled, clanking the boat against her side.

'Zachary, no!' Brookes shouted from the helm, but couldn't leave the wheel to stop him.

Despite the force of the storm, Zach climbed up onto the ship's rail and offered his first mate a farewell salute. 'Wait for me!' he ordered, but didn't linger to hear Brookes curse in reply. He slipped over the side and slid down the ladder, pausing at the bottom to gauge the shifting gap between the *Hawk* and the longboat. If he missed ...

The *Hawk* rose, the longboat fell. The longboat rose, the *Hawk* fell.

Zach jumped.

Wood smacked him hard in the chest, knocking the breath from his lungs. A wave crashed over his head, but they didn't go under. He was aboard.

Behind him he could hear the dying screams of the wrecked ship and with an oar in each hand he pulled hard towards her.

It was madness, he knew, but it didn't matter. All he could think of was Amelia and how he had to save her from such a bitter death.

By the time he reached the rocky waters where the merchantman lay, impaled, Zach's shoulders burned, his boat was half swamped, and he began to fear for his life as well as his sanity.

'Amelia!'

He yelled her name until his throat was raw, sick with rising despair and panic. He tried to keep the longboat from being crushed by the wreck as he searched the mountainous waves for one lone woman, but it was impossible. Madness.

And yet ...

Amid the black water he glimpsed a ghostly face and flailing limbs, someone exhausted, struggling for their life. Picking up the oars he fought his way through the storm towards that slender hope. He rowed until his muscles screamed, and then, balanced precariously and lashed by the storm, he reached down into the raging sea. Fingers closing around a limp arm, Zach began to haul with everything he had left.

He hoped it would be enough, for death would take them both if he failed.

Chapter Ten

Amelia awoke smothered in blankets, the familiar pitch and roll of a ship beneath her. It wasn't the *Sunlight*, of that she was certain. She knew her own ship and this ship was heavier and deeper in the draft. She opened her eyes. Yellow lamplight swayed in time with the movement of the ship, sending shadows dancing across an unfamiliar cabin. It occurred to her that she should be frightened, but she was warm, dry and safe, though her throat was scoured raw by seawater.

She shifted and realised that, beneath the blankets, she was naked. Her hair was still damp, which meant she couldn't have been long pulled from the sea.

Memories were hazy, but clearing. There'd been a wreck, men stranded. And she'd saved them. She remembered the dreadful noise of the ship breaking up; she remembered her desperate dive into the water, the cold clamp of the sea around her body. Waves like mountains, deadly rocks looming out of the night. She remembered going under, fighting for the surface, knowing that she'd never see her father again. Never see the dawn.

And she remembered hope, brighter than the sun, as an impossible hand reached out of the darkness to grab her arm and haul her to safety. Zach Hazard, wild as the ocean and just as fierce, had battled his way back to the *Hawk* while she'd huddled, coughing up seawater, in the bottom of the waterlogged boat.

After that, memory eluded her. He must have brought her aboard, must have stripped her of her wet clothes and stowed her here, swaddled like an infant.

As if summoned by the memory, the cabin door opened and Zach entered amid a squall of rain. He shut the door hard against it and for a moment rested his head on the wood, as if summoning strength. Then he turned and glanced towards her. For a reason she couldn't fathom, Amelia closed her eyes and feigned sleep. She lay still until she heard him move across the cabin, then slit her eyelids enough to watch as he opened a trunk in the corner and pulled out dry clothes. Her pulse skittered when he stripped off his sodden shirt and britches and she grew warm beneath the blankets, a guilty flush blooming on her cheek. She didn't look away.

He'd not changed in the months he'd been gone, though perhaps his hair was a little longer. His damp skin glistened golden in the lamplight and she found her breaths coming short and fast. Her blood, still burning from her adventure aboard the wreck, pulsed with a deeper heat; he was not the first man she'd seen naked, but he was by far the most beautiful. There was no denying it. Many an island girl had wrecked herself upon the infamous beauty of Zachary Hazard. She'd nearly done so herself, would have done had he not left. The memory of that painful night in her room brought a different heat to her cheeks, the old sense of loss renewed by the desire he stirred.

Grabbing a blanket of his own, Zach dried off and dressed, moving with the easy grace of a man born to the sea. As he turned away from her she noticed a hash of scars running across the back of his shoulders; someone had taken a cat to him in the past. She winced at the idea, tried not to think of the whip curling over his shoulders, breaking that golden skin. The cat-o'-nine-tails had long been outlawed on Ile Sainte Anne, but Zach hadn't lived his whole life on the island and his body was marked by the harsher world beyond. On his left shoulder he was inked, a bird in flight – a hawk, of course – and around one bicep ran the words 'The poor will wear the crown.' She knew the saying well, had learned it at her father's knee, and was surprised that Zach would keep it so close to his heart.

Perhaps his father's principles meant more to him than he would have the world believe?

In a flurry of linen he pulled a shirt over his head, and she was shocked at her own disappointment. She closed her eyes and lay perfectly still, convinced suddenly that he knew she'd been watching.

There was silence in the cabin. Outside, the storm blew hard, but she could tell they were running with the wind now and out of danger. The *Hawk* under Captain Hazard's command could handle these seas.

He sighed and muttered something beneath his breath. Then light footsteps approached the berth and, unable to feign sleep any longer, she opened her eyes. Zach stopped, watching her with a guarded expression. 'You're awake then.'

Amelia nodded, cheeks blazing. 'I was—' She cleared her throat. 'You saved my life, I think.'

'You think right.' His tone was stern, lacking its usual humour. 'And it nearly cost me my own.' Still studying her, he braced one hand on the low beam of the ceiling and glowered at her. 'What the bloody hell were you doing out there, Amelia?'

Very aware of her own nakedness, she clutched the blanket to her chest and sat up. She would not be intimidated. 'I was saving the lives of five men.'

'And very nearly losing your own – and mine – into the bargain.'

'My life is my own to risk, is it not? I didn't ask you to risk yours.'

Zach lifted an eyebrow. 'Could hardly sail past and leave you to drown, now could I?'

There was no retort that wouldn't have sounded petulant, so she said nothing at all and they simply glared at each other. After a long moment Zach seemed to give up. He let out a breath, shook his head, and sat down on the edge of the bed – his bed, she realised with a sudden rush of heat.

'Bloody stupid.' He sounded weary. 'Reckless.'

Afraid that she'd appeared ungrateful, Amelia reached out and put her hand on his. 'Thank you. Truly. It was brave of you.'

His gaze, hooded beneath long lashes, flickered down to where their hands rested on the blanket. 'Brave?' He gave a low laugh. 'Brookes has another word for it.'

She was very aware of the warmth of his skin, and the heat in her cheeks, as he slid his fingers out from beneath hers and began to trace a path along her knuckles. She dared not look at him, afraid of what he might see in her eyes, and so she couldn't see his face when he said, 'I suppose Captain Géroux will be grief-stricken by your apparent loss.'

Amelia started, struck by a sudden memory. Luc had helped her board the wreck; he must have seen it break up. 'He will think me drowned.' She pressed a hand to her mouth in horror; her father would believe her dead.

Zach's fingers stilled and in a cool voice he said, 'We'll make port by dawn, he won't grieve long.'

His words were no comfort. Her recklessness had caused Luc and her father pain – and had risked Zach's life, albeit unknowingly. Stupid, rash deed! Yet five men lived who would otherwise be dead. How could she regret that?

'Do you think me foolish?' She risked a look at Zach's face, wanting to gauge the truth of his answer.

He was staring across the cabin towards its dark windows, out into the storm, and she couldn't read his expression. 'Foolish?' A humourless smile curled one corner of his mouth. 'Yes, entirely so.'

'Then you'd have let those men die?'

'Who's to say I'm any less foolish?' He glanced at her, met her eyes briefly. 'Saved you, didn't I?'

A complex silence grew between them, part expectant, part barbed. Amelia found herself at once confused by his meaning and unable to take her eyes from the tar-stained fingers that lingered upon her hand. Nor could she deny the shameful desire she felt, her blood still burning from her dance with death. Never in her life had she felt more alive than at this moment, with his hand on hers and the storm driving them on through deadly seas.

Zach looked at her again. His chest was rising and falling fast beneath the open neck of his shirt and there was a question in his eyes that she didn't understand and couldn't answer. 'Perhaps we're both bloody stupid,' he said suddenly. 'You the Pirate Queen and me your Fool.'

The heat in his voice took her aback. 'I'm no queen.'

'Princess, then.'

'Captain,' she corrected. 'Like you.'

He lifted a hand, traced the line of her collarbone, making her shiver. 'Yes, you *are* like me.' His hand stilled, fingers curling around her shoulder. A pickpocket's fingers, long and elegant.

He could steal me, she thought. He could steal me right now and I would let him take me. Such traitorous desire, with Luc mourning her ashore. She was ashamed of herself.

'All that pomp and nonsense at the fortress. Géroux preening himself like it's bloody Versailles. That's not for you, no matter what you call your duty.'

'It's not nonsense, it's my home. And Luc Géroux is an honourable man.'

'Are you sure of that?'

Angered by his tone, she was confused by the feelings he aroused. 'Of course I'm sure. Luc and I are engaged; we're to marry by the end of the year.'

He was surprised. She saw it in his eyes before he rose from the bed and paced to the other side of the cabin, where he stood, with his back to her, so taut it made her wish that she'd kept silent. When he eventually turned around, his expression was guarded. 'I wish you joy, then. No doubt it's a profitable match.'

'You know I don't marry for money.'

'For the prosperity of Ile Sainte Anne, you do.'

Had she been dressed she would have stood to defend herself against the accusation, but in her current predicament all she could do was sit upright in the bed, blankets clutched to her chest. 'What I do, I do for the future of my people.'

'Duty, money: call it what you will, there's no love in the case.' He gave her a serious look, then turned away and waved his hand towards a corner of the cabin. 'There are dry clothes in the trunk. Help yourself. Storm's abating; we'll dock by midday, and I doubt your father – or your betrothed – would be happy to see you disembark naked.'

He walked quickly to the door but she stopped him. 'Captain Hazard?'

Turning around he regarded her with studied indifference.

'I'm in your debt. Whatever else lies between us, you saved my life tonight.'

Zach scraped a mocking bow. 'A Fool can do nothing less for his Queen.'

Chapter Eleven

The men were singing as they unstowed the anchors, sent down the top ropes and unslung the lower yards, readying the ship to make port. Whatever they thought of their captain's reasoning, there was no doubt that the *Hawk*'s crew were happy at the prospect of spending time and money in the taverns of Ile Sainte Anne.

Zach did not share their enthusiasm.

For four months he'd been stalking the eastern trade routes, determined each day not to think of Amelia Dauphin and her adventurer's eyes. Or of Luc bloody Géroux, with his courtier's grace and weasel words. Yet he only had to get within sight of the island and the bloody woman was there, flinging herself off a shipwreck and into his path.

With one hand on the wheel, he glared at the storm-battered town as he steered his ship into port and wished he were anywhere else. 'Don't know what I've done to deserve this.'

At his side, Brookes snorted. 'Do y'not, lad?'

'I told you, I couldn't let her drown. Her father and mine are like brothers; she's almost a sister.'

'Hardly that.'

'Cousin, then.'

'I'd worry less if she were.' Brookes spat on the deck. 'Bad luck, bringing a woman aboard.'

'Her father will be grateful. There'll be a reward.'

'What reward? We're already sitting too low in the water to cross the Atlantic without risk; there's no manner of reward we can carry.'

Zach smiled. 'Captain James Dauphin in our debt, Mr Brookes. That's a reward we can carry, is it not?'

Brookes grunted. 'What currency is that in the world beyond Ile Sainte Anne?' His eyes narrowed, and not against the morning brightness. He was suspicious. 'You don't plan on staying here, do you? To win the lass.'

Zach barked an unconvincing laugh. 'To win *her*?' He jerked his head towards Amelia, who stood at the rail, no doubt eager for the first sight of her dutiful fiancé. 'Why would I want to do that?'

'Because you've been struck by calf love these past four months, and not twelve hours ago you flung yourself into the bloody sea to save her!'

Startled, Zach glanced around to be sure that none of his crew had heard Brookes' scandalous accusation. 'Calf love? Me?'

'I know what I see, Zach.' He cast a dark look in Amelia's direction. 'I see trouble.'

Her shirt fluttered in the breeze, hair salted as any sailor's. She was beautiful and Zach turned away, ignoring the pain that bloomed at the sight of her. 'There's no trouble.' He sighed. 'We'll drop her off on the island and be underway tomorrow morning. A day's delay is all.'

Brookes snorted in disbelief.

'Believe me, if I'd wanted her I'd have had her. I'm Zachary Hazard, am I not? Fathers lock up their daughters when I'm in port.'

'James Dauphin may wish he had.'

He grunted his agreement. 'Very possible, for I hear she's betrothed to Luc Géroux.'

'Géroux?' Brookes' face lit. 'Is that so?'

'Not that I care. They'll all be dead by summer's end anyway. Too bloody stubborn to run ahead of the storm.' He lifted his gaze to the horizon, half expecting to see a forest of masts already massing there, but it was a clear azure line, the threat still hidden. Yet coming nonetheless, as inevitable as winter.

'Then we'd best be long gone before the blow falls,' Brookes said.

'We will be.'

They were close enough now to see people on the quay, hear the distant calls of surprised greeting. Amelia gave a cry, waving as she climbed up onto the rail. 'Father!' she shouted. 'Luc! I'm here!'

Zach turned away, handing the wheel off to Brookes. 'I'll be in my cabin.' He'd no stomach to witness this reunion. Come the morning, he promised himself, he'd be gone, never to return. For there was nothing that could make him stay in Ile Sainte Anne, nothing at all.

That evening they built a huge fire upon the beach and set two cattle to roasting on the *boucans* to celebrate Amelia's safe return. Sunset streaked out over the cliffs of the island, casting Runaway Bay into a premature twilight, lit only by the dancing flames. Children flitted in and out of the firelight, excited and squealing, begging the men who tended the meat for an early taste of the feast. Women of all ages fluffed their skirts and sang short verses, waiting for the music to begin, and the *Gypsy Hawk*'s crew threaded through them with an eye, no doubt, for later pleasures in the woods and huts beyond.

Zachary Hazard himself, however, sat quietly on the edges of the festivities and that alone was enough to draw the attention of Adamaris Sesay. She'd always held a soft spot for Zachary in her broad heart. Perhaps it was the gift of her mother's mother, but where others saw a wayward gypsy, she saw a lost soul, always in motion, always looking for something he could not find. Until now.

She watched him watch Amelia and Géroux across the fire, his heart in his eloquent eyes. He held a bottle in his hands, though rarely lifted it to his lips, and sat with his arms on his knees, more serious than she had ever known him. Addy smiled to herself; she'd never seen Zach Hazard in love and in doubt of his power over a woman's heart.

The music started, Old Jones on the fiddle and O'Reilly striking up a merry song. The girls were on their feet as soon as could be, pulling any man willing into the dance. Zach declined a dozen invitations with a good-natured wave of his rum, his attention held only by Amelia.

With a sigh, Addy climbed to her feet. Dusting sand from her skirts, she went and planted herself between Zach and the fire – obscuring the view of his lady love. To her amusement he craned his neck slightly, as though he might look around her.

'Well, Zachary,' she said, keeping her smiles inside, 'you'll not turn down a dance with me, I hope.'

'I'm not much inclined to dance tonight,' he said with a grin that wasn't as quick as it should have been. 'Mostly intend to be drinking, and the closer I am to the ground the better in that regard.'

'You've not drunk more than two mouthfuls, and there'll be no brooding this night, hmm? Eat, drink and be merry, Captain Hazard.'

He canted his head, offering her a curious look. 'For tomorrow we die?'

'Is that what you want?'

'Most definitely not.'

'Then don't tempt the Devil.' She nodded towards the dancers whirling around the fire. 'Dance with me, and make me the envy of all the girls.'

'You're already the envy of all the girls,' he said, rolling gracefully to his feet. 'Or you would be, if they knew what was what.' His smile was as warm as the hand that took hers, his touch ever gentle; he'd always been a tender lover, for all his bravado. And she might have been tempted to keep him for herself tonight had she not seen the ache in his heart. There was only one woman he wanted.

So, instead, she pulled him into the dance, and of course he performed as Captain Hazard always did: outrageously.

He twirled every girl as they passed around the circle, stealing a kiss where he could and making them shriek and giggle, somehow keeping himself on his feet through it all. Addy kept a close eye as they moved in opposite directions through the dance, and when at last she was his partner again she pulled him to the side.

'Oh!' she gasped, fanning herself. 'I think the girls are jealous enough!'

'Not nearly enough,' he smiled, the heat of the fire and the dance glimmering in a faint sheen across his brow and chest. 'Come on, we'll—'

'No,' Addy insisted, pulling away. 'But look.' She didn't try to hide her triumph. 'Here's Amelia all forlorn and in need of a dance.'

Zach's startled gaze darted to where Amelia sat in the shadows. He said nothing, just fixed Addy with a narrow-eyed look.

Ignoring him, she gathered her skirts and sat down in the sand. 'Time was when I danced till dawn, but not tonight. You dance, Amelia. I'm sure Captain Géroux will keep me company.'

'Of course,' Géroux said, though his attention darted between Amelia and Zach with a keen interest. If he objected, however, he said nothing.

Amelia's eyes lifted to Zach's. He hadn't moved, though his gaze was now fixed entirely on her. 'Won't be the first time we've danced together,' he said, and held out his hand, 'though perhaps it will be the last.'

'Perhaps.' Her echo was as sad as her smile as she took his hand and he led her into the crowd of laughing dancers.

Addy lost them for a moment, her attention shifting to Old Jones as he ended the tune to a ripple of clapping and shouts for more. Zach and Amelia were almost on the far side of the fire, but she could see them standing close, see their hands still clasped when another tune began to play.

Slower, this one, the words familiar and the beat strong. A few cries of recognition greeted it, other voices joining in to sing of the *Raggle-Taggle Gypsy* and the lady he stole. Addy smiled and watched them dance, spinning and laughing, stumbling in the sand as the dance moved faster around the fire. She saw when Amelia tripped and Zach caught her, pulling her close, and she saw them stop amid the whirl of other dancers, faces lit by firelight and the only point of stillness in the frantic rush of movement.

In that moment, she knew that Zach was anchored here as surely as his precious ship. Unless Amelia herself broke the chain, he would never sail free again. For better or worse, Zach Hazard had bound himself to her fate.

Géroux watched them too, from where he sat at Addy's side, his face impassive and eyes calculating. Nothing good, she knew, could come of his presence here. She sighed and turned away, back to the fire.

A sudden squall startled the flames into a wilder dance, an onshore breeze racing up the beach. The wind had changed direction; it was blowing now from the north and bringing a distant tang of cold on its wings.

It felt like an ill wind, sharp with foreboding, and she feared what it might mean for Zach and Amelia – and for them all.

Chapter Twelve

Two weeks later, at sunrise, the ships were spotted. Grim-faced, her father roused Amelia from sleep and together they walked to the cliffs atop Black Church Rock and watched the navy approach.

'Now's the time,' Captain Overton said, appearing out of the dawn to stand at her father's shoulder. 'Here we must make our stand, James, or lose everything.'

'As did those who came before us?'

Overton folded his arms, defiant. '*A Deo a Libertate.*'

'For God and Liberty? Is war our only choice, Zechariah?' Her father sounded weary and old. It frightened Amelia almost as much as the approaching ships.

'You both know there's another way,' she said, turning around. 'Father, we must do as Luc says. We must offer to trade with them.'

Overton spat his contempt onto the rocks. 'What would you have us trade? Our freedom is the only thing of value we possess, and they'll take that by force.'

'We must at least hear what they have to say,' she insisted, turning back to the ships, tall and imposing against the rising sun. 'We cannot fight them. They will destroy us if we try.'

Her father sighed. 'It may yet come to that. If they ask of us more than we are willing to give, then it may come to that. However—'

'James ...' Overton's voice was stiff with warning.

'Peace, old friend,' her father said. 'I will not trade our freedom, or the Articles, not for my life – not even for Amelia's life. But if there is truly another way ... Are we such old men that we reject the future and cling only to the past? Maybe we can trade more than mere sugars and silks with these people. Maybe our freedoms will also spread along the trade routes, bringing men here to see how we live and sending them away ready to demand the same freedoms for themselves.'

'Yes!' Amelia jumped in. 'Yes, that is what Luc says will happen. Ideas travel faster than ships, he says. We will do more to spread our ideas of freedom through trade than through war —'

'You think they'll tolerate that, do you?' Overton glared at her. 'You think they'll let our notions of liberty reach those wretches upon whose labour their wealth is built? Do you think they'll let any in the filthy streets of London hear our call for freedom?'

'I think they care less about our ideas than our goods. If they meant to destroy us, they would have sent more than three paltry ships!'

Overton shook his head. 'Folly.' His bright eyes turned on her father. 'Folly, James. Mark it, now. I say this is folly. We should fight.'

'Perhaps we will,' her father said. 'First, we will hear what they have to say. I make no greater promise than that, Amelia. We will hear them and then choose which path to take.'

She took a deep breath, full of relief. 'Thank you, Father. You won't regret your decision.'

He made no answer, only shared a serious look with Overton, who shook his head and turned away.

The sun was above the horizon now, chasing away the remains of the night. In the pale morning she could see the ships of Ile Sainte Anne bobbing in the harbour, fishing boats and single-masted sloops mostly – nothing to challenge the might of the British warships.

Behind her she heard her father's boots scrape on the stone as he began to walk back towards the fortress. A breeze rose and caught at her hair, whipping strands into her eyes and tugging at her shirt and britches.

She turned her face into the wind and breathed deeply. Despite her assurances to her father, she was afraid. She could not deny it. Part of her couldn't help worrying that Zach was right. What if they had nothing to trade with the British but their lives? What if they should have run, like he'd said all along?

But Zach hadn't run in the end. The *Hawk* was still anchored in the harbour and now it was too late; the enemy was at the gate. Briefly she wondered why he didn't run now, but then she remembered how he'd looked at her while they danced in the firelight and she knew the answer.

He stayed because she stayed.

'Sometimes,' Overton said, startling her, 'those ships what run most heavily armed are the most vulnerable to attack. They have a weakness beneath the waterline, a tender spot powerless against a single strike, and once they've been holed the weight of their cannon drags them into the deep faster than many a lighter ship. There's no coming back from that.'

She glanced at him, but his attention was not fixed on the advancing enemy. He was watching the *Hawk*.

'You fear for your son,' she said. 'Of course you do.'

His sharp gaze darted to her, and for a moment she saw Zach in the sardonic tilt of his lips. 'Aye, I do, for he's already sunk, isn't he?'

She felt herself colour and looked away. 'I don't know what you—'

'I'll die for the Articles, Miss Dauphin,' Overton said. 'I'll die for Ile Sainte Anne. But mark this – I'll kill for my son.'

With that he left her, picking his way along the cliff towards the fortress. Amelia watched him go in confusion, not sure what he meant by his warning. Did he think she intended to harm Zach? Perhaps he blamed her for keeping him here? But Zach Hazard was his own man, and whatever feelings had grown between them he could come and go as he chose. She had made him no promises.

Yet Captain Overton's warning had been clear; he thought she posed a threat to his son. Was it possible that he was right?

It was not the armada Zach had been expecting. The horizon was not crowded with sails and there were no bristling East Indiamen bearing down on Ile Sainte Anne with their cannon run out and primed.

Instead, dawn broke upon three sleek ships of the line, white sails gleaming and British colours snapping as they hove into view. From where he stood on the foredeck of the *Hawk*, Zach could hear the alarm clanging in the fortress, loud enough to drive his sleepy crew on deck with muttered curses as they yawned and squinted in the dawn light.

Zach lowered his spyglass, uneasy. Was this the vanguard? Did the real fleet lie concealed beyond a headland, waiting to draw out the pitiful island defences? 'Shiner,' he shouted, rousing the rangy young crewman from where he stood rubbing sleep from his eyes at the rail. 'Get aloft, tell me if you see more sails.'

'Aye, Captain.' He was scaling the rigging as he answered, scrambling up to the crow's nest like a monkey. Zach shaded his eyes as he watched Shiner pull out his own glass and study the horizon in every direction.

'It's clear,' Shiner called down, 'save a merchantman nor-nor-west of us, and some fishing scows to the south.'

It should have been good news, but somehow it only tightened the knot of unease in Zach's belly.

'Not what you were expecting,' Brookes said, coming to join him. His eyes were slits against the low morning sun, and he lifted a hand to shade his face as he peered out beyond the harbour.

'Not what you were expecting, either,' Zach said. 'You

heard the talk in Hispaniola. You heard what they were planning.'

'Aye, I heard. But this ain't no combined action – there ain't no French nor Dutch here, just the British.' He spat on the deck and cast a sideways glance at Zach. 'Maybe Géroux was right, then. Maybe they *are* here to trade.'

Far above, a pair of gulls wheeled around the mainmast, their cries clashing with the alarm tolling atop the fortress. It sounded like a warning, an omen.

The ships had entered the harbour now, slipping expertly between the boats still at anchor. On their decks Zach could see ragtag crews lined up along the rails, the occasional flash of steel betraying a defiant blade. 'Géroux is a fool,' he said. But he couldn't ignore the doubt that lurked in a corner of his mind. Was it possible that they had come here to trade? Was the British Empire grown so mighty that they no longer feared the pirates of Ile Sainte Anne and the freedoms they proclaimed? He almost laughed at the idea. 'My father will be gutted to know they care so little about his precious Articles.'

Brookes grunted a response. 'Depends on what they've come here to trade for.'

That was the material point. He met the dark look in his old friend's eyes with one of his own. 'Warned her of that. Warned her she might not like the terms of their trade.'

'They'll ask for her father,' Brookes guessed. 'And yours. That'll be the price of saving the island.'

'She won't accept it.' He was certain of that. 'She'd never hand them her father, not for any price.'

Brookes didn't answer, just scowled down at the deck.

'What? You think she would?'

He let out a low sigh and shook his head. 'What do I know of it, or her?'

'Little more than me, but I'll have your thoughts anyway. Out with them.' He'd known Brookes too long to dismiss his opinion on anything; the wily old sailor was clever for all his protestations otherwise.

After a considered pause, Brookes said, 'I've known that girl since she first set foot on the island. Sailed here with her father, didn't I? This place is in her blood, Zach. It's in her bones. Just like it's in her father's and in your father's too. They'd all die for it and call it honour. James Dauphin would willingly trade his life for the island and I think Amelia would let him. I think there's nothing she wouldn't trade to keep Ile Sainte Anne safe.'

A breeze rippled across the water, warm vanilla-spiced air from the island. It caught at the rigging, setting it jangling like old bones. 'She'd not be fool enough to trust them. Nor would my father, or Dauphin.'

'No? Géroux's honeyed words have been sweetening their ears for many a month, and they trust him. Dauphin certainly does.' Brookes frowned, and more quietly said, 'So does Amelia.'

It seemed even Brookes had noticed how Amy chose to take Luc's advice over his own. She was led by her so-called duty, he knew, and that was the bitterest part of the truth. No matter where her heart lay, she would put her duty first. Even so, Zach could not believe she would trade her father's life on so slight a promise. 'She's no fool,' he protested. 'She wouldn't—'

'She's young,' Brookes interrupted. 'Raised here, on little more than her father's dreams. What does she know of kings and their plotting? What does she know beyond pirating and the sea?'

Zach shifted, uncomfortable to hear his own thoughts leaving Brookes' mouth. Amelia Dauphin was no fool, but she was summer's daughter; few dark clouds had blighted her days and she lived far from the cold, bleak places that had shaped his life.

'We should leave,' Brookes said into the silence that had

fallen between them. 'We should sail now, put this place to our stern and not return. There's nothing to keep us here, Zach. You know there isn't.'

He flicked a glance at the fortress, imagined Amelia atop the black cliffs, watching the navy approach. He could go to her again, beg her to sail with him one last time, but she would only refuse. She'd made that clear all too often; she'd chosen to trade with the enemy, she had chosen duty and Luc Géroux, and she would never leave Ile Sainte Anne. Brookes was right, there was nothing to keep him there any more. Not even hope. And yet ...

He sighed. Was this love, to be so shackled to another that you couldn't leave them even when they had chosen another? If it was, he wanted nothing more to do with such a perilous emotion.

Angrily, he kicked at the base of the wheel. He felt like a fool and could not understand it. Never had he been such a flat-headed cully. 'Should never have come back. Should never have plucked her from the sea.'

Brookes grunted. 'Should have bedded her when you had the chance, and got her out of your system.'

Zach forced a smile, but his heart wasn't in it. Whatever this was, this yearning he felt, it went deeper than seduction. A mere tumble in the sand would have done nothing to ease the ache in his chest. Perhaps it would have only made it worse. Of all the women he had known – and there had been plenty – he'd lost his heart to the only one to put her duty ahead of his charms. There was irony in that, though he supposed others might call it justice. 'Brookes, I—'

But Brookes' attention had shifted. He was staring intently at the naval ships as they began to weigh anchor; they'd positioned themselves to block the harbour entrance. Zach's unease sharpened.

The largest of the ships was close enough now that he could see the flash of officers' braid upon the deck, watch men high in the rigging, reefing the sails, and read the ship's name, glinting gold in the morning sun.

'God's teeth, Zach,' Brookes hissed. 'It's the *Intrepid*.'

'Morton.' For a moment, dread swamped all other feelings. 'So that's why they're here.'

'How could he know?' Brookes objected. 'How could he know you were here?'

Zach let his gaze slip to the ship berthed off their stern: Géroux's sleek brigantine. 'I'm sure he got a good price for the information.'

Cursing, Brookes slammed his fist against the rail. 'Damn him, damn the man to hell! I knew we should have left, I told you we should—' He levelled a finger at Zach. 'The girl. She knew – she did this! She kept you here with her smiles and her—'

'No.' That he couldn't believe. That he refused to believe. 'No, this is Géroux's work. Amy is innocent.'

'Innocent?' Brookes muttered, fist clenching on the rail. 'Zach, lad, you're—'

'Enough.' He didn't want to think of that, didn't want to imagine she might have been complicit in this. 'Doesn't change the facts, does it? Morton is here and the harbour is blocked.' He took a breath. 'We're trapped.'

Chapter Thirteen

Standing on the quay beneath a savage midday sun, Amelia was grateful for the tricorn that shaded her eyes – grateful too that she wasn't trussed up in stays and skirts. Too hot today for such flummery, and too serious.

The naval longboats were close to shore now, oars moving with intimidating precision, and Amelia forced herself to show no fear. These men, small in their uniforms, had the might of an empire behind them. She must not forget it.

At her side, Luc tugged at his cuffs. Unlike herself, he had dressed in his best coat today and stood sweltering in the heat. He said it was important to impress these people, to appear like men of business. Amy hadn't been sure if he judged her a 'man of business', but she had determined to come to this meeting no matter what, dressed as she chose. The future of Ile Sainte Anne was at stake and she would not sit by idly while others decided her fate.

Further along the quay, just out of earshot, her father stood in close conversation with Overton. Heads together, they talked in voices not pitched to carry but she could see enough to guess at the meat of their conversation; Overton was talking urgently and her father was listening, nodding. Placating. Captain Overton, like his son, did not think this meeting wise.

She would show them both that they were wrong; she would make them see that this was the way of the future. It was certainly a good sign that the officers of Her Majesty's navy had not arrived with a fleet at their backs. Surely, if they meant to destroy Ile Sainte Anne, they could have done so without preamble?

'I will speak first,' Luc said, cutting through her thoughts. 'I will welcome them on behalf of yourself and your father.'

She glanced up at him, his handsome face marred slightly by his creased brow and the sheen of sweat on his skin. 'You're nervous,' she said, feeling her own unease bloom at the sight of his.

Luc shook his head. 'Just hot,' he said, with a smile that didn't fool her. 'All will be well once the deal has been struck.'

'If,' she said, correcting his assumption. 'If a deal is struck. We don't yet know what it is they would trade for.'

Luc smiled, but it was a thin-lipped expression. 'No, of course not, but we will know soon enough. Here they come.'

Turning back to the sea, she watched as the longboats reached the quay and lines were thrown to her men who waited on the dock to tie up the boats. The oarsmen were dressed in the customary slops preferred by most sailors, but in the stern of each boat sat men of a different sort: a dozen marines in their scarlet uniforms and two men of obvious rank, one with brocade and gold trim gleaming beneath the midday sun, the other dressed head to toe in black. Amy imagined their wool coats must be intolerable in the heat.

All but one of the men stepped out of the longboats with the agility of men used to the sea; the other man required assistance. She judged him to be close to her father's age, although different in almost every other way. Whereas her father was lean and sun-weathered, this man was fleshy and florid. His neck seeped over the top of his collar, and his britches were stretched so tight they revealed far too much. Amelia kept her eyes on his face, determined not to smile as he levered himself to his feet and was helped out of the wobbling longboat and onto the quay.

He did not seem best pleased with his method of arrival, brushing off the assistance of the sailors with an irritated tut as he was hauled ashore. Then, after looking about him with the air of a priest in a brothel, he adjusted his uniform and turned to face them.

'Ah,' he said, with a slight nod to Luc, 'Monsieur Géroux. Well met, sir.'

Stepping forward, Luc offered a bow. 'Your Lordship, the honour is mine.' Then, with a quick glance at the black-clad man, he said, 'Mr Scrope.'

Amy looked on in surprise. Scrope was the dour man Luc had talked to in Porto Novo. Uneasy, she glanced at him; how was it that he knew these men? But Luc's attention was fixed entirely on their guests.

Gesturing towards her father, he said, 'Lord Morton, allow me to present Captains Dauphin and Overton, and on their behalf welcome you and your officers to Ile Sainte Anne.'

'Honoured, I'm sure,' Morton said, looking anything but. He reached into his pocket and pulled out a handkerchief to mop his face.

Amy's father stepped forward. He did not bow, merely said, 'You are welcome, in peace, to Ile Sainte Anne, Lord Morton.' Overton said nothing, just watched with his arms folded over his chest. 'I hope,' her father added, 'that we can come to an arrangement that will benefit us all, sir.'

'No doubt we will,' Morton said, dabbing at his brow. He was red as boiled lobster, cooking in his uniform.

'Perhaps we could discuss it inside, and out of the sun?' Amelia suggested, afraid the man might collapse before the deal was done.

Morton stared at her, astonished, and Luc suddenly appeared between them.

'My apologies, Lord Morton, I failed to introduce Captain Dauphin's daughter, Miss Amelia Dauphin.'

It bridled to be introduced as her father's daughter, and not as captain, but before Amy could correct Luc, Morton said, 'Daughter, eh? I took you for a lad.' He lifted an

117

eyebrow and looked her up and down. Amelia doubted very much that he had mistaken her for a boy. 'Well, well, we have come to a savage place indeed,' he said to the man standing next to him. Mr Scrope smiled and murmured words beneath his breath that Amy didn't catch.

Luc cleared his throat, tugging at his sleeve. 'Lord Morton, if you please, we have refreshment awaiting you in Captain Dauphin's home. There we can discuss business.'

'Business, yes.' Morton's attention left Amy, darting quickly out into the harbour. 'I see that we can, Géroux.'

Luc merely smiled his answer and bowed.

The walk to the fortress was long. Morton set a slow pace, his breathing reduced to wheezing gasps long before they reached her father's court. Luc paced anxiously at Amy's side the whole way, darting surreptitious glances through the trees towards his ship where she sat at anchor just past the *Hawk*. Amy tried to catch his eye, to ask him what he was looking for, but he was lost in his own thoughts.

At last her father led them inside the grand hall, the cool shade a welcome relief, and as he talked to Morton of the fortress, Amy joined Luc at the window and followed his gaze out across the harbour. The British ships were resplendent in the sunshine, pristine and new, their sails neatly reefed and brass gleaming. The *Hawk* sat to their larboard side, elegant and well seasoned. A grand old lady of the sea, she was, and—

Amy blinked against the glare and looked again. There were men in the *Hawk*'s rigging, all along the yards. She was preparing to sail. Zach was going to run.

It was then she noticed how the British ships had placed themselves between the *Hawk* and the harbour entrance – if Zach wanted to leave he must pass through the British line.

The skin prickled on the back of her neck. 'Father—'

'Not now,' Luc hissed in her ear.

She looked at him in surprise. 'But do you see what—?'

'Of course I see it. Don't worry. Hazard won't try to sail yet; he won't risk running the blockade in daylight. We have until nightfall to secure the deal.'

She stared at him, a sick feeling fluttering in her chest as she remembered Zach's warning. *For every deal you make there's a price to be paid. Take care it is not so high that you lose everything you value in the bargain.*

'What do they want?' she said. 'Luc, tell me what they want here.'

He touched her arm, casting a cautious glance towards Morton. The chairs that were usually gathered around the fireplace, or hidden in the hall's shadows, were now arranged around a long, scrubbed table that was laden with the best fruits and meats Ile Sainte Anne had to offer. Morton sat at one end, flanked by his lieutenant and the lank-haired man, Scrope, drinking down a clear draft of chilled wine while her father exchanged a cautious glance with Overton. He had retreated to his customary place in the shadows, watching proceedings through cynical eyes that reminded her all too much of Zach's. Suddenly she wished very much that he were here.

'Now we come to it,' Luc said, guiding her towards the table. 'Take your seat, Amelia, and you will hear their terms.'

As they joined the table, Morton was sucking on a piece of mango. He cast the skin aside and reached for another slice. 'So,' he said, dangling the fruit from his fingertips, 'to business, then.'

Her father sat down opposite him. He ate nothing, only watched Morton. 'As you can see,' he said, 'We have many exotic fruits and spices that—'

'So does every other sandbar from here to the cape,' Morton said. He dropped the fruit onto his plate and sucked juice from his fingers. 'Let me be honest with you, Captain Dauphin. We've not come here to trade in fruits or spices.'

From the fireplace Overton made a scornful sound. Morton ignored him. 'You have much here,' he continued. 'Much to protect for so small and insignificant a place.'

'If it's so small and insignificant,' Amy said, 'I wonder that you trouble yourself to come so far.'

Morton looked at her down the length of the table, and then glanced at the other men as if waiting for someone to rebuke her. No one did. His eyebrows rose. 'You're a very forward young lady, Miss Dauphin.' He bit into another slice of mango, the juice running down his chin.

'I say what I think. And it's Captain Dauphin, if you please.'

He laughed. 'Is it indeed? Singular.' He dabbed juice from his face with his handkerchief. 'Very well, *Captain* Dauphin, I shall tell you why I have come so far. I am here to make an offer. This place, this so-called Ile Sainte Anne, poses a threat to us.'

'We pose no threat!' her father objected. 'We simply wish to live free.'

'Well, you do more than that, don't you?' Morton said. 'You shelter pirates.'

'Free men of the sea who refuse to be shackled by the powers of this world. Men who are left to rot in the great cities of your empire, sir. Men brave enough to stand up and take from those bloated with greed in order to feed their children.'

'Criminals.' Morton took another drink from his cup. 'Petty criminals for the most part, I concede, but one ...' He bared a shark's smile. 'There is one who is of interest to the Admiralty.'

Amy went cold. 'Who do you mean?'

'I think you know, Miss Dauphin. The pirate who escaped our nets in the Caribbean, the pirate whose ship is currently moored in your harbour.'

'You mean Zachary Hazard?' her father said. 'You expect us to surrender Zach to you?'

From the fireplace came the steel hiss of a sword being drawn. 'He's my son.' Overton's voice was as sharp as the blade he held.

Her father glared at Luc. 'This is the deal you expect us to make?'

'No.' He was pale with alarm. 'Listen to the trade he proposes.'

Morton lifted a hand to quiet them. 'Gentlemen, there's no need for concern – it's a proposal I have for Captain Hazard, not the noose.'

'What kind of proposal?'

'The days of piracy are over,' Morton said, leaning back in his seat. The wood creaked alarmingly beneath his weight. 'But the days of war are not. Why waste Captain Hazard's notable talent for the stopping and taking of ships when we can use it to our own advantage?' He cast a look at Géroux. 'Against the French.'

Luc didn't answer, face impassive save a twitch of his jaw.

Amy narrowed her eyes. 'You're offering him a privateer's commission?'

'What better man to capture scoundrels and liars than a scoundrel and liar himself?' Morton reached for a large piece of pineapple and began to suck the juice from its flesh. 'It is a simple enough trade, is it not? Bring me Hazard, and we shall leave your island alone.'

It seemed an unlikely bargain, and Amy stole a disbelieving look at Luc. But his mouth was set in a grim line and he said nothing.

'Why come to us?' The question came from the shadows, where Overton still nursed his bared blade. 'Why not go straight to Zach?'

Morton spread his hands. 'We are civilised men, Captain Overton. We've no appetite for unnecessary violence.' He smiled again. 'In my experience, sir, your son is somewhat reluctant to talk to the navy.'

That, Amy could well imagine.

'He won't come,' Overton said. 'He knows your ship; he's probably already sailed.'

'That would be unfortunate,' Morton said. 'For him, for you and for your island.'

With a beat of panic, Amy remembered what she'd seen aboard the *Hawk*. Zach was going to run the blockade, the *Hawk* against three ships of the line. It would be carnage.

'Of course,' Morton continued, 'if Captain Hazard resists I will be forced to send men ashore to dig him out of this little rat's nest.'

'If you do,' Overton growled, 'we'll cut them to ribbons and send your ships to the bottom. Don't think we ain't ready to fight.'

But they weren't ready, not really. Amelia's panic rose into her throat and she half climbed to her feet.

Luc stopped her with a hand on her shoulder. 'He'll come,' he told Morton. 'Hazard will come if Amelia asks him.'

'What?' She turned to him in horror. 'No.'

'Hazard won't fight for this place, Amelia,' Luc hissed. 'You owe him nothing.'

'I won't betray him.'

'It's of no matter,' Morton said, laying his napkin on the table and pushing himself to his feet. 'Captain Hazard is not the only brigand on this island.' His cold gaze came to rest on her father. 'Who knows how many others my men might uncover among the beggars and whores when they come ashore?'

'I do not fear you,' her father said, also rising. 'I am willing to die for what I have built here.'

'Very well, then.' Morton gestured and one of his men stepped forward. 'Take this felon—'

With a whisper of steel Overton's blade came to rest against the soldier's red coat. Everyone stopped moving.

Violence crackled through the air; it danced across Amelia's skin like lightning. Luc's fingers bruised her shoulder and from the corner of her eye she saw the man behind Morton reach for his weapon. The storm was about to break.

'Wait!' She held up her hands; stepped in front of him. 'Wait.'

'Amelia.' Her father growled the warning and behind him Overton gave a grim shake of his head.

Yet what choice did she have? She'd seen enough of the world to understand what would befall the women and children of the island if Morton's men came ashore. And she knew very well what fate awaited her father and Overton, and all who called themselves pirates. Their lives, the future of Ile Sainte Anne itself, lay in the balance.

One man in exchange for over three hundred lives; her duty was clear, though it clamped like irons about her heart.

Turning away from her father and Captain Overton, unable to meet their eyes, she matched Morton's calculating gaze instead. 'Very well,' she said, refusing to allow her voice to shake, refusing to betray her anguish to this man. 'I shall summon Captain Hazard.'

And God have mercy on my soul.

Chapter Fourteen

She would expect him to come from the trees, of course, to land on the south beach and make his way past the fortress, up onto the cliff top above Black Church Rock.

That was why Zach skulled his small boat past the hulking wreck of the merchantman and into the treacherous waters at the foot of the cliff, trusting to the sliver of moonlight and his not inconsiderable skill to guide him ashore. Surf boomed against the great rocky arch, hissing its retreat over stone and gravel. The sounds filled the night, but neither was loud enough to drown the memory of the curses thrown at him by Jedidiah Brookes as he'd left the *Hawk*.

Never a more loyal man than Brookes; he deserved a better captain. Perhaps he'd soon have one.

A flash of surf ahead warned him he was close, and he rose carefully to his feet as the boat was lifted by a wave and thrown forward, towards the rocks. He timed the jump perfectly, must have done because he didn't find himself smashed between the stones and his longboat. Instead, his bare feet landed on shale, water snaking up to his knees as he waded onto a narrow slice of beach, the only place it was possible to land this close to Black Church Rock and only then at low tide. Within an hour, the beach would be gone and his boat with it.

Zach doubted he'd need half that time.

The boat was heavy and he grunted with the effort of hauling it far enough out of the water to keep it from washing away immediately. He pushed his hair back from his face, damp with sea-spray and sweat, rolling his shoulders to loosen them for the climb. To either side of the little inlet the cliffs rose sheer and black until, far above, they gave way to a wedge of stars. He'd done the climb before, although not for many years and not in the dark. He flexed his fingers and quelled a queasy foreboding.

'The things I bloody do for you, Amy Dauphin. The things I bloody do.'

Running his fingertips across the rock, he found his first hold and started to climb. He didn't look down, he didn't look up – trouble, he knew, lay in both directions so he kept his attention on the rock face and the climb. Time enough for trouble later.

By the time he could feel the cliff-top breeze ruffling his hair, his arms and legs were shaking with effort and his shirt clung to his skin. He kept his breathing quiet, however, as he scrambled up onto the stony tip of the headland and lay flat against the rock. He'd chosen a black shirt and britches, so as not to be seen in the dark, and kept his knife sheathed for the same reason. Once he'd caught his breath he rose into a crouch and peered out from behind the scattered boulders towards the swath of grass where Amy was wont to sit and think. Trees cut a dark line across the sky, wind whispering through their leaves, carrying with it the sweet tang of loam and land. It made him uneasy.

As he watched, he heard a sound in the trees – footsteps, light and firm. He knew them well, had listened for them too many a morning on the shore of Runaway Bay. Despite everything, the sound lifted his heart, fool that he was.

He waited for her to step into the open, watched her emerge from the shadow of the forest. Moonlight robbed her of colour, rendering her skin waxen and her eyes black as midnight. He'd always suspected her of witchcraft, but tonight she truly looked the part, a perilous, unearthly beauty that all but stopped his heart. He clenched his jaw to keep from making a sound.

Amy was dressed in her usual clothes, a linen coat thrown over her shirt to ward off the night air, mild as it was. Never known true cold, this girl of the summer; never known winter's bite. He prayed she never would.

Unseen, he stood up. Her back was to him as she gazed east, towards the distant mainland shore, and for a moment Zach considered running. This time, he would leave her to her fate. He would ignore the note she'd sent, blot those few words from his mind and leave her to the future she'd chosen. Only ...

Come to Black Church Rock tonight – you can save me.

Brookes had thrust the paper into a lamp as soon as he'd read it, sending it flaming overboard and into the water. 'Don't go,' he'd growled, grabbing Zach's shoulders and staring into his face. 'It's a trap.'

But how could he ignore such a plea when it was written on his soul in letters more indelible than any ink?

You can save me.

A trap? Maybe. He watched her now, hair raven in the moonlight and arms wrapped about her chest, and he wondered what it would cost him to save her – and what it would cost him to abandon her to her fate. His soul, he decided. Leaving her now, with the wolf at the door, would cost him his soul and that was too high a price to pay.

'Amy.'

She jumped at the sound of his voice. 'Zach.' Relief and agitation mixed in her smile. 'I knew you'd come.'

'Did you?' He stepped over the rocks and onto the grass, let the wind catch at his damp shirt. It was almost cool enough to shiver. 'I didn't.'

Silence fell, the wash of surf at the base of the rocks filling the emptiness between them. Amy smiled again, but it wasn't her sunshine smile, it was tense and afraid. The hair on the back of his neck stood up and he had to fight the instinct to run.

'When I saw the *Hawk* preparing to sail, I was afraid you'd leave without saying goodbye.' She walked towards him, hair whipping across her face, and stopped just out of arms' reach. 'You know who's here,' she said. 'You know whose ship is in harbour.'

Zach grunted. 'A friend of Captain Géroux's, no doubt.'

'I don't know if they're friends,' she said, lips pursed. 'They have certainly met.'

'Géroux always did have friends in high places.' He glanced out towards the *Intrepid*. 'In low places too, come to that.'

From the docks a swell of distant laughter washed over them, drunken singing and good-natured shouts. Another night in paradise. 'So,' Zach took half a step closer. 'You brought me here with a purpose. Out with it.'

He found himself holding his breath, waiting. There was still a chance that she had changed her mind, that she would sail with him.

Amy licked her lips; he tried not to let his gaze linger there, forced himself to look her in the eye as she said, 'You can save us, Zach. All you need do is listen.'

Us. You can save *us*, not *me*. Something closed inside his chest. 'Listen to what?'

'A proposal.'

He laughed, hollow with disappointment. 'From who? Morton? I don't think so. He wants me dead.'

She shook her head. 'He says he wants to offer you a commission as a privateer.'

It was a joke. It was a great big bloody joke. 'That's what he's told you, is it?' His bitter laughter dried up and he took another step backward, away from her. 'Arrant nonsense, that is. Arrant bloody nonsense. A commission! Don't you know who he is, Amy? Don't you know how many men he's sent to the gallows? And not only men.' The idea that Morton, of all people, would offer him anything more than a hempen necklace was nonsense. 'Is that why you brought me here? Is this how I'm to save you, by handing myself over to Morton?'

Even in the darkness he could see the colour rise in her cheeks and knew he'd hit upon the truth. 'Not hand yourself over. Just hear him out, listen to what he proposes.'

'I'll not come within cannon range of that man, Amy. Not even for you.' He flung his arms up and backed further away. 'I'll not let you trade my life to further Luc Géroux's career.'

'This isn't about Luc,' she protested. 'Please, Zach, you can't leave.'

'Watch me.'

'No—' She seized his arm, slender fingers strong around his wrist. 'If you go—' Abruptly she changed tack. 'You'll never get past the blockade, Zach. Not even the *Hawk* can best three ships of the line.'

'Better to die an honest death than swing from the *Intrepid's* yardarm.' He backed up again, but she followed and wouldn't let go.

'Please. Just hear what he has to say. What harm can come of that?'

'What harm? I'll not—'

She stopped his protest with a kiss, her lips urgent and warm. Not as he remembered her, gently yielding, but better, stronger and more ardent. He couldn't hold against her, he couldn't think past the fact that she was in his arms, her slender body in her man's coat pressed against his chest as she curled fingers into his hair and held him right where she wanted him. Held him there until ...

Cold metal touched the back of his neck, the click of a cocked pistol stilling him in her arms. Her warm breath fluttered quick and panicked against his cheek, but when he opened his eyes and looked into her face he saw no surprise there. 'This was the only trade they offered,' she whispered, so close he could feel her lips form the words.

He studied her, ignoring the scarlet uniforms slipping silently from the trees. For now, it was only the two of them and he hoarded the moment against what must come. Her eyes were bright and fearless, her mouth a taut line of defiance. If she felt guilt at her betrayal it didn't show; he admired her for that, if nothing else.

'This is my home,' she said. 'These are my people. I had no choice.'

He wanted to touch those defiant lips, trace their contours with his fingertips, but instead when he raised his hands it was in surrender. 'Yes you did,' he said as someone pulled his arms behind his back, locked iron about his wrists. 'You chose them.'

Chapter Fifteen

Every muscle in her body was tense, her mind churning a dozen different emotions around and around. She'd kissed him. She'd kissed him to keep him from leaving, to uphold her side of the bargain. She'd had no choice.

He'd understand. Once they reached her father's fortress, and Morton had offered him the commission he'd promised, then Zach would understand. Then he'd forgive her.

Though she'd taken the path from Black Church Rock to the fortress a hundred, hundred times, this time the journey seemed interminable. Behind her she heard the harsh clank of the manacles as Zach walked, each sound deepening her distress. She'd not expected him to be manacled. Morton had said nothing of that. She supposed they were afraid Zach might run, which she couldn't deny was likely. So it wasn't unreasonable that they'd tie his arms. He'd be freed soon enough, once Morton granted his privateer's licence.

At last the lights of the hall came into sight, and Luc met her at the entrance with obvious relief.

'All went well?' he asked, glancing back at Zach and then at her. 'No one was harmed?'

She shook her head, wrapping her arms around herself in the cool night air. She was shivering. 'Let's get this done,' she said, moving past him, but Luc caught her arm.

'You made the right choice.'

Angry, she pulled away. 'I *had* no choice.'

Inside, her father was waiting anxiously by the fire, Overton no more than a patch of darkness in the shadows. Only the gleam of his eyes, black as his son's, gave him away. Morton sat in her father's chair, a sight that gave her pause, with Scrope standing by his side. His dour gaze followed her as she crossed the room.

Amelia spoke only to her father. 'He is here.'

'Willingly?'

She couldn't bring herself to answer, and didn't need to for at that moment Zach was led into the room. She tried to catch his eye, but he was glaring at Morton. Never had he seemed so dangerous, even though he was barefoot and manacled. There was murder in his eyes.

Morton smiled, his tongue flicking out to wet his fat lips. 'So, here you are at last. Nowhere left to run, eh, Captain Hazard?'

Zach said nothing.

'Cat got your tongue? Last time we met, as I recall, the cat had you talking aplenty.'

A muscle twitched in Zach's jaw and Amelia remembered the scars on his back. Morton had left his mark. Her stomach churned. 'Why are we talking of the cat?' She stepped between them. 'You've come here to make Captain Hazard an offer, sir. I suggest you do it and be done.'

Morton spared her a glance, as a man might glance at a servant who had spoken out of turn. 'Your daughter has a lively tongue, Captain Dauphin.'

'She speaks the truth.' Her father was angry; she didn't need to see his face to know it. 'Unshackle Captain Hazard, sir, and make your offer.'

'That sounded rather like an order, Captain,' Morton said, heaving himself out of the chair. 'I'm sure you didn't intend to give orders to a commander in the Queen's navy.' He threw her father a cold look. 'Did you?'

Her father was poised to respond, but Luc jumped in ahead of him.

'Captain Dauphin meant no offence. We are all eager to strike this bargain.'

'Not all of us.' The words were Zach's, the first he'd spoken in half an hour.

They made Morton smile, an avid parting of his lips. 'Very

well.' He walked closer and Zach straightened his shoulders, arms still bound behind his back, defiance in every muscle. Slender in his dark shirt and britches, he made a stark contrast to Morton's scarlet-coated overindulgence. 'Zachary James Overton, I have in my possession a privateer's commission which bears your name. Will you accept it, sir, and assist in the final extermination of the piracy that threatens the trade of her Britannic Majesty's subjects?'

Amy found herself holding her breath, waiting for his reply, as Zach slowly nodded his head and said, 'I will not.'

Her chest constricted, a tight pain that stopped her breath. At her side, Luc cursed. 'Don't be a fool, man. Accept the offer.'

Zach turned to him. 'You know what I think of men who trade in other men's lives. I won't do it.'

'Not even to save your own life?'

'Evidently not.'

'Zach,' Amy exclaimed. 'Don't be stupid!'

His mouth curled into that familiar sardonic smile. 'What's the matter? Did you think you were the only one with principles worth dying for?'

'I—' Her voice choked. 'Zach, please.'

But he turned his head away and all she could see was his profile behind a tangle of dark hair.

'Take him to the *Intrepid*,' Morton ordered. 'And have my longboat ready. I mean to sleep in comfort.'

The soldiers pulled Zach away, towards the door, a man on each arm. 'Wait!' Amy cried, grabbing at one of their sleeves, stopping them. 'Wait, give him more time!'

Morton lifted an eyebrow. 'Time, my dear, is a commodity I do not possess. And I suggest you move aside unless you wish to join Captain Hazard in the brig.' He tugged at his coat, straightened his sword belt, and turned to her father. 'It has been a pleasure doing business, Captain Dauphin. Now, if you'll excuse me—?'

'I don't think so.' In a flash of steel, his blade was drawn and levelled. 'Let him go.'

Amy had never been more proud of her father, or more terrified for him.

'James, don't!' Zach struggled against the men pulling him out of the door. 'Don't do this.'

Her father didn't back down and no one else moved. Morton looked along the length of her father's blade, impassive. Then he took a deep breath and in a bored voice said, 'Arrest him. If he resists, arrest the girl too.'

Someone grabbed her, pulling her close. It was Luc, face milky. 'Stop!' he shouted, hopeless as a drowning man. No one was listening.

Soldiers seized her father, his gaze finding hers across the room. 'Amelia ...' He dropped the blade, let them shackle his wrists.

'No!' She flung herself forward, but Luc was still holding her back. She struggled and fought, but he was too strong.

'Don't!' he hissed in her ear. 'He'll hang you too.'

'Father!' she screamed, but he was already being shoved towards the door. She caught a glimpse of Zach, fury on his face as he was dragged outside, and then her father was talking, calm over the storm.

'Amelia,' he said, pinning her with a weighty look. 'Save our people.'

'But Father ...'

'All will be well.' Then he was gone.

Into the terrible emptiness, Morton said, 'Well then, I'll bid you goodnight.'

She wanted to kill him, she wanted to take her blade and pierce his throat. She wanted to watch him die. She wanted—

'Look around,' Luc hissed in her ear, his grip biting into her arms. 'They're waiting for your cue. This is what Morton wants.'

Breathing heavily, she glanced around and saw the men of Ile Sainte Anne, blades bared against the marines' muskets. One word and the tinderbox would ignite – the very thing she had been trying so hard to avoid.

Save our people, her father had said. To fight, here and now, would be to die.

'You don't yet know what the morning will bring,' Luc whispered.

Horror and grief clotted in her throat; she could hardly breathe around it, but somehow she found voice enough to say to Morton, 'We shall speak further in the morning, sir. Goodnight.'

She didn't leave, though, refused to accept the humiliation of walking away. He must do that, and after a tense pause he did so, Scrope trailing him like a shadow.

It was only when the last redcoat had left that Amelia wheeled on Luc. 'You brought them here,' she hissed, stabbing him in the chest with her finger. 'You betrayed us!'

'No!' He held up his hands, backed away a step. 'Amelia, they were coming anyway. I simply brokered the deal.'

'And Zach was the price?'

'You know what he is!' Luc said, looking around him in appeal. A dozen drawn blades glinted in the firelight. 'He has made powerful enemies. And they wanted the island, Amelia. I offered them Hazard in its place.'

'I would *never* have accepted that bargain,' she spat. 'Nor would my father.'

His chin lifted, eyes narrowing. 'Did you not make the very same choice tonight, when you summoned Hazard here?'

Her jaw clamped shut on her own guilt and anger, but she couldn't deny the truth of his accusation.

Luc let out a breath, lowered his arms. 'Morton wants Hazard for— well, let us say he has his own history with the captain of the *Gypsy Hawk*. It was the only thing that kept

Morton from coming here sooner, Amelia, and in force. Without this deal, the island would already be burning.'

'And now?' she said, her voice starting to shake. 'What stops him now?'

'Me,' Luc said. 'The deal is struck, Amelia. Ile Sainte Anne is safe.'

'And you trust Morton to uphold this "deal"?'

Luc spread his hands, rings glinting in the firelight. 'I am not such a fool, but I do have some influence. Once we are married, you will be safe. I swear it.'

'And my father?'

His gaze slipped away from hers. 'I will speak with Morton,' he said, rubbing a hand across his mouth. 'It is a pity your father interfered.'

'He would not be my father if he had not,' she said, and with that the first dry sob escaped, raw and bitter in her throat.

She let herself cry for no more than a minute. Luc tried to comfort her with an arm about her shoulders, but she shook him off. 'No.' Her voice was harsh in the silent room. 'No.' Wiping her face, she stared around at the men watching her, waiting. Did they really expect her to lead them?

She scanned the shadows for Overton, but he was gone. Even now, with his son in the hands of the British, his first thought was of the Articles, of keeping them safe from the enemy. She felt a stab of anger, for Zach and for herself, because with Overton gone there was no one else who could lead, not if Ile Sainte Anne was to remain all that it had been. Putting aside her terror and grief, she said, 'My father has ordered me to save our people, and so I shall. We must protect Ile Sainte Anne and the Articles at all costs. That is more important than the life of any one man.' She swallowed thickly. 'Even if that man is my father.'

Or Zach Hazard.

Chapter Sixteen

Amelia stepped aboard the *Intrepid* at dawn, refusing to wait any longer. The young officer who met her bowed politely, something like sympathy in his eyes as he led her down to the brig, where her father was being held.

Her heart broke to see him there, behind bars, and she might have cried had she not wanted to spare him the sight of her tears. Instead, she turned to the soldier. 'What is your name, sir?'

He looked surprised. 'Lieutenant Walker, miss.'

'Very well, Lieutenant Walker. I would speak with my father alone.'

He shook his head. 'I can't do that, miss. Under orders.' She said nothing to that, just held his gaze until he started to crumble. 'I, uh ... I'll just wait over here, at the foot of the steps.'

So he did, his back turned. It was a kindness, she supposed, as much as a man in his position was able to offer. At least it allowed her some privacy, enough to talk quietly with her father.

He stood at the bars, his hands seeking hers past the iron. 'Are you well, my child? Did they hurt you?'

'I am well.' She squeezed his hands, reminding herself that they'd held cold steel not twelve hours ago. He did not seem so old now, but strong and weathered. She had never loved him more. 'Our people are nervous, Father. If Morton does not release you ...'

His lips pursed. 'He will not release me, Amelia. You must harden yourself to that.'

'I can't. I won't accept that, Father. I won't let him—'

'How will you stop him? Will you take the *Sunlight* to engage a ship of the line?' He glanced at Lieutenant Walker's

136

turned back, lowering his voice. 'You know I would gladly die for Ile Sainte Anne – but you, my child, you must live. You must do everything you can to protect the Articles and to pass them on when it is time. They cannot die here – we cannot let that happen.'

The weight of what he asked was huge and it bowed her shoulders. 'Father, I can't. I don't know how to start.'

'Amelia.' He tilted her face upward and smiled. 'You are already a captain, are you not? I simply charge you with a larger ship. Steer her into safe waters, my child. Overton will help you.'

'Overton is gone. I've not seen him since you and Zach were taken.'

'That is ill news. I hope he does not plan something reckless.' Her father frowned. 'Keep a weather eye open, my dear. Overton is not likely to have strayed far.'

Above them she heard a distant sound, the rattle of a drum. 'Perhaps he is with Zach? I thought he would be here, that I might be able to— What? Father, what is it?'

Dismay carved stark lines into his face, around his eyes and open mouth.

'Father?' She clutched his hands. 'Father, please, what is it?'

'Stay here, child,' he said, anguished. 'Stay with me below.'

Above, the drum rattled again. Something sick curled in the pit of her stomach and she looked over at Walker. He was staring up the steps, a tight expression on his face.

Again the drum rattled and stopped dead.

'Father,' she said. 'What's happening?'

He was silent, and when she looked back at him she saw tears on his kind, weathered face. 'Oh, Amelia, my child … They took him up just before dawn. I thought— I hoped Morton would—'

The world spun and she had to hold on to the bars to

stay upright. Then she was breaking free of her father's desperate grip, pushing past Walker and racing up the steps.

'Amelia, don't!'

Nothing could stop her. On deck, daylight momentarily blinded her and she skidded, disoriented. Then she saw Morton, brash in his red coat, and Luc standing before him talking urgently, gesturing. His words came to her in snatches.

'... not part of the deal ... swore you'd leave Dauphin and his daughter alone, if I brought you—' Then he saw Amy and stared in shock. 'Dear God, why are you here?'

Behind her, louder now, the drum rattled once more and she saw a marine in dress uniform wielding drumsticks like weapons. Behind him, flanked by two other soldiers, stood a man in a dark shirt and britches, arms tied behind him and—

'Oh, please, no.'

—and a noose about his neck, the rope slung up over one of the foreyard arms.

Shock turned her knees liquid. If Luc hadn't appeared at her side, she might have fallen. 'Zach ...'

At the sound of her voice he turned, and for a blistering moment their gaze met. Fear, anger and hurt – they were all there, seething in his eyes. Then, deliberately, he turned away; he couldn't bear to look at the woman who had lured him to his death.

The drum rattled for the last time and stopped. Far above, a breeze set the lines clattering against the masts and into that bright blue morning Morton shouted, 'Run him up.'

The rope began to tighten.

Amy surged forward, but a marine was in her path, blocking her. 'No!' she screamed as Zach's toes were lifted from the deck, legs kicking. 'Mercy! I beg you have mercy! Please!'

The marine cursed thoroughly, shoving her backward so hard only Luc's arms kept her on her feet.

. 'Don't look.' He pulled her into his arms, turning her away from the grizzly sight. 'For the love of God, Amy, don't look.'

She didn't, she couldn't, she just sobbed and sobbed as behind her they hanged Zach Hazard.

Part Two

1720

Now hung with pearls the dropping trees appear,
Their faded honours scatter' on her bier.
See, where on earth the flow'ry glories lie,
With her they flourish'd, and with her they die.

'WINTER', ALEXANDER POPE

Chapter Seventeen

Four years after Zach Hazard was hauled to the yardarm, death came to Ile Sainte Anne.

Smoke lingered over the ruined harbour for months after the guns fell silent, drifting down from the smouldering fortress that had once been her power and glory. They said the island burned for a week and a day, lighting up the sky like a portal to hell, and she did not lie quiet yet. For she seethed with the anger of the dead, the unquiet spirits of men who would be free.

'*A Deo a Libertate*.' Jedediah Brookes curled his lip as the *Gypsy Hawk* ghosted through smoke, flotsam bumping mournfully against her hull. Here and there the shattered ribs of a ship breached the water, the sea lapping softly around the bodies of her dead. 'God and Liberty – feeble enough reasons to die.'

'Hell's teeth, Mr Brookes.' Shiner's voice was rough-edged in his throat. 'There's nothing left.'

Brookes kept his fingers tight on the wheel and didn't spare him a look. 'Why would there be? If you want to be rid of a rats' nest you dig the buggers out and poison the hole.'

Shiner touched his arm. 'Look, there.' He was pointing towards a cockeyed mast sticking out of the water. A bedraggled flag hung limp in the warm air, but its colours were clear enough. 'It was the British, then.'

'Not only them.' Close by, rolling a little in the wake of the *Hawk*, was a fragment of hull. Visible clearly, and brave in gilt paint, was the ship's name: *La Furieuse*. 'French ship o' the line, that one.'

'British and French working together?' Shiner frowned and scratched his head. 'They did it then, in the end.'

Brookes smiled, though the expression felt grim as the devil's. 'This place was always more dangerous than any one king's navy.' He tapped his head. 'Dangerous up here.'

'It was enough to drive a man to Bedlam, to be sure,' Shiner said. 'Even so—'

'They bowed to no flag, belonged to no nation.' In his mind's eye he could see the white flag flying from the fortress, a proclamation of liberty for all men who had the stomach to claim it – a promise, an impossible promise. 'Too many men start believing they can live as they please and those who spend their days getting rich off the back of other men's labour begin to get nervous.'

Shiner cast him a doubtful look. 'Don't *we* get rich off the backs of other men's labour?'

Brookes sniffed. 'We simply redistribute it to those in more need of coin.' He fell silent then, his gaze caught by the blackened ruin that had once been Dauphin's fortress. 'This was *her* doing.' He spat on the deck and cursed the woman's name. 'She should have run when they took her father. Run straight away and kept on running. A fool's game, to defy them.'

'Got her comeuppance, though, didn't she? In the end.' Shiner peered down over the rail, as if he might see the girl's corpse floating in the water. He scratched at the thin stubble on his jaw. 'It weren't just her. If Géroux—'

'Shhh.' Brookes waved him quiet, glancing towards the only other ship at anchor in the harbour: a lean and predatory privateer. 'Bad luck to say his name, son.'

'Bad luck?'

'Aye, it is if the captain hears you.'

Looking away from the *Serpent*, Brookes ran his eyes over the solid strength of the *Hawk*, unharmed and safe by virtue of her absence when the crisis came. They'd heard talk, of course, in the dockside taverns that ran the length of the Spanish Main and down into the South Seas. They'd even heard it up north, in the Atlantic colonies, and as far east as the Mediterranean: Amelia Dauphin was raising a fleet in defence of Ile Sainte Anne and the freedom it claimed as every man's birthright. Four years after her father had hanged at Execution Dock, she was raising the white flag of liberty against the fist of empire.

They'd heard the talk, heard defiance yelled by many a voice. *For God and Liberty! We are free men!* But the *Hawk* had not joined Amelia Dauphin's fleet. They'd stayed as far as possible from Ile Sainte Anne and for that Brookes had been grateful. It was a pity, then, that they were here now, picking over the bones of the dead.

'We'll get no closer than this, Mr Brookes.' Shiner gestured down into the cluttered water. 'Seems as what was once in the city is now beneath the waves, and the harbour's fair choked with wreckage.'

'Very well, then.' Brookes gave the order to weigh anchor and handed off the wheel to Shiner. With a sigh he straightened his shoulders, determined to do what must be done, but he couldn't keep from glancing towards the harbour mouth and wondering how fast they could come about and escape this place of catastrophe.

'Best do as he says,' Shiner warned, no doubt guessing the path of Brookes' thoughts and fearing the consequences.

'Aye, true enough.' He clapped Shiner on the arm in reassurance. 'Ready a longboat, then.'

As the lad scampered off, Brookes fixed his eyes on the door of the Great Cabin and forced his reluctant feet to move. Better to get it done and be gone. He rapped twice on the door and waited. After a short pause it opened and there he stood, dressed in coat and boots, a flash of silver in his ear and a blade at his side: Captain Zachary Hazard.

In appearance he was much like he used to be, but how a man looks and how a man is are two different things. Brookes knew well enough that no warmth had touched the captain's eyes in the long four years since he'd stared death in the face and seen Amelia Dauphin looking back.

He made himself meet that bleak gaze. 'We're as close as we can get. You'll have to take a longboat from here.'

Zach answered with a curt nod, glancing past him towards the ruined township. What he felt was impossible to guess, for his face revealed nothing. He didn't even flinch when an offshore breeze swept the stench of festering decay across the *Hawk*. As it ruffled the collar of Zach's shirt, Brookes' eyes were drawn to the fading scar that ringed his neck. The sight provoked a bitter sorrow. 'Let me come with you, Zach. It's a grim business alone.'

Zach smiled, harsh as winter. 'It's a grim business in company, too. Stay here, bring the ship about and be ready to make sail when I return. I've no desire to linger.'

'No more than I, not in this place.'

Brookes' memories of that dreadful morning cut as deep as the scar about Zach's neck. The image of his lifeless body, hauled dripping from the water, was no less horrific than the memory of him dangling from the yardarm. Only moments and a miracle had saved him from death and Brookes could not forget it. Nor could he forgive those who were to blame.

Zach clasped his shoulder. 'Wait for me.'

'Aye. That we will.'

As he made his way to the longboat, a silent, grave crew surrounded the captain. Several hands reached out to pat his back or arm and a number even doffed their hats, a gesture of respect he rarely garnered in better times.

But these were far from better times. Ile Sainte Anne had fallen, the last pirate stronghold had been destroyed and its inhabitants had scattered to the seven seas. All that remained was the *Gypsy Hawk* and her crew. These were the worst of times indeed, worse than anything they'd ever known.

* * *

The oars were heavy as Zach rowed through the ships' graveyard towards the blackened remains of the Ile Sainte Anne.

Under the hand of Amelia Dauphin, it had been a place of light and laughter, so men said, but Zach had never seen anything of it. He'd not returned since the day she'd traded him to Morton for – as it turned out – a measly four years of peace. He wondered if she'd thought his life a reasonable price for such a paltry respite, or if she'd thought of him at all, here at the end of everything. He imagined not. He'd certainly made a point of not thinking about her over these long four years, and nothing but the current disaster could have persuaded him to return.

Amelia was dead, her fortress had become her funeral pyre, and Zach could think of nowhere else to be but here, where she had lived and died.

Close to what had once been the island's riotous docks, the wreckage was so dense – with ships scuppered in their berths and taverns pitched wholesale into the water – that even the longboat could not pass. Zach tied up against the rail of a drowned schooner and scrambled over splintered wood until he reached what remained of the quay. There were dead here, trapped amid the detritus of battle, and the stench was intolerable. He spat to try and rid his mouth of the taste.

His eyes stung, too, from the acrid smoke: a miasma of death that lingered over the pirate colony, bitter as sin. Bitter as his heart. He'd been drunk in Port-au-Prince when his brothers died; what right did he have to stand on their graves?

'Zachary Hazard.'

The voice was close behind him, disdain in the arrogant French drawl. Zach stopped, bracing himself, before he turned to face its owner. 'Géroux. Seems like there's no need for you and I to talk – not now, nor ever again.'

Géroux regarded him from a pale, impassive face. Like still water over sharp rocks, he was treacherous beneath the surface. Always treacherous. 'There is every need.'

Silence descended, thick as the smoke that drifted between them. Eventually Zach spoke. 'You were here then, were you? When it happened?'

'In my position? You know it is impossible.' Géroux looked up at the cliff top, the ruin of the fortress just visible. 'I told her they would come if she raised the flag against them, but she would not listen.'

'No,' Zach said, his fickle heart twisting at the memory of her beautiful, defiant eyes. 'She never did.'

'So I gave what warning I could and came to offer passage to the survivors – Adamaris Sesay is aboard, many of the children. Some men.'

'Very noble, I'm sure.'

Géroux tilted his chin, looking at him down the length of his nose. 'And where were *you*, Captain? Where were you in Amelia's hour of need?'

Zach flinched at the sound of her name; it still had the power to hurt. 'As far away as possible. I learned my lesson four years ago, and had no desire to be traded to the British again.' He offered Luc a sly smile. 'Or, worse, traded to the French.'

Géroux's brow creased and he took a step closer. His footsteps rang loud on the floating quay, the only sound in the ruined docks. 'Ask me, Zachary. There is not much time.'

'Ask you what?' He couldn't look at Géroux as he spoke; he knew what the man meant.

'Ask me about Amelia. You have come here to learn her fate, have you not?'

Zach forced a false smile past the old anger and grief. 'What's her fate got to do with me? She was *your* wife. I'm only here for my father.'

'Ah. Captain Overton, of course.'

Zach jerked his head towards the *Serpent*, sitting at

anchor closer to the dock than the *Hawk.* 'Don't suppose you have him aboard, do you? Can't imagine the old bugger let the navy-boys take him home.'

'Your father fell,' Géroux said, without pity. 'He's buried on the north slope. His men saw to it before they left, three weeks ago now.'

Even though he'd known it – heard the tale told and felt the truth in his heart – grief tripped him up. His chest grew tight, making it difficult to speak. He'd hated his father, cursed him for his sins, and yet loved him despite them all. Somehow that made it worse. 'They said—' He cleared his throat. 'I heard he kept the Articles with him to the end. Is it true?'

'Yes. And they're here now, your birthright I suppose, if you want—'

'I *don't* want.' Zach laughed, a mirthless rasp that teetered on the brink of a howl. 'To Old Hob with his bloody Articles! Look what they brought him. Look what they brought *her*!' He waved his hands at the devastation. 'Nothing but death. Never anything but bloody death.'

Turning his back, Zach stalked a few steps away and stopped. 'They died for nothing.' He drove the point home with a vicious kick at the wood rotting beneath his feet. 'They died for no more than an idea, the foolish dreams of an old man and a girl. I want no part of it.'

Silence returned, broken only by the lap of water against the quay and the far-off cry of a gull. Zach closed his eyes and tried not to think of his father's face – tried not to think of *her* face, fierce and beautiful. Gone now, both of them. Forever gone.

'There will be time later to grieve for your father,' Géroux said quietly. 'Today I need your help.'

'My help?' Zach looked at him over his shoulder. 'Why do you think I would ever help *you*?'

Géroux fixed him with a flat stare. 'Because Amelia is not dead.'

'Not dead?' His lifeless heart jolted painfully. 'What do you mean—?'

'She's been taken.'

'To England?'

'Yes. For trial.'

'For the hangman's noose, you mean. Like her father.' He backed up a step, struggling to think around the surge of painful hope. 'You let them take her to England?'

Tight-lipped, Géroux looked away. 'How could I prevent it? Was I to attack a ship of the line and kidnap her?'

'Yes! Why not?'

'Because I am no pirate!'

'Oh, yes, I forgot. You're so much *better* than us.'

'*Ta Gueule!*' Géroux's stormy eyes darkened as he levelled an accusing finger at Zach. 'I cannot betray those who sign the Letters of Marque when my life – when much more than my life – depends upon their patronage.' He lowered his hand, collecting himself, and more quietly said, 'Yet, it is true, Amelia lives.'

Zach wiped a hand over his face, jittery with a sudden terror he couldn't bear to face. 'Then go to her now; you can free her and—'

'How? How can I free her? A French privateer, free her from an English naval ship? From an English gaol? Impossible.'

'She's your *wife*! You can't let them—'

'*You* can save her.'

Zach shook his head, holding up his hands in instinctive denial. 'Answered that call once and look where it got me – dangling from the yardarm and a heartbeat from death.'

'This is punishment, then?' It seemed a genuine question, his head tipped sideways and cold curiosity in his eyes. 'You would see her die because she betrayed you?'

Zach didn't answer, uncomfortable with the truth in Luc's accusation. 'I couldn't help her anyhow. They'd hang me before I reached Spitalfields.'

'Then who?' Géroux pressed. 'Who will save her?'

You. If you loved her, you would go. Nothing would stop you.

The thought chimed clear as a bell, but he didn't voice the accusation, afraid it might reflect too harshly upon himself. Instead he said, 'What makes you think she needs saving at all? Amy has always—'

Lightning fast, Géroux reached out and snatched Zach's shirt in his fist, pulling it away from his throat. 'They hanged you, Zachary Hazard. Your neck still bears the scar. And for what? For the theft of sugar and gold. How much more do you think they will do to her, she who raised a standard against their king?'

'Warned her against that, didn't I? Told you both how it would end, and so it has.' He wrenched his shirt free of Géroux's grasp. 'Why should I risk my life for the woman who traded it for her own?'

'Because otherwise she will die. And you love her.'

He scowled his denial, as if by convincing the world of it he could convince himself. 'Maybe I did, four years past. But only a saint or a fool would love her still, and I'm neither of those.'

'Then you'll let her hang? This is your choice?'

It was, though his heart hammered in protest. He ignored it, determined not to think of it, or of her bound in irons, or of the gaol, or of the stench and circus of a Tyburn hanging. 'The choice was hers.' He swept his arm wide, encompassing the ruined haven and its smoking shroud. 'She chose this.'

She chose you.

Géroux didn't answer, his expression becalmed and flat. Even so, it looked like a promise of vengeance. Zach turned away from him, finding comfort in the familiar lines of the *Hawk*, solid and strong against the sun bleeding red into the horizon.

Chapter Eighteen

Amelia Dauphin's misery was absolute.

Hours ran into days ran into nights ran into weeks. The chafe of the irons about her wrists, the throb of her ankle, injured when she fell in battle, and the heavy weight of guilt and loss pressed like the darkness of the brig, thick and unremitting.

But she would not cry.

She'd shed no tears since the day her father had been taken from the golden shores of Ile Sainte Anne to hang beneath the cold, grey skies of England. It was a place she barely remembered, a place where she too would meet her end.

Of that, at least, she held no fear. Her father was long dead, Overton had fallen, and Ile Sainte Anne was destroyed. What fear could death hold now? When she closed her eyes she could still see the flames, the smoke-stench of it clinging to her shirt and hair even now, weeks later. She had traded her very soul for the safety of her people, but she should have known better than to make deals with the devil; he never upheld his end of the bargain.

So she had failed and her father's dream had failed with her. Ile Sainte Anne was aflame and there was no freedom left in the world, only avarice and the slavery it carried in its wake.

If only she had died, as Overton had died, free beneath the sky with a sword in her hand. Not like this, shackled and humiliated. It was her only regret.

No, not her only regret.

Alone in the stinking hold of the *Intrepid*, she could be honest with herself. Though she did not fear death, it pained her to die with her sins unforgiven – one sin especially.

There was no chance of forgiveness now, for not even God could absolve her of her greatest crime. There was only one man who had that power, and she knew full well that he would never forgive her.

In the dark Amelia let out a breath, a sigh against the sighing of the ship, and gazed at the daylight slicing into the brig. They were far from Ile Sainte Anne now, far from its golden heat and vanilla-scented breezes. They'd rounded Africa's west coast some weeks past – a rough passage, but not the worst she'd known in those troublesome seas – and the light that crept through the hull was pale and northern, the air biting cold. Above, she could hear the creak of masts, the taut slap of luffing sails in a headwind, and beneath her the ship pitched as she ploughed through a heavy sea.

North Atlantic. She knew it, though she couldn't see the horizon. Perhaps they planned to make port in Lisbon, before the crossing to England?

The heavy wrench of iron hinges drew her eyes to the hatch above. It was early for food, or what passed for food here – a ship's biscuit dropped through the bars each day, a sour slop of water little cleaner than bilge. However, it wasn't the usual leering seaman who stumped down the ladder – it was a lobster-back, looking green about the gills in his scarlet coat.

Amelia rose, taking care to put no weight on her injured ankle. She grasped the bars of her cell with bound hands and the shackles struck the bars, iron on iron, ringing loud. 'If you're going to vomit,' she said, 'best do it over the side and with the wind.'

The marine gave her a sour-eyed stare, lacking the lascivious gleam of the deck hands. 'Lord Morton wants to see you.'

Deliberately she made no response, though her heart kicked hard against her ribs. She'd known he was aboard and been glad to escape his attention. Until now. 'Tell his lordship I'm not at home to visitors.' Backing away, she eased herself down onto the scabby heap of straw that was her bed.

'It wasn't a request, miss.' The soldier had a kind face and she was struck by sudden recognition – there was something familiar about the man. The ship pitched sideways and he turned milky. 'On your feet. Now!'

Of course she had no choice; she just needed to buy a moment to compose herself. Morton was a vile, scheming creature. She should kill him for what he'd done to her father and Ile Sainte Anne. To Zach. But if he'd asked to see her it meant she had something he wanted, and that meant she could trade.

The soldier pulled a ring of keys from his belt and fiddled with the door, unsteady on his feet. The door swung open as the ship rolled again and, with a lurch, the lobster lost his lunch. Had she been armed, unshackled and not lame in one leg it would have been the perfect opportunity to escape – had she not, also, been on a navy ship somewhere in the North Atlantic. As it was, she let the moment pass and leaned against the open door, waiting as he wiped a hand over his mouth.

'I'd stick to soldiering, if I were you. Leave the seas to the sailors.'

'Believe me, miss, I'm hardly here by choice.'

'Then we have something in common.'

He gave a grim laugh and made his way back to the hatch. She followed as best she could; the pain in her ankle was severe. The stairs looked an impossible climb, until her seasick escort took her arm and let her lean her weight against him as they went.

'Thank you,' she said, breathless from the pain and the hunger in her belly.

He nodded, but in his eyes she saw pity; Amelia tried not to let him see her sudden fear.

When they reached the deck, the wind almost knocked her sideways. A fierce nor'easter was raging, the ship making little headway against it. She wondered that they didn't turn and run with it, rather than risk losing a mast to the storm. Morton had always been a stubborn bastard, though, and she imagined he'd never stand aside, not even in the face of the sea itself.

'This way!' The soldier's hair was whipping about his face and in the sudden daylight he looked younger. No more than four-and-twenty, perhaps – her equal in age, if not experience. Suddenly she recognised him. He'd been aboard this very ship the day her father was taken, the day they tried to hang Zach Hazard. She looked away, grief and guilt still sharp.

Struggling to balance on the slippery deck, Amelia shuffled after him towards the great cabin at the stern of the ship. The door was opened a sliver and she felt the soldier's hand on her back, pushing her inside. When she looked up she could see wind-stirred papers settling as the door slammed behind her, an ornate desk and gilt chair dominating the cabin. They looked like they belonged in Versailles, not aboard a ship of war. She took a limping step forward, but the cabin appeared empty.

'Miss Dauphin.'

She froze at the sound of the voice, behind her and to the right.

'Or should I call you captain?' With heavy, deliberate footsteps the man walked into view. 'How long has it been since last we met? Four years, I dare say.' Lord Morton smiled, fat-nosed and florid, as he carried a decanter of port to his desk. 'My, how you've grown.'

Amelia ground her teeth until she thought she could taste bone.

'What?' Sitting, he poured ruby wine into his glass. 'No fond greeting for an old friend?' His eyes, little gimlet slits, studied her. 'Must say, the years have been kinder to you than they have to me. Positively ravishing, you are, despite the filth.'

Willing herself not to swing for him with her manacled hands, Amelia forced words past her teeth. 'What do you want?'

He sat back in his chair, raising his glass and examining the contents with a thoughtful air. 'Many things, my dear. Power, wealth. Influence.' He smiled. 'You, swinging from a rope.'

Silent, she met his smile with a glare.

'Ah, I know what you're thinking. There must be something more, else why bother dragging you up from the brig, eh?' He took a sip of port, smacked his odious lips. 'You're right, there is. One more thing.'

The pain in her ankle was intense, even with most of her weight shifted onto her right foot. She longed to sit, but refused to show weakness before Morton. 'You promised us peace, but reneged on our bargain. Why would I trade with you again?'

'To preserve your life.'

'Take my life. I'm sick of it.'

'Ah.' Again, that infernal smile. 'To save another's then.'

'There is no other I would—'

'Hazard.'

'But he—' Her words collided and stopped, betraying her in an instant. After a pause she said, 'He wasn't at Ile Sainte Anne.'

'No. But we will find him – the last pirate upon the high seas. How long do you think he can evade us, Miss Dauphin?'

'He has evaded you these past four years!' Relief made her giddy and she laughed. 'You must think me a simpleton. You propose a trade for something you do not have.'

'Something I do not have – yet.' He set down his glass and

rose, coming around the table towards her. 'In exchange for something you do not have – any more.'

Her laughter evaporated, fear twisting a tight knot in her gut. 'Speak plain.'

'A certain book,' he said, drawing closer. She could smell the wine upon his breath. 'A certain set of Articles filled with such treacherous calumny that His Majesty wishes to see them destroyed. Forever.'

'The Articles are set beyond your reach, My Lord. They are meant for the eyes of free men, and you are a slave to your king.'

'You would die, I suppose, before betraying their location?'

'People have died for lesser causes.'

'And you would let Hazard die too, for this silly little cause? When you have the power to save him, to guarantee his freedom, you would let him die?'

She paused before she answered, not because she wavered but because she sought the right words. 'Four years ago,' she said, 'I traded his life for our freedom. It was a poor exchange and I learned a harsh lesson. I learned that men like you are not to be trusted. What makes you think I would make the same mistake twice?'

Chapter Nineteen

Zach could feel Brookes watching him as he picked his way across the flotsam towards the longboat and started to row back to the *Hawk*, a slow pull of the oars and a long, silent drift among the dead.

He wanted to be gone from this place, to sail south and feel the wind tearing through his hair and the power of the *Hawk* beneath his feet. He wanted to be free again, as he'd been in the days before Amelia Dauphin had snared him and thrown him to the sharks.

But he was beginning to realise he would never be rid of her, that nothing short of his own death would be sufficient to untangle his life from hers. Perhaps even that would be insufficient and she would continue to plague him in the life beyond.

This close to the equator, night fell like a curtain and by the time Zach climbed up from the longboat the dying sun was turning the smoke a dull umber.

'What news, then?' Brookes said as Zach gained the deck.

'None that we didn't know.' He avoided the man's clever blue eyes for fear of revealing too much. 'My father fell here, buried on the island.'

Brookes touched his shoulder. 'Ah, Zach. He was a fine man.'

'He was a selfish, conniving bastard.'

'Aye,' Brookes nodded. 'And a fine man to boot.'

Zach answered only with a grunt, turning towards his cabin, eager to be gone before Brookes asked the other question hovering about his lips. He had taken no more than three steps when Brookes called after him.

'What of *her*?'

Zach stopped, steeling himself. 'Dead, as we heard.' He swallowed. 'Or soon will be.'

From above came the shouts of men making fast the sails; others lit the lamps, while from the foc'sle he could already hear the reedy piping of music. Even in this miserable place, life went on all around him. He wasn't part of it, though. He hadn't been part of anything since the day he'd woken up aboard the *Hawk* with a hole in his memory, seawater in his lungs and the abiding image of Luc Géroux pulling Amelia into his arms as the rope had tightened about Zach's neck. He didn't know what had happened after that and didn't much care. Brookes said the rope had broken – a stroke of uncommon luck – and Shiner had dived in after him, keeping him afloat until Brookes threw a line.

Perhaps he should be grateful, but in truth there were times when he wished they'd let him drown. This was one of those times.

Angrily, he pushed the memories aside as he stalked to his cabin and shoved open the door. Brookes caught it, bracing it open before Zach could close it in his face. 'What do you mean, "soon will be"?'

Inside, the lamps were unlit and Zach withdrew into the gloom. 'She's to hang,' he said, 'if she's lucky. If it's treason they charge her with ...'

'Quartered.' Brookes' face twisted in disgust. 'That's not a fate I'd wish on anyone, not even her.' He jerked his head towards the *Serpent*, still anchored in the gathering night. 'He couldn't save her then, despite all his promises to her father.'

'He didn't dare.' He spat the words with more venom than he'd intended and Brookes' eyes widened in sudden panic. He, more than any of the crew, understood the power Amelia once held over him. Still held over him.

After a pause Zach turned away from the door and let Brookes follow him inside. Some matters were best discussed in private.

Above, he heard a call for the port lamps to be lit. Inside, Zach struck flint and the lamp on his chart table flared into life. He slumped into his chair, but didn't reach for the rum as usual. Instead his fingers steepled, tapping against his lips. There was no hiding the truth – Brookes would drag it from him one way or another – so Zach took a breath and said, 'They took her three weeks ago. Bound for London and the gallows.'

Pulling out a chair, Brookes sat down uninvited. 'Not our concern.'

'No.' What did he care for her suffering? She had watched him hang from the shelter of another man's arms.

'So, I was thinking we should head west,' Brookes said, as if the matter was closed. 'We could pick up some—'

'They'll take her to Newgate, most likely.' In his mind's eye he could see it, the thick oaken door that slammed behind you like the very gate of hell. The darkness, the rank despair. Names scratched into cell walls, pathetic remnants of the condemned. 'Cursed place, Newgate. Cursed, stinking place.'

'Aye, well, gaol's gaol right enough.' Brookes sounded nervous. 'West, Zach. Merchant ships, running full—'

He dismissed it with a wave of his hand. 'Too heavily armed. And they'll have a navy escort now.'

'Aye, that's true enough. With Sainte Anne gone, the navy won't—'

'He asked me to save her,' Zach said. 'Can you believe it? He wanted me to fetch her out of gaol and bring her to him.'

Brookes stared. 'Géroux?'

'As if I could just walk into Newgate and take her out with me!' He found himself on his feet, pacing. 'As if I would, even if I could, after what she did.'

'Feculent sod. If he wants her, he can fetch her from the bloody gallows himself!'

'He won't do it.'

'Too scared?'

'Too bloody French.'

'So he wants to send you?' Brookes' outrage was as sharp as Zach's own. 'Let her hang, I say. Not like the wench didn't earn it.'

'Maybe.' He looked away, thinking of the quartering.

Following the path of his thoughts, Brookes said, 'Probably treat her kinder, though, for being a woman.'

'Kinder? Have you ever been to Newgate?' He could remember it still, every detail, the stink and the terror. Death, all around. He reached for the rum and swallowed a mouthful, letting it burn away the bitter taste of his memories.

'When it was you in the brig, awaiting the noose, she didn't save you.' Brookes' voice was cold, flat with anger. 'She put you there and then she watched you hang.'

Zach paced to the wide windows across the stern and took the rum with him. The horizon was ablaze, an echo of the night Ile Sainte Anne burned. 'She traded one life in exchange for three hundred. That's a bargain only a fool would refuse.'

'You wouldn't have traded her life so easy.'

'No, but I always was a fool, Mr Brookes. I always was a bloody fool for her.'

In the twilight gloom of his cabin, Zach caught the scent of vanilla on the breeze. He licked his lips and they tasted of salt and rum. Behind him, Brookes stirred, his boots shuffling uneasily on the deck. 'Do you have a mind to sail for England then, Captain?'

'I'd rather pluck out my own eyes and pickle them.' He turned to Brookes with a sigh. 'Ready the men. We sail for Portsmouth at dawn. And we sail fast.'

Chapter Twenty

'Oi, Miss Dauphin, wake up.'

She wasn't sleeping; she couldn't remember the last time she'd slept. Lifting her head from her knees she saw the wan face of Lieutenant Walker peering at her through the bars. The seasick marine was the closest thing to a friend she had left in the world and she knew he'd come to warn her.

'So soon?' she said, rubbing her eyes. Outside, a thin light filtered into the brig from the open hatch, bringing with it a sharp cold and the tell-tale cry of gulls.

'Docked an hour ago,' Walker said, confirming her fear. 'There's men here for you.'

She tried to smile, but couldn't muster one through her exhaustion and hunger. 'At least I'll get out of this stinking brig,' she said, though she knew gaol would be no improvement. 'I've not visited London since I was a child, and even that I don't remember.'

'You've not missed much.' Walker unlocked the door and held it open for her. 'Filthy and full of disease. Even I'd rather be at sea.'

'There's no better place.' Pushing herself to her feet, Amelia braced herself against the hull as she hobbled towards the door, coming to a halt before the lieutenant. She studied his pinched and hungry face and thought that, but for the toss of a coin, he could have been one of her own men. 'Have you no desire to be a free man, Lieutenant Walker? To sail where you will, not where your master sends you?'

'I've a desire to see my Mary again, and not to swing from the end of a rope.' He stood aside so that she could pass. 'I'm an honest man, miss. And loyal to His Majesty.'

'It's a shame, then,' she said, making her slow way to the steps, 'that His Majesty is not more loyal to you.'

Walker followed, helping her to climb the stairs. 'Them's treasonous words.'

'*For the poorest man that is upon the Earth has a life to live, as the greatest man.*' She turned halfway up and looked him boldly in the eye. 'Have you not heard as much said?'

Walker cast an uneasy glance towards the hatch. 'No, and I don't want to hear it neither.'

'We are all born free, Lieutenant, and rich men have no right to make us otherwise. For that notion, my father died.'

'And so will you, if Lord Morton has his way.'

'Little good will it do him.' An icy wind swirled down the steps, making her shiver. 'Let him kill until the seas run red, but he cannot kill an idea. *The poorest man that is upon the Earth has a life to live, as the greatest man.* It is a simple truth and I will happily die for it. Many better than me have already done so.'

A shadow fell across her as she spoke, and looking up she saw a figure silhouetted black against a white sky. 'Your death is certain,' said a cold voice. 'All that remains is to determine its method.'

Morton. Amelia didn't answer, concentrating on getting up the steps without crying out. Once on deck, she had to squint against the light even though the sky was a uniform white with no sign of the sun. She'd been too long in the dark and her eyes watered in the sudden brightness. Furious, she dashed a hand over her eyes, afraid that he might think she wept. 'What? No trial? In this free land of England, do you have no courts?'

Morton smiled, his face florid in the cold wind. 'The trial is over. You were found guilty. Hanging is the penalty for piracy, but treason requires a different fate. Raising a flag against your king ...?' He cocked his head. 'The crowds do love a quartering.'

Fear and bile rose in her throat. 'Death is death,' she said, forcing her voice not to shake. In the distance she could hear the shouts of dockers, a familiar sound strange in this alien world. Her gaze left Morton, raced out across the vast city of London that crouched beneath a haze of smoke. The air was acrid with the stench; it made her think of Sainte Anne, of how it had burned at the order of this man. Of how her father had died at his hand, hanged in this faceless place. Of how Overton had died, how they had all died for the sake of the simple right to breathe free.

Walker moved to stand next to her. At his side there was a dull gleam of metal, his sword knocking against his hip as he walked. In a flash, it was in her hand and with a cry she launched herself at Morton. The blade connected with his face and he roared, falling back. She saw a stripe of scarlet across his cheek, lifted the blade for another blow, but someone had her wrist, twisting her arm until she dropped the sword. Then she was on the deck, boots kicking her ribs and back, hands pulled painfully behind her.

'See to Lord Morton!' someone was yelling. 'See to his lordship!'

From where she lay, she could see blood dripping onto the deck. Not enough to be fatal, but his blood nonetheless. She watched it seep into the wood and swore to herself that, somehow, she would spill it all. One day, she would make him pay for all that he had done to those she loved.

Iron bound her wrists and she was hauled upright. The pain in her ribs made it hard to breathe, the edges of her vision turning grey. Morton had a cloth to his face, covered in ruby blooms. 'Vile creature,' he spat, backing away. 'Get her out of my sight.'

Someone pushed her from behind and she stumbled, landing badly on her injured ankle. Pain jolted up her leg and she cried out, pitching forward into a sudden, absolute darkness.

Chapter Twenty-One

In the twenty years since Zach Hazard had last set foot on English soil, he'd not missed it for a moment. The December chill cut deep, despite the wool coat and heavy boots he'd purloined along the Portsmouth Road, and he cursed every step he had to take through the muddy streets of London.

There were few in the city that knew him now, but his objective was stealth and there was little benefit in advertising the fact that he'd been basking under a golden sun for most of his adult life. His hair had been cut – much to the objection of Brookes, who'd looked nervously skyward as Zach wielded the knife. In his three-and-thirty years, Zach had seen enough strangeness in the world not to dismiss Brookes' superstition out of hand. He'd once seen sharks follow a ship for three days and nights before the bloody flux broke out among the crew and half of them succumbed to death. The sharks had enjoyed the feast and ever since he'd dreaded the sight of a shark's fin off his stern. But needs must and no ill luck had befallen the *Hawk*, despite her captain cutting his hair at sea. No ill luck, that was, beyond the fact that she now skulked off the rocky shores of England, avoiding the navy and the Revenue men, in daily risk of discovery. All because her captain was unable to let Amelia Dauphin face the gallows, despite all she'd done to deserve it.

So here he was, loitering outside a coffee shop on Tyburn Street, with his hair tied more or less neatly at his nape, and a long muffler, wrapped several times about his neck to hide most of his face. He kept his hat pulled low over his eyes, as much for warmth as for disguise.

But despite it all he was chilled to the bone night and day. The *Hawk* had fair flown north, into the British Sea, and Zach's sun-soaked body had been given precious little time to grow accustomed to the seeping damp of a London winter. His lungs were already choking on the foetid air, clogged with the soot of half a million fireplaces, and he spent his days coughing and cursing the fate that had brought him back to this scabrous city.

He'd taken lodgings in a garret on Tyburn Street, so as to be close to both the prison and the Tyburn tree where Amelia was due to meet her fate. He had little chance of freeing her from the prison itself, but the cart that would carry her to the gallows passed along this very street. Custom had it that the condemned procession would call at the Mason's Arms for a parting cup en route to the hanging, and it was there that he planned to pluck her from death's embrace.

Amid a mob of thirty thousand souls eager to see her collared, it would not be easy. But he was still Zachary Hazard and, though he'd not set foot in London these past twenty years, he'd not forgotten how the city worked.

The next hanging day – the eighth, and last of the year – would fall on Christmas Eve, three days from now. It would draw a bigger crowd than usual, not least because it would see the end of the infamous 'Pirate Queen'. Her tale had spread throughout the city, told in lurid and ludicrous detail in the *Courant* and the ha'penny pamphlets that littered the streets. None of it true, of course, but Zach knew better than to expect the truth in this city of lies and hypocrisy. Besides, what were pirates at all if not the sum of their legends? Especially in these dark days.

'Sir? Mister Brookes, sir?' Zach looked down at the black-footed scrap of a boy standing before him. 'I done what you asked.'

'Good lad. How many did you find?'

The boy frowned in concentration. 'More'n thirty, I reckons, sir. I told 'em there was half a crown in it, sir. Like what you said.'

Zach nodded, his gaze drifting back to the prison. 'And they'll be there?'

'Yeah. If you'll give 'em the money.'

'I will. And twice again, after.' He studied the boy, reminded painfully of desperate nights in the knife-sharp winter wind. 'It'll be cold tonight,' he said, fishing a shilling from his pocket and tossing it to the lad. 'Get yourself somewhere warm.'

Blue eyes widened in the urchin's grimy face as he eyed his pitiful treasure. 'Yes, sir! I will, sir.'

'And don't forget – if you're not at the Tyburn Fair, I'll find you and cut your bloody ears off. Understand?'

'Yes, sir. I ain't gonna forget, sir.'

'Make sure you don't.'

With that, he pushed himself away from the wall and headed back to his room to wait. Newgate itself loomed in the distance, a terrible hulking presence, and he found himself dreading passing through its black gates. He could still remember the stench of it and a child's fear beat in his heart once more. Vivid despite the passage of twenty years, he could still picture the vast door with its enormous iron lock. He could still hear it slam shut with a clang like the bells of hell. There were few things that could have driven him back to this place. In truth, there was only one thing and he cursed her for it with his very soul.

The lodgings that Zach had taken felt far from the sultry heat of Ile Sainte Anne. He pulled his coat tighter and stood by the window, wiping a clear spot with his sleeve to look out upon the smut-covered buildings spread out below. Not a speck of blue sky or emerald sea to be seen, only the Thames running dark and sludgy through this great abomination of a city.

He longed to be gone, he longed for open water and open skies. For heat.

For her.

But that was an old and futile longing. She'd made her choice four years ago and he was only here now because his heart wasn't cold enough to let her hang. 'Bloody fool,' he muttered, his breath misting in the damp air. 'Weak-willed bloody fool, she'll be the death of you yet.'

Outside, church bells tolled the hour. It was midday, and time to be about his business. He'd a plan in mind, but she needed to be warned for it to work. Which meant he must enter that godforsaken hole of a gaol and speak with her.

He didn't know what he feared more: Newgate, or what the sight of her within its walls might do to him – the sight of her at all, after four years' absence. Though she had chosen another and betrayed him to his death, he still feared the power she wielded over him.

Funny, how the world turned and yet nothing ever changed.

With a sigh, he moved away from the window as the chimes reached twelve and fell silent. All across the city rang the echoes of tolling bells. It was a maudlin sound indeed.

On the flea-bitten sack that served as his bed lay the clothes he needed for the day's adventure, and reluctantly he stripped off his coat to put them on. The previous evening he'd made the acquaintance of a wayward and somewhat frustrated young blackcoat. The parson had caught Zach's attention the moment he'd stepped into the Mason's Arms, and the flutter of confused desire in the young man's eyes had given Zach an idea.

It had only taken half a bottle of gin to divest the curate of his vestments, and little over half an hour to divest him of the wish to tarry longer in the service of the Church. He'd left the Mason's Arms newly enlightened and no doubt bent on a path to ruin – or, perhaps, to the sea. Either way, he'd also left behind his coat and hat, both of which Zach now wore as he strode purposefully towards Newgate Prison.

He rapped hard on the side gate and waited with feigned

patience for the beetle-eyed marshal to open up. 'State your name and business, sir.'

Zach pressed his hands together and affected a polite bow. 'Reverend Jedidiah Brookes, sir. Sent to hear the last confession of Miss Amelia Dauphin, condemned to hang in three days, sir.'

'Dauphin, eh?' Beetle-eyes spat on the floor. 'That whore'll keep you busy 'til they take her to the gallows, eh? With all she 'as to confess.'

'It's my duty to serve the Lord, sir,' Zach said, smiling as he imagined running the man through and cutting out his foul tongue.

'Someone will take you.' The man nodded towards another building beyond the gate. Zach assumed it housed the prison offices. 'Though you might want to cover your nose, sir. Stinks somethin' powerful in the condemned cells.'

'With God's help, I'll endure.' Zach offered a parsimonious bow, and then turned and walked carefully towards the offices. He paused once, glanced over his shoulder to ensure that Beetle-eyes was occupied, and cut sideways across the courtyard. He knew this prison well.

It wasn't long before he was approaching the condemned cells, his flesh like ice from the dank air and dark memories. He'd last seen his mother here – abandoned while his father cavorted across the waves, heedless of the misery and poverty he'd left behind. He was dead too now, and there was another soul locked in this mortal hell.

A gate barred the corridor to the cells, guarded by a thickset man with a belt full of keys. He eyed Zach with more suspicion than the imbecile on the gate; Zach was instantly wary.

'Where's Reverend Harper?'

'If it please you, sir, I'm here with special dispensation. I tend to the pastoral care of the Dauphin family and they have asked me to hear Miss Dauphin's last confession. I've known her since she was a child, sir. Her mother was a dear friend. Intimate, you might say.'

The man's eyes narrowed. 'Was she now?'

'Indeed she was, and my heart is broken at how Miss Amelia – or Amy, as I was wont to call her – has fallen from God's grace. It's my humble desire to bring her to God again, before she is cast forever into damnation.'

The guard considered for a moment, then shrugged. 'Much good it'll do you. The banshee's been here a se'night and ain't tolerated a word from Reverend Harper all week.' As he spoke, he tugged on a chain about his waist and unlocked the gate. 'You'll find her at the end, Reverend. I wouldn't get too close, if I were you.'

'Good advice, sir,' said Zach, sidling through the gate and into the corridor. 'Yet always difficult to follow.'

The stench was, as predicted, almost intolerable. The mutters and pitiful groans of the inmates seemed to thicken the foul air, making it difficult for Zach to breathe as he picked his way along the narrow corridor that ran the length of the condemned cells. Hollow eyes blinked at him in the smoky lamplight, and he imagined these men would think the drop a blessing.

He drew closer to the doors as he reached the corridor's dead-end, peering through the window in each one in search of—

His stomach lurched, a deep swooping dive. There she was, hunched against the back wall of her cell. Her hair was filthy, hanging like rat-tails almost to the floor as she sat with her knees pulled up to her chest and her forehead resting against them. Her coat and britches hung from her like rags from bones and Zach's hand tightened about the cold iron of her prison.

'Miss Dauphin.' It took some effort to keep his voice from shaking. 'Amelia.'

She lifted her head abruptly, as if roused from a dream,

and stared directly at him with clear, astonished eyes. 'Za—Reverend?'

'Reverend Brookes, Miss Dauphin. A friend of your mother's.'

She smiled, a flash of island sun amid the gloom, and he was lost – entirely, completely lost. His walls couldn't hold against her, they never had.

'I knew you would come.' Gingerly, she uncurled her legs, wincing in a way that made Zach's grip on the bars tighten. Then she hauled herself to her feet, pausing before she moved, as if close to swooning. She steadied herself against the wall and gritted her teeth; none of the fight had left her. She was unbowed, although she *was* half-starved – as he'd known she would be. With no one to buy or bring her food, she'd have had nothing to live on in this hellish place.

'I'm here to nourish your immortal soul,' he said, as she limped unsteadily towards him. 'And your mortal flesh too.' From his pocket he produced a loaf of bread and a hunk of hard cheese. Amelia snatched them from his hand and sank to the floor, cramming food into her mouth.

He crouched too, on the other side of the bars, and watched her eat. Nothing but the seasons had changed in the four years since he'd left her in Luc Géroux's arms, and the pain of that loss was as sharp as ever.

Her eyes lifted to meet his and after a moment, with her mouth full of bread, she said, 'I'd almost given up hope that we'd meet again, before the end. But I longed for it.'

Feeling too much, Zach was forced to drop her earnest gaze. 'It's not the end yet,' he whispered. 'Be ready when—'

'Will you hear my last confession?' Her bony fingers clutched his arm through the bars. 'There may be no other chance.'

'No.' He closed his hand over hers. 'It's not time for that, Amy. Trust me.'

Her eyes filled with tears. 'I do. But please ... Zach, I must have your forgiveness, I must—'

'Shhh.' He squeezed her hand, quieting her as the guard looked towards them. 'God forgives all your sins, my child,' he said in a louder voice, 'if you will but repent.'

Amelia ripped another mouthful of bread from the loaf. 'I care nothing for God's forgiveness, only yours. Do you – can you – forgive me?'

His heart thudded in sudden, unbidden hope. 'For what?' *For betraying me to Morton? Or for doing your duty and marrying Géroux?*

'You know what, Zach.' She blinked and rubbed the back of a filthy hand over her eyes. 'They hanged you.'

'Ah.' He pulled his arm from her hand, looking away in case she'd seen the rise and fall of his foolish hope. 'That.'

'You can't know how it's haunted me, how it's tormented me to—'

'Long forgiven,' he said quickly, standing up. 'Long forgotten.' Then, in a lower voice, 'At the Mason's Arms, there'll be one chance. When the time comes, ask for rum.'

She nodded, her understanding immediate and complete. 'I knew you would come,' she said. 'I knew it.'

'The shadow moves as the sun commands, does it not?' He sketched a farewell bow. 'Be ready.'

Chapter Twenty-Two

Be ready.

Those had been Zach's last words to her and perhaps the last friendly words she was to hear this side of eternity – or damnation, depending on what fate had in store for her.

Be ready.

And she was. As ready as she could be given the way her head spun from hunger and the pain of the wound she'd taken in the battle.

She felt a flutter of panic as she remembered the fire and death, the destruction of all she'd built from the ashes of her life, and forced the memories away. It would do no good to dwell on such thoughts now. She must be ready.

Instead, in the predawn grey, Amelia conjured an image of Zach's dark, guarded eyes and the promise they held; he would save her, or die trying. Though she didn't deserve his loyalty, her heart soared to know that she had it anyway. In this, her darkest hour, Zach was the only light left in the world.

They led her from the cell a little after dawn. Two others were with her, shuffling manacled along the corridor until another door swung shut behind them. The priest was there again, but Amy paid him no mind as he administered last rites to the condemned. One of the men with her sobbed, the other cursed God and the priest both. Amelia was silent. Her salvation lay in another's hands – in the conniving, clever hands of Captain Zach Hazard, and in him she had more faith than the priest had ever deserved.

Sunlight split the room when the doors were opened, lancing through the thick air with a snow-bright glare. Amelia sucked in a deep, icy breath and it felt like the end of the world. They were loaded into the sombre cart that would take them to their end and Amelia did her best not to look at the men who accompanied her. She dreaded seeing her own terror reflected in their eyes, was afraid that what courage she had would flee at the sight of their panic.

So she thought of better things: of Zechariah Overton's defiance, of Luc Géroux's careful loyalty, and of Zach Hazard, who had come once more to save her.

Quietly, she began to hum an old tune, the battle anthem she had learned at her father's knee. The anthem she had sung in defiance of an empire, standing shoulder to shoulder with the free people of Ile Sainte Anne as they braced for attack. Then, as now, her courage rose as she sang.

'*Your houses they pull down. Stand up now, stand up now ...*'

She moved to the front of the cart, holding on as it lurched into motion. The wide doors of the prison yard opened ahead of her, revealing a cityscape frosted with Christmas snow. Her voice grew stronger.

'*But the gentry must come down, and the poor shall wear the crown ...*'

This time, no one else took up the song. Amelia sang alone.

Thousands of people clogged the streets, eager for a view. Hawkers plied their trade at the tops of their voices and even though it was barely ten in the morning, Zach had already seen a dozen fights break out in the heaving, drunken crowd.

'Worse than bloody pirates,' he said, turning away from the window to the garret in which he'd slept. Or, rather, not slept. The straw pallet was a veritable menagerie of biting insects and he missed the comfort of his own bunk aboard the *Hawk*.

The curate's clothes now lay discarded in a heap on the floor, today's ensemble involving an innkeeper's shirtsleeves and leather apron. Although it would be an ignominious fate, he knew it was highly probable that he would meet his end dressed as a seedy London innkeeper on a seedy London street. Not for the first time, he cursed the ill luck that had ever brought the name Amelia Dauphin to his ears. 'Bloody things I do for you, Amy,' he grumbled, as he tied the apron about his waist, slipped his heavy coat over it, and headed for the door.

He could hear the roar of the crowd getting closer, like a monster wave in a turbulent sea. There was no need to look to know that the cart grew nearer and that soon it would be stopping to give the condemned one last drink. The final dregs of sand were slipping through the hourglass and the time approached to turn everything upside down.

The landlord, Mr Tobias Kendall, was exactly where Zach knew he would be on such an auspicious occasion – behind the bar, selling out his stock of ale and gin. The crush was so great that Zach could barely move through it as he pushed to position himself between the cellar door and the storeroom that lay behind the bar.

Outside, a horse whinnied and the crowd roared, jeering and applauding, laughing and screaming. Zach sank deeper into his coat and waited.

A sharp-eyed man was the first to enter the Mason's Arms, the city marshall himself, followed by six of his armed men, pushing back the crowd inside the inn and standing, arms linked, to form a corridor through which the condemned walked. Amelia led the way, of course – always a leader, even when she had only the walking dead to lead. She held her head high and in the inn's light Zach could see bruises and welts that had been obscured by the gloom of the prison. His fist curled and he looked away, turning his gaze on the men who followed; it was too risky to dare a moment's eye contact with Amy.

Ashen and shaking, the men who shuffled in her wake

looked like most men did when facing their end – catatonic with fright. He tipped his hat to them. Though he no longer feared death, the dying still held terror. For he remembered all too well the bite of the hempen necklace, the desperate struggle for breath as the deck disappeared from beneath his feet, the relentless choking of the rope about his neck. He swallowed, fingers running along the scar about his throat.

'Mr Marshall, sir.' Kendall's voice, close behind him, jerked Zach free of the memory. Cursing his wandering mind, he watched as the innkeeper scurried to welcome his eminent guest, wiping his hands on his apron and smiling broadly. 'All is ready, everything's here to honour their last request. Follow, follow ...' Kendall turned and led the way towards the beer cellar where the condemned were to enjoy their last drop before *the* drop. When the door closed behind them, Zach held his breath and waited.

It would be now, or it would be never. If it were now, the plan might work; if it were never, he'd be forced to die in a futile attempt to rescue her by force. He'd do it too, rather than live to see her hang.

The guards didn't move, staring at each other blankly over the exit they guarded with their lives. Behind them, Kendall's patrons shifted like uneven sands, eager for a taste of blood.

Still Zach didn't breathe.

Then he heard it, footsteps on the cellar stairs. The door opened and the guards' heads snapped around; the crowd tried to surge forward, but the marshall's men held their line.

'Bloody woman wants rum!' Kendall exclaimed with a flap of his hands and disappeared into the back room.

'That's 'cause she's a pirate!' someone yelled, and the room burst into another round of laughing jeers.

Zach took the opportunity to slip, unnoticed, after the innkeeper. Kendall was fussing about with a crate, muttering to himself about the ingratitude of the condemned. Taking his pistol from his belt, Zach hefted the barrel in his hand and brought the handle down hard on the back of the man's head. He dropped like a stone.

Pausing only to slip off his coat, Zach picked up the bottle of rum. 'You'll thank me later,' he told the catatonic innkeeper and took a swig to steady his nerves. Then he moved to the door and pressed an ear against it.

Everything depended on part two of the plan.

At first all he could hear was the yelling, jeering crowd. Then suddenly there was chaos: shouts of outrage, panic, running feet. Zach risked a peek and saw everyone rushing to the doors and windows of the inn. The guards' neat corridor had evaporated and they were trying to push through the crush to reach the door. Outside, Armageddon had begun.

Well, as much Armageddon as two score street boys could make on the promise of a crown and a half apiece. Zach couldn't see much, but he could hear and that was enough. With a smile, he slipped out of the storeroom, past the distracted guards, and down the stairs to the ale cellar. Amelia was there, one hand manacled to the far wall and the other two men chained next to her. She said nothing as Zach entered, barely an eyelid flickered, and yet he could tell she was poised for action.

'Who are you?' The city marshall put his hand on his hilt, eyes narrowing.

'Luc Géroux, monsieur. Onion seller turned innkeeper.' Zach nodded back up the stairs. 'There's some kind of trouble outside and Mister Kendall said to fetch you while I see to the drinks.'

As the marshall eyed the stairs suspiciously, a gunshot echoed from somewhere above. Then another. He bolted, pushing past Zach and taking the steps two at a time.

When he was gone, Zach held up the keys he'd lifted from the man's belt and grinned. Heart thumping, he crossed the room and with a click of the lock Amelia was free and in his arms.

'Zach ...'

'Run,' he said, pushing her gently back. 'Now.' He tossed the keys high in the air and they landed not a yard from the condemned men. 'Help each other, and you might live to see Christmas Day.' With that he grabbed Amelia's bird-thin wrist and tugged her towards the stairs.

The riot outside was in full swing, but he didn't pause to look as he darted from the stairs back into the storeroom where Kendall lay sprawled. Amelia's mouth opened to speak, but he pressed a finger against his lips to hush her. Stripping off his apron, he grabbed his hat and threw her his coat. She put it on gratefully and he took her hand, pulling her towards the door at the back of the inn. It opened out onto an alley, dark and putrid, but on the other side of the building from the riot. Silently, they started walking and he tried not to notice how badly she limped. There was no time for that now. Later, when they were safer, he'd discover why. She just had to keep up.

'Where are we going?' Amelia hissed into his ear, her breath the only warmth in the city.

'A friend's house, but not for long. We must leave London tonight.'

'By ship?'

Zach smiled and glanced at her long-forgotten, familiar face. 'No chance. We'll have to sneak out like the rats we are.' He gestured around at the squalid poverty, the decaying buildings and haunted faces that watched them from shadowed doorways. 'This is our world now. A mighty fall for Madame Géroux I'm afraid, but there's nothing to be done about that.'

A flicker of fire lit her eyes. 'I've long been Captain Dauphin, as well you know, and this has always been my world.'

He smiled and touched his hat in salute. 'So be it, then.'

Chapter Twenty-Three

He took her to a brothel, rapping twice on the rickety door, and all Amelia could think was, *Please hurry, please let us in.*

She was frozen to the marrow of her bones. Her left ankle shot agony along the length of her leg and Zach had been helping her to walk for at least half an hour. Hunger was a fist in her belly and her head throbbed, as it had for weeks, for the want of food and water.

A narrow-faced woman appeared, glanced at Zach with a sour expression, and cracked the door just far enough to admit them. 'One hour,' she said, her accent like the scrape of dry rocks. 'Any longer and I'm fetching the bleedin' coppers m'self.'

Zach pushed open the door with one hand, his other arm tight about Amelia's waist, keeping her upright. 'Everything is as I asked?'

'Course. Now hurry up. I'll not swing for ya, Zach Hazard.'

Her dragging left foot caught on the threshold and Amelia stumbled hard, clamping her jaw shut to keep from crying out. Zach's arm tightened about her waist.

'Upstairs,' the shrew-faced woman said. 'First room on the right.'

Amelia coughed as they moved through the dim corridor, the air thick with the groundnut scent of opium. She breathed deep, hoping it might dull the pain.

'None of that,' Zach warned. 'Need your wits, Amy.'

'Not much use if I can't walk.'

He didn't answer, just led her towards the room to which they'd been directed and shoved open the door. Inside, mercifully, a small fire had been lit in the grate. A filthy-looking bed dominated the room, upon which sprawled a ragged dress that may once have been red. A thin shawl lay next to it. The clothes couldn't hold Amelia's attention, however, once she'd seen the loaf of bread that sat on a small table near the window. Two bowls next to it were filled with a greasy-looking stew. To Amelia, it seemed the finest feast she'd ever eaten, and she fell upon the food, sopping the bread into the gravy and shoving it into her mouth.

Zach watched her in silence after helping her to sit on the single chair at the table. He peered into the second bowl and wrinkled his nose, before shoving it towards her and heading to the window, gazing out into the alley below. 'It's quiet,' he muttered, and then turned back to her. 'What's wrong with your leg?'

'I fell. In the battle.' Amid the fire and the flames and the dying.

Zach moved around the table and knelt to examine her ankle, lifting her booted foot onto his knee. 'Not broken.'

'No.' He set her foot back down and the lance of pain turned her stomach despite her hunger and she sucked in a breath.

He looked up at her, his expression more guarded than she remembered. 'Is it bound?'

Amelia shook her head.

'That will help. So will the rum, but not 'til we're somewhere safer. Can you bear it?'

'I bear greater wounds than this.'

He held her eye for a moment, though she could read nothing in his dark gaze. Slowly he stood, returning to the window. 'It's not my intention to offend you, Amy, but you stink of the gaol. There's water by the fire. Wash what you can and burn everything but the shirt. We'll use that to bind your ankle. The dress is for you, though it'll hang on you like a sack.'

Her eyes roved to the bed and the dirty dress, then down to the filthy rags she wore. It was a marginal improvement. 'I've not worn a dress in years.'

'Maybe not, but they're looking for the Pirate Queen, a whore in men's clothes.' He bobbed his head a little. 'Again, no offence. It's little by way of disguise, but better than nothing.'

She smiled as bravely as she could and limped towards the fire. A small tin bath sat there with little more than an inch of water within. It looked clean though, and perhaps not entirely cold. Sinking onto the bed, she pulled the boot from her good foot and sighed. 'Is that what they call me then? A whore?'

'And worse. But everyone's a whore in this city of whores and thieves. What do you care for their opinion?'

'Nothing, I suppose.' She gave a cautious tug on her other boot and hissed at the jab of pain, her eyes filling with unwelcome tears. Sniffing, she blinked them away. 'Once, I would have.'

'We were all fools once.' Crossing the room, Zach knelt again before her and gently began to work the boot free of her swollen ankle. 'Live long enough, though, and the fool is knocked out of you. For the most part.'

Gritting her teeth, she let him pull her foot free. When the pain had receded she opened her eyes and found him studying her ankle. Ugly, was her first reaction to the swollen mass of scarlet flesh.

He touched her ankle lightly. 'There's some infection, but I've ointment that will help. It'll heal, in time.'

'Time I now have, thanks to you.'

He glanced up. 'We're but half an hour from the gallows, the pair of us. Don't thank me yet.'

'I will. Even if we hang at dawn, I'll thank you for this. Things were not left well between us, Zach, and I know how you—'

'Géroux sent me.' Pushing himself to his feet he returned to the window. 'Couldn't come himself, so he sent me in his stead. Paid me a good price to fetch you back to him.'

She was silent a moment, watching his back and the set of his shoulders. He was tense. In the past she might have thought that he was lying. Now, she didn't know, so all she said was, 'You've seen Luc?'

'At Ile Sainte Anne, picking up survivors.' He didn't turn around, or look at her, but his voice softened. 'Addy was among them, so Géroux said. And the children.'

She let out a breath, felt her shoulders sag. 'Thank heaven. Thank heaven for that, at least.'

Zach just grunted and said, 'Now hurry, if you will. We must be gone from here before the mistress of this fine establishment finds a wandering constable knocking at her door.'

Amelia hesitated, despite her overwhelming desire to wash the stench of Newgate from her skin. Even aboard ship she'd had a modicum of privacy, and this was *Zach*. Why that should make a difference she didn't know, but nonetheless it did.

He made a sound low in his throat, a laugh perhaps, though there was a bitter tang of derision about it. 'Don't worry, Amy, I'll keep my back turned. Not been so starved of female company these past four years that I desire a peek at the skin and bone you hide beneath your rags.'

A faint heat burned her cheeks, a sharp pain tightening in her chest. Was it shame? 'You're an honourable man,' she said quietly, plucking at the ties about the neck of her shirt before pulling the wretched thing over her head. Not once since she'd taken her father's place as leader of Ile Sainte Anne had she thought about her appearance; she'd cared about nothing there but the safety of her people and the ideals for which they fought. Now, as she gazed down past the lank hair hanging over her grimy shoulders, to her flat breasts and skeletal ribs, she wondered what Zach must see when he looked at her. A wretch, no doubt, like those they'd passed in the alley, half-starved and desperate. Her eyes blurred and she had to blink before she could untie her britches, trying not to see the ugly protrusion of her hipbones beyond the concave fall of her stomach. The walking dead, she thought grimly and, but for Zach, she'd be the swinging dead. She should count her blessings. And yet ...

Why did she care what Zach Hazard saw when he looked at her? He'd seen nothing at all of her these past four years, though she'd made it known that his presence was welcome on the island. More than welcome.

She shivered and Zach shifted, leaning his shoulder against the window frame. With care, she stepped into the water; it had, perhaps, once been hot. With a shaking hand, she took the sliver of pearlash soap and began to work a thin lather over her body, scooping up handfuls of water to rinse her skin and her wounded ankle. Some, but not most, of the dirt came free.

She was just considering the best way to clean her hair when Zach said, 'Don't wet your hair. We'll be travelling tonight and there'll likely be a frost. Don't want you dying of lung fever before we reach your *husband*.'

There was a sardonic emphasis on the word that spoke of resentment. She could hardly blame him for it, though it gave her some pain. This was not the time to be dwelling on his bitterness, however, and his advice about her hair was sound. In truth there was little chance of getting it anywhere near clean in the inch of filthy water that remained.

So cold now that her teeth were chattering, she limped out of the bath and snatched a blanket from the bed to dry herself. Then she pulled on the dirty dress, grateful for its warmth and heedless of its stains. The shawl, too, she wrapped tight about her shoulders.

Her britches she tossed into the fire and watched them catch and burn, and for a moment it was another fire that hissed and spat before her eyes.

'Are you dressed?'

She looked up to where Zach still stood with his back to her. 'Yes.'

He turned and regarded her without comment. The dress, she knew, hung upon her as if upon a rather tall, half-starved child and she tugged the shawl tight, to hide her bony shoulders.

Zach dragged a chair close to the fire and waved her towards it. 'Sit. I'll dress your ankle; then we must be gone.'

The fire's heat was like heaven and she leaned as close as she could, trying to forget that she'd soon be back out in the jaws of winter. She could hear Zach tearing her shirt into pieces and then he crouched, pulling her ankle onto his knee again. From his pocket he produced a small vial of ointment that she recognised instantly from its honeyed herbal scent; it was one of Addy's. His hands were warm, she noticed, as he began to apply the ointment and bind her foot. He didn't look up as he worked, his nimble fingers seeming well practiced and she supposed he'd had many occasions to dress the wounds of his men. A leader herself these past four years, she knew the weight he carried on his shoulders. She knew what it was to see your people fall.

Had she known these things before, back in the golden days before her father's death, she might have understood his warning better. Might have paid more heed.

'There,' he said, sitting back on his heels. 'That will help, though we've a long journey ahead of us.'

Gently, he began to ease her foot into the boot and she clenched her teeth to keep from showing how much it hurt. 'Where are we going? Portsmouth?'

'Hardly possible for the *Serpent* to anchor in the Royal Dockyards when we're fleeing the Admiralty.' He looked up, serious in the firelight. 'There's a cove to the west of Poole. The *Serpent* is to meet us there. It's as close as we can get after …' A flicker of pain crossed his face.

Amelia finished his thought. 'After my defeat at Ile Sainte Anne? It's all right, you can say it. I've had time enough to contemplate the ruin I brought upon us all.'

'*You* brought?' There was an odd vehemence to his voice as he rose to his feet and turned to warm his hands over the fire.

'Don't blame Luc.'

He barked a laugh, then stifled the sound and glanced cautiously at the door. 'No, heaven forbid I blame Luc bloody Géroux for anything. Pure as the new driven snow, that man.'

'None of us can look back on those days without regret, Zach. Not even you.'

'I make a point of not looking back on those days at all.'

She was quiet again, watching his anger carefully. 'We built a haven there, Zach. A place of equality and freedom. A place where a man or a woman's worth was judged by the work they did, by the contribution they made to life at Ile Sainte Anne – *For the poorest man that is upon the Earth has a life to live, as the greatest man.* So say the Articles and *that's* what brought them down upon us, that simple, dangerous notion.'

'Recall saying something similar myself, four years ago.' He looked at her, firelight dancing in his eyes, beautiful despite his anger. 'You should have run.'

She rose to her feet. 'I'm not in the habit of running, Captain Hazard.'

'No.' A smile curled the corners of his mouth. 'That's why I have to keep coming to your rescue.' He nodded to the door. 'Are you ready? For tonight we do run. And we don't stop until we meet the sea.'

Chapter Twenty-Four

They slipped out of the brothel without a word to its mistress; better that she remained ignorant of the direction they walked, lest her tongue be persuaded to wag by the temptation of another's coin.

It was past noon now and the morning's sun had been replaced by a heavy, dark sky. More snow perhaps, later. The air was raw. It cut through Zach's coat like a whetted blade and he knew Amelia must be sliced to the bone by it. He'd taken the blanket from the bed and she wore that about her head and shoulders, clasped tight by white fingers beneath her chin. It was hardly enough against the December frost.

They walked in silence, mostly because she had no breath for talking. He kept the pace fast and she limped along gamely at his side, no word of complaint passing her lips. Whether it was pride or strength that kept her on her feet he didn't know, but at least the exercise would keep her from freezing. And his concern for her kept him from thinking about the streets and alleyways through which they fled.

Twenty years on, the place seemed little different, only more crowded than ever. More starving, hollow faces peered out from the dark, more miserable wretches crammed into this human abyss. The wharfs were fit to bursting, with ships waiting weeks for a berth and the shore littered with unloaded goods, just begging to be pilfered by the Scuffle Hunters and other longshore thieves. More pirates in the Port of London, he thought, than ever sailed the Spanish Main. And yet we're the ones they chased to Hell.

'Oi! You, sir!'

The voice was distant, but Zach was taking no chances and dodged quickly down an alley to his left. Amelia, though, didn't notice his move and continued straight ahead until he reached out and snatched her hand, tugging her into the gloom. Her fingers curled tight about his and didn't let go as he drew her further down the overhung passageway.

'Where are we going?' Amelia wrinkled her nose at the stench; the place was putrid with death.

'Short cut.' He hurried her along as fast as her lame leg would allow. 'Didn't you hear someone shout?'

She shook her head, lips tight.

'Nothing to do with us, most likely. We'll be at the river soon.'

Ahead, a misshapen lump blocked the alley. Zach tried not to look too closely as they approached.

'I thought you said we couldn't get away by ship?'

'We can't. Port's thick with Revenue men, and worse. They'll be checking every ship that's leaving.'

'Then why are we heading to the river?'

Zach slowed, his hold on her hand tightening. 'To pay a debt, before we leave. Hush now, wait.'

The lumpy shape that sprawled across the alley was, as he'd suspected, a man. 'You there,' Zach said, keeping his distance. 'What's your name?'

There was no answer and none likely. The stench was worse and Zach guessed the man had been dead some days. Suddenly there was a scrabble of movement and a small figure detached itself from the corpse, tearing away down the alley.

Amelia gasped. 'What ...?'

'It's all right, just a scavenger. The dead are always worth robbing when you're too small to thieve from the living.'

She made no answer, though he could feel her gaze boring into his back. After a moment she said, 'I hope the poor man didn't die of some pestilence.'

'Foot pad, more than likely. He's too fat to live hereabouts. A merchant, perhaps. Even so ...' He turned and plucked the blanket from her fingers, wrapping it across her mouth and nose. 'Just in case.'

He did the same with his muffler and together they stepped over the decomposing corpse, giving it a wide berth. Zach didn't look at the face; he'd never looked at their faces.

A little later, they emerged into the relatively fresh air of the riverside. That is, the stench of death was replaced by the stench of the river at low tide, which was just what he wanted.

He found the lad down on the flats, digging in the mud with the rest of them, and called him over with a whistle. It was risky to draw so much attention, but he'd made the boy a promise and intended to keep it.

Amelia was watching him with unveiled curiosity as he pulled a purse from his coat and began distributing coins to the urchins crowding around him. 'For services rendered,' he said, meeting her eye over the boys' heads. 'In service to their queen.'

'And a handsome reward.' The slight rise of her eyebrows told him she approved of his generosity.

'Little enough to see them through the winter,' he said, as the last of them disappeared into the crowds, eager to spend their small fortune on watered gin and chalky bread. Haunted, he turned away and found himself captured by Amelia's earnest gaze. In that moment, it seemed that a connection was made, or perhaps renewed, between them, and he heard himself whisper, 'God's mercy, Amelia, but there's nowhere in the world so miserable as this cursed city.'

She drew closer, her cold fingers finding his again. 'When we rebuild Ile Sainte Anne there will be somewhere for these people to go, Zach. A haven. *The poor shall wear the crown.*'

'Rebuild?' He tightened his hold on her hand and began

to walk, heading west along the river. 'Is that your intention then?'

'Of course. They will never win while the Articles are alive in our hearts. Your father taught me that, Zach. And he died believing it.'

'Then they will come again. And again and again, until there are none left to remember the bloody Articles.'

She was silent a while and her grip on his hand slackened. 'What are you saying, Zach? That we should just give up?'

He sighed. 'You always were a stubborn bloody wench, Amelia Dauphin.'

'I'll never give up. Never.'

'Not until they hang you.'

A soft sound reached his ear – her laugh. Her blessed, childish giggle, which he'd never allowed himself to miss until that very moment, when the sound cut a path from the pit of his belly to his heart, flipping it right over. 'I'll never hang,' she laughed, 'for I have Zach Hazard to save me, do I not?'

'It's *Captain* Zach Hazard to you. And I am, as you know, a notoriously unreliable brigand. Best to put your faith elsewhere.' He glanced at her once, seeking the truth in her eyes. 'With your very reliable husband.'

For an instant, she met his gaze, then looked down at the muddy street. 'Yes,' she said, her laughter fading. 'Of course, with Luc.'

After that they spoke no more, cutting back and forward from the river's edge as they walked, avoiding the crowds. There were soldiers in the streets and about the wharfs and the resultant serpentine nature of their route meant that, by the time the sun surrendered to the midwinter dusk, they were still north of the river. Darkness, however, would serve them well in crossing the bridge. If the soldiers had half a mind between them they'd be guarding each end, yet the haphazard collision of decrepit old shops and houses that lined London Bridge provided many a hole down which a clever rat could slip unnoticed.

For those London rats that knew it well, the journey was simple – if costly and awkward. For the right price here and there, Zach was able to lead Amelia from cellar to cellar, out onto the great sterlings on which the bridge was built, passing beneath the very feet of the soldiers standing guard. Then up a flight of stairs to the attic of one old house, scrambling across the roof that spanned the street and down again, three buildings further on, and out onto the crowded bridge just south of Nonsuch House. It was thick with people, rich and poor. Carriages pushed through the crush with frequent, loud curses from the drivers as they navigated the narrow thoroughfare. Zach kept a tight hold on Amelia's hand; she'd been silent and flagging for a good hour now. All the climbing had done her in and her limp was increasingly pronounced. She'd need to rest soon, yet they hadn't travelled half so far as he would have liked. The night watch would be out now, but he was more wary of the red-coated soldiers than of the doddery old men with their whistles and torches. Even so, they needed to leave London, and leave it tonight.

'Zach?' Amelia sounded strained, watching him from a milky face.

'A little further,' he said, drawing her closer to a shop window and out of the stream of traffic. 'Can you make it?'

She shook her head. 'I feel faint. It hurts ...'

'Not here,' he said, slipping an arm about her waist just in case. 'Too much attention. The soldiers are only a few yards away.'

But her head was lolling, her face turning from milk to snow. 'I can't hear ...'

'Shhh.' He drew her hard against him, pressing her head against his shoulder as he cast about for somewhere to take her. The South Tower, where her father's treacherous head may well have been spiked, was crawling with redcoats, weapons over their shoulders, scanning passers-by; if he had to carry her, they'd be spotted instantly and he'd be unable to run. 'Stay awake,' he hissed, feeling her knees start to buckle.

Across the road there was a coffee shop. He didn't know it, but it would have to do. Half-hauling her, he crossed the street and ducked out of sight. It was busy inside, a crush of people, and they were met by a wave of moist heat and chatter. Wasting no time, Zach grabbed the sleeve of the first serving girl he saw. 'My wife has been taken ill,' he said. 'I need a place for her to rest. Have you somewhere?'

The girl glanced at Amelia. 'I'd 'av to ask Mr Albert, sir.'

'Then ask. There's a half crown in it for you if he says yes.'

She bobbed a quick curtsy and scurried away through the crowd. A few moments later a harassed-looking man pushed towards them, ruddy-faced and with retreating hair streaking his balding head. He eyed Amelia suspiciously. 'We've no rooms to rent. This ain't an inn.'

'Just a few minutes rest. Somewhere to lie down, is all. Here.' Zach pulled coins from his pocket. 'For your trouble.'

'What's wrong with her?' the man said, eyeing her more closely than Zach would have liked. 'I'll have no fevers here.'

'No, no,' Zach assured him with a smile. 'She's ... ah, with child and can hardly keep a bite down. Faints all over the place.' He offered the coin again. 'She'll be right as rain in half an hour, I swear it.'

Avarice and caution fought a brief war in the man's eyes, and greed came out the victor. He snatched the coin and said, 'Follow me, then.'

With Amelia barely able to walk, Zach followed the man up a narrow flight of stairs and into what must have been his own bedroom. 'No funny business,' he said, standing aside to let them pass.

Zach lifted an eyebrow. 'Unlikely.'

As the door closed behind them he lowered Amelia onto the bed. 'I'm sorry,' she whispered, eyes closed and lips barely moving.

'Shh. Rest now, Amy.' Anxious, he sat down at her side and pondered their next move. Clearly she couldn't walk further tonight, and yet they must get off the bridge and out of the city. He had coin enough for a hackney cab to the outskirts of Clapham, but that would be a risk – a trail he'd rather not leave – which left the option of either commandeering a wagon or carriage, or stowing away. He glanced down at Amelia; her eyes were closed, her face white beneath the grime and her lips chalky. She would be no help whatsoever, in either endeavour.

Frustrated, and increasingly nervous, he rose and paced to the grimy window that looked out over the bridge. He could just make out the soldiers near the tower, bored now and talking among themselves. Had he been alone, he could have sneaked or charmed his way past them. Of course, had he been alone, he'd not be in half so much danger. Had he been alone, he'd have never returned to his pestilent childhood home in the first place.

His gaze slid back to Amelia, her slight form asleep on the bed, fixing him where he stood as effectively as the heaviest bower anchor.

She left you to die once, and saved herself, whispered a dark corner of his mind. *Why not return the favour?*

Yet how could he live with himself then? How could he live with her blood on his hands? How could he live anyway, after he'd returned her to Géroux and her precious duties?

The truth was, one way or another, she'd bring him nothing but misery or death. And if that was the choice, then the decision was easy.

Chapter Twenty-Five

'Escaped?' Lord Charles Morton spat the word, livid with indignation, making the new scar on his cheek stretch and sting. 'From Newgate prison?'

The man before him, a grovelling foul-breathed creature from the gaol, backed up a step. 'Not strictly from the prison, sir. From the Mason's Arms, sir, on the way to Tyburn.'

Getting up from behind his desk, Morton crossed the room to glare at the unfortunate bearer of bad tidings. Outside Admiralty House, he could hear the rattle of late-night carriages, but inside the silence grew heavy with fear.

'How?' he said, bearing down on the snivelling fool. 'She is a woman. How could she outwit your men?'

'Beg pardon, sir, but she had an accomplice,' the man said, wringing his hands. 'And him with half a bloody army – pardon the language, sir – but half an army in wait near the Arms.'

Morton narrowed his eyes. 'An army?'

'Yes, sir. Outnumbered, the men was, and—'

'Hazard.' The word was spoken in black-velvet tones from behind him. He cursed silently, but showed no reaction as he turned to see his advisor standing close to the window. In the lamplight, he looked like a shadow, dressed head to toe in his customary black.

'Mr Scrope, I did not see you enter.'

Calvin Scrope nodded towards the side door, hidden within the wood panelling of Morton's Admiralty office. 'I did not wish to disturb you, My Lord.' His gaze, dark as his lank hair, switched to the gaoler. 'It was Hazard who freed the pirate whore.'

The man's eyes were wide. 'Who, sir?'

'Zachary Hazard,' Morton repeated. Then, to Scrope, 'How do you know?'

A smile touched his thin lips. 'Who else would dare? Or succeed?' He gave a slight shrug, narrow shoulders lifting as if it were a matter of no importance. 'Besides, the *Gypsy Hawk* has been sighted off the Devonshire coast.'

'Sighted, but not captured?'

Again, the slight smile. 'Not yet.' He didn't move from his position by the window, his face cast in shadow. 'Sir,' he said, with a significant glance towards the gaoler, 'if I may have a word?'

Morton turned to the filthy swine, glad to be shot of him. 'Be thankful that I don't throw you into your own foul gaol for this!' He waved his hand in dismissal. 'Leave now.'

The creature departed with mumbled thanks and apologies; Morton half expected to see a streak of dirt in his wake rather like a garden slug marks its passage. When the door closed behind him, Morton turned back to Scrope – vile, in a different and infinitely more threatening way. 'Speak, then,' he said, returning to the chair behind his desk.

Scrope ducked his head, a meaningless gesture of servility, and moved to stand before him. In the lamplight his face was easier to see. Pallid, shadowed beneath the eyes, he looked like death in his sombre black. 'As it happens, My Lord, this turn of events may prove fortuitous.'

Sceptical, Morton leaned back in his chair. His stomach growled and he glanced at the clock on the mantle; a quarter before ten. Supper called to him, and after that a return to his family home for the Christmas feast. He had hoped this business would be put to rest by now, the harlot strung up like her treacherous father. Yet it lingered on, like the wound to his face, made by her hand. 'Tell me how so, Scrope, and make it quick.'

'Yes, sir.' He laced his long fingers before him, white against his raven coat, and said, 'Géroux has wedded the whore.'

'Wedded?' Morton absolutely stared. 'How is that possible?'

'I assure you, it was sanctioned at the highest level. Certain strategic advantages were anticipated from the match, although I fear it has disappointed in that respect.'

'You're talking nonsense, man,' he snorted. 'Géroux wedded? I would have been told.'

Scrope spread his hands, at once placating and condescending. 'For reasons of delicacy, My Lord, few were informed. You will understand, of course. Had even a rumour reached society in general ...'

'And yet *you* knew, Mr Scrope?'

He bowed, but did not answer that particular observation. 'Obviously it is no marriage in the eyes of God or the law, but it is enough to ensure that she will do his bidding. All that remains is to wait for the obedient wife to return to her husband.'

Inside the room, all was quiet save the slow tick of the clock. Morton sat forward and lowered his voice, more than a little perturbed by this turn of events. 'Géroux, again? If the Admiralty were to discover my dealings with him, a French privateer ...'

'They will not.' Scrope dipped long fingers into his coat pocket. 'Besides, I received this today.' He set down a note on Morton's desk, slanted writing on expensive paper.

Morton made no attempt to touch it; he recognised the hand. 'What does it say?'

'*He* is unhappy with our failure in Ile Sainte Anne.'

Uncomfortable, Morton shifted in his seat. 'The place was destroyed, Dauphin's nest of vermin burned. What more does he want?'

'The acquisition of the Articles is seen as more important. The threat they pose is greater by far than the squawking of one little bird.'

Morton snorted. 'Do you think they mean anything

without her? It was to Dauphin and his daughter that the mutineers rallied. It was they who raised the flag of so-called liberty. Do you think the beggars that followed them can read a single word? The Articles mean nothing to them.'

Scrope drew closer and lowered his voice. 'My Lord, the poison contained in this evil book has already slain a king. And it grows more threatening with every generation. It cannot be allowed to pass on again; it must stop here.'

'Yes, and it will stop with Dauphin's death.'

'It must stop with the Articles burned, their notions turned to smoke. Would you have us ruled by beggars and thieves?' He lowered his gaze, perhaps aware he had overstepped his mark. 'Besides, *he* wills that the Articles be found and destroyed, My Lord.'

'Does he, now?'

Scrope inclined his head. 'My duty is to serve you, My Lord. And as your humble servant, I advise—'

'Yes, yes,' Morton snapped, irritated that the man was right. '*He* must not be gainsaid, I know.'

'Indeed.' Scrope folded his hands again, calm as the grave. 'We must find the Articles, My Lord, and we cannot do it without the pirate whore. Géroux tells me the book is hidden on the island, though even he does not know where. Amelia Dauphin is the only one who knows how to find it.'

There was a pause in which Morton rose from his desk and went to stand by the window, looking out of the Admiralty towards the road. The street was quiet, it being the eve of Christmas, and Morton imagined the people of London asleep in their beds and ignorant of the danger abroad in their city.

Not looking away from the window he said, 'Perhaps there is some merit to your advice, Scrope. We do not wish to earn his displeasure, do we?' Tugging down his coat, he turned. 'See? There is a reason I keep your long face around after all. Have Géroux contacted, remind him of his duty to the cabal – tell him what we need him to do.' He smiled. 'Perhaps we shall kill more than one bird with this stone, Mr Scrope. It would make a pretty picture, would it not, to see Hazard and Dauphin hanging together on the dock at Wapping?'

Scrope bowed again. 'Yes, My Lord, indeed it would.'

Amelia woke with a start. Heart racing, she sat bolt upright and stared into a cold, unfamiliar darkness. 'Zach?'

There was no answer.

Her head was foggy, memories colliding. They'd been on the bridge, her ankle burning, vision fading and her hearing no more than the rush of blood through her ears. Zach had held her upright, hissing instructions. She'd tried to walk and then … nothing.

'Zach, are you here?'

As her pulse began to slow she swung her legs from the bed. The faintness had subsided and her ankle had been re-dressed, though it still throbbed viciously. A single lamp lit the room and outside she could see the lights of other shops on the old wooden bridge. There was no way to tell, however, how long she'd slept – or how long she'd been alone.

Cautiously, she got to her feet and hobbled to the window. The street was still busy, but in this, the world's greatest city, that told her little about the time of day or night. Scanning the throng of people through grimy glass, she saw no sign of Zach. There were still soldiers at the end of the bridge and she pulled back quickly from the window as one of them turned towards her.

Worried now, Amelia returned to perch on the bed and gingerly re-laced her boots. Despite the stew she'd eaten earlier, her stomach was hollow and she felt thin enough that the winter wind might cut through her completely. It was as if she were hardly real any more, a ghost of herself in this alien city. Ghost enough to slip past the soldiers without them glancing at her twice. What would they see, after all, but a waif in a ragged dress, clutching a shawl about her bony shoulders to keep out the night's cold? There must be ten thousand such women in this city. Had the faintness not come upon her, they would have been free and clear.

She shifted on the bed and glanced at the door; in the distance a clock chimed the half hour. 'Where are you, Zach?' she whispered into the darkness, clinging to the belief that he hadn't abandoned her. He was too good a man for that.

But a man betrayed, too.

The door swung open, lamplight flooding the room. She started, flinging her hand up to shield her eyes. 'Zach?'

'Half an hour, I said,' came a curt voice. 'It's been almost two.'

Amelia squinted at the silhouette. 'Two hours?' Zach had been gone for *two hours*? 'I was asleep, I'm sorry. I don't—' She stood, biting back a grimace of pain. 'I'm sorry, sir, I have nothing to pay you for the use of your room.'

The owner of the coffee shop lifted his lamp higher. 'No need, your husband's already settled with me.' He peered more closely into the room. 'Where is he, then?'

'My husband?' Her thoughts flashed instinctively to Luc and it took Amelia a moment to understand. 'Oh, Zach. He had some business that couldn't be delayed.'

'Did he now?' The man drew closer and in the golden glow of his lantern she could see an ugly expression twist his face. 'Funny kind of a husband what leaves his wife alone under another man's roof.'

Backing up a step, Amelia cursed the lack of a weapon at her side. 'I'm sure he believes you to be an honourable man, sir.'

'So I am. Which is why I'll have no whores in my shop.'

Her eyes widened. 'What?'

'I'm no fool. Don't think I don't know what you are.'

'I'm not—'

He reached out and snatched a handful of her hair, hauling her towards the door. 'Go on, get out, you trollop. And don't bloody well come back or I'll shop you to the coppers!'

He shoved her hard towards a set of narrow stairs, and she half fell the first couple, crying out as her damaged ankle twisted. Hobbling badly, she staggered down the rest of the steps and into the heat of the coffee shop below. Hostile eyes watched from the smoke as the owner grabbed her arm and marched her through the crowd, before tossing her outside.

'Ply your trade elsewhere,' he snarled and slammed the door in her face.

Shaking, more from fury than anything else, Amelia stood a moment in shock. An icy wind lanced across her skin and she realised that she'd left the blanket behind. All that stood between her and the falling snow was the thin shawl about her shoulders.

Buffeted by irritated passers-by, she started to move, joining the flow of traffic, her mind in a daze. Two things were now dreadfully clear: Zach had left hours ago and not returned, and she was destitute on the streets of London.

'Stand up now, stand up,' she sang to herself as she limped towards the end of the bridge and the soldiers who patrolled the grim, grey castle that loomed far above. She kept her eyes down and masked her limp as much as possible without slowing her pace. Amongst this wretched sea of beggars and thieves, how could she be noticed? Yet it felt as though she approached a fire, her skin burning with the presence of the troops – one word, and she was theirs. With no hope of fleeing or fighting, Amelia's world narrowed to the street beneath her feet. She had no idea where to go; the future didn't exist beyond the rasp of each breath and the arch of stone through which she must pass.

All around her, the mass of people moved ever onward – pushing, jostling, laughing and despairing. Behind her she heard the clatter of a carriage and moved over, closer to the shops, still not daring to lift her eyes from the muddy road. Snow was falling steadily now and she welcomed it like sea fog, as somewhere to hide. But its stinging cold bit at her bare fingers and she knew that if she didn't find shelter she might as well have hung from the Tyburn tree for—

She crashed headlong into a soldier. Panicked, she jerked back, arms flailing at the hands trying to grab her. He was strong, pushing her hard against the wall. She screamed. 'No! Don't—'

A hand clapped over her mouth. 'Quiet!'

Chapter Twenty-Six

Trying to slide from the soldier's grasp, Amelia squirmed sideways. But he grabbed her again and slammed her against the wall, holding her there with the hard length of his body. 'Amelia.'

That smoke-scarred voice, the scent of tar and sea salt ...

Her vision cleared and panic receded. There was no soldier's uniform, no musket. An involuntary sob of relief escaped her throat as his hand loosened on her mouth. 'Zach?'

'What the bloody hell are you *doing*?' he hissed, glancing both ways along the street.

'I thought you'd—' She broke off because she didn't rightly know what she'd thought. 'You were gone.'

His gaze slid back to her, though he couldn't meet her eyes. 'Why did you leave the coffee shop? It's only a matter of bloody luck that I saw you at all through the snow and the crowds. Had we missed each other ...'

She was so cold, and his hands on her arms were so warm, she couldn't help but draw nearer, closer to the heat. 'When he found you gone, the owner thought I'd been ... plying my trade. He threw me out.'

A grimace flickered across Zach's face. 'Threw you out?'

'By the hair.'

He was silent, his face immobile but for the slight tensing of his jaw. 'I'm sorry,' he said eventually. 'I was gone longer than I'd intended.'

Her head came to rest against his shoulder, so weary and cold. 'I wouldn't have blamed you for leaving. Run before the storm and the devil take the hindmost. Isn't that your motto?'

A stilted moment followed, stretching too long. He might

have drawn her closer, slid his arms about her in comfort, but he didn't move; the hand that had seized her arm seemed as frozen as the rest of him. 'You ran,' he said at last. 'Got yourself past those bloody soldiers, didn't you?'

Amelia lifted her head and looked back the way she'd come; London Bridge was a hundred yards away or more and the soldiers still guarded its entrance. She'd passed them without even noticing. A smile crept across her face, an unfamiliar stretching of her cold lips. 'So I did.'

'Come then.' He let her go, but gestured along the street with a flourish of his hand. 'Your carriage awaits, Majesty.'

'Carriage?'

Zach shrugged and began walking. 'Farmer's wagon, in fact, but it's heading for Clapham and will keep us out of the snow. He won't notice a couple of stowaways amid the milk churns. We can't hang about, though; he won't tarry long, not tonight.'

'That's why you left me?' she asked as she followed, slip-sliding in the slushy mud. 'To find us transport out of town?'

There was a pause before he said, 'Did you think I'd abandoned you, then? Thrown you over to save my own skin?'

'No. No, of course not.'

He smiled, an ironic twist of his lips. 'I'd rather face the wrath of the Admiralty Court than the wrath of Luc Géroux, that's all. Don't think there's anything I wouldn't do if it were in my own interest.' He gave her an arch look. 'Besides, he's paying me well.'

Amelia made no answer. Partly because she could ill afford to waste her breath and partly because there was a sardonic look in Zach's eye that gave the lie to his words. Whatever his reason for staying, it was not fear of Luc Géroux. Neither was it self-interest.

In her heart, she hoped that it was friendship; warmth of

feeling that could overcome the years and deeds that stood between them. If that could rise from the ashes of Ile Sainte Anne then she would not consider everything lost.

Silently she slipped her hand into his and kept walking.

The wagon sat behind a tavern off Tooley Street, just where Zach had last seen it. The horse was still hitched, its driver on the cut within. Zach could see him through the murky window, half-sprung already, and as loquacious as when he'd spoken with him earlier. Off home to his wife, he was tonight, to partake of the family feast the next day – and fairly flush in the pockets from good trade at the London markets. With luck, he'd not drink it all away before he left for home.

Quietly, Zach led Amelia to the back of the wagon, and lifted the canvas covering the milk churns and empty flour sacks the farmer was taking home. There was just room beneath it for the two of them to lie, hidden from sight and from the snow.

'Quickly now,' he hissed as she crawled beneath the canvas. With a final look around, Zach followed, pulling the cover down firm and plunging them into darkness.

Although he couldn't see Amelia, he could hear her; she was shivering uncontrollably, her breath rattling through her teeth. Making his way towards the sound, his hand touched hers and her breath hitched.

'Shh,' Zach whispered. 'Quiet.'

Awkwardly, he shifted until he lay on his back, the empty sacks providing some sort of comfort for his head. Amelia moved about at his side, very close, until she stretched out next to him and suddenly he could feel her breath against his cheek.

Glad of the darkness, he closed his eyes and tried to ignore the sensation.

She was still shivering, pressing closer, as if starving for his warmth – what little he had left. He'd shared enough bunks to know the advantage of pooling heat in foul weather, and yet it had seemed easier to lie between two unwashed sailors than it did to draw her close and keep her warm. Probably because the sailors hadn't held a knife to his heart, threatening to tear it out and feed it to the bloody sharks.

He sighed and tried to ignore the feel of her body against his, tried instead to remember the look on her face as she'd handed him over to Morton's men. *These are my people*, she'd whispered as they'd closed the irons about his wrists. *I had no choice.*

No choice. It brought a bitter smile to his lips. No choice, indeed.

The sound from the inn suddenly grew louder. A door had opened.

'Zach?' Her voice was breathy in his ear.

Blindly, he reached out and found her hand, squeezing hard in warning. Her fingers were like ice, but she stilled nevertheless.

The wagon rocked as its driver climbed aboard and, a moment later, geed the horse into motion. The wheels began to clatter over the cobbles and Zach allowed himself a smile of relief. He turned his head and whispered, 'By morning, we'll be out of London. And safer.'

'Thank you,' she whispered back, so close he could have tasted her lips had he moved an inch.

Closing his eyes against an obscene wave of desire, he said, 'Sleep now; we'll need to walk again come morning.'

Amelia didn't reply at first, but after a while, in a small voice, she whispered, 'I'm so cold. Too cold to sleep.'

God curse his propensity for doing what was right, but he couldn't lie there and let her freeze. Clamping his jaw shut against a sigh, Zach moved his arm until it encircled her, drawing her into his embrace. She moved willingly, eagerly, to rest her head against his shoulder, slipping her arm across his chest and holding tight. A drowning woman never clung to a raft so tightly.

With a deep sense of foreboding, he drew her close. It was perfect and terrible, a delight and a misery all at once; a dark shadow of a life that might once have been, but was now lost to him forever.

'Thank you,' she whispered against his chest. 'Thank you for coming back.'

He didn't answer, didn't bother to persist in a denial that neither of them believed. Yet perhaps his arms tightened a little, and perhaps his head turned so that his cheek pressed against her hair; perhaps, silently, he vowed he'd not leave her again.

Later, much later, when the rattle of cobblestone had turned to the rumble of a rutted, muddy road, he heard, in the distance, a litany of chimes; behind them, the bells of London Town were ringing in Christmas Day.

Amelia stirred, lifting her head from his chest. 'What ...?'

'Shhh.' His hand found her cheek, gentling her back down against him. 'Midnight is all. Christmas.'

'Christmas ...' She sighed, her breath an unconscious caress against his neck. 'The last time I celebrated Christmas in England, my mother was alive.'

Zach snorted softly. 'Mine too.'

She shifted again, turning so that when she lifted her head she could look at him. All he could see of her in the dark was the glint of her eyes. 'You were born here, then? In England?'

'In Farringdon.'

'Is that in London?'

''Course it bloody is.'

She stiffened, and he couldn't help smiling at her irritation. 'I don't see how I'm supposed to know that. I've visited London a grand total of twice in my whole life.'

'Is that so?' He slipped a hand behind his head so that he might look at her better; he thought he could trace the shape of her cheekbone, pale in the darkness. 'Your father didn't take you to entertainments and such like in town, then?'

'I was little more than an infant when we left, Zach. But I believe we lived in a place called Kent.'

'Never been there.'

'I don't remember much,' she said, without regret. 'I think there was apple blossom in the spring, though. I remember petals falling like snow upon the ground.'

'I remember snow falling like snow upon the ground,' said Zach. 'And a hunger that burned worse than the cold.'

She was silent for a while. Then, 'Is that why you left?'

'Had no reason to stay.'

'No family?'

'Well, my father, as you know, was called to higher duties than providing for his family. My mother and my sister—'

'You have a sister?'

'I *had* a sister. Pretty little thing, used to hang on me like—' He stopped, startled by the sweep of emotion the memory evoked. It had been years since he'd spoken of Kitty and he blinked into the darkness, grateful for its shelter. Clearing his throat, he quietly said, 'She was seven or thereabouts when our father left and she and our mother were sent to the debtor's gaol. I brought them what I could, stole what I could, but … well, there was an outbreak of typhus and it did for them both. So I left, stowed away on the first ship I could find and paid my debts with the topsail. The rest, as they say, is legend.'

'Zach …'

'Me and a hundred thousand others in that stinking hole of a city, Amy. You don't have enough pity to go around.'

She was silent again, lying back down to rest against his chest. After a little, and in an odd voice, she said, 'I don't pity you, Zach.'

'Nor should you,' he agreed. 'Two years out of Billingsgate Wharf I discovered a talent for hazard and won the *Hawk* on the roll of a dice. Captain Hazard was born and he never looked back to that miserable city, not once.'

'Until now.'

'Until now.' He let out a slow breath and closed his eyes. 'Sleep, if you can. Tomorrow will be harder than today.'

She didn't answer, just tightened her arm about his waist and made him wish that this perilous, frozen night would never end.

Chapter Twenty-Seven

Amelia opened her eyes to a soft grey light that seeped through and beneath the canvas. But it was the slowing of the wagon, rather than the dawn, which woke her. Lifting her head, she found Zach already awake and watching her. Silently, he lifted a finger and pressed it to his lips. Then he mouthed, *Time to go.*

She shifted her weight off him, a little conscious that she'd spent the night in his arms. Moving with care, Zach rolled over and made his way to the edge of the wagon, lifting a corner of the canvas. Bright white light lanced through the gap and he dropped it hurriedly.

'I'll go first,' he whispered, 'and help you down, but we've got to hurry.'

Amelia nodded, feeling her blood race in anticipation. She made her way on her belly to the edge of the wagon, praying that her ankle would hold for the drop to the ground. A slight grin played upon his lips before Zach lifted the canvas again, slipping beneath it and out. She didn't hear him land – he'd always moved like a predatory cat – and so she lifted the canvas herself until she could see the road rolling slowly beneath the wagon's wheels. There was snow everywhere, thick and dense. At least it would make for a soft landing.

Trusting to nothing but good luck, she slid from the wagon and dropped to the ground. The snow was crisp and bitter cold; she found herself up to her knees and elbows in it before Zach hauled her to her feet. 'I've seen a flounder make a more graceful landing on deck!' he hissed in her ear, eyes bright with the cold and a humour she'd almost forgotten.

She felt somewhat like a landed fish, and couldn't help smiling at the image. 'Well, I—'

Zach started, eyes fixed over her shoulder. 'Off the road.' Suddenly he was dragging her through a thick, thorny hedgerow, cursing as his clothes and hair caught, but not slowing. Then he was gone, sliding down a steep embankment on the other side of the hedge, and she was following before she had time to call out. They tumbled together, landing in a tangled heap at the bottom of a ditch. Zach's hair was wild, covered in leaves and twigs where he lay, sprawled beneath her. She would have laughed had he not clamped a hand over her mouth. Above, behind the hedge, footsteps crunched in the snow.

Heart racing from the fall, she barely dared to breathe and instead of looking up locked her gaze with Zach's. Tar-black and stark against the snow, his eyes might have said much if only she'd been able to interpret his silences. Her weight lay mostly across his chest, but she dared not move for fear of making a sound. He, though, loosened his hand from her mouth, trailing fingers across her face to cup first her cheek, then her neck, drawing her down until her forehead touched his.

Their breath mingled, white and misty, in the cold air and the only heat in the world existed in the scant distance between them. Discovery was a glance away, yet all she could think of was the last time they'd been so close. Often, over the years, she'd thought of those fleeting seconds of contact. Not of the betrayal, not of the disaster that had followed, but of the way he'd yielded to her so wholly, so willingly. Like a lover.

Now, eyes closed, she could hear his soft breathing and remembered the saltwater taste of his lips, the secret heat his touch had ignited, a heat none since had extinguished, or satisfied. It burned still, deep inside her.

Slowly, imperceptibly, she drew closer until her nose grazed his and—

His breath caught; she froze.

Above them, on the road, the farmer jingled his reins and urged his horse onward. The wagon was moving. Amelia sank back in relief.

'Gone home for the feast, no doubt,' Zach murmured, turning his face away to look up the side of the ditch in which they lay. Looking anywhere but at her. 'We're lucky.'

'Yes,' she whispered, disconcerted and flustered. 'Very.'

Lifting his head, he reached out awkwardly and tugged a twig from her filthy locks. 'You look like you have half of Surrey in your hair, love. I've seen vagabonds better dressed.'

She smiled weakly, rolling off him to sit staring at the trees all about them. 'Appropriate, then, since vagabonds we are.'

Zach stood up and made a vain attempt to dust the snow off his clothes, before extending a hand to Amelia. 'Get up, before you're soaked through.'

Ignoring his hand, her senses too heightened to risk the contact, she scrambled to her feet. 'It's strange,' she said, tugging her thin shawl about her. 'It's so strange ...'

With a frown, Zach lowered his hand. 'World's a strange place, or did you have something particular in mind?'

'This,' she said, looking up at the filigree of snow bedecking the branches. 'Being here, like this.'

'Ah.' He invested the word with a weight of meaning, then turned and said no more. He was studying the steep bank, searching for a way back to the road.

Amelia watched him, trying not to be fascinated by the way his fingers probed the earth in search of purchase. He looked quite different in the cold northern light. No island gold here to gild his skin, and the black of his hair and eyes seemed starker against his cold face. She'd always thought of him as dark, like a rum-soaked night, fire-lit and intoxicating, but here he was black as a winter tree, bleak against a snowy sky. Strong and enduring, but not soft. Not inviting.

'Last time you were in England,' he said, testing his hold on a tree root some inches above his head, 'you were Miss Dauphin and as far from the likes of ... of us as any woman of birth.'

'Yes, I suppose I was.'

Over his shoulder he flashed a snow-bright smile. 'Had we met then, your father would have run me off the road without a backward glance.'

She was silent, not deaf to the hint of accusation in his voice. 'I cannot help who I am,' she said at last. 'Or, rather, who I was.'

'None of us can do that,' he agreed, bringing his hands to his mouth and blowing on them for warmth. Guiltily entranced, Amelia found herself unable to look away. 'My point, however, is that you've never been a beggar in England.'

'Obviously.'

He shrugged, as if the conversation held little interest. 'Sometimes, who we are in one place is not who we are in another, is all. The Pirate Queen of Ile Sainte Anne might find herself a beggar in England and have some difficulty reconciling the two.'

Whatever he might believe, it seemed clear to Amelia that Zach was not talking about her at all. She'd been an infant when they left, and England was but a distant memory that held no weight. Yet to him, this was a place of grief and shadows. Gripping her shawl tight to keep from reaching out, she said, 'And what are you here, Zach?'

A bitter smile curled his lip and he cut her a sly glance. 'Nothing. Nothing at all.'

'No man is nothing.'

'There's a hundred thousand nothings in London Town. Didn't you see them, scurrying beneath your feet? Dying in corners? A whole city of nobodies.'

'Zach—'

'Enough.' He stopped her with a lifted hand. 'Less talking, more walking, unless you're looking for a quick return to the comforts of Newgate.'

With that, he started up the steep embankment with a sailor's nimble grace. Amelia sighed, at her throbbing ankle and the tangling skirts about her feet, but mostly at the emptiness she'd seen in his eyes.

Never had she understood it before, but now it was a truth as clear as the winter sky: Zach Hazard was nothing. In his own eyes, he was nothing more than the legend he'd created, a confection of exaggeration and tall tales stacked like a house of cards. And, ultimately, just as likely to topple.

She was watching him. He'd felt it all morning, since they'd tumbled into the ditch and into each other – a tug in the pit of his stomach whispering of intimacy and desire.

Her lips were not to be trusted any more than his own, but Zach couldn't fathom her intention behind that breathy promise of a kiss. Or why she kept looking at him, slyly, from the corner of her eye when she thought him unaware. Had she known him better she'd have realised that he was never unaware – especially of her.

The short day was swiftly over, the sun dipping to the horizon by mid-afternoon and the chill night hard on its heels. They were somewhere between the village of Clapham and the city of Poole – a wide canvas, indeed, but it was a clear sky and he took some comfort from the hope of glimpsing the stars between the crowding branches of England's forest sea. There'd be a frost though, and he'd seen the effect of that on many a weak and hungry body. They needed a fire, else the dawn would find her blue-lipped and curled like a child who'd never wake again.

He shook off the memory with a toss of his head, flinging back the hair that had come loose from its tie. From the corner of his eye, he could see her shivering, though she never complained – not even of the gnawing hunger he knew they both felt.

Food, shelter and fire.

He stopped and she stopped with him. 'We'll rest now,' he said, glancing into the swiftly darkening forest beside the road.

'So early?'

'Shhhh.' He nodded to the trees, succumbing to a brief smile at her confusion. 'Wood pigeon.'

Her eyes widened – like saucers in her too-thin face – and then she smiled too, hearing the soft coos. 'But how do we …?'

Zach slipped a pistol from his belt with a flourish.

'You're going to shoot it?'

'Well I'm not going to challenge it to a bloody duel, am I? Of course I'm going to shoot it.'

She frowned. 'I mean, won't that … attract attention?'

'The attention of other wood pigeons? Quite possibly. Perhaps a squirrel or two. But unless you hadn't noticed, Miss Dauphin, we are, in fact, in the middle of bloody nowhere and close to bloody starving!' He turned and stalked towards the trees. 'Stay there.'

Maybe his irritation was uncalled for, but he was hungry and, in truth, had no idea how to shoot a wood pigeon, or any other woodland creature. He'd gone direct from the streets of London to the ocean, stopping nowhere in between. Nevertheless, needs must as the devil drives, and so forth.

It took him several attempts, and had there been any of His Majesty's finest in the vicinity they'd have swiftly been on their way to put down the bloody revolt that seemed to have broken out in the woods, but by the time the gloom obscured his vision, Zach had a couple of pigeons and something that might have been a pheasant dangling from his hand.

'Supper,' he announced triumphantly as he returned to the road.

Amelia smiled, and prodded with her toe at a pile of dry wood. 'And a fire.'

There was a moment then when he couldn't help but smile, and her smile broadened in response, touching her eyes like starlight, and he— He looked away. 'We should get far off the road, so the fire's not seen.'

She laughed. 'Do you think there's anyone within ten miles who didn't hear—?'

'Do you want to eat or not?'

Without answering, she stooped and picked up the armful of tinder she'd found. 'Carry on, Captain.'

The sun had disappeared entirely now and night was upon them. They found a small clearing, sheltered from the road by a stand of evergreens, and swiftly built a fire. There was no snow on such sheltered ground, and the dry sticks Amelia had managed to find caught with the aid of pine needle kindling. Bright flames soon licked the darkness as the wood hissed and crackled, sending up sparks into the night.

Despite his inexperience as a hunter-gatherer, Zach managed to pluck and gut the birds with little difficulty. He washed his hands in the snow and then took his flask from his pocket, swallowing a mouthful of rum, while Amelia set the meat to roasting. The mouth-watering aroma of food quickly joined the pine scent of the smoke, and he had to distract himself from his eagerness to eat by hacking down branches of fir tree to make a shelter.

Amelia watched him from the other side of the fire. Its golden light lent some semblance of health to her face and reminded him, too painfully, of the woman – the girl – who had pilfered his heart so many years ago, around another fire. She was different now, more burdened, more beautiful, but just as unreachable.

Zach had often wondered whether, had he taken her that night, she would still be his, or whether she'd have shot him in the morning and run, sobbing, into her father's arms. In truth, he thought the shooting more likely than the sobbing. But sometimes, when he felt most alone, he thought it might have been worth the price to burn bright and die a swift death, like the sparks that perished on their way to the stars. He'd have saved himself a world of regret at the very least.

'They're ready, I think.'

She was crouched by the fire, prodding at the birds with a stick, and he came to sit by her side. They ate without talking, too intent on stripping every shred of meat from every tiny bone, until there was none left. Dropping the last bones into the fire, Zach sucked the juices from his fingers, eager for every drop.

'I almost feel—' Amelia broke off when she saw what he was doing, staring at him oddly. 'Um ...' She looked hurriedly away, pulling her knees up to her chest. 'Full. I almost feel full.'

He watched her as he continued to lick his fingers. 'A Christmas feast, eh? More than you've eaten in a while, by the look of you.'

'Yes.' She wrapped her arms about her knees and made a brave attempt at a smile. 'My father always said I was nothing but skin and bone.'

Zach picked up a stick and poked at the fire, sending a cloud of sparks up to their deaths. 'I like a girl with a little softness to her, myself,' he said, watching the flames dance. 'Something to get a hold of, if you know what I mean.'

He sensed her stiffen. 'That's hardly a detail I need to—'

'Come, come now, Amy. We've no secrets, you and I.' He flicked her a look, but she too was staring into the fire. 'You, for example, have a preference for respectable men.'

'For good men, yes.'

'But a good man is not always an honest man and I think, Amy, that none but an honourable man would suit you.'

Her lips twisted into a sad smile and she turned her head, resting it against her knees as she looked at him. 'That would depend on one's definition of honour. Your father, Zach, was an honourable man, in his way.'

'Overton? He was as black-hearted a sinner as any man and cunning too.' Scowling, he poked hard into the fire and watched as the flaming log at its heart began to crack, crumbling in on itself. If the old bastard had laid a hand on her ... Through gritted teeth he said, 'Charmed you too, did he?'

Amelia sat up straight and glared at him. 'Not into his bed, if that's your insinuation.'

'Wouldn't put it past him.'

'Or me, it would seem.'

Her eyes blazed and her irritation irked him. 'I'll leave the defence of my father's honour in your hands then,' he said, rising to his feet. 'You and he certainly thought alike when it came to the honour of self-preservation – saving your own skin was a virtue highly prized in your little paradise.'

'Prized by you too, Zach. Where were you when Sainte Anne burned?'

There was pain in her words, for both of them, and Zach's mouth twisted into an impostor of a smile. 'Once bitten, Amy. Did you think I'd come back and risk you trading my life for a second time?'

Large eyes looked up at him, luminous in the firelight. 'One life for three hundred – would you have made a different choice?'

'The calculation matters little when the rope tightens about your neck.' It was a hard thing to say – he knew it – but there were times when he still woke at night, choking and terrified and always, always, the sight before his eyes was Géroux pulling her into his embrace. Turning her away from him.

Stung, Amelia stared into the fire. 'Then I'm not forgiven?'

'What's to forgive?' He sighed, trying to shake free of the old anger. 'You did what you could to protect those you loved. How can I blame you for that?'

Silence fell, heavy with everything that remained unsaid. Zach scuffed his boots through the dirt and dug his hands deep into his pockets; the temperature was dropping, a frost was on its way. 'I'm just going to …' He nodded towards the trees. 'Build up the fire; then we'd better bed down for the night. Stay warm.'

Amelia nodded, but didn't look at him as she threw more wood onto the flames. By the time he returned, the blaze was high and she stood with her hands held over it. He watched her from the shadows, tracing the elegant bones in her face, the willowy length of her limbs, and felt his blood quicken despite the cold. With a sigh, he stamped out any such thoughts and returned to the circle of firelight.

A bed of pine was better than the damp ground, two or three branches braced over them trapping what little heat they had to spare. The mouth of their shelter faced the fire and Zach crawled in first, rolling onto his side and inviting her with a look to follow. With obvious trepidation, she crept into the bower beside him.

'Turn so you face the fire,' he told her quietly, closing his eyes so that he didn't need to see the sharp curve of her hip, the flash of bare skin at her shoulder. It didn't help much; he could still feel her moving, coming to rest a breath away from where he lay. When, eventually, he opened his eyes again he found himself gazing at the fall of her hair, at the glimmer of firelight on the pale skin of her collarbone. She was shivering.

Zach took a deep breath and reached down to unbutton

his heavy coat. He inched closer until he was pressed flush against her back, wrapping her against him, inside his coat. 'I'd do the same if I were stuck here with Brookes,' he whispered close to her ear.

Something that might have been a sigh escaped her lips, but she burrowed back against him nonetheless, her fingers entwining with his and holding his arm tight around her. 'Needs must.'

'Aye,' he murmured against her hair, too conscious of the slight swell of her breast beneath his arm to say more. So he just listened: to the rustle of the wind in the trees, to the scurrying of the night creatures and to the rise and fall of her breathing. When, at last, she lay heavy and sleeping in his arms he turned his head to press a forbidden kiss against her hair, drawing her closer into his embrace and – for a moment – allowing himself to feel all that he kept so well guarded.

He thought he might die from the pain of it.

Chapter Twenty-Eight

It was still dark when Amelia awoke; dawn approached but wasn't close enough to ease the gloom. The air was bitter cold and the fire had dwindled to embers that glowed softly beneath a blanket of grey ash. She should, she supposed, get up and stir the fire into life, but she was loath to move.

Zach was sleeping. She doubted he'd been asleep long and didn't want to wake him yet. His breath stirred the hair at the nape of her neck, steady as the rhythm of the sea, and the arm he'd draped around her was heavy and relaxed. He was warm, too, a comforting heat that penetrated deeper than that of any fire, and for a moment she allowed herself to imagine a life where she woke like this every morning – not buried beneath leaves and branches, but in a soft bed with his arms about her.

Fantasy, she knew, a dream built on a fiction. For what did she really know of Zach Hazard? They'd spent but a few days together, all in all, their relationship riddled with conflict, mistrust and betrayal. Yet, in the years since they'd last met, she'd grown convinced that he held her heart in his hands, in his eyes, in those secret depths no one else seemed to notice. She felt a connection to him so fundamental that she'd only understood it after he was gone. Luc had won her hand with good sense and prudence, with the promise of a future for her people, but in Zach's arms lay the fathomless comfort of a kindred soul.

It was all for nothing now, though. He might have spoken of forgiveness in the gaol, but last night she'd seen anger beating like a storm behind his eyes. If he'd ever felt anything for her, it had died that night atop Black Church Rock, when she'd handed him to Lord Morton in chains, trading his freedom for the survival of Ile Sainte Anne. Only a saint could have forgiven that betrayal, but Zach Hazard was no saint and Amelia felt his resentment in every barbed comment that left his lips.

The sun, she realised, must be close to the tree-shrouded horizon, for she could see his hand now, entwined with hers, laying close to her lips. Tanned and tar-stained, it was a sailor's hand, strong and capable. Yet she remembered those long fingers dipping into his purse and doling out silver to the packs of smut-faced children scurrying through the streets of the city, ragged shades of his own childhood spent scavenging amid the refuse of London. It almost broke her heart.

Turning to look at him, she caught the moment of his waking: heavy eyes blinking, mouth curling towards a smile that became a yawn. 'You snore like a bloody horse, woman.'

'I do not!'

He smiled again and rolled onto his back. She regretted the loss of his arm about her waist, flung now above his head, but resisted the temptation to curl up against him again. Instead, she too turned onto her back, stretched out the cramped muscles of her legs, and gazed through their bower into a sky paling from black to indigo. 'Fresh bread,' she sighed, 'and coffee, with milk and lots of sugar.'

'Mangos,' Zach suggested. 'And rum. Oh!' Awkwardly, he reached into his coat pocket and pulled out a small flask, unstopping it and taking a swallow, before passing it over. 'For a little warmth.'

The flask was light, almost empty, and she took a small sip before passing it back. Rum burned in her throat, rough and ready, reminding her of home.

'I've had a thought,' Zach said, returning the flask to his pocket. 'Considering that you're half lame and I'm too old to be tramping about in the snow, it seems like this might be an opportune moment to indulge in a little land piracy and commandeer ourselves some sort of vehicle.'

Amelia propped herself up on her elbow so that she could see him more clearly. 'Where are we likely to find a carriage in these woods, Zach?'

His smile was a crafty glint of ivory. 'Trundling along the road, where else? Is this not the season for fops and dandies to be traipsing about the countryside, feasting with friends?'

'Are you suggesting we—?' She smiled, her heart racing at the prospect, and for a moment it was as if she stood at the helm of the *Sunlight* once more, the world and all its possibilities spread out for the taking. 'Zachary Hazard, are you suggesting highway robbery?'

'Consider it a little Christmas amusement.' He grinned, eyes alight. 'I've always wanted to yell "stand and deliver".'

There was a ploy Amelia had often used aboard the *Sunlight*, which involved dragging barrels behind her on long warps, to give the appearance of an unsteady merchantman wallowing through the waves. It made her seem harmless to passing trade, allowing her to stalk her prey in full sight, and when they were board-a-board the crew would raise the black flag and terrorise the hapless victims with bloodcurdling screams and a vicious display of blade and musket. As a result, her crew rarely needed to fire a shot before the terrified merchants surrendered their cargo.

Amelia thought of that ploy as she lay sprawled on the frozen mud, one of Zach's pistols pressed between her rapidly beating heart and the road. She, not her ship, was the harmless bait this time.

Zach was somewhere aloft. He'd scaled a large oak a little upstream from where she lay, and was perched precariously on a branch that stretched out over the road.

Through the ground, she could feel the drub-drub of hooves, the rattle of carriage wheels. Their quarry approached and she prayed they would see her in time to stop. Eyes closed, she listened as the resonance beneath her cheek became a sound and in the distance a horse whinnied and a man's voice called, 'Whoa, there.'

The hoof beats slowed, reins jingled, and the carriage came to a stop some distance away. There was a muttered curse and the sound of someone climbing down, booted feet thudding to the ground.

'Sanders? What the deuce is going on?' The accent was sharp as cut glass. 'Why have we stopped?'

'There's summat in the road, sir.'

'What sort of—? Oh.' There was a pause and Amelia imagined the man's nose wrinkling in distaste. 'Looks like a beggar woman.'

'Aye, sir. Don't look in good shape neither. I'll just see what's—'

'Just move her out of the way, Sanders. We're already half an hour behind and it will not do to keep Lord George waiting. He does not tolerate unpunctuality.'

There was a telling pause. Then, 'I'll see if the wretch needs me help, sir.' The man's compassion made Amelia regret what she must do next, but these were desperate times. Footsteps approached, heavy and solid, and she could paint a picture of the coachman with those scant details alone: an honest yeoman of good sense.

'Miss?' he called, from some distance away.

She gave no answer, breathing so lightly her chest did not move. Her finger tightened on the trigger of her cocked pistol.

'Miss, can you hear me?'

'Just put her to the side of the road, man! She's probably dead, or soon will be.'

The coachman ignored his master, drawing closer and coming to crouch next to Amelia – just where she wanted him. 'Miss?' He shook her arm gently. 'Miss, can you—?'

Before the man could draw breath her pistol was pressed

beneath his jaw. 'My apologies, sir,' she said, 'but I'm in need of your coach.'

Eyes wide, he lifted his arms and together they rose to their feet. 'I have a wife,' he said, 'and three daughters, depending on me. I beg you—'

'Do as you're told,' Amelia said, 'and you'll come to no harm.'

From the coach there came a sudden thud. 'What the dickens? Sanders—?'

Amelia glanced up and grinned. Zach had landed on the roof, picking up the coachman's musket and emptying it of powder. 'Good morning, sir,' he called. 'A merry, jovial and seasonable Christmas to you all.'

From the window of the carriage, a pasty-faced gent in a powdered wig was staring in horror as Zach slipped down from the carriage roof, pistol in hand, and ran his fingers possessively over the coach's polished wood.

'I carry nothing of value!' the fop squeaked.

'I'll be the judge of that, sir.' Zach waved his pistol vaguely at the window. 'Out you get then. Chop-chop, I've not got all day.'

Carefully, the carriage door opened and out crept a young man, tubby about the waist, with a fleshy, weak-chinned face. He was dressed in festive finery of brocade and silk, and trod charily into the mud with his red-heeled, buckled shoes. 'I'll have you hunted down and shot for this outrage!'

'Not if I shoot you first,' Zach smiled. Then he peered into the carriage. 'You too, milady.'

A quaking woman, a little older than the man, also stepped out. She was dressed in a thick wool cloak that Amelia immediately coveted; her ample curves instantly – and predictably – attracted Zach's attention. 'What have we here?' he asked, slipping the tip of his pistol beneath her cloak and lifting it back, over her shoulder, to reveal a generous décolletage – decorated with a rather fine necklace.

The woman lifted her head, eyes bright with defiance and ... Something else. Excitement, perhaps?

A shameless smile curled Zach's lips and he ran his fingertip, grimy against the woman's pale skin, along the length of the necklace to where it dipped between her breasts. 'Very pretty, indeed.'

Amelia found herself breathing hard, a knot of something unpleasant in her throat. 'We only want the coach,' she hissed at him.

Zach ignored her, his slow gaze drifting to the man who stood pale with rage at the woman's side. 'Now what is it I'm supposed to say? Your money or your wife?' Zach leaned a little closer, his whisper clearly audible. 'I think I'd prefer the wife. She looks ripe for the plucking. Not been neglecting her, have you?'

'If you lay a hand on my wife, I'll —'

'No, Richard, don't do anything rash!' the woman exclaimed. 'I can endure.'

'There'll be no need for endurance, milady, I can assure you of that.' Zach's grin was wicked as he nodded towards the clasp holding the cloak in place. 'Take it off.'

With trembling fingers, the woman did as she was bid and the cloak fell to the ground. Her chest was rising and falling fast, and Amelia doubted her agitation was entirely the effect of terror. 'Do with me what you will, but do not harm my husband, I beg you.'

With a roll of her eyes, Amelia looked away and found her attention caught by the husband. He was watching the proceedings with an intense kind of rage. No, it was more than rage. It was something darker and better hidden – something more like envy. With shaking fingers, he reached beneath his coat and pulled out a small ivory-handled pistol, aiming it directly at Zach's head.

'Drop it, or die where you stand!' Amelia aimed her gun steadily at the man's heart.

Everyone froze. After a moment Zach turned his head towards his assailant, eyebrows lifting in surprise. 'Ah.'

'Richard!' the wife exclaimed. 'Don't be a fool!'

Hands shaking, his face flushed, the man – Richard – hissed, 'Unhand my wife, you hell-featured scoundrel!'

In two steps Amelia was at his side, her pistol pressed to his head. 'I said, drop your weapon.'

Zach smiled, sauntering closer and running his finger along the barrel of the man's gun. 'Sir, I'd be ashamed to draw such a very small, inadequate pistol on another man.'

Richard's eyes narrowed, face burning. 'It can still kill you.'

'Yes, but I have something much better suited to the task, both in breadth and length as well as *power*. Blast a bloody hole in anything, it can.' He pressed closer and Amelia's eyes went wide as she realised what he was doing. Leaning in, Zach whispered in the man's ear. 'Is that how you like it?'

Richard's voice was hoarse, hand shaking violently. 'You disgust me.'

'Do I?' Zach closed his fingers lasciviously around the pistol, giving it a suggestive caress. Then his wrist twisted, snapping the gun from the man's hand and dropping it to the ground, crushing the barrel beneath his heel. In the same movement he grabbed Richard's brocade coat and hauled him off balance, sending him stumbling face first against the coach. Zach pressed in behind him, holding him in place with the length of his body. A knife appeared in his hand, hard against the man's throat. '*I* disgust *you*? You, who would ride on while she died by the side of the road? You, who would stuff your face with meat while a thousand others starve at your door? No, sir, *you* disgust *me*.'

Torn between horror and fascination, Amelia watched as Zach ground his hips forward, driving a mewl from deep in the man's throat. She found her breath coming more quickly, a curling heat building in the pit of her stomach.

'Sorry,' Zach whispered, so close his lips must have brushed the other man's ear. 'I have neither the time nor the inclination to give such a lobcock what he wants.' Amelia felt her cheeks heat as Zach slowly reached around the man's waist and did something that made Richard gasp sharply. 'But I hope the *need* of it drives you to Bedlam, you dissolute son of a whore.'

With that Zach let go, leaving the man dishevelled and shocked, his wife scarcely less so. Zach swept her a bow, 'Madam, I'm sorry to disappoint, although with this molly for a husband you're no doubt accustomed to frustration. Yet you'll be able to brag to your friends that Captain— Ouch!'

Amelia kicked him and glared a warning. 'Mr *Brookes*? I think we have what we need.'

'Ah, yes. Yet not quite.' He stooped to pick up the woman's thick cloak from the ground and tossed it to Amelia. Then, to the coachman he said, 'Start walking now and you'll reach Clapham before dusk.' To Amelia's astonishment, he tossed the driver a coin. 'You're a good man, sir. My apologies for the trouble.'

He lifted his pistol again and kept it trained on the three travellers. 'Madame Géroux? I trust you know how to pilot one of these bloody things?'

Amelia smiled, although his use of that name disturbed her troubled spirits. 'I do,' she said, swinging up onto the coachbox and taking the reins. The horses looked fit and well; the coach, light and new. They would make good time. She geed the horses forward.

As they began to move off, Zach jumped neatly onto the footboard, his pistol still trained on the carriage's previous owners. 'Gentlemen! I take my leave.'

With that Amelia flicked the reins hard, urging the horses into a gallop.

They travelled without much conversation for most of the

day. Bundled in her newly acquired wool cloak, Amelia kept the reins and gazed ahead with fixed determination. At her side, Zach lounged against the seat and watched her.

He'd seen fire in her eyes that morning, the bright spirit that had lured him like a will-o'-the-wisp to his doom. It stirred his desire – a desire that had never been extinguished but could never be sated. It was a damned curse, to be sure.

Yet he couldn't look away, captivated by the reality of a face he'd pictured so often in the past four years. She frowned, thoughts flitting through her eyes, and he was just wondering what had her so vexed when she spoke and answered the question herself.

'That woman, Zach, in the carriage ...?'

'What of her?'

'Would you have really ...?' She looked uncomfortable. 'Would you have really taken her virtue? Right there?'

He smiled, admiring the pretty flush on her cheek. 'Her virtue? Little of that on display, was there not?' He sat forward and studied her more closely. 'Disapprove of my tactics, do you?'

Amelia was silent, her lips in a tight line. 'I don't—' She shot him a quick glance, then turned back to the road. 'Is there nothing you won't do to obtain your own advantage, Zach?'

He didn't answer, sprawling back in the seat again and resting a foot on the edge of the coachbox. 'Why is it of any interest to you?'

A faint smile touched her lips. 'Curiosity.'

'Curiosity's a dangerous thing, Amy. Are you sure you want to know the answer?'

'Why else would I ask?' She smiled, faintly regretful, but didn't repeat the question, or press him for an answer.

For a while longer he watched her, watched the black bones of the winter trees pass them by, and eventually he said, 'There is one thing I won't do, if you recall. I won't trade in other men's lives, not even to save my own. But beyond that I'll take any advantage I can find.'

She was silent, her hands still on the reins as she gazed along the road. 'I had heard that about you, on the island.'

'I wager you did.'

'I hear so many things about you, Zach. I don't know which to believe.'

'Believe them all, Amy. The worse, the better.'

She shook her head. 'No. I saw through the legend of Zachary Hazard a long time ago. It's the man that interests me now.'

For a moment her eyes held his, ardent with a meaning he didn't dare grasp, and then she looked away with a rueful smile. 'It's funny ... You bed any woman you choose and are made a legend from Ile Sainte Anne to Nassau Port, but when I take a lover to my bed I'm made a whore in the eyes of all the world.'

'You— What?'

She glanced at him, a glimmer of amusement in her eyes. 'Well then, now I've shocked you.'

'No, I—' Yet he felt an unwarranted blaze of anger in the pit of his stomach. 'A lover? And what of your husband? What of Luc?'

Amelia looked back out at the road. 'Luc has secrets, dark matters he will not share, and business that takes him far from the island.'

'That, I can believe.'

'He's a good man, but his heart is not easily touched, and he didn't begrudge me the comfort of another's arms while he was gone.' She glanced at him, measuring his response. 'No more than I begrudged him the same. It is an honest marriage, at least.'

The world might not have stopped turning, but Zach's mind was spinning as though he'd drunk a quart of rum in one swallow. The very axis of his world, it seemed, was balanced on the fact that her duty came before the desires of her heart. 'I thought,' he said, steadying his voice against a surge of feeling, 'that you had neither time nor inclination for such foolishness as love.'

Brittle, defensive, she flicked the reins and urged the tired horses faster. 'I did not think we were talking of love.'

Zach shifted where he sat, suddenly aware of the gnawing hunger in his belly, irritable and unwilling to examine the cause. 'So who is it then, this lover of yours? Or do you, perhaps, have a harem?'

'You're angry.'

'Why should I be angry?' He sat forward, fingers knotting together. 'It's not like I've risked my bloody life coming here to return you to your husband, only to find you've a dozen lovers who could have—'

'Oh I see! So it's perfectly acceptable for you to go knocking your way around the world, but if I dare to take one night's comfort in another man's arms—'

'*I'm* not married!'

She stared at him for a long moment. Then laughed – laughed so hard he thought she might fall from the coachbox entirely. 'Oh, Zach,' she said eventually, wiping her eyes with the back of one hand. 'Of all the preposterous ... How many women have you swived beneath the notice of their husbands?'

He folded his arms, though could do little about the laughter he knew must show in his eyes. 'That's not the point.'

'Leave the moral instruction to the parson in the pulpit, Zach – he's better suited to hypocrisy.'

He didn't answer, staring out along the road as his humour swiftly faded. It was growing darker already, the short day coming to a hasty conclusion; they would need to consider where to sleep. The sky was heavy with snow and Zach had little desire to spend the night shivering beneath the trees again. Up ahead he could see a small cluster of buildings and wondered if it were a farm. If so—

'There have been two,' Amelia said, distracting him entirely from his sober thoughts. 'Since Luc, there have been two others.' With no idea what to say, Zach held his tongue and Amelia continued more softly. 'Both visitors to the island, both ... Perhaps it makes it worse, but there was no love in either case.' She sighed, suddenly weary. 'For who would dare to love the Pirate Queen of Ile Sainte Anne?'

'Only a fool.'

She looked at him, hurt bright in her eyes.

'For only a fool would love where love's not wanted.'

With a sigh she pulled her cloak closer against the cold air. 'And you know that I could never love a fool.'

'That I know all too well.' Before she could answer, he lifted his hand and pointed. 'Look there, a farm. We'll find a hayloft or some such for the night and get out of this bloody cold.'

The hayloft was small, but warmer than Amelia had imagined, especially when she buried herself deep in the fragrant straw, wrapped tight in her new wool cloak.

Below, she could see the coach's two horses munching on oats. She'd insisted they bring them in, despite Zach's dire warnings about the noise and the risk of discovery. Fugitive she may be, but she'd not allow the animals to freeze to death on her account.

However, it was not the horses that chiefly occupied her thoughts. Rather, it was the small door through which Zach had disappeared some time ago. How long ago, she was uncertain, but she was sure it must be at least an hour. He'd gone in search of food, and for that she was grateful. Yet ever since she'd confessed her ... liaisons, he'd been acting strangely. Prickly. How he'd imagined she'd been living these past four years, she knew not, but she'd not been born for a cloistered life and could not live as though she were.

After her father's death, she and Luc had married quickly, at his insistence. The wife of Luc Géroux, he'd promised, would be shielded from Morton's malign attention. But Luc could not linger on Ile Sainte Anne in the years that followed. His own business – dark and shadowy, never spoken of – had kept him from the island for months at a time. When he did return, he'd been distant, haunted and had little time for Amelia. In truth she'd had little time for him either, or for anything beyond working to hold her community together, and once she'd come to understand her own heart there'd been only one man in the world whom she'd wanted. The one man who could never forgive her. She'd not understood it at the time, but when she'd traded Zach for the safety of Ile Sainte Anne she'd thrown all hope of happiness into the bargain.

Below, a door creaked open and the man himself stepped through. His coat was dusted about the shoulders with powdery snow and in his hand he held a full sack. Giving the horses a wide berth, he made his way to the ladder and hurried up to the loft. Lamplight cast his face in shadows, but the ivory glint of a smile told her he'd been successful.

'Bloody freezing,' he whispered as he dropped into the hay at her side.

'What did you find?' Amelia's eyes were rooted to the bulging sack; she was so hungry she could have eaten the hemp itself. 'Bread?'

'Something better,' he said with a smile. 'I found an obliging serving girl.'

She flicked him a confused look. 'What?'

With a flourish, he tipped out the content of his sack: bread, apples, something with the look of cold meat wrapped in cloth. A veritable feast! 'And this,' he said, pulling from his coat pocket a somewhat shrivelled orange. 'A little taste of home.'

Amelia picked up the bread and tore it in two, handing half to Zach and biting a hunk from her own. 'Dare I ask,' she said with her mouth full, 'why she was so obliging?'

Zach smiled, impudent and irresistible with his loose hair falling into his eyes. 'Friendly persuasion.'

With a sigh, she picked up an apple and took a bite. It was cold and sweet, and, oh, so delicious. 'Zach Hazard, you're incorrigible.'

'No,' he corrected, lounging back on one elbow and waving at his hair and clothes. 'I'm incognito.'

She smiled and thought how much, just then, she would have liked to brush the hair from his eyes and to kiss him – had the world been a different place, had they lived different lives. As it was, she could only say, 'I'm glad you're here.'

To her surprise he nodded. 'Me too, Amy. Me too.'

Chapter Twenty-Nine

They settled for the night as they had the night before, curled together for warmth, her cloak now covering them both. With her belly full and the straw warm and sweet, Amelia found herself drifting happily on the cusp of sleep with no inclination to fall deeper into oblivion.

Zach slept though, his breathing deep and even at her back. Or so she thought until he spoke softly in her ear. 'Will you go back there, then? To Sainte Anne?'

'I've nowhere else.' With a sigh, she rolled over so that she could see him. The lamps still burned below, their flickering light reflecting in his eyes and on the sharp angles of his face.

'They'll come for you again,' he said. 'The island was only safe while it was secret.'

Amelia sighed; she'd been wrestling with this herself. 'You think I should rebuild elsewhere, then? The Caribbean perhaps? Madagascar, as of old?'

'Not the Caribbean. Much too dangerous.' He was silent then, watching her thoughtfully. 'Have you considered *not* rebuilding?'

'Never. The Articles must be preserved, Zach. They're worth more than my life – more than any of our lives.'

'Are they?'

'Your father and mine—'

'Didn't write them.'

She stared at him. 'What?'

'The Articles of Agreement were written elsewhere, in another time, and by another's hand. At least, those bits most worth preserving.' His smile was a mere sardonic curl of his lips. 'Pirates, Amy. They'll steal anything.'

Amelia propped herself up on her elbow. 'Zach – what are you talking about?'

He considered her for a moment, and then said, 'What do you know of that great conflagration between the King and his Parliament?'

'As much as anyone, I suppose. The King lost his head to Cromwell, he in turn found himself corrupted by power and, upon his death, the country would have fallen into anarchy had Charles not restored the monarchy.'

'Very good, Miss Dauphin. Perfect schoolroom knowledge indeed.' A little amusement danced across his face. 'Come, come now, don't you know the history of your own people?'

'Of England?'

'Of pirates.' He smiled again. 'Now then, Cromwell was a joyless old sod, to be sure. A right tedious bore, so they say. He had no time for wine, women nor song, and banned the festive season out of hand. Almost as dull as those grindingly dreary folk over in the northern colonies. All work and no play, as they say.'

'What on Earth does this—?'

'Ah!' He held up a hand to stop her. 'Now, among his men were those who thought more deeply than the crime of a man dancing a jig or wearing buckles on his shoes. Ended in the Tower, most of them, for their talk of freedom. But one man ... One man who served in Cromwell's army went by the name of Overton.'

Startled, Amelia sat up. 'Your father?'

'*His* father.' Zach's grin grew devilish. 'Captain Overton may have sold his soul to the devil, Amy, but he's not that bloody old.'

'Your grandfather fought with Cromwell?'

'Aye, and when it became clear that the Lord Protector would have nothing to do with the ideals for which he'd been fighting, old Overton took steps to preserve those ideals before he lost his head. Sent his son on the first ship he could find to the new world, and with him went certain writings and so forth that made the bones of the Articles.' He slumped onto his back, chewing on the end of a piece of straw. 'Somewhere on the crossing his ship was boarded by pirates – my father met yours, and I imagine the rest of the story you already know.'

Amelia nodded. 'I learned it at my father's knee – how they sought to build a haven for those who would live free, based on the Articles of Agreement. *For the poorest man that is upon the Earth has a life to live, as the greatest man.* They died for that principle, Zach. How can I stop fighting for it now?'

'Because men tore this bloody country apart over it, Amy. And then what?' He looked at her, all humour fleeing. 'Then nothing. Then more war, more fighting and nothing bloody changes, Amy. They killed a king! And for what? To see another, by another name, rise in his place. And after him, the son of the first. And so it goes on, and on and on, forever.'

'So we should just give up?'

He gazed up into the dark rafters of the barn, chewing lazily on the straw. 'You did what you could, Amy. Perhaps it's for others to fight on; perhaps it's for another time and another place.'

'You don't believe that.'

'Don't I?'

'I remember—' She smiled at the memory, shaking her head at her own regrets. 'Sometimes we would sit upon the beach at dawn, you and I, speaking of freedom and what it meant. Do you remember?'

He nodded, not looking at her. 'I remember.'

Closing her eyes, she pictured him then, younger by four years and golden in the sunrise. Beautiful. He'd asked her to sail with him, begged her to shake off the chains that bound her to her father and Ile Sainte Anne, and to seek the freedom of the open seas. She'd refused, of course, and bound herself instead to Luc Géroux and his hopes for a different kind of freedom. Hopes that had ended in fire and ash.

She opened her eyes, shivering in the cold reality of this English winter. 'You told me once that the sea was your freedom. You said you'd trade your life for it.'

'For *my* freedom.' He turned his head and she wasn't sure if the glint in his eyes was laughter or anger. '*That* I'll never trade for less than my life, but I see no reason to die for the freedom of men who'd as soon live as slaves. Let them fight for it themselves, I say.'

'Then what am I to do?'

'What I've always told you to do.' He looked away, up into the rafters. 'Run, Amy. Run before the storm and the devil take the hindmost.'

She woke later in silence and darkness. For a moment she was back in Newgate, death crouching in the shadows, and only fear kept her from crying out. Then she felt the prickle of straw beneath her hand, caught the sweet scent of hay, and felt the heavy weight of a man's arm around her waist.

Zach.

In the dark she could make out the lines of the stable door, glimpsed moonlight glittering on snow beyond. Cold, bitter England. She was far from home.

And yet ...

Zach was there. He lay close behind her, still and silent. Reassuring. Her eyes drifted shut as she let herself remember the taste of him, the lightning heat of her lips against his. Never had she felt anything like it, before or since. And she ached for it now, in the soft, slow blackness that surrounded them. She ached for him.

If she turned her head, if she brushed her lips against his, would he recoil? Or was there some part of him that still felt the connection between them, that remembered the heat of that fatal kiss?

It had been night-time, like this, though warm beneath a slim moon. She remembered watching the play of moonlight across Zach's shoulders, pale against the dark linen of his shirt. She remembered his face sculpted by shadows, beautiful, stealing her breath. In his eyes she'd seen the stars and something more, something dark she'd not understood until much later.

She'd kissed him then, swept away, passionate as a summer storm.

Then the soldiers had come.

Yet the kiss had lingered. She could taste it even now, and she yearned for it. For him. Cautiously, she turned her head and found him watching her, silver moonlight gleaming in his eyes.

'I wasn't—' He took his arm from about her waist. 'I didn't mean to wake you.'

'You didn't.'

'Ah. Then, good.'

They were silent a moment, strangely awkward, vividly awake. Surely here, she thought, in this quiet darkness, he could forgive her at last? She risked a hand on his cheek; he closed his eyes as if it hurt. 'Zach, I want to—'

'No.' He turned away from her, rolling onto his back. 'Sleep, Amy. I'm too tired for more talk.'

She was silent, hurt by his sharpness, hurt by what it meant.

'I'm sorry,' she murmured into the darkness, and hoped the apology would cover her multitude of sins. But she knew it wasn't enough; she knew he would never forgive her.

Zach woke her later with a hand held firmly over her mouth. She started back and his eyes flared in warning, one finger pressed to his lips. Daylight streamed into the barn as Zach nodded towards the edge of the hayloft, at the stable below, and slowly released his hold on her.

'Zachary?' A woman's voice drifted up and Amelia froze.

236

'Zachary Brookes, don't be silly. I know you're here 'cause I see your horses, don't I?'

Amelia's eyes widened and Zach shrugged.

'Come now, my love, I've some breakfast for you.'

Zach leaned closer, his breath hot in her ear as he whispered, 'She can't know you're here.'

Amelia mouthed, *I'll hide.*

But Zach shook his head. 'Too risky. Give me a few minutes, then run. I'll distract her and meet you where the road crosses the farm track.'

He moved to go, but she caught his sleeve. *Will you be safe?*

A trace of a smile flickered across his lips and he nodded. Then, snatching up his coat and weapons, he vaulted over the edge of the hayloft and made the girl below squeal in delight at his entrance.

For a while Amelia lay there, not daring to move, while Zach's voice rumbled softly below. From time to time, the girl giggled, and then, after a while, all fell silent.

Tentatively, Amelia moved. She tugged her cloak about her and made her way as silently as possible to the top of the ladder. There she paused, ears straining to hear—

'Oh ...! Oh, Zachary ...'

Her breath caught oddly, then tightened in her chest. Surely not. Surely he wasn't—? Heart racing, Amelia crept down the ladder until her feet touched the stable floor. Beneath the overhanging loft sat a wagon half filled with hay. She couldn't see what was happening behind it, but from the sound of the girl's laughter she could guess. Amelia found herself unable to move, unable to draw breath. Her eyes misted oddly until she blinked hard, the movement summoning a gasp that scratched her throat and echoed in the silent barn.

And then she ran.

She ran out into the frigid embrace of the morning, through slush and mud, welcoming the ice against her scalding cheeks, demanding that the frost in her lungs douse the deeper heat, the ache of desire that would not be quenched.

She ran until she could run no longer and then she stopped, gasping for air, and enraged at herself, at him, at the world. Had she the energy, she'd have screamed her frustration into the sky. But she had nothing left, nothing but dejection, and so she sobbed, half a decade's worth of longing, love and loss.

At least half an hour must have passed before Zach climbed over the little stone wall that bordered the fields. Amelia didn't see his approach because she sat on a milestone, turned away from the farm, keeping her face composed. Nevertheless, she could feel his presence like the heat of a fire at her back.

He stopped some distance from her, saying nothing. The tension was intolerable.

Stiff-backed, Amelia stood up. 'We should hurry; we've missed much of the morning.'

'Yes, we slept too long.'

She didn't respond, simply started walking along the road. The sky was grubby grey, a faint mist drifting in the cold air, seeping into everything with a penetrating chill. She pulled her cloak tight about her, against the cold and the anger.

Zach caught up, easily matching her stride. After a time, he reached into his pocket and pulled out a hunk of bread. 'Breakfast?'

She shook her head, turning away to gaze into the murky trees, and tried not to imagine him sharing it with ... with that woman. So she wasn't looking when her weak ankle turned on a frozen rut in the mud, making her stumble.

Zach grabbed her arm, keeping her from falling. 'Careful, you—'

'Don't touch me!' She snatched her arm from his hand and stumbled back. 'Just— Leave me alone.'

He looked at her, face unreadable. 'Would you care to enlighten me as to why ...?'

Amelia didn't intend to answer, but somehow the words spilled out. 'How *could* you?'

'I'm at a loss. How could I what?'

'Do what you— What you just did!' Her voice had become an angry rasp and she clamped her mouth shut, daring him with her eyes to argue.

'Ah,' he said, nodding in a manner that spoke of resignation. 'I see.'

'It's ... It's disgusting!'

His eyebrows rose in a slight shrug. 'Actually, I was—'

'Stop it!' Enraged, she lashed out at him, but he caught her hand before it could touch his face.

'I was helping you.' There was a heat in his voice now, a simmering anger, and his fingers curled so tight about her wrist that it hurt. 'I was helping you to leave unnoticed, if you recall.'

'Oh, and you couldn't have just taken her outside? Or—'

With a yank, he drew her closer. She could feel the heat of his breath against her mouth when he smiled, an angry curl of his lips. She didn't want to think about where those lips had so recently been and turned her face away. 'Whatever it is you think I did, I fail to see how the manner of my distraction should concern you.'

'Let me go.'

He released her, but didn't step back. 'What harm a little kiss? It's no worse than any of your seductions, I'll wager.'

'It's entirely different! To trick a woman simply to effect your own escape—'

'It was *your* escape I was effecting.'

'Even so. To *use* her like that! To toy with her heart ...' She turned away, unable to hold his baleful glare and afraid, if he looked too deep, that he might see the root of her anger. 'It's depraved.'

There was a long silence, broken only by the mournful call of a crow in the trees. After a while Zach said, 'We're

239

much alike, you and I. Neither of us fastidious about doing what must be done.'

'I would never—'

'At least I didn't hand her over to the King's navy afterward. *I* didn't watch her hang.'

Amelia's jaw dropped. 'You can't compare— It's not the same!'

'You're right.' He turned to her, leaning closer. 'Because I didn't trade her life for those of more value. Did I, now?'

'I didn't—'

'Shall we walk, Miss Dauphin? You must be eager to return to your dutiful husband.'

With that he strode away, not looking back, and Amelia was left alone with her thoughts. She found them very unsatisfactory company indeed.

Alight with indignation, Zach stalked along the road and refused to look back to see if Amelia followed.

Let her hang! Let her gasp her last self-righteous breath from the gallows and see if he cared. Depraved? Bloody woman knew nothing of the matter. If she'd known the direction of his thoughts as they lay all pressed up together, night after bloody night ... Bloody tease, bloody treacherous harlot! How dare she be disgusted by what she thought he'd done without even asking the truth of it? How dare she condemn him for the very thing she'd done herself, when he was entirely innocent? Relatively innocent.

He was so lost in resentment that he didn't notice the drum of horses' hooves along the road until the sound rumbled in his ears like the approach of a storm. He turned, horrified to see the red and gold glint of soldiers in the distance. Amelia, her pace slowed by her injured ankle, was far behind him, almost out of shouting distance, and all his anger was suddenly exploded by a horrifying fear.

They'd found her.

Chapter Thirty

There was no time to go back; the only thing Zach could do was dart into the thick hedge and scramble beneath it, into a ditch half filled with slushy, muddy snow. His heart hammered, drowning the drumbeat of horses' hooves, fingers shaking as he pulled free his pistol and poured the powder. All thought was narrowed to one question: *will they send her back to Newgate or shoot her where she stands?*

He could hear the clink of horse tack as the soldiers drew closer and imagined Amelia slung over the back of one of their mounts. His finger tightened on the trigger and he rolled onto his belly, squirming up out of the ditch so that he might ambush the troop from behind. It was a desperate plan, to be sure, and no doubt his last. But these were desperate times. With one foot braced, and his free hand reaching for his sword, Zach steadied himself before—

A hand seized his shoulder, another clamping hard across his mouth. 'Don't move,' Amelia hissed in his ear.

His heart tripped and tumbled in a crashing wave of relief. Helpless against the emotion, he loathed himself for it nonetheless, for showing such weakness to her, of all people.

Slow and wary, Amelia released her hold on him. Neither spoke, nor looked at the other, as they settled into a wintry silence. Side by side, but not touching, they watched as a forest of legs trotted past the scant shelter of the hedge.

When the last of the soldiers was gone, Zach waited for the count of one hundred before clambering out of the ditch and peeking in each direction. The road was empty, the soldiers no more than a silver glint in the distance. He shuddered then, but not from fear. It was the icy ditch water, seeping through his clothes from top to toe, that chilled him. That was all. It was too bloody cold, this wretched land. Too bloody cold, indeed.

Behind him, Amelia scrambled up the bank. Gritting his teeth, Zach closed his eyes and calmed his shaking breaths, settling his features into a cavalier smile. When he turned around, he regarded her coolly and said nothing.

Like himself, Amelia was sopping wet and covered all over in mud. 'I went under the hedge and crept through the field beyond.' Her expression had lost none of its chill and after a moment she added, 'Did you imagine you'd need to save me again, Captain Hazard?'

He sketched an apologetic bow. 'In truth, I thought only of saving my own skin. No more than you'd expect, I suppose, from a depraved cur such as myself.'

A thin rain had begun to fall, colder than the snow, and Amelia's face grew frostier beneath a thick smear of dirt. With a sigh, she looked along the road, in the direction the soldiers had taken. 'They've been sent for us, I suppose.'

'For *you*.'

Her gaze darted back to him, more bitter than he felt was warranted. 'Are you abandoning me, then?'

Was that what he'd been doing, before the soldiers came? He didn't know the answer, so said nothing in reply.

Amelia pressed her lips into a humourless smile and nodded. 'Fine. Go ahead and leave, Zach, you do it so well.'

'Not well enough, it seems. I always make the mistake of returning.'

'And I always make the mistake of wishing for it!' With that she turned and stalked down the road, her arms wrapped tight about her body in a vain attempt to keep warm.

Irritated, he yelled after her. 'Then allow me to correct both our bloody mistakes! Find your own way to the sea!'

'Fine!' she shouted back. 'I will!'

'Fine!' He watched her go, steaming, and determined that he would not, under any circumstances, follow. He'd return to the farm, to the willing – grateful – arms of Mary Bullen and there, perhaps, do what Amelia thought he'd already done. It wouldn't be difficult to find a coach that would take him to the coast, and from there it was but a short step to the *Hawk*. He'd done what Géroux had begged and freed his wife from the noose, the rest she could do for herself. Anyway, she'd never been the sort to need his help; she'd never wanted it either. Yes, leaving the grimy shores of England was exactly what he wanted to do. He'd turn his back, walk the other way, and finally wash his hands of the irksome Amelia Dauphin.

Yet he found that he didn't move.

For there was one trifling bedevilment, an insignificant obstacle on his course towards freedom. It came in the form of his imagination, always too vivid, painting her death in stark detail. It came in the form of his treacherous heart, which had already sacrificed too much for her happiness and would gladly sacrifice twice as much again. It came in the form of his twice-cursed, wretched, godforsaken honest streak that could not see her limp away into the rain without a penny to her name nor a bite to eat. In short, it came in the form of a restless, unrequited and utterly self-destructive love.

His father had spoken of such nonsense once, back when Zach was growing into manhood. He remembered the night well, high upon the windswept island cliffs, with the *Hawk* anchored below and merrymaking lighting the beaches. It had been some celebration, its meaning lost in time and only the few words exchanged with his father lingering still. Perhaps it had been Christmas ... It mattered not. There had been women aplenty, beautiful women with light skirts and welcoming arms, and Zach, at barely one-and-twenty, had believed himself in a kind of mortal heaven.

His father, sitting behind the smoke of his pipe, had watched with dark eyes and envy, or so Zach had imagined then. Envy that his son commanded a harem while he, old and sea-worn, had only his tobacco for company.

When Zach had said as much, Overton had snorted around his pipe stem. 'A woman can do what she likes with your shiner, son. But if she don't touch your heart, it's like drinking rum with no bite – not worth the effort.'

Zach had laughed, half-cut and sated from his latest conquest. He remembered dropping down onto the dry grass, close to his father's fire. 'Love's a game for fools,' he'd said. 'And I'm no fool.'

''Tis a hazardous business, right enough,' Overton had said, sucking on his pipe and blowing a lazy ring into the air. 'But the rewards ... Ah, neither gold nor silver can compare.'

'There's only one lady I could ever love.' Above him the stars reeled and Zach had smiled at their rum-soaked dance. 'Beautiful, she is. Strong, powerful. And when I touch her ... Ah, she responds so light and delicate to every caress.' He'd glanced over then, caught the firelight glitter of his father's eyes. 'The *Gypsy Hawk*, see, is my true love. And ever will be.'

'Ever will be?' His father had laughed, rough and smoky. 'Know your own future, do you, lad?'

'Know my own mind,' he'd replied, with a glib confidence that, viewed from a decade's distance, made him wince. As if it were any more possible to deny love than it was to deny the tide. Six years later, he'd learned that truth. He'd stood like Canute upon the beach, powerless as the waves rolled in.

The tide had swept him away completely. Rudderless and without a sail, he'd been unable to do anything but follow where she led. He followed her still, even into this cold and bitter land. Followed her though reason and self-preservation spoke against it. Followed her though he had nothing to expect at the end but anguish and regret.

'Bloody fool,' he told himself, as he stomped after her through the slushy snow, head bent beneath crouching winter skies. 'Imbecilic, half-witted, stupid bloody fool. You deserve everything you get.'

The rest of the morning was spent in a tense silence and away from the road. No doubt their theft of the carriage had been reported, two and two quickly calculated and the correct solution arrived at: their location was known.

So they kept to the trees, following the line of the road from the relative shelter of the woods and fields. It was muddy, difficult walking, and, soaked through as they both were, it was achingly cold.

At about noon they stopped to rest. Zach handed Amelia bread and an apple, which she ate as though she had to the force the food down her throat – as if it were contaminated by his depraved touch.

Her hypocrisy angered him, but not so much as his own weakness in following her still. He only hoped that her anger blinded her to the root of his fallibility. Let her think him a dissolute monster, a wanton debaucher of innocent women – he was, after all, Zachary Hazard – but let her stay ignorant of the power she held over him. At least then he would retain some degree of dignity. When he'd finished eating, he stood and tried to stamp some life into his long-dead feet, but there was no warmth to be had, no warmth anywhere in the world. Amelia sat blue-lipped and shivering like the condemned, despite the cloak. She was too cold, he knew, and needed to be moving. He was about to rouse her when she spoke, her voice perilously slurred. 'Why d'you never come back t'the island, Zach?'

'Had no cause.'

She nodded and hugged herself tighter, as though her

bone-thin arms might protect her from the cold. 'Not even f'your father?'

He stamped his feet again and peered up at the heavy sky. An icy, penetrating drizzle had set in properly now and the light was already fading. 'Need to keep going,' he said, deliberately not reaching for her hand. 'It's a deadly cold, this.'

She didn't move, just sat staring ahead. 'Little longer ... so tired ...'

'On your feet, Amelia, or you'll be food for the crows.'

She made no answer, but pushed herself wearily to her feet and began to walk. This time, Zach remained close behind her and kept a weather eye open for anything that might look like shelter.

By the time dusk crept upon them, a mere blackening of stony skies, Amelia had slowed to a stagger. When she talked, it was a mumble of fragmented thoughts, and he feared she might sleep on her feet.

Not good. Not good at all.

His own feet were stumbling too, his thoughts sluggish, fingers numb. He'd seen it before, this deadly cold, and knew it for the very devil.

He had flint and tinder, but there wasn't a dry twig to be found in the whole sodden forest, and if they didn't find a way to warm themselves soon ... They said it was an easy death, but he'd had a taste of what came after and didn't care to try it again.

'Zach?' Her voice roused him and he found that he'd stopped walking. Her weight was heavy against him, shaking so hard her bones rattled, and he wondered how they'd come to be clinging together.

'Can't stop,' he muttered, dragging his feet back into motion. He'd no memory of stopping, no idea how long they'd stood there.

'No.' She tugged on his sleeve with clumsy hands. 'Look.'

Blinking and peering through the encroaching gloom, he saw nothing ahead but murk. Was she seeing phantoms?

'C'n y'see it?'

'See what?'

'House.'

He blinked, as if the fog were in his eyes and not settling between the trees. 'A house? Bloody hell, it's a house!'

There, in the middle of the forest, rose an austere house of grey stone and black windows. They struggled towards it, the promise of shelter giving Zach hope and, with it, a little heat to his blood. There was grass – a lawn, perhaps – rain-soaked and slippery, then a gravel path that passed between ominous grey statuary that watched from the mist with solemn, disapproving eyes.

Zach paid them no mind. 'Our luck, Miss Dauphin, has turned,' he said, gazing up at the big, dark house. 'Lord and Lady Muck are in town, no doubt, and their staff along with them. Tonight, we'll sleep in luxury.'

She made no answer; he wasn't even sure she had heard him at all. Her blue lips moved a little, but her eyes were glazed and unfocussed. It was as though she was but half in her own mind.

'Stay here,' he said, easing her to the ground at the feet of a dour, heraldic beast.

Amelia didn't answer, just pulled her knees to her chest and dropped her head onto them. Zach spared her a single parting look before summoning the very last of his reserves and lurching towards the great house. One way or another, he was going to find a way inside.

Chapter Thirty-One

She was sinking slowly beneath the sea, into the icy clutches of the ocean, the cool embrace of the water hushing her towards misty shores. Somewhere, in the distance, she was aware that she shook like a leaf in a storm, moments away from being torn forever from the branch and cast out into the wild world, all alone and bound for death. She knew that she should fear it, that it would take her from warmth and light and life, but she was so tired and thought that if she just let herself go, let herself drift out over the glacial ocean, among the stars that glittered above, that she would find him on some strange beach, and there would be life and light and warmth after all, because he—

'Amelia.'

—he had brought her to life, ignited the fire in her heart that burned for freedom and adventure, and without him—

'Amelia! Get up.'

—without him—

'Wake up!' There were hands on her shoulders, shaking her hard. Shaking her until her eyes opened, confused and disoriented. She was somewhere dark. Somewhere cold.

'On your feet.'

She blinked, trying to focus, trying to remember, but the hands were hauling her upright and she was shaking so hard she couldn't speak.

'Door's open, let's get inside.'

She peered at a face through rain-drenched darkness, but could hardly make it out. 'Zach?'

'Yes.' There was relief in his voice. 'Yes, that's it Amy. Now come on, walk. Too bloody tired to carry you.'

On numb feet, she staggered forward. He was holding her up, so close she could feel how he shivered too, could hear his teeth rattling. The rain was coming down heavy, in sheets that drove against her, raw with cold. And then …

Then she was stumbling over a step, stumbling into darkness, and the rain was gone. There was no heat though, just a stiller cold. She stood unmoving while Zach pushed shut the door, the noise echoing through the empty room. It was too dark to see where they were – kitchen, hallway?

'Upstairs,' Zach said, pushing her forward. 'Found blankets and wood. Bloody lucky. Come on.'

Hope surged, pushing back the cold's death-grip as she made her way up a wide, grand staircase, clinging to the banister with numb fingers. Zach walked ahead of her, leading the way, his customary swagger replaced by a weary trudge as he walked down the landing and stopped at a door. 'Here.'

She followed him inside and saw that it was a small bedroom. A large chair sat by the fireplace, which was built but unlit. The bed was carefully made, laden with blankets and an embroidered quilt, and beyond that was a window against which the rain lashed with renewed venom.

'Get your clothes off and get under the blankets,' Zach said quietly, kneeling before the fireplace and fumbling in one of the pouches that hung from his belt. She watched as he withdrew his treasured flint and a little tinder, dry as a bone. His fingers were clumsy with cold and it took him several attempts to strike a spark; Amelia held her breath and tried to stop the chattering of her teeth as he blew softly on the precious little spark, nurturing a lick of flame.

Let it light, she thought. Dear God, let it light.

The tinder burned, then the kindling caught, and the flames began to leap and dance around the logs in the grate. With a smile, Zach sat back on his heels and glanced at her. His expression changed. 'Amelia, I said take your clothes off and get into the bloody bed.'

When she didn't move, he climbed wearily to his feet. 'At

times such as this, Amy, modesty will kill you. Now get rid of those sopping rags.'

For an instant, her eyes met his and it seemed as though, for that single moment, the Earth teetered precariously on its axis. Then he turned away, back to the nascent fire, and the moment passed.

'Yes,' Amelia mumbled, too cold to care about modesty or anything else. Too cold even to remember what had vexed her earlier. Everything was an icy fog, and her only desire was for warmth.

With trembling, numb fingers she fumbled at the buttons on her dress. She could not work them free from the wet cloth, her fingers slipping awkwardly as she tugged and pulled.

'Here.' There was a glint of silver and she looked up to see a knife in Zach's hands. 'Don't move.'

With hurried, shaking strokes he slid the blade beneath each button and cut it free. Tossing the knife to the floor, sending it skittering towards the fire, he tugged at the soaking fabric. 'Can you ...?'

'Yes.' Shaking so hard she could hardly move, she began hauling the dress from her shoulders, but it clung to her wet skin, twisting tight and awkwardly.

'Turn around,' Zach said after a moment, pushing at her shoulder until she had her back to him. Distantly, she thought that she should feel ashamed as he yanked the dress down her back, over her hips, and sent it pooling to the floor at her feet, but all she could feel was cold. 'Get into the bed,' he said roughly, even as he held her hand to balance her as she stepped out of the sodden skirts.

Amelia didn't look around, tried not to think about his gaze falling on her scrawny body, as she stumbled towards the bed and squirmed herself beneath the heavy blankets. It was cold as ice and she lay there, curled around herself, shivering and shivering until she thought she might shake herself to death.

Then the bed moved and he was there too, the faint heat of his bare chest pressed firm against her back, the slow beat of his heart strong and reassuring. He clutched her to him, urgently, as though she were the last ember of warmth in the world. 'Don't worry,' he whispered, cold in her ear, 'I've no intention of stealing your virtue, only your heat.'

'I know.' She did know, but the knowledge only brought a deeper chill; she could imagine how unappealing her shivering bones must appear.

Perhaps he took it as a statement of trust, though, for he relaxed a little and said, 'Mustn't sleep yet. Try to stay awake until the fire's caught, 'til we're warmer.'

'Yes,' she agreed, and thought she could never sleep while she shook so badly. Or while he held her thus, his arm pressed tight across her naked belly.

'There might be food in the kitchens,' Zach added. 'Tomorrow, I'll look.'

'Coffee, maybe?'

'Dry clothes somewhere, too.'

She closed her eyes and pressed closer to him, her fingers curling over the strength of his arm. 'I'm glad you didn't leave,' she said after a while, and it was only when she spoke that she realised her shivering had subsided a little, that a brave glow of warmth was blossoming between them. Light flickered on the wall and she saw that the fire had caught. Relieved, she sank deeper beneath the blankets. 'Today was a terrible day.'

'I've had worse.'

His quiet reply made her sigh; would he never forgive her?

'We're close though,' he added, perhaps sorry for raising the spectre once more. 'Just two days from here, at most.'

'Until the sea?'

'Yes.' His arms, she noticed, drew back as he spoke. 'Then you'll be free to go where you will.'

'And what about you? Where will you go?'

'Anywhere I like, I suppose.' He sighed, his words lacking conviction. 'But where is there left for us now?'

She was silent, not because she had no answer, but because she didn't know if she dared speak it. But if she couldn't say it now, in this room, where it seemed that every convention was turned on its head, when else could she say it? Closing her eyes she said, 'You could come back to Sainte Anne with me.'

His breath was warm against her shoulder. 'And do what?'

'Help me. Help me rebuild.'

'You know my thoughts on that. If you rebuild, they'll tear you down again and this time they'll not hesitate to hang you from the nearest yardarm.'

'Then what ...?'

'Run, as you should have done from the start.'

Bristling at his gentle reproof, she said, 'What kind of life would that be?'

'A free life, Amy,' he murmured sleepily. 'A free bloody life.'

They must have slept then, for Amelia awoke later to find herself alone in the bed. Seized by a sudden alarm she sat up, clutching the sheets to her chest. The fire was piled high and none of Zach's clothes or effects were missing. Outside, the sky was lightening into a solid, intransigent slate-grey and the rain still fell. It was morning, of sorts; she must have slept the whole night.

Satisfied that he hadn't left, her heartbeat slowed and, with a grateful sigh, she sank back into the bed, burying herself deeply into the warmth. The blankets pressed heavily against her legs and she had no wish to ever leave such a cosy cocoon. Her eyes drifted shut once more and, lulled by the crackle of the fire and the rattle of the rain, she decided she would sleep longer.

However, as she floated towards her dreams' gentle shores, her mind seemed determined to take her into unsafe waters. The pale curve of his shoulder on the moonlit beach swirled before her eyes; she remembered how he'd looked when he'd drawn her down into the sand, the roguish desire in his eyes igniting a heat that had little to do with the fire or the blankets. Irritated, she rolled onto her back, the brush of linen against her heightened senses seeming a sudden torture.

Now the cold had receded, her body burned with another heat, an unquenchable fire that had the potential to unhinge her entirely. Yet she'd spent the night naked in his arms and he'd not been stirred. Four years ago, she thought, things would have been different; in such circumstances much might have changed between them. But that had been before her betrayal, before Luc, and everything was different now; everything but the way she could trace the curves and angles of his face in her mind's eye, everything but the burning memory that time had done nothing to dim, of his hands upon her skin, his lips …

She drew in a deep breath as beneath the blanket her fingers trailed across the sensitive skin of her stomach.

His fingers …

Drawing lower, skimming her hip. Soft, gentle.

Lower still, until she shivered.

His fingers, there, teasing and—

'All sorts of delicacies in the kitchen,' Zach announced as he barged through the door. 'We'll eat like bloody kings!'

She jerked awake, half sitting up, her face as red as the apples Zach held in his hands. Oh God, his hands.

He gave her a curious look, but said only, 'The place is so well provisioned, I'm thinking the owners must soon be returning. We must plunder and be gone.'

'Yes,' Amelia agreed, falling back, flustered and frustrated, into the pillows.

'Found some clothes too,' he said, setting down all he'd been carrying by the fire and indicating the mismatched britches and shirt he wore, a fine brocade coat thrown over the top, so large it reached below his knees. A couple of rings, she noticed, now adorned his fingers. 'Lots of women's stuff next door,' he added.

Staring at the ceiling, trying to banish her errant thoughts, she said, 'I think I'd kill someone for the chance to bathe.'

He bit into an apple, the crunch loud in the quiet room. 'No need for such drastic measures, Amy. There's a huge bloody bath down the hall, if you're willing to heat enough water.'

She sighed. 'I had maids once, to do such things.'

Zach was silent, chewing his apple. After a moment he said, 'I might be your disloyal subject, Amy, but I'll never be your bloody servant.'

'No.' She sat up. 'I didn't mean— You know that's not what I meant.'

He didn't answer, just stared into the fire. 'Keen enough to give orders, though,' he said after a while. Then, in a voice she assumed was a mimicry of her own, '*Captain Zach Hazard is requested to present himself at Ile Sainte Anne with all due haste, by command of Captain Dauphin*. Had that bloody note thrust into my hand in a dozen different ports.'

Her bare shoulders were cold now and Amelia drew the blankets up towards her chin, wishing she were dressed. 'I missed you,' was the honest answer, and she was surprised to hear it on her lips. Exhaustion and hunger, perhaps, were the cause. Even so, Zach seemed not to hear, or else chose to ignore her.

'Never been one to do things by command of any man – or woman,' he said, slumping down into the chair by the fire and extending his feet towards the flames.

'I meant no insult,' she said quietly. 'I just needed ... your counsel.'

He slid her a doubtful look. 'Regarding what matter?'

'Every matter!' she exclaimed. 'My life was turned upside down: my father dead, Luc gone. You were— You and Addy were the only friends I had left in the world.'

A flicker of disquiet creased his brow and he turned back to the fire. She was reminded, painfully, of his father, and how he would sit by the fire in the fortress, puffing on his long-stemmed pipe and staring into the flames. She'd often wondered what – or who – he'd sought in their depths.

'I don't blame you for not returning,' she said after a while, pulling one of the heavy blankets up about her shoulders. 'You had every right to be angry – to distrust me. You still do, I suppose. Perhaps I had no right to ask, after luring you into Morton's trap.'

'I knew what I was doing,' he said into the flames. 'Don't think I didn't know what I was doing that night – I'm not so big a fool as you might think.'

'Yet you're still angry. That's why you never returned to Ile Sainte Anne, isn't it? Because you couldn't forgive me.'

'It's best forgotten.' He stood up. 'Let it go with the tide, Amy.'

'I can't forget when—'

'I'm going to make a fire in the kitchen. If you've the arms to carry it, you can heat water for the bath.'

With that he stalked from the room, leaving Amelia frustrated and hurt by his anger. How could he tell *her* to let the matter go when he clung to his resentment like a drowning man?

Zach found wood outside and lit a small fire – no point in advertising their presence to all and sundry. With luck, in this rain, the smoke would not carry far. Then he filled a pot and set the water to warming, even before there was much heat in the flames. Let her carry it to the bath herself, though; he was nobody's bloody servant.

He slumped into a large wooden chair close to the hearth and stared into the flames as they slowly consumed the wood. Just as Ile Sainte Anne had been consumed, piece by piece, and turned to ash. Just as his father had fallen, and with him the Articles.

The world was changed, though Amy didn't see it yet. The edges of the map were joined in endless circumnavigation and there was no room left for freedom. Nor pirates. Their time was passing; the hourglass was almost empty and a new age was drawing closer with each silver dawn.

What did it matter, then, that his fool heart still ached from the blow she'd dealt him four years past? Why should he care – why nurture his resentment – when all around him their world was ending?

He tugged at the collar of his pilfered shirt, felt the scar about his neck, carved there by the noose that had so nearly ended his life. It brought back a flash of memory, vivid as day: the deck, a bright blue morning, terror like nothing he'd known before. Slow strangulation. Amy, in Géroux's arms, turning away from him as blackness crowded the edges of his vision. Death. He'd seen that dark spectre for what it was, felt its shadow even as his body kicked and fought for life. And then a crack like doom itself and falling, falling ...

He surfaced from the memory with a jerk, gasping for air. Harsh in the quiet room, his breaths were ragged and raw and seemed to fill the kitchen. Lifting shaky hands, he pressed them over his face until, slowly, his breathing returned to normal.

It's over now. Let it go with the tide. Let it go.

After a while he dropped his hands back into his lap, exhausted. Staring once more into the fire he had a sudden and profound wish for rum, so hauled himself to his feet and went in search of something to take the edge off his black mood. There was no rum to be had, but there was brandy.

A little Oyl of Barley would have to do, he supposed, as he uncorked the bottle and took a long swallow. Coughing, he wiped his mouth on the back of his hand.

It burned nicely on the way down, thawing some of the lingering cold within, until he could examine what lay beneath the ice. Old wounds aside, he knew why he was glaring into the fire as if he might worm his way back into hell; the bloody wench had tweaked his guilt, turning the tables when he was the one wronged!

My life was turned upside down: my father dead, Luc gone. You were— You and Addy were the only friends I had left in the world.

Would she bleed him dry? She had stolen his heart and traded his life; would she take the rest of him, too? Of course she bloody would, for she was a better pirate than he had ever been – more ruthless, more wily. More treacherous.

Yet, even knowing that, he still felt guilt – at not heeding her call, at not returning to Ile Sainte Anne, at abandoning her to the very fate of which he'd warned her so fervently. Witch of a woman, to have wound such a confounding spell around his heart.

'Zach?'

He turned with a start to find Amelia standing in the kitchen doorway, dressed in a shirt that came no lower than her knees. He could see her ankle, the wound healing and less angry, and looked away before his gaze could rove the length of her slender body.

'Water should be warm,' he said, taking another swig of the brandy and reclaiming his chair by the fire. 'Careful you don't burn your hands on the pot. It's bloody heavy.'

Amelia said nothing, just slopped water into a bucket and carried it, banging against her leg, out of the kitchen and up the stairs. She came back a few minutes later and repeated the process, then again with a bucket of cold water, and once more after that.

He tried not to notice how she struggled with the weight and told himself it would do her good to do such things for herself.

There was a sheen of sweat on her face when she returned again, pouring another bucket of hot water. At first bemused by her obstinacy, Zach soon realised she was making a point. Despite himself he smiled, his perfidious heart racing. After she'd left again, he rose slowly from the chair, took the last of the water from the fire, and followed her upstairs.

The bathtub stood in a bedroom full of frill and fancy that must have belonged to a lady of little imagination. All sorts of worthless porcelain figurines cluttered the mantel and dressing tables, most of them silly little dogs adorned with bows and suchlike, and there was lace as far as the eye could see. It was just such a silly woman, he supposed, who would see fit to keep a bathtub in her bedroom.

He remembered his mother frequently warning him to stay clear of water and the pestilence it bred – she'd had a kind of morbid fear of it. As a nipper she'd seen both parents succumb to the Great Plague and had held an unnatural fear of water ever since. A life at sea had cured him of that notion, and he'd often strip down to dive into the warm waters of the Indies, just for the sheer pleasure of it against his skin. Nonetheless, it seemed passing strange to keep a bathtub in a bedroom – how often could the woman possibly need to bathe?

Such thoughts were preoccupying him when he shouldered open the door and stepped inside, the pot sloshing a little hot water over his leg. Just as he did so Amelia walked from behind a dressing screen, naked as the day she was born.

For a split second she didn't respond, simply stared. He met that stare, held it until, with a gasp, she snatched up the shirt she'd been wearing and pressed it to her chest. It fell narrowly before her, covering the essentials yet leaving the slender lines of hips and legs exposed to his gaze. He didn't look away, though he did set the pot on the floor, curling his lips into a deliberate smile and attempting to hide the sudden pounding of his heart. 'Should have locked the door, Amy. Unless you wished for company ...?'

'A gentleman would have knocked.'

'True,' he agreed. 'Too bad there're no gentlemen hereabouts.'

She sighed, and Zach saw that the hands clutching the shirt to her breast were shaking. From the cold perhaps, or from something else? He walked closer, further into the room, but she didn't move back. Steam rose from the bath, misting the windows, and he felt hot suddenly. Unsettled. Amelia's shoulders squared and she met him with defiance, as if expecting something. He wondered if she thought him capable of taking her against her will; she seemed to think him capable of every other depravity.

'If you've come to mock me,' she said stiffly, 'then get it over with so I might bathe in peace.'

'Mock?' He frowned at the strange idea. 'Why would I wish to do that?'

'Because you can. Why else do you ever do anything?'

'Oh, so many reasons.' He drew closer, punctuating each step with a word. 'Amusement. Boredom. Vengeance.' She held her ground, eyes sparking fire, and he could see the rapid rise and fall of her chest, the colour in her cheeks and an intensity in her face that—

He stopped dead.

Desire, like before – seductive, terrible, glorious desire. His smile faltered, his mind overtaken by a sudden heat.

He could take her, right here. Right now. Taste those lips again, make her his own, make her gasp his name and—

Fast as it swept upon him, the heat was overtaken by a wave of anger. Did she think him such a fool as this? To be taken in twice, made a fool of twice?

Deliberately, he took a breath and sharpened his tongue. 'What is it you want, Amy?' He lifted a finger to touch her face, but held off at the last, simply ghosting the line of her jaw. Even the slightest touch would undo his resolve.

'Nothing,' she answered unsteadily.

'Fortunate,' he whispered, leaning in as if to kiss her. 'For that's all I have to give.'

She let silence linger a moment, then said, 'I thought we were friends, you and I. Allies.'

Her words were a breath on his lips, an agony of thwarted desire. 'Never that, Amy.'

'Why not? You thought we were alike, once.'

'Ah yes.' His gaze lingered along the length of her shoulder, so close he could see the arc of her back and the sweet curve below. 'But that was before.'

At the base of her spine she had a tattoo – a dolphin, sleek and beautiful. Muscles clenched at the memory of how, that very morning, he'd woken to find himself hard against the soft heat of her back. Against that very spot. He'd burned with the slightest movement until, with a silent curse upon his lips, he'd been forced to slip from the warmth of the bed before she woke.

Zach licked at dry lips and thought, for a wild moment, that he should just take her now, hard and fast, and be done. Like every other encounter for the past four years, it could be a thing of soulless gratification. An itch scratched and no more.

'Before what, Zach?' Her voice was soft and breathy, a seductress's purr.

He drew back, cautious. How easy, how very easy, to lose himself here. For he could not take her without being taken himself, and then he'd be undone forever. He sketched a smile onto his lips, kept it cold, kept it cruel. 'Think me a whore if you like, Amelia, but never think me a fool. You made your bargain four years ago and I see no reason to think the terms have changed. You'll need to find another of your humble servants to scratch your itch.' He leaned closer and whispered in her ear. 'I fear I'd find the pleasure unequal to the peril entailed.'

Her cheeks flushed with anger and her eyes, once molten, cooled and cracked into fragments of pain. She turned away. 'Please leave.'

Despite himself, he felt a pang of shame and found that he wanted to say something to take the sting from his words.

But he could think of nothing, and it was clear from the way she stood, head turned and rigid, that she wanted nothing more than to have him gone. So he offered a bow, theatrical and out of place, and left without another word.

There were those who'd have called him a bigger fool for leaving than for staying, but they knew nothing of what beat in his heart as he stalked the length of the elegant hallway.

Some men might be content with one night in her arms, but Zach Hazard was not. He wanted more. He wanted everything, body and soul. Or he wanted nothing at all.

Amelia sat in the water until it was cold, her skin scrubbed raw, her hair soaped and soaped again. Yet nothing she did could cool the anger that burned in her heart. Zach's needless, intentional cruelty had cut her to the quick. His words hurt her, even if they were the truth – perhaps, *because* they were the truth.

I fear I'd find the pleasure unequal to the peril entailed.

She sank back in the bath and stared at the ceiling. It seemed he would never forgive her betrayal, she had resigned herself to that, and yet hadn't he countered her outrage at his apparent seduction of the farm girl by claiming that they were the same? That neither of them was fastidious about doing what must be done?

His hypocrisy riled her. For a man, she supposed, such seductions were acceptable. For a woman? Oh no, heaven forbid a woman used her natural advantage to best a man. Especially a man like Zach Hazard, who believed himself so bloody irresistible. Was that why he couldn't forgive her? Because she'd played him at his own game and won?

Was that why he taunted and humiliated her?

Well, no more. She'd had enough. She was Amelia Dauphin, leader of Ile Sainte Anne, defender of the Articles, and she had done what was necessary to protect her people. She did not deserve his anger, and she would have his respect.

Getting out of the bath, she dried herself and dressed. She'd found a shirt, britches and a black coat that was only a little too large; she assumed there was a lanky boy somewhere in the family. She was grateful to be out of the wretched dress that had tangled her feet and stank of their miserable flight through London, and was warmer, too, in men's clothes.

A silver comb and brush sat upon the dressing table and she sat down to brush out her hair, leaving it loose to dry. The face that gazed back from the gilt mirror was not one she recognised, narrow and angular with eyes that seemed too large. Her collarbone was too pronounced, her chest barely noticeable beneath the shirt and coat. As lean as a blade, she thought, and just as deadly.

Let Zach Hazard beware.

Straightening her shoulders, she marshalled her anger and turned away from the mirror. It would end now, one way or another. For good.

There was no sign of him when she returned to the room they had shared, but she knew he must be in the house because he'd left his sword and pistols on the chair. Snatching up an apple from the pile of food he'd left by the fire, she stalked off in search of him.

The house wasn't so large that it was impossible to track him down, and she soon found him poking through an elaborate bedroom, examining all the *objets d'art* that littered shelves and tables, occasionally dropping something into the sack that dangled from the fingers of one hand.

She stood in the doorway and watched as he carefully scrutinized a golden candlestick. Then, braced for what was to come, she said, 'You have no right to hate me, Zach.'

He froze, but didn't look away from the candlestick. 'Only gilt,' he said, tossing it aside. 'Ugly, don't you think?'

'I did what I had to do, I've apologised, and that's enough.'

'Oh look!' Zach ambled across the room to a shelf full of ridiculous china dogs. 'Even worse.'

'Did you hear me?'

He glanced at her, dark and sly. 'I swear, this whole house is a shrine to mediocrity and not a single thing in it of any value.'

So this was how he wished to play it? Very well, then. 'Don't expect me to apologise again, Zach.' Her voice was hard, icy. 'I did what I did and – all things considered – I don't regret it.'

He was half turned away from her, toying with one of the ornaments. His fingers curled about the porcelain figurine as if he might strangle it. 'Never imagined you did.' She could only see him in profile, but still caught the bitter smile that flitted across his lips. 'Told you before: we're the same, you and I. Had our positions been reversed, it would have been you swinging from the yardarm.'

His words tripped her; she felt herself stumble into confusion. 'Then why won't you forgive me?'

'Already have, told you that too.'

'Don't lie to me, Zach. At least show me that much respect.'

Carefully, he replaced the china dog on the shelf, hoisted

the sack over his shoulder and turned, fixing her with a swaggering stare. 'Are you quite finished?'

'No!' She curled her fingers into fists. 'No, I'm bloody not! How dare you treat me like this?'

He blinked. 'How *dare* I?'

'You humiliate me—'

'Amelia—'

'—punish me—'

'Leave it, now.'

'Lie to me!'

'*Enough!*' His shout echoed in the silent house, seemed to rattle the very windows. 'Enough.' He glared at her, smouldering with a rage she'd known was there all along. With a clatter the sack fell to the floor and he prowled towards her, slow and deadly. 'Very well then,' he hissed, 'you're right. I don't forgive you. I'll never forgive you for your theft, because you stole something you can never return, no matter where in the world you sail. And after you stole it, you broke it beyond repair. Cast it aside.' He reached out as if to touch her face but stopped at the last moment, making no contact, his gaze seeming fixed on her lips. 'I can't forgive that, Amy. Can't forget it, neither.'

'I don't understand,' she whispered, refusing to back away from him despite the way her heart was hammering. 'What ...?'

His gaze lifted from her mouth, that bitter smile lingering in the black depths of his eyes. 'You chose *him*, Amy. You chose Luc bloody Géroux. What else did you think this was about?'

Chapter Thirty-Two

Zach left as soon as the words were spoken, pushing past her and out of the room, leaving Amelia standing rooted to the floor. She barely trusted herself to interpret his meaning. What had she stolen from him? What had she broken? Could it be ...? Could he mean his heart?

Her breath returned in a gulping gasp and she turned on her heel, racing from the room. 'Zach!'

He was already halfway down the stairs, taking them two or three at a time, and didn't turn when she called. She could only stand on the landing and watch him stride across the entrance hall and slam through the door towards the kitchens without a backward glance. Amelia was left alone with only the fading echoes of his anger.

For all his flamboyance, Zach was a private man. She knew that following him now would achieve nothing, might even drive him off entirely, so she didn't move from where she stood; they'd speak later, when he'd cooled and they'd both had time to consider the significance of his words. Even so, Amelia felt something ignite in her chest, a heat – a hope – that had not burned for years. If it were true that, against all expectations, he still harboured some feelings for her ...

Pressing her lips together, she turned and made her way slowly back to the cosy room they'd shared. She had much to think about, and before she spoke to Zach again her own mind would need to be clear.

She stayed the rest of the day in their room, building up the fire and watching the rain against the windows. Eventually daylight succumbed to the deeper darkness of night and the room plunged into dancing shadows. Amelia dragged a couple of blankets from the bed and sat close to the fire, wrapped up against the cold and thinking on Zach's words.

You chose him.

And so she had, in those golden days before her father's death. She'd chosen to stay in Ile Sainte Anne, to trade not run. She'd chosen hope over despair. Then the storm had come, her father was taken, and Zach ... Even now, she shied away from the image of his hanging, the hurt, fear and sorrow in his eyes as they'd tightened the noose. Her doing, all her doing.

There was not enough hubris in the world that could have convinced her Zach would feel anything less than contempt in the aftermath of her betrayal, nor that she deserved anything more. In those dark days, only Luc had defended her against Overton's bitter anger, only Luc had held her as she wept for her father, only Luc had shielded Ile Sainte Anne from Morton.

In truth, *then* there had been no choice at all.

Now, however ...

She closed her eyes and rested her head on her knees, remembering Luc's earnest face. He was a good man, honest in his heart if not always in his deeds. He claimed to have been as misled by Morton as herself, though she didn't know how much credence to give his words. He was full of shadows, his soul as enigmatic as his manners were plausible. He'd felt responsible for what had happened to her – that much she did know – and bound to protect her as best he could.

He'd sailed far and often though, chased by something she didn't understand and that he refused to discuss. While he was away, she'd embraced her role as the new leader of Ile Sainte Anne. With Overton at her side, she'd read and re-read the Articles until their profound truths had marked her heart like the ink beneath her skin. She'd taken lovers to her bed, distracted herself with the pleasures of the flesh, and all the while not felt a heartbeat of guilt. For Luc, she knew, did much the same.

But this? This was different. This was her soul longing for the touch of another; her heart aching to be filled after so many empty years. This was love. She was brave enough to name it so at last, but was she brave enough to claim it for her own?

She knew there was only one way to do so and the thought of it was terrifying. Zach must be told; her heart must be laid open to him. Though the prospect made her tremble, Amelia Dauphin had never been a coward. She owed him the truth, and he would have it.

Gathering her resolve, she left the warmth of the blankets and went in search of Zach.

There was no sign of him in the kitchens, but there was a lingering thread of cold air that betrayed the slightly open door. It was bitter outside with only her light coat, and she knew he couldn't have gone far. Sure enough, when she rounded the corner, she found him.

He stood near a log pile, stripped to the waist and wielding an axe with precarious precision. The pile of chopped wood at his side and the sheen of sweat on his skin told her he'd been working hard.

He didn't stop as she approached, just picked up another log and swung the axe, sending splinters flying. Amelia kept her distance, watching him in silence. In the dim light of the single lamp that hung from the eaves of the woodshed, he seemed to glisten in gold and ebony, a tangle of ink about his arm and back. He moved with curt, angry strokes, slamming the axe into the wood as though dispatching an enemy in battle.

She wondered how long he would ignore her, if she'd be forced to brave the flying axe and stop him before he'd listen. In the end, after he'd splintered yet another log, he drove the axe into the stump and, breathing hard, lifted his eyes to look at her. He said nothing, revealed nothing.

'You're right,' she said quietly. 'I chose Luc. I chose duty over love. But I am my father's daughter, Zach, and I cannot be any different. You must take me for what I am, or not at all.'

His gaze dropped, brow creasing as he stared at the top of the axe handle, scrutinising it in great detail.

Amelia drew closer. 'Those were dark days, for us all. Did any of us truly know the consequences of our actions? Did you?'

He didn't answer, just looked out into the night, and in the icy wind that blew she saw him shiver.

'Come inside,' she said gently. 'Come in where it's warm, Zach. I'm so tired of the cold.'

With that she turned, arms hugged about her chest against the biting wind, and didn't look back to see if he followed.

She returned to their room and curled up by the fire. Wrapped in a blanket, on some pillows from the bed, she lay in the warmth and watched the flames dance. She didn't doze though, despite the gentle crackle of the fire and the patter of the rain outside, because all she could see in the flames was the darkness in his eyes and the depth of his anger.

Would he come to her now, or had her confession come too late? Had their time passed, their lives been swept too far apart by the same relentless tides that had borne death to Ile Sainte Anne?

As she gazed into the fire, her mind drifted back to those dark days, when the might of empire had been thrown against her and she'd had to face it alone, without Luc and without Zach. The island had fallen, toppled in an inferno worthy of Dante himself, and as she lay by the fire, watching the logs spit and hiss in the flames, she realised how futile was their protest. The flames were unstoppable, like the turning of the world, and the fate of the logs was sealed – as was hers, as was Luc's, as was Ile Sainte Anne's. They all burned, helpless against their destiny.

So lost was she in her thoughts that she didn't notice the door open, and it seemed that Zach appeared out of nowhere. She simply looked up and there he was in the doorway, watching her. In his arms he carried wood for the fire, his shirt hanging open as if flung over his head without him caring how it fell.

When she caught his eye he glanced away before stepping further into the room and kicking the door closed behind him. Amelia said nothing as he walked towards her, though she sat up to make room by the hearth when he crouched to put some wood on the fire and to pile the rest nearby. In the firelight, he was gold once more, rum-dark eyes catching the glint of the flames and reflecting it like long-lost sunlight. He didn't look at her, though, not for a long time. He just gazed into the flames as she had done.

When he spoke at last, his voice was quiet and not at all like Captain Zach Hazard. The legend was discarded and the man who spoke was no more nor less than that – a man. 'I'll not argue with you about those days,' he said, 'nor about who has the greater share of blame. Whatever you thought, I knew well enough that it was a trap, but I came to you anyway when you asked. That choice was mine.'

He was silent then and Amelia wondered if that was all he had to say. She wondered whether he was expecting some kind of answer from her, but she had nothing to add; he'd spoken the only truth they both knew.

Then he shifted, wiping the fingers of one hand across his mouth as if the words he was about to utter displeased him. He glared deeper into the flames. 'I have sworn', he said, in a voice quieter still, 'not to love you. I have sailed the world to be free of you, yet always you bring me back and I cannot—' His voice broke and for a moment he said no more. The only sound between them was the crackle of the fire. 'Amy, I must know. If I had stayed all those years ago, would you have chosen differently?'

He went very still as he waited for her answer; not a muscle moved and his shoulders were a rigid line of suspense. Because she would have no more truck with half-truths and lies, Amelia said, 'I don't know. I don't know what I would have done then. I can't answer for the child I was.'

Zach nodded, or perhaps he just bowed his head. A stray lock of black hair fell forward, hiding his face. After a moment, in a strained voice, he said, 'Now, then? If you can't answer for four years past, then answer for now. Answer for this night. Would you choose differently, if you could?'

She closed her eyes. Suddenly it was as if she were standing on the very tip of the mast, ready to dive and dizzy in anticipation of the fall. 'Yes,' she said softly, feeling the air start to rush past her face. 'This night I would; this night I do.'

His breath caught and then there was silence. When she opened her eyes, he had turned from the fire and was watching her intently.

'I choose you, Zach,' she said. 'My heart has always chosen you. It always will.'

'And what of Géroux?'

'You think me cruel.' She didn't make it a question, for she wasn't in any doubt of the answer. 'A woman's heart cannot be bound, Zach. It must roam free.'

'Not a woman's heart,' he said, and for the first time a smile touched his eyes. 'A pirate's heart. That, you've always had.'

'Do you despise me for it?'

He shook his head and drew closer, a cautious predator. 'How could I when it's the mirror of my own?'

'Fickle?'

'Free, once.'

'And now?'

His answer was a shaky breath against her lips, a whisper of her name. She ached to lean in, to close the gap that had opened between them so many years ago, but it was a breach only he could cross.

His forehead touched hers, long fingers tracing patterns on the bare skin of her wrist. 'The world's turned upside down, Amy, and I hardly know which way to fall.'

'To me,' she urged, slipping her hands across the taut muscle of his shoulders, drawing him closer. 'Always to me.'

He shivered and closed his eyes, a butterfly kiss of lashes against her cheek. 'You can't catch me, Amy.'

She wanted to deny it, to tell him that she would always catch him, but she had no words for lies; she was bound to her duty and to another man. She could not save him. 'Then we'll fall together. Fall with me, Zach.'

'To the end, I swear it.' And with a soft sigh of surrender he bridged the void between them, his mouth closing over hers in a scalding kiss that claimed her as his own at last. Pickpocket fingers tangled in her hair, caressing her neck, tilting her head so his lips could blaze along the line of her jaw, her throat.

She slipped her arms around his neck, holding him close as he lowered her down into the pillows and blankets, kissing her breathless. Kissing her as if it were the end of the world.

One hand slid beneath her shirt, his rough palm grazing her nipple, teasing and glorious. He growled her name low in his throat and she gasped as she felt fabric ripping. Then his mouth was there, hot on her breast, and she arched towards him, fingers knotting in his hair as his tongue and teeth drove her to distraction. It was almost too much to bear, her heart was too full. 'Zach ...'

Breaking free, he lifted his head to look into her face, eyes liquid with desire. And behind that something else, something darker and deeper. Doubt. Despair.

With trembling fingers she touched his cheek, his lips, his throat, lingering on the scar about his neck. 'I did this,' she realised, sudden tears in her eyes.

He shook his head, took her fingers from his throat and pressed them to his lips. 'Not you. It was never you.'

Forgiveness, at last. She hardly knew whether to laugh or cry as a bittersweet wave of relief washed away years of remorse and regret, but she could do neither because Zach was kissing her again. Her torn shirt pooled around her as he skimmed her belly with his lips, kissed her breasts, her throat. His breath was hotter than the fire that cast dancing shadows over his skin and she craved his heat, his touch.

Curling fingers into the linen of his shirt, she pulled it over his head, desperate to feel the heat of him next to her bare skin. He helped her, kneeling up and casting his shirt aside. Reaching for him again, she tried to pull him back down, but he resisted. Instead, he just gazed at her, drinking in the sight of her lying there naked and wanton. She watched his pulse quicken in the hollow of his throat, chest rising and falling, eyes reflecting firelight from behind a fall of black hair. 'Tomorrow,' he said in a scratchy whisper, 'nothing will have changed.'

Though the truth broke her heart, she could not deny it. 'Yet now is not tomorrow.'

Zach closed his eyes in an expression akin to pain, then cursed softly and pulled her into his arms, crushing her against his chest and kissing her until her head swam with starbursts. There was no more talking after that, only feeling – his mouth on her throat, her breasts, trailing kisses lower still. Clever fingers stripped her, rendered her naked in the firelight, making her writhe and whimper beneath his adept touch. Driving her to the edge, but too skilled to let her fall. Not yet.

At last, when she could bear the torment no longer, his eyes locked with hers, asking a single unspoken question.

Her answer was the nip of teeth against his collarbone, the scratch of fingernails along his back, and with a ragged groan he buried himself deep inside her.

She gasped as he began to move, steady and measured at first, then harder, deeper, less controlled. Urgent. 'Amy ...' It was a plea, a curse. 'Oh God, Amy ...'

But something was wrong. She felt it in her heart, in the depths of her soul; they were racing for a horizon they could never reach, seeking something that could never be theirs.

Desperate, she held him close, wrapped herself around him, yet somehow it wasn't enough. She couldn't get close enough to fill the emptiness at their core.

And then he slipped a finger between them, touched her right *there*, and tore a cry from her lips as he tipped her over the edge. He followed while she was still falling, muscles tensing like iron as he gasped her name in hot breaths against her neck, over and over and over.

Clinging to him as the storm abated, Amelia found her face wet with tears. For though their bodies had found incandescent release, their longing went unsated, their hearts remained but half-filled; deep down they both knew that it was too late, that the world had shifted and their time had passed.

Afterward, as he lay sweat-damp and glistening in the firelight, it didn't surprise her when he said, 'God, Amy, but that was a sweet death.'

'Shhh,' she scolded, putting her fingers to his lips. 'Don't say that.'

He spoke no more, just gathered her into his arms and held her there against the slowing beat of his heart; in a matter of days they would reach the sea and this glimpse of what might have been would be swept away by the remorseless tides that had always torn them apart.

Amelia woke first, as dawn crept into the room, a mere

lessening of the darkness beneath heavy clouds. The morning was thin and grey, cold despite the fire, and Zach looked pale in its light. He slept by her side, in the bed to which they'd retreated as the night grew colder, one arm curved above his head and the other resting on his stomach. The ink that wound about his arm was black in the early light, black as the hair that sprawled wild across crisp white pillows, and he seemed too vivid for this bleak winter landscape.

He didn't belong here, neither of them did, and soon they would be gone.

Pulling the blankets a little further up his chest, she slipped from the bed and tugged on the clothes she'd found. Then she built up the fire and went to stand at the window, gazing out over leafless trees into a fine, grey mist. The rain had stopped, at least. Somewhere beyond the woods lay the sea, and with it her duty to her father's legacy.

After a while, a hand touched her shoulder and she found Zach standing close behind her. 'We've stayed here too long.'

'I know.'

She didn't say more, just leaned back against him and felt relief when his arms slipped about her waist and pulled her tight against his chest. Her head came to rest against his and in a quiet voice Zach said, 'He'll never hear of this from my lips, I swear. Nor will anyone else.'

Amelia closed her eyes, lifting her palm to cup his cheek. 'Does this have to be the end?'

He was silent; she could feel his chest rise and gently fall. 'Where will you go now? Where will you have him take you?'

'To Ile Sainte Anne, I suppose.'

'There to rebuild your court and wait for death in all her imperial glory?' He drew back, and when she turned, she saw sorrow in his eyes. 'I'll not follow you there, Amy;

don't ask me to. Ile Sainte Anne is gone; I've seen it with my own eyes. There's nothing there but death.'

'The Articles are there.'

'Those days are over. Can't you see that? The days of piracy are gone, there's no place left for us in the world. We must find our freedoms elsewhere.'

'But where else — ?'

Zach started, his attention darting over her shoulder. 'Get down.' Tugging her to the floor, he crept up to the window and peered out.

She could hear it too, the drum of horses' hooves and the rattle of a carriage. Someone was returning – the staff, most likely, in advance of the family.

Zach's smile was crafty as he turned back to her. 'A hasty departure would seem prudent, Captain Dauphin. What do you think of the window?'

'That it might prove a long drop.' She was smiling too, already tugging on her boots. 'Yet preferable to a short drop from the Tyburn Tree.'

Without further comment, Zach pulled on the rest of his clothes and weapons, pausing only to toss Amelia one of his pistols. She tucked it into her belt with a nod of thanks, and then quickly wound her hair into a plait to keep it from her eyes as they made their escape.

By the time Zach pushed up the window, the sounds of horses' hooves had been replaced by the low murmur of conversation; whoever had arrived, they were at the front of the house. It would not be long before evidence of their presence was discovered.

Sure enough, just as he climbed out onto the narrow ledge, a shout went up from below. He stopped and his eyes met hers for an instant, filled with an unexpected glee, before he abruptly dropped from view.

Amelia gasped, leaning out of the window and half expecting to see him sprawled on the path below. Instead, he was crouched on the flat roof of a bay window only ten feet below and looking up at her with a grin. Then he was over the edge and clambering down.

From inside the house, Amelia heard voices – raised and angry. Quickly, she climbed through the window until only her fingertips held onto the sill. With a muttered curse, she let go and fell – forever, it seemed – to the flat roof below. She landed with a crunch that jarred her healing ankle and made her spit a curse out loud.

'Shhhhh!' Zach was making frantic hushing gestures from the ground and the sight was so comic that she couldn't help but smile.

Less elegantly than he, she scrambled down from the roof. His hands steadied her for the last part, and when her feet touched the ground she found that she was all but in his arms. Despite, or perhaps because of, the current danger she reached up and kissed him quickly on the mouth. Then glancing over his shoulder she grabbed his hand and whispered, 'Run!'

A moment of surprise registered on his face, and then they were both pelting towards the trees.

'Hey!' A man's voice yelled from behind them. 'Come back here, you filthy buggers!'

Amelia didn't look back. The trees were very close now and Zach was outpacing her – only because of her ankle, she told herself. She followed him into the woods, ducking branches and scrambling through scrub. Then, out of nowhere, a hand grabbed her arm and tugged her sideways.

'Loop around,' Zach whispered breathlessly, his fingers finding her hand and holding tight, pulling her through the trees to cut back around the clearing in which the house lay. They weren't far into the wood, but far enough to be hidden, and she could see his logic; they'd make their escape in the opposite direction and need not worry about pursuit.

She could hear people shouting, disturbingly close. Once,

when the voices seemed as if they might be lurking behind the next tree, she hauled Zach to a halt and they stood there together, listening. In that suspended moment his eyes met hers and held them, as if he were still getting the measure of her. His hand tightened around hers and she squeezed back, hoping he understood, better than herself, the complexities of her heart.

The voices moved away and they started walking again. At last, Zach judged they had gone far enough and they headed deeper into the woods, away from the house and all that had happened there.

Perhaps that was why they walked in silence, their hands linked by unspoken consent. It was that same tacit intimacy that had always defined their relationship, an unvoiced certainty of their closeness that had never been discussed.

Zach talked briefly about taking a room at an inn for the night, but that afternoon they saw soldiers on the road again and decided it would be safer to stay in the woods. So they built another shelter and a small fire and ate the food they'd taken from the house.

They sat close, though, and when Zach leaned his back against a tree, she rested her head on his shoulder and smiled at the warmth of his arm about her. The fire popped and crackled, and far above, through the winter-black branches of the trees, Amelia thought she glimpsed the stars. It reminded her of nights on the cliffs of Sainte Anne, with Overton at her side as she learned the fine art of celestial navigation. With the whole ocean laid out before her, she'd sometimes imagined she could see the entire world and everyone in it – everyone lost to her.

With a sigh, she slipped her arm about Zach's waist and turned her face against his neck. 'Where will you go?' she asked, the first one to speak for hours, it seemed. 'If not to Ile Sainte Anne, then where? The Indies again?'

His head came to rest against hers. 'I find I've lost my

appetite for the pleasures of the Indies, and gold only has value if you've a mind to spend it.' He made a soft sound that might have been a laugh. 'My father could attest to the emptiness of plunder.'

She was silent a moment, steeling herself, and then said, 'Not sure he ever lost his appetite for treasure, Zach. Though he gave up something more valuable at the end, for the Articles.'

'Yes,' Zach said after a while. 'How uncharacteristically noble of the old sod.'

'You think his life wasted?' She bristled under his accusation, lifting her head so that she could look at him.

'He abandoned me twice, Amy. Don't expect me to mourn him.'

She studied his serious face, confused. 'Once, I know about. That he left you as a child in London, but a second time ...?'

With a shake of his head, he looked away into the fire.

'Zach?' She touched his cheek, but he wouldn't look at her.

'On the *Intrepid*,' he said at last. 'He— What father would die for a book yet watch their son hang and not—?'

Amy gasped, a hand to her mouth. 'My God,' she breathed as he turned to look at her in surprise. 'Can it be that you don't know?'

'Don't know what?'

'Oh Zach.' Tears filled her eyes and she dashed them away, swallowing hard before she could speak. 'Don't you know that it was your father who saved you?'

He absolutely stared at her. 'My father? I thought Brookes ...'

'Brookes fished you out of the water, yes, but it was Overton who fired the shot that cut you down. From the deck of the *Sunlight* – an incredible shot.' She hung her head, eyes filling again at the memory. 'He knew what

Morton was; he knew what the dawn would bring. If he hadn't ...' She shivered and looked up. 'He loved you, Zach. Never doubt that.'

He was silent for a long time, lost in the flames, and only roused himself when she touched his hand.

'Your father would have wanted you to have the Articles, Zach. He always spoke of them as your inheritance.'

Zach shrugged and looked away, out into the night. 'You know my thoughts on that. It's a new world we're living in now and we'd best change with it, or die.'

'Is that what you're planning to do?'

He glanced at her from the corner of his eye. 'Die? Not partial to the taste of that, as it happens. But there is a place ...' He smiled and lowered his gaze into the flames, drifting slowly away. 'There's a place, Amy, a slice of paradise. Hot sun, blue seas ...With a sloop and— Well, a man could be happy there. Live free of interference from His Majesty, or any other majesty who might poke his beak in.'

She laughed, a little uneasily. 'Not you, Zach. You were born for the sea, for a pirate's life.'

With a sigh, he turned to her. 'So it seems. Doomed to my father's fate.'

'He died free.'

'Aye, completely free. Unfettered by a single chain, save the one that bound him to the Articles.'

His eyes had turned as black as the night and not a single star lit their depths. There was bleakness there, an emptiness she felt echoed in her own heart – the pain of being alone, unconnected in the wide world. Perhaps it was that sudden, desperate loneliness that made her reach for him again, that made *him* reach for her, as eager as herself to fill the void.

This time his kiss was achingly tender and her body flowered beneath his touch, needing him more than she could bear. His hands didn't leave her, sketching a lover's dance against her skin even as he moved slow and steady inside her. After a while he stilled, carefully, and she opened her eyes to find him watching her. Never breaking eye contact, he began to move once more, slowly at first, and she wondered if he was showing her something of himself in that velvet gaze – or if he was seeking something of her. A truth, perhaps. Whatever it was, he hung on as long as possible – long after he'd drawn her crashing over the edge – until he was trembling with the effort of not giving way. Then she spoke his name, a soft whisper infused with all that she felt, and it was enough. He fell, kept on falling, and she held him tight as he gasped her name, over and over, against her neck, his words drifting slowly into drowsy kisses.

Above her, Amelia found the stars misting with tears and wondered how she would bear the separation that dawn would bring.

Chapter Thirty-Three

The sun was at its zenith when Zach first caught the scent of the onshore breeze. Fresh and clean, it swept in from the southwest and blew away the clouds that had lingered through the morning. The afternoon was bright and clear, colder, but what did that matter now they were at journey's end?

He glanced over at Amy to see if she sensed it too. From the set look of her jaw and the pallor of her face he suspected that she did. They walked a discreet distance apart, as they had since dawn, both thinking on what the day would bring. And the months and years beyond that ...

Though he knew it to be folly, he'd given thought to returning to Ile Sainte Anne. But in that fortress he couldn't be all to her that he wished to be, and he couldn't bear to be anything less. For she was still wife to Luc Géroux and mistress of that island, that's as it was, and despite her talk of choices past and present, what was done was done. Wishing it otherwise was a fool's game.

Yet he'd always been a fool.

They walked now through a narrow ravine that lead across a peninsula and down to the cliffs, shadowed on each side by trees and, far above, by the melancholic ruin of a castle, laid low, no doubt, during the troubles of his grandfather's years. Zach looked up at its dour grey walls and tilting turrets, not sorry to see it in a state of such dereliction; it had the look of hanging, and worse, about it.

As he looked away, he caught Amelia's eye, caught the strange wonder in her face as she, too, looked up at the castle walls. In that moment, he realised that she was more a child of the sea than he, for this was a strange and foreign land to her. 'How old do you think it is?' she asked, squinting against the bright winter sun.

Zach shrugged. 'A few hundred years, I suppose.'

'Amazing, to have stood for so long.'

'And to have been brought down so fast.'

She smiled a little. 'All things must pass.'

'Aye,' he agreed, casting her a hopeful look. 'So they must.'

But she wasn't watching him, her gaze now on the treacherous path they walked and her face set.

After a while he said, 'I've seen things older than this, though. Statues and jewellery from Rome, the Greeks. Makes this look like a child's blundering construction.' He paused, casting her a sly look. 'Have you never sailed the Mediterranean?'

Though he asked the question, Zach already knew the answer. Amelia Dauphin had ventured little from Ile Sainte Anne, too busy with her ideals – or her father's ideals – to leave her seat of power. That was exactly why he'd spent so many of the past years sailing the Barbary Coast.

Amelia frowned as if she understood his game, and he felt a pang of guilt for playing it at all. 'Perhaps one day I will,' she said with a thin smile.

'When duty permits?'

She looked away and stopped suddenly, her hand reaching for his arm. 'Look.'

Ahead of them, he could make out the path widening into a track, and beyond that a few stone cottages clustered together. It was not that which drew his eye, however; it was the scarlet flash of a soldier's coat. 'We'll have to go around,' he said.

'Do you think they know where we're heading?'

Zach shook his head. 'Not unless the *Serpent*'s been spotted. Géroux will have men ashore by now, waiting for you, and his ship will be hiding. Come on.' He began to climb the steep bank towards the tumbledown castle, keeping low among the scrubby trees.

'And you?' she asked, clambering after him.

'The *Hawk*'s hereabouts – I dare say I'll find her.'

There was a pause from behind him, then: 'Why not let Luc take you to the *Hawk*, Zach?'

He smiled, glad she couldn't see it, for he doubted it was a pleasant sight. 'I can find my own way.'

'But Zach—'

'Shhh.' Ahead, there was an open stretch to cross before they reached the shelter of the castle. He waited, listening, then ran, Amelia on his heels. He stopped in the shadow of a fallen wall, crouching low as she crowded in behind him. From their vantage point, he could see the small village swarming with soldiers, but if they cut through the ruined castle and down the other side, they'd miss the lot. 'Follow me.'

Carefully, they picked their way through the mournful ruins, climbing over stone and beneath precariously tilting walls, until they reached the other side of the hill and scrambled down and back into the shelter of the trees.

'A short cut,' Zach said, breathless from the climb, as Amy joined him in the woods. 'You'll be in your husband's arms before sunset, no doubt.'

She frowned and he regretted his words – regretted the harshness of them, at least. Grimacing, he reached out a tentative hand. 'Amy, I—'

'Stand still, if you value your life, sir.'

Zach froze, his arm still outstretched. From the corner of his eye, he saw a red coat and a musket.

Bugger.

Amy lifted her eyes to his and they flared a little, as if saying: *Take him*. He dared not smile, however fierce the desire, and so instead lifted both hands and turned to get a better view of his enemy. There were two of them, no more than two score years between them. One seemed like he'd still to sever the apron strings, the other had a hang-gallows look about him. That one, Zach kept his eye upon. 'Honest travellers, sir,' Zach said, by way of introduction. 'Me and my ... brother here.'

'Very honest, skulking around such as you are,' said the boy. 'What's your name?'

'Jed Brookes. What's yours?'

But the devilish one wasn't listening, his attention – as Zach had feared – was fixed on Amelia. 'You,' he said, 'come here.'

She moved closer, poised, Zach could tell, for a fight. His own fingers itched for a weapon but he dared not move, not with the other man's musket aimed at his head.

'Brother, you say?' The soldier eyed her carefully, and Zach knew from the lascivious glint in his eye that he was not fooled. Indeed, few would be.

'Is it them?' the other boy said. 'Is that her? Shall I fetch the captain?'

'That depends,' the soldier said, 'on what the pirate whore is prepared to do to persuade us otherwise.'

Before Zach could react, Amelia had stepped forward. 'Oh, I'm prepared to do a great deal,' she said softly. 'A very great deal.'

Zach held his breath.

'I learned much,' she purred, 'among the ... *pirates.*'

The soldier's eyes were widening, musket drooping even as other things were rising. 'Yes,' he breathed. 'I bet you did.'

She smiled and licked her lips in a way Zach would have found intoxicating had the situation been different. 'Shall I show you?'

'Yes ...'

She ran the fingers of one hand across the polished buttons of his coat, 'This was my first lesson.'

'Go on ...' His eyes bulged, oblivious to the fact that, in Amelia's other hand, Zach's pistol appeared.

She leaned in with a devilish smile and suddenly the pistol was jammed beneath the soldier's chin and the musket yanked from his limp fingers. With a sharp crack, she slammed the butt of her weapon into the lad's head and he dropped like a stone. 'And that,' she said, 'was lesson two.'

Oh, Zach could have kissed her, but he was forced to restrain himself in view of the fact that the other soldier was staring at them both with eyes like plates, his hands trembling as he waved his gun at them.

Zach sauntered closer, pulling his own pistol from his belt. 'You were right: we are pirates,' he told the boy. 'Fearsome, ruthless bloody pirates. If I were you I'd scarper before I let her have at you. Lesson three's quite something to behold.'

With that, the boy was off, struggling up the hill towards the castle. Zach glanced briefly down at the lad on the ground, then back up at Amelia. He tipped her a brief salute, 'Very well done, Captain.'

She just smiled.

Stupidly, helplessly, he let himself fall into that smile, and for a blissful moment there was peace – perfect understanding between them – but it was too painful to bear and with a sigh Zach looked away, towards the beckoning sea. 'Now,' he said, 'we need to run.'

So they did.

The sun was low on the horizon by the time they left the sparse woodland and the low roar of the sea reached Zach's ears; never before had he cursed the sound. The land sloped gently down to the cliff edge, scrubby grass and thistles thick beneath his boots and the air tart with the salt-scent of home.

Pale blues and purples coloured this winter sunset, not the glorious ochre of the Indies, and the water gleamed like white gold beneath a violet sky. Ancient cliffs, sculpted by waves into coves and arches, marked the rocky shore of this island he had once called home, and Zach was struck by its melancholic beauty.

Amelia bumped against his shoulder as they walked and he glanced over. In the day's dying light she looked ghostly, a phantom passing through his life, soon to be gone. Soon to be in the arms of another.

The thought made him grit his teeth and turn away, back to the silver horizon. That's when he saw the ship, sleek and bright, half hidden behind the great arch of rock that reached out from the cove. He touched Amy's arm, getting her attention, and pointed. 'Géroux.'

She looked and said tensely, 'I can't see the *Hawk*.'

'We're somewhat east of her, I imagine.'

'Then how will you find her?'

He cut her a look. 'Do you think I can't find my own bloody ship?'

'I think you're being stupid. Why won't you come aboard the *Serpent*?'

'You know why.'

She was silent, frowning. 'I won't leave you here, with the soldiers so close.'

'Then we have an impasse, for I'll not be a passenger aboard the *Serpent*. Don't ask me to witness that fond reunion, Amy.'

'Would you rather face—?'

The crack of musket fire echoed over the grassland, sending them both sprawling to the ground. To their right, and behind, he saw soldiers, their coats bright in the dusky light, bearing down towards them on horseback.

'Stop where you are!' one of the men shouted. 'Stop, in the name of His Majesty the King!'

Zach was on his feet, hauling Amelia after him. 'Run!'

The cliff edge was only a few hundred feet away, but there was no cover save the falling darkness and they had no choice but to run full tilt. Another musket shot rang out, and again it missed.

Amelia turned and fired her pistol as she ran, the gunpowder scent mixing with the salt-tang and reminding him of every other battle he'd fought. He fired too, and smiled to see the soldiers break formation, slowing.

Too late, he realised it was because the cliff edge was beneath their feet.

With a yelp, he pitched forward and found himself skidding down a steep, but not vertical, drop. He came to rest on an outcrop of grass, Amelia slip-sliding to land next to him.

Above, he heard the rumble of hoof beats and knew they weren't safe.

'Come on.' Tucking his pistol back into his belt he made his way down the steep, rocky cliff. Below curved an almost circular cove. A pale glint of sand was all he could make out in the twilight, but it was dark on the beach and tonight darkness would be their salvation.

Above them, someone was shouting orders and from the dark he heard the soft crack of steel on flint. A torch was lit, flaring bright into the night sky, but its light was too feeble to find them now.

They were so close to the beach that he could hear the soft lap of the waves against the shore and all too soon his boots crunched into the shingle at the base of the cliff. He stopped and let the feel of it fill him; in moments Amelia would be safe – in moments she would be gone.

From the other side of the cove he heard movement, clumsy footfalls on what was probably a path down to the shore. The soldiers were on their way.

Amelia scrambled down the last couple of feet and crowded close to him. There was no moon yet, though it wasn't quite dark and he could still see her face as she looked across the flat sea.

Neither of them moved.

After a long silence, Zach said, 'Walk to the shore. He'll have a longboat in the water by now. They'll find you.'

'And the soldiers will find you.'

'Unlikely.' He took her arm and began to lead her to the sea. 'If I can't outrun this rabble, I'll bloody deserve to swing.'

They were almost at the water's edge. A vast stone doorway arched out into the sea – black against the deep violet of the sky – and beyond it the horizon faintly glowed. A promise, Zach thought, or a warning. All things must pass.

Behind them, muffled voices whispered and a foot stepped onto the beach.

'Go,' he said softly, releasing her arm and stepping back.

Amelia stared straight ahead, across the water. In a low voice she said, 'How can I?'

'How can you not?'

When she didn't reply, he knew it was because she had no answer to give.

The soldiers were creeping along the base of the cliff, but he didn't think they'd seen them yet, standing close to the water and beneath the shadow of the vast arch. Nonetheless ... 'Go, Amy. Hurry.'

'No.' She turned around to face him. 'I won't. I won't leave you.'

He drew in a deep breath. 'Amy—'

'I won't leave you here!' Her fingers wrapped about the fabric of his shirt, pulling him close. 'Do you hear me?'

'Aye, I hear you, and so will His Majesty's finest if you don't lower your bloody voice.'

'Come with me.'

He knew he could. He could stride with her into the waves and Luc Géroux would take them both aboard his ship. He'd take them aboard and take his wife for his own, and *that* Zach could not witness. Would not witness.

So with a deep breath he took her face in his hands and

drew her closer, drew her into a kiss that broke his heart for a second time. She softened beneath his touch, her fingers loosening on his shirt and coming to rest against his shoulder as she melted into him, languid and beautiful. Slowly he drew back, enough to see her face once more. 'I've got no choice,' he murmured, and with a sharp push he sent her stumbling backward, stumbling to her knees in the surf. Stumbling back to Luc.

Amelia gasped, more from the shock than the cold he supposed, and stared down at the water swirling about her. 'No—'

Stepping backward, Zach raised his hands. 'Go, now.'

'Zach, no.'

A gunshot rang out across the beach. Zach flung himself against the cliff, watching as Amy scrambled to her feet. 'Come with me!' she pleaded. 'Zach!'

From behind the rocky outcrop came the low shape of a boat, oars dipping and moving fast through the water. Sent from the *Serpent*, no doubt. A shout rang out from the foot of the cliff, but Zach ignored it. All his attention was fixed on Amelia as she glanced from him to the longboat and back again, her face splintering into a dozen different emotions. Zach retreated further. 'Run,' he said. 'Run, Amy, and keep on running.'

She looked at him, heartbreak in her eyes, and for a moment he thought she might throw all her duties aside and come to him. Her hand lifted, reaching out, and he took half a step towards her. Then she turned, striding out through the waves, back to the longboat and Géroux.

Back to everything that held them apart.

His breath left him all at once, sending him sagging, gasping, against the cliff, and had the soldiers shot him in the chest at that moment, he would have felt no pain. For his heart had beaten its last, and now lay like stone in his chest.

It was over. She was gone.

Chapter Thirty-Four

Jedediah Brookes was sitting on the quarterdeck steps, chewing the end of his pipe, when he heard the first gunshot. It rang out over the flat sea with the precise crack of a soldier's musket. He cast a sharp glance across the deck and found himself fixed by Shiner's nervous stare. The second shot came a few moments later, another musket, and then a third and fourth – and those, he recognised. 'Zach.'

Shiner unwound his gangly legs and climbed to his feet. 'I know the sound of them pistols right enough,' he said, scampering across the deck to lean out over the starboard rail. 'Sounds like the captain's in trouble, Mr Brookes.'

With a sigh, Brookes pushed himself to his feet. 'When isn't the captain in trouble?'

Shiner cocked his head. 'Well, there was that time, three year ago, when —'

'It was a rhetorical question,' Brookes growled. His old bones weren't suited to the cold and damp of the British Sea and they'd ached like the devil since they'd entered the North Atlantic three weeks ago. He felt like an old man as he stumped over to where Shiner was shivering and peering out into the gloomy evening. 'About five or six miles east, I'd say,' Brookes ventured, hearing no more gunshots. 'Too close to Poole for my liking.'

With a sigh, he turned away from the rail. It seemed Zach had chosen to make a dash to the sea somewhat sooner than planned, far closer to the busy seaport and its Revenue men and navy frigates. Too close for the *Hawk* to venture safely, especially in these troubled days. Zach would have to make his way west, into less perilous waters.

Brookes pulled his flask from his coat pocket and took a swig of rum, but its fierce burn wasn't enough to warm him.

'D'you think they got him?' Shiner asked fearfully. 'I don't hear no more shots.'

Brookes wiped his mouth on the back of his hand and put the flask away. There was a time when he'd have laughed at the notion – Captain Zach Hazard wasn't likely to be captured by a handful of redcoats – but the world was a different place now and Zach Hazard had become a different man these past years; Brookes wasn't entirely convinced he'd want to get away if it meant leaving *her* behind. 'We stick to the plan and wait for the signal,' was all he said, and prayed they'd not be left waiting forever.

Though she didn't recognise the sailors who manned the longboat, the *Serpent* was just as Amelia remembered her: sleek, well ordered, her brass fittings bright in the lamplight. Like her master, the *Serpent* was always immaculate.

Amelia, though, climbed the ladder onto the deck without seeing anything of her glory. Her mind's eye was focussed still on Zach, standing on the foreshore, coat caught by the winter wind, whipping out behind him as he watched her leave.

A gunshot rang out from the beach and she spun so fast she almost lost her footing. Another shot, the flash of a musket barrel in the dark. She strained her eyes, but could see nothing more. It was too dark.

Sick with loss and fear, she had to stop for a moment, clinging to the ship's rail for support as she gathered her strength. Duty. She clung to that, too, as surely as she clung to the rail. She could not abandon her duty to Ile Sainte Anne, to the Articles, and to her father's legacy.

As much as she might want— No, she would not think about it. That was done. Her choice had been made and so had his. Zach would not return to Ile Sainte Anne, and she would not abandon it. Fate marked two paths and they had each chosen to walk a different one. She would not regret or repent.

Taking a deep breath, she straightened her shoulders, let go of the rail, and turned to face her husband's crew. She couldn't see his first mate, so addressed one of the men who'd fetched her in the longboat. '*Où est le capitaine Géroux?*'

The man smiled, an unpleasant expression, and said in native English, 'You'll find him below, miss.'

His accent was educated, surprising given his ragged appearance. Surprising too among Luc's French crew. Her hand found its way to the pistol tucked into her belt – Zach's weapon. 'Take me to him, then.'

'Delighted,' said the crewman, and gestured towards the steps that led down to Luc's cabin.

The hair rose on the back of her neck as she began to walk, eyes watching her from the darkness. She licked her lips, kept her hand on her weapon, and told herself it was ridiculous to be uneasy aboard Luc's ship. He was her husband, was he not?

The deck below was dark, only the light creeping out from around the edges of the cabin door provided any guidance, but she knew this ship well and in a few steps she was at his door, pushing it open. 'Luc.'

He turned around with a start. 'Amelia.' His face was white, his expression more akin to horror than joy.

'What is it?' she said immediately. 'What's happened?'

'I ...' He took a step closer and she noticed his crumpled clothing, the ashy circles beneath his eyes. 'Amelia, I'm so sorry.'

'Good God, what's happened?' Her first horrified thought was of Zach – he'd been killed on the beach. 'Tell me at once!'

'Forgive me, I had no choice.'

She opened her mouth to speak, but the hard press of a gun at her back cut off her words. 'Captain Dauphin,' said a familiar, loathed voice. 'How kind of you to join us.'

Luc turned away, unable to look at her.

'It's unnatural still,' Shiner said, glancing up at a clear sky awash with northern stars. 'Do you feel Neptune's hand in it?'

Brookes sniffed and pulled his coat tighter. 'Not in these waters, lad. There's other creatures what rule these chilly depths, if you believe the stories.'

'What stories?' Shiner blinked worriedly. 'What stories, Mr Brookes?'

'Well, they do say, King Llŷr rules these seas – and a terrible king he is, too, so old it seems his face is carved of driftwood, his hair floating out like tangled seaweed. When he's in a rage the seas boil, but when he's calm ...' Brookes gestured about him.

'Boil?' Shiner repeated.

'Aye, and he has himself a daughter – the fairest you ever did see – sent to lure unsuspecting sailors to their death at her father's hands.' He glanced back towards the land. 'No doubt possessed of near-black hair and a fiery spirit, with a habit of dressing like a lad and putting her nose where it don't belong.'

Shiner blinked. 'Like the sirens luring sailors onto the rocks.'

'Aye, something like that.' Brookes sighed and stumped to his feet. 'Or onto land.' He looked out, towards the black cliffs. 'Come on, Zach, where are you?'

After a while Shiner said, 'Perhaps he sailed with the *Serpent*, back to Ile Sainte Anne?'

Brookes slid him a sceptical look. 'He'll not go back there. Turned his back on all that, didn't he?'

'I'm thinking, Mr Brookes, that if he'd turned his back on it we wouldn't be sittin' here freezin' to death.'

It was a good point, Brookes was forced to concede. 'He'd not abandon the *Hawk*,' he insisted, turning back to stare at the shore once more. 'Nor his crew. If he don't come back, it's because he can't.'

He said no more than that, couldn't bear to think of what that might mean.

Lord Morton.

He sat in the captain's chair, hands clasped over his belly, smug and self-satisfied. Amelia loathed him with every bone in her body. The only slight satisfaction she felt in seeing him again was the jagged scar across his cheek, left by the blade she'd wielded the day she'd first landed in London.

Her fingers itched for a weapon now, to finish what she'd started.

'Isn't this charming?' Morton said. 'A husband reunited with his wife. Delightful.'

Luc said nothing, standing to one side of the desk with his face set like stone. Amy spared him a single glance; whatever his motives for this betrayal, she'd not discuss them in front of Morton. 'What do you want?' she said instead. 'If you think to set a trap for Zach then you have the wrong bait.'

'Zach Hazard?' His faux surprise revolted her. 'Did you not hear the gunfire? My dear, Captain Hazard is already dead.'

Horror clamped in her gut, but she kept her face immobile and said only, 'So you say.'

'See the body if you wish. I'll have it tarred and gibbeted in Wapping until it rots. Alongside your own, in due course.'

Lies. It was lies. It had to be. Gritting her teeth, she turned her gaze once more on Luc to see if she could read the truth in his face, but he would not look at her. She'd never seen a man more crushed by guilt. She could almost pity him.

'No,' Morton said, rising with effort and strolling closer. 'It's not Hazard I want, Miss Dauphin; it's you.' His warm breath washed over her face, making her turn away in disgust. He laughed. 'Oh don't worry, I've higher standards than that. I've no desire to strum a common street whore.' He leaned closer, lowered his voice. 'It's what's in your head that interests me, not what lies between your legs.' When she said nothing, he added, 'The location of a book. A scurrilous book.'

'The Articles of Agreement?' The mere mention of it brought her father to mind and she faced Morton with renewed defiance. 'That is what you want from me? I don't have it. It's not here.'

'Obviously.' He moved away, circling the table and exchanging a look with Luc. 'I understand that this book, these Articles of Agreement, are hidden on Ile Sainte Anne – and that only you know where to find them.'

Luc hung his head still further, fingers clenching into fists. His lips moved in silent apology, but Amelia had to look away, so hot was her anger. To have betrayed *that* to *this* man! Every other treachery paled in comparison – Luc had betrayed everything upon which her life was built.

Voice shaking with rage, she said, 'My father died to protect the Articles and the freedom they represent. So did Captain Overton and a hundred other good men. Do you think I could ever betray their memories?' She squared her shoulders, finding strength in her certainty. 'Do what you like to me, but I will *never* tell you how to find the Articles.'

'Yes,' Morton sighed, 'I thought you might say as much.' He signalled over her shoulder and from behind her another man stepped forward. Tall and brutish, he wore a stained leather apron and stank of blood and despair. 'Tonight we sail for Ile Sainte Anne,' Morton said. 'Mr Crouch, take her below and make her talk before we dock.'

An iron fist closed about her arm, pulling her towards the door. Weak-kneed with terror, she recoiled. 'No. Please ...'

'*Mon Dieu!*' Luc burst out. 'Please, Amelia, just tell him where to find the book!'

She stared at him, at his grey face crushed by remorse and fear, and in his weakness she found her strength. She stopped struggling and in a firm voice said, 'I'd rather die.'

'How fortunate.' Morton gave an ugly smile. 'For that is your only other option.'

Three hours passed, the moon had long since set, and the night was black as pitch and cold as the devil. Brookes blew on his hands, but there was little warmth to be had as he leaned against the rail and scoured the cliffs for any sign of Zach.

Some of the crew whispered that he'd sailed with the *Serpent* or been felled by the Revenue men, or by those in pursuit of Amelia Dauphin. But not Brookes. He'd known Zach too long – seen him dead-drunk and dead-dead – and knew that he'd not give up his life so cheaply. If the noose could not claim him, then nothing could. So said Jedediah Brookes.

That's why, when he saw the flicker of light on the beach, he was relieved, but not surprised. 'There!' he said softly, touching the sleeve of Shiner's coat. 'Do you see?'

Rubbing his eyes, Shiner peered into the night and for a moment they both held their breath. It came again, a flame – bright, and then gone. Bright, and then gone. A lantern or a burning torch.

Brookes grinned. 'That's it, that's Zach's signal.'

'He made it!' Shiner laughed. 'Captain Hazard made it!'

'Shhh, now,' Brookes scolded, glancing about as if he might see the navy board-a-board. 'Don't know who's in these waters tonight, eh? Go, quietly now, and lower a longboat. Fetch the captain.'

With a quick bob of his head, Shiner scampered off and Brookes heard him gathering someone to help him row ashore.

From the land, the light came again – bright, and then

gone. Bright, and then gone. Stooping, Brookes picked up the dark lantern he'd kept at his feet all night. Lifting it high, he slid back the panel for a count of ten and closed it again. He did it twice more and then the light on the beach disappeared and Brookes doused the lantern; Zach knew they were on their way.

Yet it seemed a cold eternity before Brookes heard the soft splash of oars that heralded the longboat's return. With hushed voices the boat was tied up, and from the darkness Zach Hazard emerged. Bereft of his usual swagger, he looked a different man as he climbed the ladder to the deck.

'Zach,' Brookes said, grasping his hand to help him the final few steps. 'Glad to see you in one piece.'

'More or less,' Zach agreed, looking about him as if surprised to be there at all. 'Have you had any trouble?'

'Only dragging Shiner out of the *Wink* at Lamorna, Captain. We stayed westerly, you see, though it's less friendly even down there than I'd like. Bloody Revenue men everywhere.'

'It's less friendly everywhere in this poxy country, Brookes. It's less friendly in the whole wide world.'

'So it is, Captain.' Brookes paused, catching Shiner's eye as he clambered back aboard. 'That being as it may, Zach, the crew and I was wondering what our heading might be – now that you've settled your business here.' But from Zach's morose demeanour Brookes feared that the business wasn't settled at all, and with a sigh he said, 'Talking of which, where is Miss Dauphin?'

'Safe with her husband,' Zach said, turning towards his cabin. 'Sailing back to Ile Sainte Anne. Plans to rebuild it herself or some such nonsense.'

'And what of our course?' Brookes persisted, following. 'Where do we sail now, Zach?'

He stopped abruptly, head bowed as if he studied the deck. After a while, and in a flat voice, he said, 'In truth,

Mr Brookes, I have no bloody idea. Take us somewhere warmer.'

'Warmer?'

'I'm cold, Brookes, and tired of it. Tired of it all.' With that, he pushed his way into his cabin and slammed shut the door.

Slowly, Shiner moved to stand at Brookes' side as all around them the crew exchanged uncertain glances. 'I'd say Old King Llŷr's daughter has him fair wrecked, Mr Brookes.'

'Aye, so she has.' He sighed and looked over at the rangy crewman, seeing more understanding than he'd expected in his narrow features. 'Ain't just her, though, is it? There's no room left in this new world for the likes of us. No room at all.'

Chapter Thirty-Five

Despite his brutish features, Crouch was an artist. His touch was delicate. He knew exactly how to administer pain, how to seed terror and nurture its growth. And he knew when to use violence, when to overwhelm her with his size and ferocity.

Thus, he made Amelia talk.

But he could not make her speak the truth. When he left her shivering and broken in the brig, she clung to the fact that everything she'd told him was a lie. Morton would never find the Articles from her directions, and with luck she would die before he realised as much.

Dark days and dark nights bled together; she knew not when one ended and another began. She cared not. Her only hope was death, but Crouch was too clever to let that come quickly.

Then one night, in the thick black, she heard another voice, soft through the bars of her cell. Her father? Perhaps she was close enough to death that he could speak to her? She half rose from the floor, stomach twisting with sickness. Hunger and pain, she supposed, conspired to add to her misery. Her throat was raw, voice scratchy as she whispered, 'Who's there?'

'Amelia ... Dear God, forgive me, Amelia.'

'You!' Peering through the gloom she saw pale fingers on the bars, behind them a haunted face staring out of the dark. 'What do you want here, Luc?'

He drew closer. 'I have food. Can you eat?'

He held out bread to her, through the bars, and it reminded her too much of Zach's visit to her in Newgate Gaol. The memory pierced her, sharper than any of Crouch's blades, and her eyes filled with tears. But though her pride recoiled from taking anything from this man, she was not so foolish to obey it and shuffled closer to the bars. Her left hand was useless, the wrist broken, clutched to her chest. With care, she reached through the bars for the bread he offered and began to nibble. 'Water?'

'Yes.' He pushed a skin through the bars, hands shaking, glancing over his shoulder every moment. He was afraid. 'Amelia, I have no words to— How can I explain to you? My God, it's impossible.'

The water was fresh and soothed her ragged throat. 'Then don't,' she said, wiping her mouth with her good hand. 'I've no stomach for your explanations.'

'But I must—'

'You betrayed me!' she hissed. 'You betrayed Zach, my father – all of us. If I had a blade I would kill you!'

He drew back, pallid as a ghost. 'I would do it myself,' he said, 'if I did not have another to protect. But Morton is a powerful man, he has powerful friends, and if I do not do as they command, then—' His voice broke and he dashed a hand across his eyes. 'They have other men such as Crouch.' Though it was dark, and her mind was clogged with fear and pain, it seemed to Amy that she could see him clearer now than ever before. Gone was the suave exterior, gone was the confident façade and reserved smile; she felt as though she were seeing Luc Géroux for the first time. He was a damaged, broken man.

'My father is dead. Zach is dead, and I am soon to follow. Yet you fear for your own life?'

'No, not for *my* life.' Luc looked up, distraught. 'For my daughter's. Amelia, they took my daughter from me.'

For a moment she couldn't speak, just pressed the water skin to her lips and swallowed. Her wrist throbbed like the devil, her back burned from a dozen lashes from the cat, yet she found that her heart ached for the man before her – for the sorrow she saw in his eyes. 'What do you mean?' she said at last. 'What daughter? Why didn't you tell me?'

300

He shook his head, turning away in shame. 'How could I? I fell under Morton's power ten years ago and have been his creature ever since. How could I tell you, or anyone, and risk the life of my child?'

'Ten years ago? Then ...'

'Yes, yes, of course. Now you know why I first came to Ile Sainte Anne – it was in search of Zach Hazard and at Morton's command. This much is true. But I did not— You must believe me, I did not know he would take your father. When he had done so, and you were alone ...?' He shook his head. 'It would have been better, perhaps, had I gone too. But how could I leave you alone when I had been the means of taking your father from you?'

She was silent, thinking. All along, Zach had warned her against trusting Luc, but she'd been so sure of him, so sure his heart was good. And perhaps she had been right after all. 'Your daughter,' she said, picking through the facts, 'she is how old?'

'Eleven years, now, and beautiful. He lets me see her once every twelvemonth.'

Amelia nodded. 'And her mother ...?'

'Élise. She was a maid in the house of Morton's wife.' He looked up, into Amelia's eyes. 'I loved her very much.'

'Loved?'

His gaze slipped away from hers. 'It is a dark story, and there is no time to tell it. All that matters is that she is gone, dead at the hand of Morton's men. A punishment for my—' He stopped, shook his head, then reached through the bars and took her hand. 'Forgive me, I may have no other chance to tell you this and you must hear it.

'There is a man in this world that even Morton fears, and this man hates me. He hates me because I betrayed his daughter.'

'How so?'

'She— Amelia, she was ... she *is* my wife.'

She felt her eyes widen in the dark, but said nothing, waiting for Luc to continue. After a moment he did so, his voice full of anger and grief. 'My father made the match, and what could I do but agree?' He made a sound – it might have been a laugh, but it was bitter as wormwood. 'Though I loved another, I believed a dutiful son must obey his father no matter what his heart desires.'

She took another swallow of water. 'And now?' she said. 'You think differently?'

'Of course, how can it be otherwise? Now I know that if a man acts against the will of his heart, he will always act wrong. What else can guide us true, but love?'

She was silent, the dark of the hold pressing in around her yet somehow it was less oppressive than the terrible truth in Luc's words. For she had long denied the will of her heart and let duty govern her choices; had it brought disaster down upon them all?

'My wife is a vain and ignorant woman,' Luc said, 'and I grew to hate her. I could not bear to be with her. And ...' His voice sank so low she could hardly hear him. 'And Élise was always in my heart. Beautiful, gentle Élise. Money and wealth, they were nothing to me. I thought only of Élise, of how to make her mine. And I did. I persuaded her to run away with me and for two years we were happy together – I believe she was happy.' After a pause, and in a stronger voice, he said, 'You can guess how it ended. We were discovered. She was—' He cleared his throat. 'Élise died and our child, our precious Josette, was taken. Thus I was to return to my wife, to act the good husband and save her from a society scandal. The life of my daughter was held as surety, to make me the slave of this man and his cabal. That is the truth, Amelia, all of the truth. That is why I am here now, why you are here. The fault is mine, all mine.'

Throughout all this speech, his hand had clutched hers in supplication. Now she pulled free, back through the bars.

'But this man – your wife's father – did he know of our marriage?'

'He knew of it, encouraged it in fact.' He shook his head and could not look at her. 'God forgive me, but I played a double game. I persuaded him that by masquerading as your husband I could wield power over Ile Sainte Anne – that, in time, I could destroy the Articles and everything for which they stood. You see, I thought it would stay their hand, keep them at bay. But when you raised the call to arms ... There was no more I could do. Nothing more I could say to stop them. Forgive me, Amelia, for in that I failed, too. I could not keep you safe.'

She said nothing immediately, not sure what she felt. Yet death was close and there was no time for recriminations or injured pride; there was no time for anything but honesty. After a little thought she said, 'Perhaps duty has led us both astray, but we did what we thought we must. There is no shame in that.' Taking his hand once more she squeezed his fingers, drawing his eyes back to hers. 'I forgive you, Luc. If my forgiveness is worth anything to you, then you have it.'

Astonishment covered his face before a ghost of a smile touched his lips. He pressed his hand to her bruised cheek and drew her closer until their heads were almost touching, separated only by the bars. 'Amelia, you can have no idea ...'

'I do. I know a great deal about betrayal and regret, Luc. About the longing for forgiveness.'

He pulled back, looking into her face. 'You are talking about Zach? Of course you are. I hope he has forgiven you. When last we met he was very bitter.'

'Yes,' she said, too tired to hide her feelings. 'He has.' Then she remembered what Morton had said, and her heart sank. 'He had, at the end.'

'I have not seen his body,' Luc said. 'Morton lied, I am sure of it. Zach survived. He always survives, does he not?'

She tried to smile, but it hurt and only roused a flurry of

fear when she thought of the pain yet to come. Tightening her hold on Luc's hand she said, 'Help me. I know, for the sake of your daughter, you can't free me, but at least bring me a blade. I can end it now, before Crouch comes back.'

'What?' He recoiled in horror. 'Amelia, no. Don't ask me to do that.'

'Luc, please. I'll die anyway, here or at Tyburn. It doesn't matter. But I can't endure any more —' Sudden tears clogged her throat. 'Please. Help me.'

Shaking his head, he backed away and she couldn't keep hold of his hand. It slipped through her fingers. 'I can't ...'

'You must!' she hissed, struggling to her feet. 'You owe me this!'

'There must be another way.'

'You know there isn't. If you free me, they'll hurt your daughter. Give me one of the knives he uses – there, on the table. They'll think I took it somehow.'

He looked at Crouch's dark blades and shuddered.

'Please, Luc. It's the only way you can save me.'

For a dreadful moment, she thought he would refuse, that he would turn and leave her alone to suffer and scream. He took a step to the door, then stopped and in one quick movement snatched up one of the knives and dropped it onto the floor. She fell to her knees and with her good arm stretched out fully. Just touching the tip, she dragged it through the dirt until she could pick it up. Pulling it through the bars, she sat back and looked up at Luc.

Misery marked every feature; she could see how much guilt he carried. Forcing a smile she said, 'Thank you. Luc, you've done all you can. Thank you. From my heart, thank you.'

He couldn't speak. His eyes shone liquid in the faint dawn light that began to creep down from above.

'Go,' she said. 'Before you're discovered.'

With a nod, he turned, hunched over in grief as he disappeared into the darkness.

Amelia listened to his feet on the ladder until he was gone, and then sat a good deal longer with the remains of the bread he'd brought in her hand and the knife resting on her lap. It would be the work of a moment to open a vein in her wrist and watch her life spill out.

Would there be time before Crouch returned? She didn't think she could slit her own throat, though it would be faster. Sitting there, in the dark, with the cold metal on her lap, she began to be afraid. Afraid, now it came to the point, of venturing into that shadowy land all alone. Afraid of abandoning life and hope.

Afraid of never seeing Zach again, of never telling him the single truth in all of Luc's many truths that had touched her most deeply: love, not duty, should be her pole star.

For what else could guide her true, but love?

Zach slept upon the deck. He breathed easier there than in the confines of his cabin, haunted by some half-lost suffocating memory of the ocean closing over his head and death wrapping her icy arms about his neck.

Or perhaps it reminded him of those nights beneath cold English skies with Amelia at his side, in his arms. He'd learned the art of celestial navigation in these northern skies, at his father's knee before duty had taken him away forever. He thought of it now, of the old sextant in his father's nimble hands, of his gruff voice and of the pain Zach had felt when his father left him behind in London's stinking streets. Left him for Ile Sainte Anne, just as Amelia had done. Duty, always duty.

You could have followed, a small voice whispered in the back of his head. *You chose to let her go.*

He shifted, irritated by the thought. That child, the half-starved lad he'd once been, could not have followed. He'd had no ship, no coin.

Unlike you.

'Will you be taking the early watch, sir?' The question came from Brookes, holding up a lamp and looking down at him with an irritating all-knowing scowl.

'Shiner has the watch,' Zach growled pulling his hat over his eyes to hide from that look. 'I'm sleeping.'

'Aye,' Brookes muttered. 'A fine place for the captain to be sleeping.' Nevertheless, he put down the lamp and lowered his old bones to the deck at Zach's side with no apparent intention of leaving. 'Dawn's almost here.'

Giving up on sleep, Zach sighed, propped himself up and cast an eye to the horizon. It was turning steel grey, like the blade of a knife.

'We should bear east,' Brookes said. 'If we're heading for the Floridas.'

'Heavy crossing, at this time of year,' Zach said, with a glance up at the *Hawk*'s foremast, still lost in the dark.

Brookes grunted. 'Precious few other places left in the world, Zach, for the likes of us.'

There was more truth in that than Zach wanted to admit. It made him think of Amelia – what didn't, these days? – and the impossible utopia she was determined to rebuild.

Perhaps Brookes saw something of it in Zach's eyes, for he said, 'It would be worth the voyage, though, for some good Cuban rum.'

'So it would.' A chill wind cut across the deck and he pulled his coat closer. 'I've been thinking about my father,' he told Brookes. In the lamplight he could see little but the weathered lines on his old friend's face. It was an honest face, one of the most honest faces he knew. 'Amelia told me it was him who saved me that day, his shot that severed the rope that would have hanged me.'

'Is that so?' Brookes rubbed a hand through his scraggy grey hair. 'He always was a good shot, your father.'

'I wish I'd known it,' Zach said, turning his eyes back

to the horizon. 'I wish I'd known it before he died. Things were not left well between us.'

Brookes huffed a sigh. "Tis always a bad thing, unfinished business.'

Unfinished business indeed.

He glanced at Brookes, to find his friend watching him in return, washed of colour in the grey dawn light. 'You've been a shadow of yourself, Zach, since you came back from London.'

'Seems that I left something of myself behind,' he said with a listless smile.

Brookes grunted. 'Not like Captain Hazard to leave behind that what he wants to keep for himself, even if it did belong to another.'

'Perhaps not,' Zach said. 'But Captain Hazard wasn't there, Jed. It was only Zachary Overton, and he never had much luck in London Town.'

Brookes shifted where he sat, sniffed a little in the cold wind. 'Well, we ain't in London now, are we? And Captain Hazard is the best pirate these seas ever saw. Perhaps it's time he claimed back what he left on England's shores?'

'It's not in England any more.'

'Mother and child, Zach,' Brookes growled. 'You know where she is!'

'Aye, amid the dead of Ile Sainte Anne! Throwing her life away on that dream, again. I'll not be part of it.'

'Why not?' Brookes said. 'God knows, Zach, if I had my way we'd put the wench to our stern and never look back. But if being apart from her leaves you like this, a ghost in your own bloody life, then why not go to her?'

'Because—' His jaw worked but he found the words were not there to argue. 'She is too much like my father.'

'Your father loved you.'

'He abandoned me.'

'Aye, and saved you in the end.'

Zach sighed, leaned his head back and gazed up at the fading stars. 'Amelia will never leave Ile Sainte Anne.'

'And you will never stay?' Brookes pushed himself to his feet. 'She ain't the only one too much like your stubborn bloody father.' With a shake of his head Brookes stomped across the deck, heading for the galley and breakfast.

Zach didn't move, he just sat in the cold morning light and thought on Brookes' words, thought on the moment Amelia had left him on the beach – the moment he'd let her go. Thought on the prospect of never seeing her again.

To the east, the sun was breaking over distant French shores; to the west the wild North Atlantic spread dark beneath the stars. But to the south ...

He took a breath, the air icy in his lungs. To the south lay the woman he loved, the woman he had risked everything to save and then let go at the last. Perhaps Brookes was right; perhaps he was fooling himself to think he could ever live in this world without her.

Perhaps he had been a fool all along to think it better to have none of her than that part of herself she could give.

Before he could think better of it, Zach scrambled to his feet. 'Brookes!' His first mate stopped and turned, the lantern swinging low from his hand and bumping against his leg. 'It's a foul time of year to cross to the Floridas,' Zach said. 'And the Bay of Biscay will be little better.'

'Aye,' Brookes agreed. 'We'd do well to find a friendly port for the winter, Captain. The crew's tired and the *Hawk* in need of careening.'

'As it happens,' Zach said, 'I've some unfinished business in a port close to these waters.' He cleared his throat, did his best not to notice the wary resignation in Brookes' eyes. 'That is, I've a mind to pay my last respects to my father.'

Brookes gave a solemn nod, an odd mixture of unease and relief. 'Then we sail for Ile Sainte Anne after all.'

'Where else?' Zach said with a weary smile. 'Where else in the world would I go but there?'

Where else would he go but to her?

They'd been a week at sea, heading south along the Portuguese coast, and already the weather was warmer. Luc Géroux sat with his back to the mast of the ship that had once been his and tried not to listen for sounds from below.

Instead he closed his eyes and thought of Josette, of her dark curls and sweet smile. Everything he suffered, the guilt and shame, he suffered for her – and gladly. If he could have saved her from danger by laying down his life, he would have done so, but his sacrifice was not so simple, his pain so much greater. He must deceive and betray; he must watch others suffer because of him, and he must not lift a finger to help them. That was his fate; that was his punishment for youthful pride, ignorance and naivety.

A shadow fell across him and he opened his eyes. Morton was there, cold-eyed in his scarlet uniform, flanked by his lieutenant. 'On your feet,' he said. 'We have matters to discuss.'

Luc didn't move. 'What matters?'

'Lieutenant Ashton is not happy with your navigator.'

'In what respect?'

Ashton glared, grabbing Luc's arm and hauling him up. 'On your feet, man, when you speak to Lord Morton.'

Shaking off the man's hand, he said, 'What is wrong with my navigator?'

'We should be close to Lisbon by now. Yet, by my reckoning, we're still a day's sail north.'

'So we are. In these winds our progress is not so fast. Do you think I sail my ship slowly on purpose to delay you? You can see how the sails are set. What is your accusation?'

'On an English ship—'

'This is a French ship.'

'Yes, as we're painfully aware.' Ashton looked Luc up and down, making a show of his contempt. 'What is that, on your knees?'

He looked down at the dirt marring his britches. His heart lurched. 'I— It's—'

'I sincerely hope,' Morton said, dripping menace into each word, 'that you've not been visiting our prisoner. That would be most unwise.'

'No.' He licked his lips, knew the lie was blatant. 'That is, I—'

From below, there came a muffled scream. Luc flinched, blood running cold. Morton only smiled. 'You realise, of course, that she is of great value. If anything were to happen – should she escape ...'

Another cry drifted up and then sank back into a deathly gurgle. Morton frowned, listening. 'What the devil is he doing to her?' He jerked his head at his lieutenant. 'Ashton, go and see. Remind the fool that she's to be kept alive until we actually have the Articles.'

The lieutenant nodded, disappearing quickly down the steps and Morton returned his attention to Luc. 'If it should get back to Paris that you hindered our search for this wretched piece of calumny ... Well, I dare not imagine the consequences for dear little Josette.'

Luc said nothing. From below he heard footsteps – the lieutenant returning – and held his breath. Had she used the knife? Or had it been discovered before she was able to take her life? Would they suspect him? Damn the dirt on his knees, he should have been more careful. If they suspected he had played any part in this ...

Morton turned towards the steps. 'I hope the brute hasn't damaged her too badly, I—'

He stopped dead.

For at the top of the stairs stood Amelia Dauphin, bruised and beaten but fierce as a new dawn with the lieutenant's sword and pistol tucked into her belt and another aimed straight at Morton's head. 'Not too badly,' she said, by way of an answer. 'Certainly not so badly that I can't kill you where you stand.'

Silence. The whole world held its breath, even the sails were frozen for a single, breathless moment.

Then Morton said, 'Géroux, disarm the harlot.'

A dozen thoughts raced through his mind – a hundred options, all with the same dreadful consequence for his daughter. But he had no time to act, no time even to make a choice.

Amelia pulled the trigger. In a flash of powder and shot, Morton fell dead upon the deck.

'That,' she said, with relish, 'was for my father.'

Dropping the pistol, Amelia pulled the other, cocked and ready, from her belt. It was aimed at Luc. 'I don't want to hurt you,' she said, 'but if you stop me from leaving, I will shoot.'

He raised his hands, gazing down at Morton's body. Lifeless eyes stared into the bright morning sky, dead. Lord Morton was dead.

'Dear God,' he said aloud. 'Josette.'

Confident of Luc's cooperation, Morton had brought only his lieutenant and his inquisitor, Crouch, aboard the *Serpent*. Both lay dead, throats cut, in the brig. Which left only Morton's body in need of disposal.

'Throw it overboard with the other two,' Amy said, teeth gritted as she sat on deck and let the ship's surgeon examine her wrist and tend her other wounds. 'Let the sharks feed on his guts.'

Luc shook his head. 'No, if he disappears how am I to explain it? They will know – at the very least they will suspect – that I am involved. It is too big a risk. We must think of something else.'

'This will pain,' the surgeon said in heavily accented English.

'*Ce n'est pas grave*,' she said with a smile. 'I am strong.'

He moved her wrist, and it did hurt. A great deal. She didn't cry out, though, and after a moment the pain began to ease as the surgeon quickly bound her wrist. When she could speak again, she said to Luc, 'Pirates. Tell them that the *Serpent* was raided and he was killed in the attack.'

'Maybe,' he said. 'Though the *Serpent* is undamaged.'

'Set him adrift, then, in one of the longboats. Let them find him adrift.'

Luc was silent, pacing away to the ship's rail.

Behind her, the surgeon lifted her tattered shirt. She hissed as it came away from the lash wounds on her back.

'Hmmm, I will need to clean this,' he said in French, light fingers probing the wounds.

Amy winced. '*D'accord*.' Although she knew the cleaning would hurt far more than the setting of her wrist.

They took her down to the surgeon's quarters, where he stripped the shirt from her back, bathed and salted her wounds. Unlike Crouch, the surgeon was no artist in pain – he didn't have the skill to keep his patient conscious long enough to endure every last moment of the torture and Amelia quickly, gratefully, sank into oblivion half way through the process.

It was some time before she was able to think or talk again. Longer still until she could stand. Queasy from the pain, she resisted the surgeon's efforts to keep her below and sought fresh air on the deck.

Dusk had turned the winter sky to violet and in the far distance she saw the glitter of a city on the coast.

'Lisbon,' Luc said from behind her.

She turned with a smile, let him take her arm and lead her to the ship's rail. 'Have you ever been there?'

'Of course. It is a beautiful city.'

'Perhaps one day I'll see it for myself.'

'Once Ile Sainte Anne is rebuilt?'

She shook her head. 'Perhaps, but there is something more important to be done first.' She darted a quick look at him. 'I must find Zach and make things right between us. After that ...' She looked out towards the distant shoreline. 'Somehow I have to preserve my father's legacy, Luc, pass on what the Articles promise. I can't let them die with me.'

After a moment's thought, he reached into his coat pocket and pulled out a chain on which hung two familiar keys. 'Morton wanted these. His men could not find them when they sacked Ile Sainte Anne.'

Amelia's heart raced at the sight of them. 'You mean that you took care they shouldn't find them.'

Luc gave a slight smile. 'Perhaps I did,' he said, watching the keys as they swayed on the end of the chain. 'Were I to deliver them to *him* it might be enough to— But, no.' He caught them up in his hand and said, 'Zach has saved your life; now you must save his.'

Alarmed, she said, 'He *is* in danger then.'

'Only from himself.' With a serious look he offered her the keys. 'No man – not even a pirate – can live for silver and gold alone. Zach Hazard is in need of greater treasure, but knows not how to claim it.'

With a shaking hand she reached out and took the keys from his hand. One gold, one bronze, they felt warm and heavy in her palm. 'He'll not thank me for these,' she said. 'He never wanted this legacy. It's not the treasure he seeks.'

'No,' Luc said. 'You are, Amelia. And there is more than one way for the legacy of Ile Sainte Anne to endure.'

Her cheeks flushed, but she did not look away. 'And what of us, Luc? What of you and me?'

He took her hand where she held the keys, closed his fingers over hers. 'We sail on different courses, Amelia. I would not have you follow where I must go.'

'Then we must say goodbye?'

'Not goodbye,' he said, letting go of her hand. 'Not yet. You have a destiny to fulfil, and so do I. Our paths will cross again, one day, and perhaps in happier times.'

He took a step backward and called, 'Lower the longboat.'

With a creak of rope, the longboat made its slow descent into the sea. Aboard was Morton's body, the single shot to his head stark in the fading daylight. Amelia watched him until the boat hit the water and found not a shred of pity or regret in her heart.

'Will you cast him adrift?' she asked, keeping her eyes fixed on the body as Luc climbed down the ladder and into the boat.

He looked up. 'No. I dare not. I must speak with them, make them believe we were attacked. If they do not, if they suspect— This is the only way. I can be in Lisbon in a few hours, if we're not picked up sooner.'

'But the *Serpent* ...'

'She's yours until you reach Ile Sainte Anne; then she belongs to the crew. That's our way, is it not, under the Articles?'

He spoke calmly, but she could see the sadness in his eyes and realised that it had always been there – fear and sadness, cleverly masked, but always visible in his stormy eyes if you knew how to look. 'Luc,' she called, moving to the top of the ladder. 'Wait.'

Sitting in the boat, he cast off the last rope and took hold of the oars. 'Live well, Amelia. Be happy.'

From her belt, she pulled her pistol. 'Luc, wait!' Taking aim, willing her hand not to shake, she said, 'Your left shoulder. From this distance it won't be bad. Better if you're picked up wounded. We'll sound the cannon, get their attention. It'll sound like a raid if we leave fast and run dark. No one will know what happened here, but there will be stories – stories you start when they find you.'

He smiled – a brief, bright expression. 'You always were a better pirate than me, Amelia Dauphin.' Then he nodded once and turned his head away. 'Aim true.'

Holding her breath, arm braced on the rail to keep it steady, she took the shot. He fell back, crimson blooming on his coat, and for a dreadful moment she feared she'd missed, hit too close to the vital blood vessels. Then after a moment he sat up, hand clasped over his shoulder. 'Thank you,' he said, and laughed a little woozily. 'A glancing blow, I think.'

'Bind the wound,' she called as the longboat began to drift. 'Be safe!'

'*Au revoir*, Amelia Dauphin!' he called back. 'Tell Zachary I am in his debt, and yours!'

Tears threatened again, but she dashed them away with the back of her hand. The *Serpent* was hers, for now, and she would act like her captain. 'Fire the starboard cannon!' she barked. 'Find every pistol or musket to hand and shoot across the starboard rail – let them think war has come to Lisbon!'

It was a fitting salute to the *Serpent*'s departing captain.

Slowly, the longboat drifted away, growing smaller and smaller against the backdrop of the Portuguese coast until Amelia could see it no longer. There were other ships, though, pouring out from the port, heading for the commotion.

Amelia smiled. 'Douse the lamps,' she said. 'And send six men aloft. Tonight, we hunt the *Gypsy Hawk*.'

315

Chapter Thirty-Six

It was only after the *Hawk* had been at anchor in the remnants of the harbour for the best part of two days that Zach emerged from his cabin. He said nothing and, to Brookes' weary eye, he seemed disturbingly sober as he walked to the rail and studied the wreckage of the fallen city. There was no smoke now, just the maudlin slosh of waves breaking over shattered ships and spilling across the ruined quay. No other ship was moored there, not a living soul remained in Ile Sainte Anne. Flocks of gulls, however, roamed the heaping wreckage and Brookes tried not to think about what they feasted upon.

In silence, Brookes joined his captain at the rail and, after a few moments Zach said, 'My father is buried on that slope, so Géroux told me.'

'Not buried at sea?' Brookes sucked in a breath.

Zach glanced at him with bleak eyes and said, 'A son should pay his respects, even when his father was a black-hearted devil, eh?'

'Aye,' Brookes agreed, and so Zach left.

That had been two hours earlier, and Brookes now found himself marvelling at the remarkable prescience of Zach's departure. For not long after he'd taken the longboat and pulled hard for the island, the *Serpent* had appeared off their port bow, the very ship for which the captain had been waiting.

The *Serpent* sat still in the water, some distance hence, and among the rest of the crew Brookes sensed a tangible unease, though, in these unsettling times, such disquiet was more usual than not. In the weeks it had taken to sail from the British Sea to Ile Sainte Anne, they'd seen none of their kind afloat – seen naught but naval ships and merchantmen, running heavily armed. On the captain's orders, Brookes had kept well clear of the trade routes and sailed mostly at night, with the lamps doused, so the *Hawk* could disappear into the darkness.

What future lay ahead of them, none of the crew knew. The ruin of Ile Sainte Anne set every man thinking about the days to come and about their place in a world intent on spinning too bloody fast.

That Zach's thoughts had been bent in the same direction, Brookes had no doubt. But what could he do? What could any of them do? Brookes would sleep with Old Hob before he took the King's shilling, that was for good and sure. Freedom, once tasted, was impossible to relinquish – for Zach Hazard and for them all. But with the might of the Empire turned against them, how could an honest pirate make a living?

'Mr Brookes?' The voice was Shiner's, warbling nervously as he pointed towards the *Serpent*. 'Looks like she's making sail.'

So she was, much to Brookes' astonishment. He watched the sails billow as she came about and began to race towards the mouth of the harbour and the open sea.

Brookes watched her go with mingled emotions. If *she* had been aboard, then the fact that she'd not sought Zach out spoke loudly of everything Zach kept silent. Brookes was glad the captain had not witnessed such a pointed rebuff, though what he would tell him when—

'Brookes!' A startled hand grabbed his sleeve and Shiner pointed wide-eyed towards the remains of the quay. There, staring out after the departing *Serpent*, stood the woman herself. It was here that Brookes' feelings abruptly gybed, for he had the sudden fervent wish that she had sailed with her husband and not lingered to torment Zach further. What the devil did she mean by staying? She had no ship, could not live here alone …

When at last the *Serpent* had disappeared behind the rocky curve of the island, Amelia Dauphin turned around and Brookes could have sworn he saw an avaricious glint in her eye as her gaze fell upon the *Hawk*. His hand reached instinctively for his pistol, though in truth he could not see her face well enough to judge its expression. Still, the wench had all but killed his captain once and he'd not trust her again, no matter what Zach Hazard felt for her. The world was different now and each man must protect that which he valued most.

'Watch the ship,' he said to Shiner, pushing past the man and walking down the gangplank to the quay. He waited for her there as she made her way towards him, dressed, as always, in men's clothes with her hair tied back into a loose pigtail. Her wrist was bound and her face, though healing, looked bruised and battered. She was not the girl he'd once known, and with a scarf tied about her head she looked more pirate than ever she had. Stopping some distance from him she held out empty hands and said, 'Mr Brookes. It's been a long time since we met.'

'Aye,' he replied, not shifting his hand from the pistol in his belt.

Her gaze travelled briefly to the *Hawk* and with obvious trepidation she said, 'Where's Captain Hazard?' Perhaps Brookes glanced up at the ruined fortress, for after a moment she answered her own question with a smile of relief. 'With his father, of course.'

'And wanting to be alone while he makes his peace,' Brookes added, moving to block her path. 'Your business with him can wait.'

To his surprise, Amelia smiled. It was a genuine, warm smile. 'You're a loyal friend to Zach, Mr Brookes.' She stepped forward and touched his arm before he could move back. 'You have no reason to trust me, but know this – I'll never again do your captain harm.'

'Seems as your very existence does him harm, *Madame Géroux*.'

She looked away. 'Much has changed, Mr Brookes. More than even Zach knows.'

'Has it now?'

Her eyes met his, fierce as he remembered. 'Whether you trust me or not, Mr Brookes, I will go to him. Don't think you can stand in my way.'

He held that gaze a moment, before stepping out of her path. 'And don't think I won't have my eye on you, Captain Dauphin. You dazzled him once. I won't let you do it again.'

With a nod, she dropped her hand from his arm and glanced up at the cliffs. *'Then you shall know the truth, and the truth shall make you free.'* She glanced at him again and smiled slightly. 'I do love him, whatever you might think.'

Brookes nodded, unable to help a sigh from escaping. 'Then I suppose you'd best be telling him that, for he's been flat as the doldrums these past four weeks.' He paused and scratched his whiskers. 'Actually, for these past four years, now I think on it.'

'The world keeps turning, Mr Brookes,' she said as she walked past him, 'and somewhere the sun is always rising. Today, perhaps, it is here.'

Though she'd not seen the grave, Amelia knew where Overton was buried. It had been on the third day, when all hope had been lost and they'd fallen under the shadow of defeat.

She'd still been in the fortress, though by then it was already burning and men were flinging themselves into the arms of the ocean – or of the navy, whichever they imagined would deal them a kinder fate. The message had come from the cliffs that Overton had fallen and that the marines advanced. There'd been no time to bring him to the sea and his men had refused to leave their captain's body behind.

So they'd buried him, safe from the invading horde, and stood their ground. As far as Amelia knew, none but the boy who had borne the Articles back to her had survived the onslaught.

It had been then that she'd ordered the island abandoned.

The memory was vivid and haunting; she could still feel the cold clamp of iron about her wrists and ankles, the heavy weight of defeat hanging like a chain about her neck. So many dead, so much lost.

But not all.

The Articles were preserved and she bore now a new hope for the future that shone as bright as the sun. There was much to tell Zach, much to pass on.

It was a steep climb up to the west cliffs and by the time she reached the top she was breathless. Despite the three weeks since they'd left Lisbon, her body was still recovering and her chilled bones weren't yet used to the heat of the equator. She was forced to stop and strip off the jacket she wore. For a moment, she closed her eyes, basking in the sun's heat upon her face, but she could not be distracted for long.

About half way down the jagged slope was a stand of trees and it was beneath their branches that Overton lay. Tying her coat about her waist, Amelia picked her way down the rocky cliff towards the softer grass and trees, beyond which spread a wide beach. The glitter of the morning sun upon the water was bright; it hurt her eyes, and she was forced to look away.

It was then that she saw him, leaning his shoulder against a tree close to his father's grave. Sunlight bronzed his skin and set the sword at his waist flashing silver; four years, it seemed, had faded away and he looked more like the pirate she had once known than the dour man who had come to her rescue in England. Here, she thought, he was himself again.

Though Amelia's heart soared at the sight of him, she quelled the urge to run and throw her arms about his neck. Instead, she slowed, walking quietly, and watched as Zach gazed down at Overton's rough grave; she would not intrude. After a while his shoulders rose and fell, and in a soft voice he murmured, 'If you saved my life, then I owe you thanks. Rest in peace, if you dare.' After a moment he added, 'Amen, I suppose.'

With that he turned away, only to stop with a jolt. 'Amelia!' His astonishment stripped away all artifice and for a moment his truth was laid bare – loss, yearning, grief and a glimmer of wild hope. She thought her heart might break at the sight of him. There was so much she wanted to say, but no words seemed adequate to the task. So she found herself standing, watching him as he watched her.

At length he cocked his head towards the grave. 'I came for my father ...'

She nodded and said, 'I came for you.'

Zach took a step back, regarded her cautiously, as if she were a treacherous creature once more. 'I've not changed my mind,' he said in a voice that shook more than he probably knew. 'I still think returning here is madness, but it seems I cannot be anywhere that you are not. So I'll help you and Géroux rebuild—'

'For *you*, Zach,' she said, finding certainty in his declaration. 'Not for Ile Sainte Anne, nor Luc, nor the Articles. For you.' She moved closer, her heart leaping. 'I choose you, Zach. Do you understand? I choose *you*. Now. Always.'

He stared as though he looked at her from the very depths of his soul. Then he was moving, and she was moving, and they crashed together like the sea against the shore. His breath washed warm and quick on her neck, fingers clenched in her hair as his heart hammered against her chest. 'Amy ...'

The whisper of her name released something deep inside; a sob of relief rose to her throat and she buried her tears against the thick fall of his hair. 'I choose you,' she repeated, over and over. 'I choose you, Zach.'

His arms tightened, desperate in their embrace, and for a long moment they stood lost in each other. At length he moved back, holding her shoulders and studying her face. 'You're hurt,' he said, touching her bruised face, her wrist. 'What happened? Did Luc—? I'll kill him if he hurt—'

'No,' she said, quelling him with a touch. 'No, this was Morton's work.'

'Morton?' He looked aghast. 'For the love of God, Amy, what happened?'

She shook her head. One day she'd tell him, when he was sure of her and would understand what had driven Luc to betray them. But not yet; it was too soon, too raw. She shook her head and said only, 'Morton's dead, by my hand. And Luc's ... Luc's gone.' She sucked in a shaky breath, trying to steady her voice. 'Zach, my heart has always been yours. And always will be.'

His hands were on her face, sea-rough and tender, his lips following with reckless desire. Melting, drifting, floating, she traced the elegant lines of his face with shaking fingers as she kissed him, dizzy with the absolute knowledge that he was *hers*. Now and always. She would never let him go again.

Like the tide, their kiss ebbed and flowed until eventually they came to rest forehead to forehead, lips a whisper apart. 'It's a new world, Amy,' he breathed against her mouth.

'I know.'

'And we must find our place in it.'

'Together,' she smiled, the words almost a kiss. 'Our place is together.'

'Always.' He drew her tight against him, as though he might never let go; she almost hoped that he wouldn't, for she felt that she could live an eternity in his arms. Eventually, however, he pressed a gentle kiss against her neck and drew back to look at her, a strange half-smile touching his lips. 'You've turned my world upside down again, Amy. I hardly know what I'm about any more, where to go, what I'm doing.'

'You were saying farewell to your father,' she said, smiling sadly as she glanced over at the rough mound of earth beneath the trees. 'As should I.'

Zach's smile faltered, his brow creasing into a frown. 'He should have been buried at sea,' he said. 'Not right for him to lie in the ground like this.'

'It's where he fell,' she said gently, 'and there was no time. I'm sorry.'

'No.' His arms tightened around her again. '*I* should have been here. If I had—'

'Then you'd have died at his side, Zach, and I'd have hanged broken-hearted from the Tyburn tree.' She pulled away and looked into his face. He was beautiful in the sunlight; she'd always thought so, even at his worst, but never more so than now. For there was a light in his eyes that burned brighter even than the sun and she knew, in her heart, that it was for her alone. She smiled despite his gravity and kissed his mouth, her fingers brushing his cheek. 'Come,' she said, taking his hand. 'There is something we can do for him at least.'

Leading him back to Overton's grave, she crouched down and dug her fingers into the loose soil, scooping up a handful of dirt. After watching her a moment, Zach did the same and then followed her as she scrambled down towards the beach at the bottom of the cliff. There were rocks there, leading out into the crashing waves, and Amelia led him along them until they stood as far out as possible. The waves roiled close to their feet, the spray blowing up and over them like a strange kind of baptism. 'Lord, I commend to your care a true son of the ocean!' she called over the roar of the sea. 'Let him sail once more, and always, under your protection!' With that, she scattered the soil from Overton's grave across the water, and glanced over at Zach. He was watching her with a smile that lurked between amusement and pleasure; then in a loud voice he shouted, 'But keep the old bugger away from the rum!' and flung his own handful of dirt into the sea.

His smile faded, turning into something more sombre, as his gaze drifted across the ocean. 'So it ends,' he said at last. 'Ile Sainte Anne is no more and our time is over.'

Amelia turned so that she might face him, drawing his eyes back from the horizon. 'No,' she said firmly. 'It doesn't end here. It just passes on.'

He frowned. 'What passes on?'

'Let me show you,' she said, and took his hand to lead him back to the fortress.

The walk was long, but they were neither of them in a rush; after their days of travelling together it seemed natural to walk side by side in relative silence. This time, though, they walked close, fingers touching, eyes meeting often, and, occasionally, lips meeting, too. It was a quiet happiness she'd not anticipated, and, from the somewhat bemused expression on Zach's face, it was a new experience for them both.

As they drew closer to the fortress, however, their mood grew more sombre, for it was a grim sight indeed, blackened and twisted. There were few features she could make out, but the bones of her father's court stood proud, like the skeletal ribs of some vast creature of the deep. So much had been lost, but not all. Not all.

Far below, she could see the *Hawk* at rest in the harbour and Amelia imagined old Brookes watching her with a disapproving eye. She held no animosity towards him, though – no matter how much he might distrust her. He loved Zach as much as she did, in his own way, and for that she would love him, too. When Zach waved in the general direction of the *Hawk*, she knew she'd been right.

Keeping hold of his hand, she led him around the foundations of the fortress until she had her bearings, and then set out deeper into the forest, pacing her steps with care. When she had found the right place, she crouched down and swept aside the fallen leaves and other rotting vegetation to reveal an iron trapdoor embedded in the earth. From around her neck, she took the keys Luc had returned to her during her sojourn aboard the *Serpent* and turned the bronze key in the lock.

'What is this place?' said Zach, the first words he'd spoken for some time.

'The vault.' Amelia hauled open the door and let it fall with a thud onto the ground. Cold, damp air flooded out and she slipped on the coat she'd earlier tied about her waist. 'I had it built soon after my father was taken.'

He nodded, but said nothing in return.

Steps disappeared into darkness, but a torch sat ready close to the door. Amelia lifted it out as Zach produced a flint and soon the brand burned fiercely. 'It's not far,' she said, leading the way down steep steps carved into the bones of the cliff, the torch flickering before her as she walked.

Soon, she reached the bottom of the vault, cold air nipping at her nose and fingers. From above, a shaft of sunlight gleamed on the far wall and it seemed as though she looked up from the bottom of a well. Resting the torch in a sconce on the wall, Amelia made her way across the small chamber to the sea chest which lay on the floor. Her fingers came to rest on the lid and she frowned, remembering the despair with which she had locked it so many months ago.

'Amelia?' Zach's voice was a soft growl, warm and immediate. His hand rested on her hip and she thrilled at the hint of possessiveness in the action.

She turned and, in the firelight, he was all dark shadows and glitter. 'Take the key,' she said, offering him the golden one. 'Open the chest.'

'What's inside?'

'Don't you know?'

Zach made no answer, simply crouched down and turned the key in the lock. It opened with a smooth click and, carefully, Zach lifted the lid. Peering over his shoulder, Amelia was irrationally relieved to see the contents undisturbed.

With an unenthusiastic sigh, Zach sat back on his heels. 'The Articles.'

'Everything we fought for,' she insisted, her hand coming to rest on his shoulder. His skin felt warm beneath the thin fabric of his shirt, though she thought he must be cold in the chill air. 'This is what we must pass on, Zach.'

Slowly he stood, brow furrowed. 'Pass on to whom, Amy? There's none left who want to hear. The navy owns the seas now, there's no room for an honest pirate or—'

'It's not about piracy, Zach. You know that as well as I. The ideas in the Articles, the ideas of your grandfather, they must be passed on. *For the poorest man that is in upon the Earth has a life to live, as the greatest man.* We are born free creatures—'

'We are crushed, Amy, and our colours banished to the depths. Our time is passed.'

'I know. I understand that now.' She smiled, couldn't help but smile despite her own fears. 'Don't you see? We must pass this on to others.'

'Pearls before swine, Amy. You can't free a man who shackles himself, and the likes of them are ten a penny these days. Too many men are content to wear a golden chain if it makes them rich enough. We'll be passing nothing to them but our necks for stretching.'

'Not to them, Zach. Not to men of this world.'

His lips twisted into a sceptical smile. 'Then to whom?'

Now that the moment had come, she found herself uncertain. Yet there was nothing to be said but the truth and it was a truth that could not lie hidden for long. She took Zach's hand and raised it to her lips, kissing his palm, before she pressed it against her belly. 'To her,' she said quietly. 'Zach, to our child.'

His hand jolted beneath her touch. 'Child?'

She nodded, watching with trepidation the play of disbelief and wonder that danced across his face.

'Our child?' He pulled her hard against him, fingers bunched in the fabric of her coat. 'Bloody hell, Amy, *our* child?'

'Yes,' she laughed into his shoulder. 'Our future, Zach. Our immortality.'

Long fingers cupped her face, eyes tight shut as his lips pressed shakily against her forehead. 'Our hope,' he breathed against her skin. 'An improbable, incredible bloody hope!' He laughed then, a quicksilver flash in the torchlight, before quickly sobering. His dark eyes were bright with firelight as he fixed her with a steady look. 'I'm a rootless, faithless blackguard, Amy, wanted for crimes from Nova Scotia to the end of the bloody world. But tell me this: do you trust me?'

'I always have.'

'Then throw off these chains, Amelia. Throw off your duty here, and I'll show you what freedom really means.'

Chapter Thirty-Seven

It was a balmy night shortly before Ashia's first birthday and, through wide open doors, the distant hush of the Tyrrhenian Sea drifted on a rosemary-scented breeze. Amelia woke slowly, aroused by the feather-light touch of Zach's lips on her neck, the tender stroke of his fingers along the curve of her hip. Sighing, she stretched and rolled onto her back with a smile. 'It's early,' she whispered.

'Mmmmm ...' His breath was warm, fingers trailing devastating patterns across the sensitive skin of her belly, igniting a familiar and irresistible fire. 'Didn't mean to wake you.'

'Yes you did.'

She felt him smile against her mouth as he kissed her, the soft fall of his tangled hair caressing her face and shoulders. 'Go back to sleep then,' he murmured, even as his lips found that spot beneath her ear that made her just ...

'Fiend!' she hissed, arching helplessly against him, relishing the pressure of his taut, hard body against hers. He was oil to her flame, an incendiary touch that she craved like the very air she breathed.

His lips found her breast just as his fingers slipped between her legs, making her gasp. He grinned, 'Wanton doxy ...'

'Well, you'd certainly know, you ... Oh *God* ...' He was too good, played her like a fiddle, and she was helpless beneath his practiced touch.

Almost helpless.

He rolled willingly onto his back when she pushed against his shoulder, knowing what she wanted as she claimed his mouth for the deepest of kisses and pressed herself, for a moment, against the entire length of him, as if it were possible to make themselves one in body as well as in soul. Then slowly, still lost in his kiss, she sat up and took him inside her, grinning at the rasp she drew from his throat. His head sank back, eyes heavy-lidded, and hands resting loosely upon her hips as she began to move, to find their rhythm.

'Beautiful,' he murmured, stroking her skin almost absently.

She watched him, letting the heat build slowly, deliciously. Capricious as the sea, Zach Hazard had many moods and loved her differently with each. At times he was a tempest, all stormy passion and towering seas. Other times he danced like sunshine on the waves, light and teasing, laughing and adventurous. Then there were times such as this, with deep, calm waters and the sense of a storm on the horizon.

She leaned down and kissed him, delighting in the feel of his fingers threading through her hair. He could be so gentle at times, so tender, so in need of her love. Yet so far away. 'Where are you?' she whispered against his cheek. 'Where are you, Zach?'

He smiled, unfocused and distracted, and she knew he was close to the edge. 'The end,' he breathed, fingers tightening on her hips as he began to move with her, quickening their pace, 'the beginning ... It's all the same, Amy. It's all the bloody same ...'

Their breathing grew ragged, tumbling together as they both reached for release. The heat was a fire now, raging in the pit of her belly and desperate for freedom. Her hands braced against his chest, their pace urgent, his heartbeat a frantic tattoo beneath her fingers.

Suddenly he was lifting her up and off, rolling her onto her side. 'Like this,' he growled into her ear, moulding her body to his.

She gasped her agreement as he pushed in from behind, his clever fingers dancing like liquid fire across the place where they met, his kiss biting down hard upon her shoulder.

Head spinning, filled entirely and completely by him, she clutched a fistful of his hair in one hand, arching back to meet the thrust of his hips with her own until the world began to tremble. She thought she might die there, on the cusp, poised like a bird about to take flight. Her lungs begged for air, his name a whimper, a plea, a curse, a command, until, with a touch of magic, he drew her slowly, inexorably over the precipice, sending her thrashing and shuddering into a white-light bliss that blinded and deafened, transporting her to the heavens. But even as she fell he was still moving, hard and hot inside her, his fingers holding her tight against him until, with an inarticulate cry, he fell gasping and sweat-slick against her shoulder.

Heavy limbs draped across her then, and she sank gratefully into his arms, letting herself drift among the stars awhile.

Later, just as the sun broke the horizon, she surfaced again and felt his fingertips tracing a thoughtful line along the length of her arm. She said nothing, though threaded her fingers with his and burrowed back against him, waiting.

After a while, in a quiet voice, he said, 'Today I'll do it, then.'

Amelia rolled over, unsurprised yet heartsick nonetheless. 'Zach, are you sure?'

'Must be done, lest we wish to lose this slice of paradise to some prince or other. That frigate passed too close last week.'

'They didn't see her.'

'Only a matter of time.'

She didn't argue, for she knew he was right. With a sigh, she said, 'The Articles, too?'

'What's in it that's not inked upon us, Amy? Nothing that's worth remembering, that's for sure. Ashia's taken it with her milk; we've done our duty by her, but perhaps others will have a need of it, in time.'

She studied his face, the curious certainty in his eyes reminding her how he'd always skirted the edges of the world. 'You really believe that?'

'I do.'

She traced a finger across his shoulder. 'Shall I come with you, on the *Serenità*?'

'No. It's a leave I must take on my own. A lady of her age deserves that respect.'

Amelia lifted her lips to kiss his forehead. 'So she does.'

With a sigh, Zach got up and began to dress.

'We'll wait for you,' she said. 'We'll wait on the cliffs.'

He nodded and pulled a shirt over his head. 'At sunset, then. I've a mind to spend the day with her first.'

Tears tightened Amelia's throat, stealing her voice.

He glanced over, as if suspecting her weakness, and she forced a brave smile. 'I love you, Zach.'

For a moment, he studied her, dauntingly perceptive. When he spoke, his voice was measured. 'The greatest treasure I ever stole lies within these walls, Amy.' He crossed the room and took her hand. 'What I lose today is nothing to what I would lose should our haven be discovered.' He reached down and touched her cheek, as if wiping away the tears that had not yet fallen. 'All will be well, I swear it. This is nothing but the severing of ties with a life long gone.'

'I know.' Hanging her head, she let a tear fall on the sheet before wiping it away with a finger. Then she sniffed and looked up. 'Go then, and let it be done.'

Zach squeezed her hand once, and then let it fall into her lap. He glanced at Ashia's crib and drew a steadying breath, then he was gone, bound for the rocky shore and the sea.

Zach walked her from prow to stern, walked every inch of his beautiful ship.

She had sat at anchor in this azure sea for almost two years now, too big to sail without a crew, too deep in the draft to come closer to shore.

He'd offered her to Brookes, but the old goat had shaken his head and muttered of a secret hoard north of Haiti and a woman waiting in Port-au-Prince. Too old, he'd said, to captain buccaneers, even had there been any left in the dazzling waters of the Caribbean. How could Zach argue with that, when he'd found his own secret treasure and planned to live in paradise the rest of his days?

The others, too, had gone their own ways. Shiner, he'd heard, was somewhere in Venice, although what he might be doing there Zach could hardly imagine – haranguing passers-by with his profound observations on life, perhaps? Or perhaps robbing them blind. More than likely a devilish combination of the two, and he'd not condemn the man for that. Zach Hazard had done worse, and ill-deserved the glorious happiness he'd plundered from the *Serpent*'s captain, wherever he might be.

So the *Hawk* had come to rest here, beautiful against the blue skies, a memento of life past. The world had moved on, Ile Sainte Anne was no more, and the *Gypsy Hawk* was as anachronistic as the old salts that still clung to the remains of Port Royal and called themselves pirates.

Much worse, though, was the fact that she drew the eye of passing ships and Zach knew it would not be long before some eager young lieutenant recognised her for what she was – the last great pirate ship left afloat. Zach Hazard and his Pirate Queen were still wanted and, where once he might have dared the hempen collar with a gleam in his eye and a challenge on his lips, now all he could think of was Ashia left alone.

The *Gypsy Hawk* had been his first love, his teacher, his mistress, but he was a grown man now and saw her for what she was – no more than a ship. She'd given him freedom, yes, but her freedom had never been more than the freedom to run, to leave everything behind and reach for the horizon. As soon as he'd held his child in his arms he'd understood that running was no freedom at all. He wanted to live now, to see Ashia grow beautiful like her mother, to see a son born, or another daughter – to live a life so much deeper than the vain chase for fortune and glory that had marked his youth.

He walked the deck, fingers trailing across the sun-warmed wood and the lines unused for too long, and it occurred to him then that the *Hawk* had never really been his at all. She'd always belonged to the ocean, to the misty world between sunlight and shadows, and he thought she always would. Her destiny, perhaps, had always been greater than his.

The sun was low on the horizon, a golden ball in the west sinking behind the rocky isle of Salina and the far-distant Filicudi. He stopped and gazed awhile, feeling the rise of an evening breeze from the east, sensing the *Hawk* chafing at the anchors with which he had bound her for so long, for too long.

'Soon,' he told her, quietly. 'Soon you'll be free.'

Turning away from the sunset, Zach headed into the great cabin that had once been his – and before him had belonged to other captains long since past. On the chart table there was nothing but the ironbound chest he'd carried from the vault beneath Ile Sainte Anne, and beside it the Articles themselves.

He ran his hand over the aged leather cover, remembering sharply his father's gnarled fingers as he'd pored over the text in search of some hidden nuance about which Zach had cared so little. Even now, Amy cared more about the aged tome than he. Though here, at the end, Zach could see beauty in it – and a future too, perhaps, when all men subscribed to the ideals that quickened Amelia's heart.

They'd not live to see it themselves, of that he was certain. But he hoped Ashia, or her children, might live in such a world.

The thought comforted him as he lifted the book and set it inside the chest, closing the lid and sealing it with the lock he'd had made especially for the purpose. He was still Zach Hazard, after all, and he would leave his mark.

When it was done, he rested both hands on the chest and, for a moment, bowed his head. No profound words came to mind, beyond the most simple of all – farewell. His heart, though, was clenched tight as he walked back on deck and saw the sun like fire on the horizon.

With care and precision, he let loose the anchor chains and felt the ship roll beneath his feet as if she could sniff the wind already. 'Easy,' he said gently, returning to the mainmast. 'Not long now.'

On the deck, he'd set three flagons of oil and he lifted them one by one, strewing the content over the main deck, over the quarterdeck steps, and down to the forecastle. It would be enough, in this dry heat.

His hands shook and his throat was tight with a sudden and overpowering grief as he returned to the main mast and freed the lantern that hung there. He tried to take a deep breath, but it was no more than a shudder and he found himself leaning into the warm wood, pressing a kiss to her mast as his fingers stroked the familiar wood for the last time.

After a moment he calmed and, collecting himself, drew his knife and slashed the line that released the mainsail. It unfurled and caught the wind, billowing and snapping like life itself. 'Farewell, my *Gypsy Hawk*,' he whispered. 'May you always have fair winds and following seas.'

With that, he dashed the burning lantern onto the deck and watched as the flames danced over the wood, licking and curling across the deck as the *Hawk* caught the wind and began to sail.

Maybe it was the smoke that stung his eyes then, or the flames that blinded him, for suddenly everything was a blur and Zach was forced to turn away – to leap onto the rail and suck in a cool breath. There he paused a moment, arms outstretched and face lifted to the dying sun as, behind him, the fire crackled and spat. On the rocky cliffs of Panarea, he thought he saw the glint of Amelia's hair and he knew that she stood waiting for him, waiting with Ashia for his return. He closed his eyes, felt the roll of the *Hawk* beneath his feet for one last time. Then he dived.

It seemed for a moment that he flew, free as the birds, before he plunged deep and deeper into the crystal waters that refracted the fire of the sun and of his burning ship, and somehow he swam through them both.

Zach broke the surface with a gasp, but did not look back as he stroked hard for the *Serenità* and thence home. He docked the sloop easily on the ancient quay and determinedly climbed the steep path up the cliff, to where Amy would be waiting. Until he had her in his arms he could not look back – would not look back.

She greeted him silently, with Ashia on her hip and her arm outstretched. For a moment, he clung to her as if she were all that kept him on his feet and a strange broken sound came from his throat, but then Ashia squirmed and complained and it was as if his heart started beating again.

'Come here,' he said roughly, taking her from Amy and pressing a kiss to her rose-petal skin; warm and soft and real, this glorious life he'd forged.

He sniffed and steadied his breath, finding Amelia watching him with her heart in her eyes. 'All's well,' he said, taking her hand and drawing her towards the cliff edge. 'Come with me and we'll watch her leave.'

'I'm not sure I can bear it,' she whispered, resting her head against his shoulder. 'I'm not sure I can bear to see the end.'

'It's not the end. Not for her, nor us. It's just the beginning of a new story, a new and glorious story, Amy. It's the beginning of a whole new world.'

With his daughter in one arm and his love in the other, Zach Hazard drew close to the edge of the cliff. The sky was aflame, but its shades of gold were nothing to the brazen conflagration of the *Gypsy Hawk* as she sailed, brave and beautiful, to the far horizon and beyond.

Epilogue

'So it ends?'

Samuel Reed smiled at the disappointment in the Frenchman's voice. 'Aye,' he said. 'So it ends for Captain Zach Hazard and the Pirate Queen, but the Articles ...' He looked pointedly at the leather-bound volume in the young man's hands. 'They live on.'

'To what purpose, I wonder?' He lifted the cover, studying the inscription within. 'In France we say, "*Liberté, Égalité, Fraternité*".'

'And then separate a man's head from his body, so I understand.' Reed sniffed and climbed to his feet, stiff from sitting so long with a cold, damp wind blowing across his old bones.

'The sentiment is the same, is it not? *The gentry must come down, and the poor shall wear the crown.*' His lips twisted in an ironic smile. 'I had not thought the English so enlightened.'

'Then clearly you know little of the English.'

The lad acknowledged it with a shrug, holding the Articles close to his chest. He didn't seem to want to let them go. 'Tell me,' he said. 'What happened to my compatriot? What happened to Monsieur Géroux?'

'Ah. Well now, that's another story. They say he—'

'Reed!' The captain's voice bellowed across the deck. 'What are you men doing, standing about flapping your lips? If you've no work to do, there's the bilge to be pumped!'

Sailors scurried in all directions, leaving Reed alone with their passenger. 'Sorry, sir,' he said, stepping in front of the young man to shield what he held from the captain's eyes. He couldn't explain why, but he didn't want to see the Articles in another's hands. 'Just answering some questions from the young man, sir.'

'You're not paid to answer questions, Reed. Now get about your duties.'

'Aye, sir.' Turning away, he glanced at the lad and saw him tuck the Articles into his coat. For a brief moment their eyes met and held. 'Find me later,' Reed said as he headed off about his work. 'Find me later and I'll tell you the tale of Luc Géroux, though I warn you it ain't for the faint-hearted.'

The Frenchman smiled. 'Then it is well that my heart is strong.'

With a nod, Reed hurried away, but he stopped when he was out of the captain's sight and turned to look back the way he'd come. The young lad stood once more at the ship's rail, raven hair curling about his ears and the old sea chest at his feet as he gazed out into the fog.

Slowly he raised his hand as if in greeting or salute and for a moment it seemed to Reed that he saw the old square-rigger in the mist again, her sails billowing in a phantom breeze as the *Gypsy Hawk* bade them farewell and good fortune.

He smiled and thought of the Articles tucked safely inside the lad's coat, a legend passed on, a new story begun.

Perhaps it was not such a bad day to be at sea, after all.

Historical Note

Although the events in *The Legend of the Gypsy Hawk* are completely fictitious, some of the ideas and words are borrowed (without permission) from history.

Amelia's song, including the much quoted line 'The gentry must come down, and the poor will wear the crown', is actually the 'Digger's Song'. This seventeenth-century ballad was sung by members of the radical Diggers and Levellers groups, agrarian protest movements which advocated the kind of radical social change we might now call communism.

The Articles of Agreement, of course, are based on similar ship's articles, to which pirates, and other sailors, signed up on joining a crew. Typically, they included arrangements for the equitable sharing of prizes, rules of communal living aboard ship and sometimes a pension for the dependents of those maimed or killed in action. However, the text quoted from Amelia's Articles – *For the poorest man that is upon the Earth has a life to live, as the greatest man* – is based on the discussion that took place in the 1647 Putney Debates, between members of Oliver Cromwell's New Model Army. The actual quote, startlingly forward-thinking, was spoken by Thomas Rainsborough:

> For really I think that the poorest he that is in England hath a life to live, as the greatest he; and therefore truly, Sir, I think it clear, that every Man that is to live under a Government ought first by his own Consent to put himself under that Government; and I do think that the poorest man in England is not at all bound in a strict sense to that Government that he hath not had a voice to put Himself under.

Although Rainsborough and his fellow Puritans would certainly have disapproved of any kind of novel, let alone a romance novel, I hope they won't mind me borrowing a few of their inspiring words and putting them into the mouths of some distinctly un-puritanical characters.

About the Author

Sally lives in London, England with her American husband and two children. She is co-founder and commissioning editor of Fandemonium Books, the licensed publisher of novels based on the American TV series Stargate SG1, Atlantis and Universe. Sally is the author of five of the Stargate novels. She has also written four audio Stargate dramas, and recently she completed work on three episodes of the video game Stargate SG-1: Unleashed which were voiced by Stargate SG-1 stars Richard Dean Anderson, Michael Shanks, Amanda Tapping and Chris Judge.

The Legend of the Gypsy Hawk is Sally's first historical romance and Book One in *the Pirates of Ile Sainte Anne* series.

Follow Sally on:
Twitter: https://twitter.com/sally_malcolm
Facebook: https://www.facebook.com/sally.malcolm.3
Blog: http://sallymalcolm.blogspot.co.uk/

More from Choc Lit

If you enjoyed Sally's story, you'll enjoy the rest of our selection. Here's a sample:

Fool's Gold
Zana Bell

Winner of 2015 Koru Award from the Romance Writers of New Zealand

Love – is it worth its weight in gold?

It's 1866 and the gold rush is on. Left to fend for herself in the wilds of New Zealand's west coast, Lady Guinevere Stanhope is determined to do whatever it takes to rescue her ancestral home and restore her father's good name.

Forced out of his native Ireland, Quinn O'Donnell dreams of striking gold. His fiercely held prejudices make him loath to help any English person, let alone a lady as haughty and obstinate as Guinevere. But when a flash flood hits, Quinn is compelled to rescue her, and their paths become entwined in this uncharted new world.

Though a most inconvenient attraction forms between them, both remain determined to pursue their dreams, whatever the cost.

Will they realise in time that all that glitters is not gold?

Visit www.choc-lit.com for more details, or simply scan barcode using your mobile phone QR reader.

Highland Storms
Christina Courtenay

Book 2 in the Kinross Series

Winner of the 2012 Best Historical Romantic Novel of the year

Who can you trust?

Betrayed by his brother and his childhood love, Brice Kinross needs a fresh start. So he welcomes the opportunity to leave Sweden for the Scottish Highlands to take over the family estate.

But there's trouble afoot at Rosyth in 1754 and Brice finds himself unwelcome. The estate's in ruin and money is disappearing. He discovers an ally in Marsaili Buchanan, the beautiful redheaded housekeeper, but can he trust her?

Marsaili is determined to build a good life. She works hard at being a housekeeper and harder still at avoiding men who want to take advantage of her. But she's irresistibly drawn to the new clan chief, even though he's made it plain he doesn't want to be shackled to anyone.

And the young laird has more than romance on his mind. His investigations are stirring up an enemy. Someone who will stop at nothing to get what he wants – including Marsaili – even if that means destroying Brice's life forever ...

Visit www.choc-lit.com for more details, or simply scan barcode using your mobile phone QR reader.

The Silver Locket

Margaret James

Book 1 in the Charton Minster series

Winner of 2010 Reviewers' Choice Award for Single Titles

If life is cheap, how much is love worth?

It's 1914 and young Rose Courtenay has a decision to make. Please her wealthy parents by marrying the man of their choice – or play her part in the war effort?

The chance to escape proves irresistible and Rose becomes a nurse. Working in France, she meets Lieutenant Alex Denham, a dark figure from her past. He's the last man in the world she'd get involved with – especially now he's married.

But in wartime nothing is as it seems. Alex's marriage is a sham and Rose is the only woman he's ever wanted. As he recovers from his wounds, he sets out to win her trust. His gift of a silver locket is a far cry from the luxuries she's left behind.

What value will she put on his love?

Visit www.choc-lit.com for more details, or simply scan barcode using your mobile phone QR reader.

From the author of *The Road Back*

LIZ HARRIS

A Bargain Struck

A Bargain Struck

Liz Harris

Shortlisted for the 2014 Romantic Historical Novel of the Year Award

Does a good deal make a marriage?

Widower Connor Maguire advertises for a wife to raise his young daughter, Bridget, work the homestead and bear him a son.

Ellen O'Sullivan longs for a home, a husband and a family. On paper, she is everything Connor needs in a wife. However, it soon becomes clear that Ellen has not been entirely truthful.

Will Connor be able to overlook Ellen's dishonesty and keep to his side of the bargain? Or will Bridget's resentment, the attentions of the beautiful Miss Quinn, and the arrival of an unwelcome visitor, combine to prevent the couple from starting anew?

As their personal feelings blur the boundaries of their deal, they begin to wonder if a bargain struck makes a marriage worth keeping.

Set in Wyoming in 1887, a story of a man and a woman brought together through need, not love …

Visit www.choc-lit.com for more details, or simply scan barcode using your mobile phone QR reader.

Introducing Choc Lit

We're an independent publisher creating
a delicious selection of fiction.
Where heroes are like chocolate – irresistible!
Quality stories with a romance at the heart.

See our selection here:
www.choc-lit.com

We'd love to hear how you enjoyed *The Legend of Gypsy
Hawk*. Please leave a review where you purchased the
novel or visit: **www.choc-lit.com** and give your feedback.

Choc Lit novels are selected by genuine readers like yourself.
We only publish stories our Choc Lit Tasting Panel want to
see in print. Our reviews and awards speak for themselves.

Could you be a Star Selector and join our Tasting Panel?
Would you like to play a role in choosing which novels we
decide to publish? Do you enjoy reading romance novels?
Then you could be perfect for our Choc Lit Tasting Panel.

Visit here for more details...
www.choc-lit.com/join-the-choc-lit-tasting-panel

Keep in touch:
Sign up for our monthly newsletter Choc Lit Spread for
all the latest news and offers: www.spread.choc-lit.com.
Follow us on Twitter: @ChocLituk and Facebook: Choc Lit.

Or simply scan barcode using your mobile phone QR reader:

Choc Lit   *Twitter*   *Facebook*
Spread